Awakened by Betrayal
The Saga of the House of Warwick

Margarete A. Keeling

PublishAmerica
Baltimore

© 2006 by Margarete A. Keeling.
All rights reserved. No part of this book may be reproduced, stored in a retrieval system or transmitted in any form or by any means without the prior written permission of the publishers, except by a reviewer who may quote brief passages in a review to be printed in a newspaper, magazine or journal.

First printing

All characters appearing in this work are fictitious. Any resemblance to real persons, living or dead, is purely coincidental.

At the specific preference of the author, PublishAmerica allowed this work to remain exactly as the author intended, verbatim, without editorial input.

ISBN: 1-4241-3460-9
PUBLISHED BY PUBLISHAMERICA, LLLP
www.publishamerica.com
Baltimore

Printed in the United States of America

DEDICATION

I would like to dedicate this novel to the entire Watson family. Especially my two wonderful girls, Lakesha and Kelly, who truly are an inspiration to me; To Fruzzy, Shirley, Rickie and Louise my special loves who will never know of this accomplishment. Finally, thanks to Herman and Ronnie for their support.

Through many years of loss and pain, we have survived to become more thankful…

ACKNOWLEDGMENT

Thanks to my church family with whom I have been privileged to receive so much.

Also special thanks to everyone who supported my efforts.

Thanks so much to Etta, Georgia, Margaret S., and Stanford Montessori staff.

A special thank you to Loraine O., for sharing the name of Publish America.

I will always be grateful to each of you.

"AWAKENED BY BETRAYAL"
The Saga of the House of Warwick

The Warwick saga began on a bitterly cold winter day in the year of our Lord 1500 A. D.

King Charles accused his brother Darius Warwick of being too weak to rule in his stead, a kingdom built from war and bloodshed.

He then looked for another who could take his place, but found none equal to the task. Even though Charles was dying being a warmonger, he continued to send his army into battle after battle. Risking everything, he sought to gain as many Provinces as possible.

A few years later Charles had one last scrimmage, for soon after members of his own army weary from the taste of war killed him. Sometime in the night as he slept each betrayer took up his sword and left their mark, then proclaimed Darius king of England.

The reign of Darius was very short lived however, for as a result of his brothers' broken treatise, he was left no choice, but to establish England's borders by going to war with Spain.

His queen Cassandra died months before of pneumonia, leaving only his son Lyonus I, who took up a sword and rallied by his side.

In this great battle king Darius paid a heavy toll, for a sword meant for Lyonus took him.

In the battle, many of young Lyonus' friends who fought by his side shared the victory. In exchange for their loyalty and courage, he granted them positions as his ministers.

Lyonus I, made peace with Spain and captured one of its daughters, Rosa.

In this, would be the first sign that a crevice would appear in the House of Warwick.

CHAPTER ONE
A Rift Begun

It was spring, the year 1509, and the place somewhere in England. All the flowers in bloom, and the trees were singing their songs of green leaves. With leaves so green, it was as if they were veils that covered the face of the sun. So wonderful it was to look through their branches. This was indeed a peaceful time for England; at least for a time war had ended.

Lyonus Warwick I was now king of England. In his early reign he was a good and thoughtful king. He grew mighty and the people loved him. As he passed through their villages, they would throw out rose peddles, cheer his name and shout.

"King Lyonus the mighty…King Lyonus the merciful…Long live King Lyonus!"

Rewarded as advisors to the king were: Lord Fredrick Guy, tall and ruggedly handsome. He was said to be of noble birth, however none of his relatives were alive to contradict the fact. Lord Guy was very knowledgeable in matters of tax collections and accounting. At the very least, he fought side by side with the king. But even with his rich rewards, he remained dissatisfied. Along with lord Guy, there was Lord Richard Biltfry, political strategist. Lord Biltfry was neither married, nor desired the company of young maidens. He was responsible for the discovery of certain indiscretions. Then, there was Duke Westmoreland, a man of law. He was useful in writing documents for the king. The Dukes' wife died giving birth to their daughter

Kathryn. There was also Lord William Du'Voe one trusted by the king and was a great diplomat. Lyonus would always use him as High Lord, or Regent, in his absence. Then lastly the root of one heroine of the story, lord Thomas Hendly Graybourne. Lord Graybourne was a very skillful man, in fact he taught the art of the sword to many members of the king's army. He was known throughout the realm as "Thomas of the Blade," and was known for his battle strategies. Thomas became one of the kings' closest friends and confidant. Lord Graybourne married Lady Claire Norwick, and rewarded with the plush land of the Hilton estates. They had a beautiful daughter named Melinda.

Now Lyonus I was so favored by the people that it caused great jealousy among his ministers. A tare could be seen throughout the kingdom. Lyonus noticed that something had to be done to ensure his solvency.

He wanted to find a wife, a queen who would give him comfort. Perhaps even a son who would continue to rule and protect the land.

So King Lyonus I took as his wife Rosa Juanita Valdez, the granddaughter of a Spanish noble, Luis Regard Valdez.

Their marriage did not begin out of any great love, but rather out of obligation to the people of England. It began as a pact between the two countries, but later, the king had hopes that Rosa would fill the emptiness in his heart.

Queen Rosa was very slender, pale at a glance. She had long black hair, as black as a raven's wing, that reached the back of her knees. She seemed almost ghostly for lack of the sun's rays.

Because of the lack of attention from king Lyonus however, she took her devotion elsewhere.

Rosa loved to dabble in the black arts, and grew in close association with the king's Seer.

In the court of Lyonus I, was one who had the sight, Ivan Fellows. Ivan gave the former king Darius' army an edge in many battles by use of his visions. The visions somehow lead to a victory for England. Ivan, though never quite rewarded, as were the other advisors, became an invaluable consort to the king…and to the queen, Rosa.

Ivan taught her the art of potion making, spells and how to enter dreams, though he did not use the art himself. King Lyonus however, condemned its' use.

After trying so many times to have sons, and being rewarded with failure, king Lyonus was not very happy with the queen. He became estranged, and spurned her even more. He sought the maidens of the court to comfort him and gave them token gifts.

Rosa found it more difficult each day, to hear the gossip about the king. She'd even overheard her chambermaids discuss the kings' affairs with other servants.

Then one day Rosa decided to force his hand. She began to make regular visits to the kitchen, to sample the king's food. It went unnoticed by many, but Roger the cook, took notice of her every move. As she mixed her powder to give the kings stew it's savor. Roger was forced to remain silent.

When the queen glanced over to see him staring, he walked over to see what she was doing.

"Good morning your majesty…do you find the stew to the liking of the king…?"

"Hum…I have added a tad bit more of this special spice to the mixture…it's his favorite you know?"

"Indeed…" said Roger, as he turned to walk away from the queen. Roger knew that no good thing would come of what the queen was about to do. But silence ruled the day.

With my potions thought Rosa, the king will not be able to control his love for me.

But instead of growing more loving, Lyonus became even more evil towards her. He suspected her witchcraft and would not even look her way. The king flaunted his affairs more openly than before.

One day Rosa came to the king as he slept, as Ivan had taught her, and entered his dreams there they lie together. But her presence in his dreams seemed to unsettle him.

Rosa became so upset by the embarrassment it caused her. She was afraid that now the king might get rid of her once and for all if he realized what she had done. So she went straight way to Ivan and asked for help.

When she told Ivan what had happened, he began to scold her, as if she were a little child. Rosa however flared up in a rage.

"Why not indulge myself, after all the king is my husband, I have a right."

"Your majesty…" said Ivan, those potions are deadly…the king should not be drugged to do his husbandly duties."

Rosa turned her head with tears in her eyes, and then said.

"I've tried so many times to talk to Lyonus, to get his attention…I don't know why he loathes me so…"

"My queen, the king truly loves you. I believe the king has no thought of right or wrong in this matter. I feel he cares so much for England that he has forgotten love, and warmth…and…"

"Oh!" said Rosa, in a voice of indignation. You play me the fool Ivan? He then should love England more than me? Is that what you are telling me Ivan…England is more to love than I…his queen? Do not think for one second that I am not aware of the young ladies he entertains."

Then Ivan lifted his eyes upon the queen and said.

"Can I question the queen about her feelings? No…I may not. I only say be very careful of the art, it is very dangerous. Some…it took a different route, than what was intended…some…have destroyed their love, and still others their lives with such a powerful device. It could be quit simply overdone."

"Well…" said Rosa, while she dried her eyes with her fingers, and flung her head in the air.

"Thanks for the warning Ivan…I'll try to remember that the next time I want my husbands attention and his affection…and he rejects me…"

Rosa picked up the bottom of her dress, and made her exit from the room.

Subsequently the queen made another attempt with the king.

"Your majesty!" said the guard, "the king has said he should not be disturbed…wait!"

Rosa walked right pass the guard, and intruded on Lyonus with two young maidens one on each side of him sitting on his bed. She flung the door wide opened. The guard came in behind her. "Sorry your majesty, I tried to stop my lady." The king furious yelled at the guard. "Get out you idiot…and close the door!" Then Rosa shouted.

"Lyonus! I can not believe you have spurned me yet again."

"Rosa!" said the king, as he rose up to see her face. "You have come at a most inconvenient time. I did not send for you! I was not to be disturbed!"

"Disturbed? You did not send for me? Lyonus I am your wife!" Then Rosa yelled at the maidens while she swatted them away. "Get out! Get yourselves out now!"

Both young ladies looked at the king for his sanction before they moved. Then Rosa continued to shout. "Remove yourselves from these quarters, or I will have you thrown in the dungeon!" Then Lyonus looked at the girls and moved his eyes toward the door and then said. "Just go for now." The girls prodded the king for their gift. Rosa swatted at the girls once again.

The girls leaped from the bed tugged for their clothes, and fought for the door.

The guard rushed in the room. He walked right into the girls as they ran out.

"Go! I said all of you out!"

Then the guard quickly closed the door.

"I dare you intrude!" said the king, outraged at Rosa' behavior.

"Dare my lord? Was this why you found it so taxing to come to me?"

"I am the king." Rosa interrupted him and then said.

"I care not. I am your queen, your wife Lyonus, what of that? Being king does not mean you should ignore your wife and take the chastity from young maidens."

"I have taken nothing!" said Lyonus, as he raged on. "Those ladies loved me."

"Have you heard what you have said Lyonus? They love nothing but the gold and jewels you have given them." Rosa held the bedpost and dropped her head as if in despair "Don't think I haven't been ashamed when they've laughed at me behind my back, while they flaunted the things you'd given them in my face."

"Listen Rosa!" said the king. I have privileges that are ordained by…"

Rosa immediately cut him off by saying. "Oh no you don't! Don't you dare put God in your evil my lord."

Lyonus responded with a very careful indignation when he said.

"You might won't to choose your words more carefully my dear. Life is quite a fragile thing you know.

"As king, the example would fall to you. As their leader, whom else should the people have looked to for that which is right?"

The king rose from the bed and put on his robe and then remarked.

"Do you think this little farce would honor your husband?"

"Is that questioning for me my lord? Perhaps you should ask the question of yourself."

"You mean to hurt me then is that it?"

"For months you've ignored me Lyonus. Did you not think that would hurt me? You have all these maidens, and yet you can mention hurt."

"Well, I've asked because you seemed intent on making me a pig."

"I've made you nothing!" said Rosa, as she remembered the kings warning. Rosa's memory, helped her softened her voice. She moved close to him and then said. "I've merely pointed out to my lord that you are bound to me. I am here for your pleasure…for you my king." Rosa pulled off her robe revealing her tight sheer nightgown that highlighted her silhouette.

Lyonus almost groping fastened his eyes on her. She kissed him and they starred the one into the eyes of the other, and then the king said. "Why my lady, it has been such a long time…too long, I can hardly remember…"

The queen walked to the table and then poured Lyonus a drink of wine, making sure to draw his attention. She did not forget however, to shake in a little of her special powder.

"Yes…now it is time for you to re-acquaint yourself with me." Then she handed him the drink.

"Here you are my husband, drink this wine, and remember me, remember the love of your queen…"

Lyonus took the goblet and drank until it was finished and then threw the goblet to the floor. Rosa pulled off his robe and laid him back on the soft bed with many fluffy pillows. She climbed along side him and began to whisper in his ear making a chanting sound, as they finally spent a night together. That night king Lyonus I, would sire and heir.

The next day Rosa went to her chamber for her bath in realization of what had happened.

I *have conceived*!" she said to herself. *Now there will be an heir to the throne…!*

She laughed, as if having gone completely mad.

Some time had passed since the queen talked with the seer, then one very early morning before the sun showed its' face; Rosa came to Ivan with the news of her pregnancy.

"Ivan…Ivan, I want to tell the king of my pregnancy. Should I tell him now, or have you foreseen some calamity? Please, tell me quickly! I don't want to chance another miscarriage."

"Your majesty, it's rather early. He yawned loudly and then asked. "Will the king even remember being with you?"

"Ivan…" said the queen.

"There could be great blame here…!" said Ivan.

"Have you ever known of anyone to get pregnant from a dream?"

"Well…" said Ivan, as he hunched his shoulders.

"Silence! You fool! Are you aware to whom you speak…I am the queen of England!"

"Yes…certainly…my lady."

"Besides Ivan, I have taken care of the kings memory, he will recall what ever I need for him to. You just tell me what lies ahead…"

"Your majesty…" Then Ivan took a step forward, and bowed to the queen.

Then Rosa interrupts.

"And again tell me…why do you always have to sneak about with…that lord Guy? It has caused some to wonder if perhaps your loyalties may have been a little misplaced…Ivan."

"Utter nonsense my lady. I've never been disloyal to you…why I've kept your every confidence. Why do you suggest?"

"I suggest nothing…I want to be assured that the things we've discussed will remain in your heart."

"No place else my lady…no place else." Ivan answered bowed to the floor.

"Good! Let's keep it that way shall we…Get up!" Then she looked him in the eyes and said. "Very good Ivan, for the day you reveal my secrets, will be the day you no longer see." She followed with a smug expression and said, "Now then, since we've settled the question of trust, on to the matter at hand."

"Your majesty…" said Ivan.

Rosa quietly closed the door behind her.

"Now…what have you seen…in those dreams, or visions or whatever you call them…?"

He stared into space for a moment, as if deciding what to say.

Ivan had seen something, which only a few days ago he had reported to Lord Guy and the other ministers. He was told not to reveal it because it would alarm the queen and king.

"Ivan…! Shouted Rosa, I am speaking to you!" Ivan thought back on what lord Guy had said. He shuttered for a moment then said.

"My queen, I see nothing in the future of you or your unborn."

"What? You lie!" said the queen. "I demand to know what I am sure by now every one else already knows!"

"Please my lady!" Ivan backed up across the room then folded to his knees. "Please!"

"I demand to know! It is likely that you have already told Lord Guy and those other idiots. I command it…now!"

She pushed her way across the room and moved in closer to Ivan.

"I…van!" said Rosa. I have a right to know everything that concerns my child."

"Mi lady…then I can only say that the child will not be given a royal welcome.

Then Rosa interrupts.

"What…what do you mean not receive a royal welcome, I don't understand?"

"Your majesty please…to tell you more would cause lord Guy to have my head."

"Ivan…if you don't tell me, I will have your head myself, and use it as a table ornament…now speak up! Do it quickly, I have lost my patience with your nonsense."

Queen Rosa spun around the room, paced back and forward, then stopped just short of Ivan. Both of his hands flew up to his face, as to protect it from a blow.

"Put down your hands…you fool."

"All right…all right, you want to know what I've seen in the darkness. Then listen until your blood freezes and your heart pounds to stop it's beating"

He encompassed her as he proceeded to impede her thoughts. "Look deep, deep into my eyes, into my dreams that you may see…you will see what I have seen!"

Rosa tried to take a step back, in what seemed to be some sort of spell. Then Ivan came closer.

"Look deep, deeper, your child, not male or female, but a child, then there were two."

Ivan walked closer to the queen, with his eyes stretched. He grabbed her shoulders and looked into her eyes all the more as he continued.

"One covered in blood—blood that came not from the child—but flowed onto the infant. The place we cannot see—only the eyes—they are of crystal blue. For the darkness cannot give way, and it covers everything. Here you see wild beasts that stand over the child, whose mouths snarl and foam, as if waiting for a bit; each beast had a sword between their teeth. Now they are digging a deep pit one filled with blood…they cast in the blue eyes of the night…"

Ivan quickly loosened the queen.

"There…There now it is finished. Ivan closed his eyes again, and walked away panting, and then shook his head saying.

"I can see no more, it is done."

Both continued to their labored breathing.

"Ha…ah…!" Rosa gasped and then said. Why that was…horrible, so much blood. And this…you would want to keep from me? "

Rosa shook her head and then sat herself down.

"What…what does it all mean?"

"My queen, I cannot say. I could not interpret it. What I have seen, I have merely seen."

"Merely seen…? The life of the heir to the throne of England, and you say, you have merely seen…?

The queen leaped from her seat.

"You must have had some idea…Surely there must be a meaning to this horror?"

Rosa, wrung her hands in and out frantic, she remembered what the relationship was like between her and the king during the last miscarriage.

"There must be an answer…" she insisted.

"Surely you are correct, my queen, but it has not yet been revealed in my visions."

"Your visions…"

Said Rosa with disgust, then began to question all the more.

"Well have you told anyone of this? Have you sought the king…did he advise you not to say anything, was it he? Or did he say what he thought of your…dream?"

"Dreams…No mi lady, they are visions of the future. I have entertained visions that have taken me deep into the hearts of men. I have seen into their very souls." Then Rosa interrupts.

"Yes…you can do all that, yet, you can not do so a simple a thing as interpret one for me!"

"Your majesty…I have made manifest the deepest desires of some, and sealed the graves of others, but this I can tell you my queen, nothing that is fated can be changed, but that which is intended can be altered."

"What…you come to me with riddles…?"

The queen began to grit her teeth.

"I need to know…Is there perhaps some spell that could change this for my son…I wish to know it."

"There is no great potion any magic to use that can tamper with the fates."

"I don't wish to know about the fates, but rather let them take care of the things that matter to them. I want to know what can be done to save my child from death. That is my wish…"

"I only know that the heart of man changed, can sway the act of fate. That is the only thing I know…"

"Useless then!" said the queen, forging her way passed Ivan.

"Unless of course…maybe I should use more potions to silence your fates."

"My lady no!"

"If I could change the fate of the kingdom with an heir, then I can find some way to protect that same heir from your fates…"

"Not mine your majesty…"

"Then whose? For they have disappointed me, and taken many a seed to the grave. But this time I will have my way. I will not see my child destroyed by you or the fates or anyone else…is that quite understood?"

"Your will is mine…great lady."

"Good…then we must precede with great care. I must tell the king at once."

"Wait!" said Ivan, "let us think this through…"

"This vision can not be kept from my lord Maybe he could make some since of it."

"Mi lady, please…lord Guy ordered me to keep it until it was time to be revealed."

The queen turned to Ivan, with one brow raised and said.

"Well Ivan…I thought perhaps there was another reason you could not share your visions with us. Is Guy the king, or is he a servant Ivan, even unto me?

"Majesty." Ivan said as he bowed.

"Then…consider it time…!" she demanded.

For Ivan feared the wickedness of lord Guy, even more that the king, but he did not dare to face the wrath of the queen. Ivan made one last bow as the queen made here exit, then said.

"Just has you have ordered, your majesty."

"Come with me Ivan."

"Yes great queen."

"We will inform Lyonus at once…then you may take your leave, I have grown tired of your presence. A word of warning Ivan," she said as she paused from her stride. "You had better make sure there is no miscarriage involved in this vision before you tell the king…"

They immediately continued to make their way to the hall that lead to the king's chambers. Queen Rosa began to lag behind. Ivan dreaded to go inside, but he knew that the only way the queen would be contented would be that the King be informed. So Ivan addressed the guard that stood at the door of the kings' chambers.

"Good day there." Lowly nodding his head at the guard.

"Good day Ivan…state your business."

"You know my business is with the king!"

"He asked not to be disturbed."

Queen Rosa finally made her way to the door.

"What is this?"

"I merely asked if the king has awakened."

"I believe the king can see you now your majesty."
"Has he not awakened?" said the queen.
"I will announce you."
"You do just that." scoffed Rosa.

The guard rapped then tapped at the chamber door. "Your majesty…your majesty!"

"Yes…"answered the king, while he grunted to clear his throat. Yes I'm awake…what is it Hudson?" The king crossed, as if pulled from a deep sleep.

"Ivan the Seer, and her majesty, bid audience with you this morning sire."

"Who? Who did you say…Ivan? Said the king, well…then have them enter."

While they entered the room, the king began to mutter. "It must be pretty important

If they have come at this ungodly hour, the rooster has not yet crowed."

The king looked at Rosa and kissed her on her forehead. "Good morning my dear."

Then looked at Ivan, and cleared his throat. "Um…um…hum…what brings you two here together? Could it not wait for the king to have his breakfast?

"My lord," said Ivan, still shaking from Rosa's threats. "I have had yet another vision."

"Oh…my old friend, the time for war and battles are over for a time, can we not enjoy the blessing of peace."

"Begging His majesty's pardon, but it has nothing to do with war."

"No!" groaned the king. "Of what then? Spit it out man, for goodness sakes, I haven't all day!"

"Sire…it has to do with your unborn children. My lady feared to tell you because of her past miscarriages."

"What…my un…born…what have you been conjuring? You get out!" Lyonus annoyed pointed to the door. "Rosa what is this?" he asked sharply.

"My lord…" said Rosa, while trying to clam him.

It could hardly be explained for the king was still ranting around about the room, and then he paused and said.

"Such foolishness…I've never heard of such. Ivan, it is too early for these kinds of games. You and I both know, Rosa has not been able to have a child, since her last miscarriage, two years ago…Rosa…Explain this!" said the king.

Ivan spoke up in her stead.

"Listen your majesty…the fates had a different ending for you. The queen herself told me just moments ago that she was indeed pregnant. She wanted to know if I had foreseen anything in the future for the child."

Then Queen Rosa spoke again.

"Yes Lyonus…and he told me such a ridiculous story, I had to let you hear it."

"Wait…! Now…just wait, slow down Ivan. You're saying…that my wife…the queen, is now pregnant…and she asked you…to come tell me?"

"Not quite sire, please, just a minute more."

"I'm sorry Ivan, go on and continue."

"When Mi lady came to me, I was not at all surprised at what she had to say. Because only days ago, I had envisioned something that was not yet clear. Oh I had seen well enough, but I did not know what to make of it."

"Did you receive just a glimpse of it or what?"

"No my king, it could not be detailed in my mine. So I went to lord Guy, he asked me to keep the matter quiet until he should tell me. He said to tell you would cause a problem if queen Rosa were to have one more miscarriage. And that is why I did not come directly to you both with this before."

"Now I'm lost Ivan. How is it that my lord Guy could dictate what you should or should not say to me or my queen…Is he now a seer of dreams…can he lay hold on the future…?"

"No sire."

"Then I ask you…is he king of England?"

"I'm sorry your majesty, I feared him…what he would do if I were to come to you with my vision. But when the queen asked it of me, I could not refuse her will. Queen Rosa came to me after I had already spoken with lord Guy. She bided me show her the vision. When it frightened her, she insisted I tell you everything. But my lord king."

As he stopped to look around the room, said.

"I cannot suffer through it again, my lord…please do not require it of me."

"Oh…said the king. But you will do it again!" he insisted.

King Lyonus demanded the vision be told, and not one detailed deleted. Ivan tried his best to reveal all to the king. When they were finished, the king was so shaken, that he fell back into the large chair that sat at the end of the table.

"Ivan…your powers…a great mystery," said the king in utter amazement.

"Indeed sire…"

"Does this mean that my son will die by the hand of some wild animal or something?"

"My lord, it is not clear to me what it means."

"Hum…" mumbled the king. Then perhaps…when it comes to you, and I trust it will be soon Ivan…you will not hesitate to reveal it to me…first. Do we understand each other?"

"Without fail, your majesty."

"Ah…there then my dear…the matter is settled Ivan knows exactly what to do…"

"But what about the…?" Before she could finish the king put up his hand for her to stop.

While he caught his breath, Rosa moved around the breakfast table rather slowly. She chose all the king's favorite things, she made sure to shake enough power to enhance her potion, and then she sat them down in front of him.

"This is nice Lyonus…it's wonderful being together like this again. It's been so long since we've had breakfast together. I've missed those times Lyonus." Rosa confessed, as she walked around his chair her pressing her lips against his ear. Remember how you treated me…but remember our love," she whispered.

The king glanced up at Rosa, with a look that seemed to pierce her.

"I'm sorry my lord, I haven't given you a chance to say anything."

Then just as suddenly a look of admiration came over his face, then he said with a smile.

"First of all I want to say, my dear…I'm so sorry. I want to apologize for my neglect all this time. But I want you to know you could still have come to me with anything you needed. Well what ever may have been the bother my dear, what I'm trying to say is…I've wronged you." Then once again the king seemed confused and then said. However Rosa, I do remember you coming to me my dear. Well…can you ever forgive me…?

"Do you have to ask my king…I forgave you each time I wanted you to hold me and you turned your back, or when I smiled your way and you dropped your face from me only to smile at other maidens. But I must rid these things from my heart."

"Then all is as it should be, let's not dwell upon the miseries of the past."

"I agree my lord…we should embrace the future…"

"Well, I am just so happy you are with child…I must celebrate!"

"Then my love…let me give you one more reason…!" said Rosa.

"More…what more could there be…?"

"The surgeon said there might be two."

"Ho…ho…oh!" laughed the king. He reared back in his chair, and then stood with a proud stance. It's wonderful…finally a chance, there will be two heirs to the throne."

"Yes, I am happy you are so pleased my lord." They embraced each other, and used that moment for several long kisses. Then as was the practice of Lyonus I, he celebrated good news with a hunt followed by a feast.

"I'm more than happy my dear. I think it is time for a hunt…I feel great!"

"Hudson…!" shouted Lyonus.

"Yes your majesty…?" said Hudson.

"Send for the wine maker…"

"Jacob Corley my lord?"

"Yes…I want enough wine for the feast when I return. He knows just what I require."

"Yes your majesty…at once."

"All right Lyonus…" said Rosa. But at least finish your breakfast first dear."

Lyonus and Rosa embraced each other again.

Just then Lyonus opened his eyes and saw that Ivan was still standing there, so quiet and still, as if he was a fixture in the room. Then the king said.

"Oh Rosa darling, we have forgotten Ivan is still waiting."

Then Rosa strolled toward the window looked out at the garden and then said.

"Well…just dismiss him." While she flaunted her hands, she then turned and said.

"Or maybe take him hunting with you. Perhaps he can show you where the deer are hiding with one of his famous visions, or dreams or whatever he calls them."

Rosa voiced her sarcasm, then sat down in the chair to eat.

Lyonus and Ivan turned to leave the room, when the king spun, and walked over to Rosa—then while he held her shoulders—he leaned in to whisper.

"My dear, don't take his visions too lightly, he's brought us many victories…" The king paused for a moment then said. "Wait…I'll be right back."

The king took a minute to walk Ivan out. Rosa tilted her head slightly around the chair and then spoke aloud.

"It doesn't matter what he has seen, I will have my children!" She stood a second and then said to herself. I *will place a spell to protect my child from the womb*. Then she said aloud again while she walked to the window, as if speaking to the wind. I will secure their survival, and ensure no one will harm them. They alone, would have to shed blood one from the other before harm would befall them."

When Rosa stood from the table, king Lyonus was entering the room.

"I'd like for us to dine alone this evening my dear…when I return from the hunt." The king stepped closer to Rosa. "It will be a rather late supper, do you mind?"

Rosa beside herself with glee could not wait. "It has delighted my heart. I look forward to the time we will share my lord. It will be wonderful to be with you again…"

"Then until tonight."

"Till then my king."

Lyonus walked Rosa out of his chambers. Rosa was sure to make her way to the kitchen.

Then the king shouted for the guard.

"Guard!"

"Yes…yes your majesty."

"Oh…it's you Hollands."

"Yes…my lord."

"Gather my things and make ready the horses, we're off to the hunt my lad!"

"Your majesty, did you say hunting…?"

"I did indeed my boy, it's a fine morning for it to…a mighty fine morning!'

"Yes sire, a fine morning." The guard was amazed at the king's behavior. It had been so long since the king had shown that type of happiness; he knew it must have been something very special. Hollands smiled at Lyonus and shrugged his shoulders at the other guards; they were all trying to find out why the king was so elated.

"Oh my boy, what of the wine…His father makes the best?"

"We have sent a messenger to the wine maker as we speak sire…"

"Good…good…!" said the king.

King Lyonus was on top of the world, and why not? After all, the woman he chose as his queen finally announced a pregnancy of twins no less. The spark of love rekindled, and to top that off, the kingdom was at rest from war. The land was green with plenty. It indeed would be a new beginning for the royal family.

CHAPTER TWO
Rosa's Last Testament

The days, weeks then the months passed quickly. It was nearing the time for Rosa to deliver. But something was wrong. Rosa continued to have nightmares that she would not live to see her children, some ill will possessed her dreams.

She had also dreamed that there were two children that played in a field; she was there beside them. Then suddenly one child would jump up and smash his foot against the neck of the other. The more she shouted for him to be released the tighter he would press. Then just as suddenly wolves came and ran the child away leaving the other bloody and badly wounded. Then she would awaken from her nightmare.

The next time Rosa dreamed that terrible dream she awoke and arose from her bed, and open the wall behind her fireplace. It revealed the room where she would practice her art. She called upon the power of the night, and traded her life for the lives of her children. She began to chant.

"Into the night…search the night, draw back the life that would be taken…bring the death to me, that no harm should befall the life in my womb. Protect that which waits in my womb, that I may see its face before my end. Into the night, I search the night…!"

She continued as a great storm arose and the winds howled a terrible sound. The winds came through the trees, and into the room of the queen. There the breeze seemed to have possessed her.

Very early the next morning, there was a scream like never before.

"Help! Help me!" yelled Rosa. "They're coming…ha…ha…my babies."

With a cry and then a laugh, again and again until finally she called.

"Please, I need the surgeon. Please get me the surgeon!"

Rosa's screams could be heard down to the end of the corridor. A dark figure of an old woman moved slowly toward Rosa with her arms stretched toward her. She stood near and seemed to tug at the child inside her.

Rosa continued to scream.

"Are you a surgeon? I say are you a surgeon…you bag of old bones…!" she cried.

"No…" she replied in a whispery voice.

"Then who are you?" asked Rosa.

"I am someone you have called for…"

"I called for the surgeon, you idiot!" said Rosa, while she screamed in great pain.

As a result of her pain, the woman, grabbed Rosa hands and then said.

"Come to me…don't push."

"Oh…I…I've got to push…oh…ho…!"

Just then the surgeon entered the chamber.

"Stand back…woman…let me see. What is going on?" said the surgeon.

Then the woman as a shadow suddenly left the room, and the surgeon stood alone with Rosa.

The King was in the outer chambers. He paced back and forward, forward and backward. With every scream, the King walked more and grunted with every step.

"Please your majesty," said one of the guards. "Please sit down sire, before you're worn out from pacing."

"It's hard…the waiting," said the king. I can recall before when Rosa miscarried, it was awful. Indeed, I want to be here for her now."

"I understand my king, I missed the birth of my two sons…the war…you know."

A voice called from the doorway.

"My king…!" Lord Graybourne approached. The king spun around on his seat, with a great smile.

"Ah…my lord Thomas…what a delight my friend."

"Yes your majesty, I share your gladness…but I have some bitter news to share as well."

"Graybourne, on a day like today…with Rosa in delivery. I know it can wait."

Just then Graybourne stepped to the side and revealed the royal cook. This was much to the king's surprise.

"What? Roger, what pray tell are you doing here? Graybourne...what's this all about?"

King Lyonus turned to dismiss the guard waved him out of the room.

"All right Roger, you may speak, what's going on?"

"Your majesty it was brought to my attention some time ago, that the queen made regular visits to the kitchen." The king looked rather puzzled.

"And why would that be so noteworthy of the queen, she often times would go to the kitchen to see how things were prepared, she always said she was fascinated with cooking."

"Please my lord," said Graybourne. Allow him to finish."

"...Sire, when I walked over and asked her how was the stew, just to get a glimpse of the powder, I saw that it was a green substance."

"Oh...now I'm confused."

"The green powder alone is nothing, but when mixed with ambrosial root!"

Then the king chimed in. "One of the spices I love so much in venison stew?"

"The very same sire..."said Roger. After that your majesty, I did not know whom to trust, except of course my lord Graybourne, so I told him what I had seen."

"Thank you Roger, you have nothing to fear from your king. I don't understand why Rosa would want to do such a thing. We've been happy these last seven months, or at least it seemed so...Graybourne?"

"Yes your majesty...after talking with Roger, I went to see the surgeon. I got him to at least agree with Roger that this root combined with others..."

"Like ambrosial root?" the king added.

"Yes my lord like ambrosial root. When added to others, it could, in small doses be used as a sedative in small animals. The affect in humans over a period of time my lord, would act as a slow moving poison...very slow."

"This is just preposterous! The more the king objected the more Rosa seemed to scream. "Why would she? She would not dare! She would not harm her king!" Suddenly the king headed for her chamber door, when he heard a yell.

"Wait, your majesty...this is not the time or place to address the queen on the matter...sire...!"

King Lyonus turned and without a word, stormed out into the outer room.

Just then he heard the most heart-wrenched scream that came from Rosa, as if it were a last breathe.

"Ah…hah…"said Rosa, who now seemed at peace. Let the night bring them…let the darkness obey…come, bring forth from the womb…ah…hah. I have seen them…they are born…Ah…Now death may run it's course."

As she gasped the last drop of air, her hand fell passed her and dropped to the floor.

There could be heard, the sound of air being released from her lungs that gave off a hideous sound.

Then Lyonus stormed into the outer room, pushed the guard out of the way, and

Pulled open the door to Rosa's room. When much to his dismay, queen Rosa laid in a puddle of blood, the surgeon stood over her. The chambermaid ran over and fell at the feet of the king, and then screamed with tears.

"Oh…oh my lord, our queen is gone…is gone!"

"No…!" said the king. No, this cannot be! What trick has fate played against me?" At that moment the surgeon replied.

"Yes, your majesty, I'm afraid queen Rosa is dead. We could not stop the bleeding sire. I've never seen so much blood…it was not possible, she should not have bled so much."

"But your majesty, your sons, twins…are okay…they will be just fine."

Lord Graybourne rushed in to lead the king to his chambers. The surgeon prepared a drink for the king, and told him to drink it and rest. Then the king turned back to the midwife and said.

"Victoria."

"Yes, your majesty," she replied, as she hurried to join them.

"Why…do my eyes deceive me, were you not here but a moment ago?"

"I have just arrived my lord. I was told the queen was ready to deliver, I came with all speed sire."

"Then who was that woman here with the queen?"

"I cannot say my king…should I ask the surgeon?"

Then the surgeon reached out to Victoria, and handed the king a drink. Then said.

"Come Victoria, take the children and clean them up…Sire you should drink…"

"Yes my lord," said Victoria, a little surprised by the questions.

"Would you take care to bring my sons,…bring them to me later…? I think I will rest now."

Lyonus looked back at the surgeon. "Whatever that drink was...it's got me a little...well it's been a trying day, perhaps for everyone."

The surgeon never looked up at the king, but said.

"You will feel better after you have rested. I'll come and check in on you later, my lord."

"Come...my lord king," said Graybourne. We will all grieve for our queen. But for now, let the weight of today's troubles be lifted with rest."

"Yes...yes, always you are here for me. The surgeon did give me drink." The king began to fade.

"Sire." The king became drowsier as he walked to his room.

"Always you are here by my side...even in battle...remember my lord Thomas. Side by side, the great Thomas of the blade."

Graybourne smiled in great content.

"I remember, my lord. We were au pair, ha...ha...ha!"

Finally, the guard opened the door for Graybourne and the king.

"Here we are your majesty." Graybourne slowly helped the king to his bed.

"Oh let us remove this robe. I'll come back, when I think you've had enough time to sleep sire."

The king so slurred in his speech, for the drug had now taken effect.

"Thomas..." he muttered. "M...my boys...watch out for them please."

Graybourne answered with great pride.

"With my life, my king...with my life, now rest." Then proceeded to close the chamber door that would creek just a little.

Lord Thomas took pains to make sure the twins were okay. He started to trot, to the royal nursery. In his haste, he ran straight into lord Fredrick Guy.

"Oh...my goodness...I'm sorry." Now taking a moment to notice. "Why Lord Guy, what...I thought you were still out of the city. His majesty has been making inquiry all day. Where were you old friend?" Lord Guy stumbling over his words.

"Well...I...um...Tragedy, isn't it...the queen so young. Leaving the king with two boys to raise, it will be difficult for him. He'll need us now...hey Graybourne?"

"Tragic indeed Guy," he said, as he rubbed his chin. I'll inform the king you've returned, but for now the surgeon gave him a sedative to rest." Graybourne walked away.

"Oh I see...well."

Thomas yelled back to lord Guy.

"Sorry...lord Guy, I must attend the young princes'."

"Ah…quite right lord Graybourne…"

Now when lord Graybourne entered the nursery, Victoria had already cleaned, fed and dressed the children. She had them tucked safely in their cribs, waiting for their nurse Jeanine to arrive.

"Thanks Victoria for all your care. I know how hard this must be for you."

Victoria dropped her head, then inch by inch; she raised it again with pride then said.

"No, my lord, I have found it not at all the way you have pictured it."

Thomas stood there with a look of confusion on his face.

"Well I meant about the queen and the boys, and everything that has transpired."

Victoria cut him short, and then said.

"Well indeed, I knew exactly what you meant Thomas…my heart has had plenty of nights to heal, and plenty of days filled with the sight of other folks children. Their tears and the groans…it's all a bit much now. Let us just not go over it Thomas…not here, and certainly not now!"

Thomas sprang closer to Victoria, close enough even to kiss.

"Victoria," he whispered faintly in her ear, in his all too proper tone. There is no need for this. I was…we were young. And I was committed too…"

"Yes…yes, I know, you were committed to yourself, and your damned glory. You left me…I made a decision based on what was right for me!"

"Wait Victoria…"

"No…! Did you think I would be stupid enough to live as an unmarried pregnant girl forced to live as an outcast…Thomas Hendly Graybourne, where was your mind? Or did you lose it when you became betroth to Lady Claire?'

Thomas took a deep breath, and paused for a second, but Victoria chimed right in.

"Did you think I could not get the picture? Good enough to bed but not good enough to wed! Well Thomas, I got the picture…I certainly got that!"

"Stop! Just stop it Victoria…please! If you'd hold on for a moment, I'd explain."

"Go right ahead…or did you think I would turn away and not allow you to! Oh…I can't wait to hear this. Make it good Graybourne…" She showed what was meant to be an attempt at sarcasm. But out of breath from her venting, she leaned over even closer to Thomas. The heat from their bodies made it almost impossible for Victoria to stand still.

By now Thomas was more than eager to explain.

"As I said before Victoria, being in the king's service, was no place for a married man, especially at the time. But after I read your letter about our child, I went to the king, and begged him to let me leave my post to come to you...and Victoria, I had planned to run away if he refused me...commit desertion to be with you."

"Well...what happened?"

"I was wounded, and lay unconscious they tell me, for six months."

"Then wh...where did they take you...why didn't some one tell me? They must have known I'd worry."

"Victoria, listen to yourself...you know where we were. In the time of war, no one was spared. Men lost their body parts, their lands, children, and families not to mention their lives. No one wanted to face another loved one. Besides you were simply one out of thousands who felt the loss. You must try and understand! I met Claire at a time when I too needed to be saved. I realize, this may not be what you thought or wanted to hear, nevertheless, it's the truth."

Just as Thomas finished, Victoria kissed him with a great swelling embrace. Even he was surprised at their tender moment of passion as he retuned the kiss.

Thomas knew Victoria had held such anger in her heart, that words alone could not ease the strain of it. He slowly released her from his clutches, and then said.

"Never again...can we dare to do this my love..." Tears began to stream from both their eyes. They began to back slowly away from each other...their arms releasing then their hands...until finally...their fingertips. Then Victoria spoke up, with a tremble in her voice.

"Never, ever can we...Thomas my love."

As soon as Thomas and Victoria patched their relationship, trying to place old feelings behind them, there came a knock at the door. Then it opened, with nurse Jeanine peeking her head through the door.

"Oh...sorry," she said, with a giggle and bounce. "Am I interrupting something...this is the nursery isn't it?" Thomas seemed a little offended, replied.

"No...you haven't interrupted anything...aren't you a bit too young to care for babies?

"Begin' your pardon sir...I had small brothers at home. I care for them. I had great references. The queen's lady gave me the job...but if you don't want me to stay..." When she turned as if to leave the room, Victoria said.

"Wait now, I don't have any problem, if the queen had chosen you, then by all means come right in. Here they are, England's little heirs."

Jeanine looked at Victoria, and then over into the crib. One at a time she peered into the crib, back and forward, until finally she said with great awe.

"Blimey, my lord…no one told me they were two of a kind…aren't they beautiful? I'll have to fine some way to tell them apart."

"Yes," said Victoria. "When I see them together, one seems to look…oh I don't know…a little." Gasped Jeanine. Ha…look at that!" Both Thomas and Victoria said almost in unison. "Wh…What is it child?"

"Why one of them has brown eyes and one has blue eyes. Imagine that…can you see them? Just come very close and look…Hold his eyelid open. There you see! Can you see them? Look!" she said, as she pointed down into the crib at the babies.

"You're so right!" said Victoria.

"Lord Graybourne?"

"Yes…I see it. I guess now you have found your way of telling them apart."

"Ha…ah…oh!" laughed Victoria. "Now you need only know their names…Ah?'

"Right you are there ma'am, right you are," said Jeanine. "I have a thought about that too, that is if nobody minds me stepping in to say so sir."

Victoria then pulled Jeanine to her. "What do you to want to say Jeanine?" Victoria seemed anxious to hear.

"Well ma'am…sir, you could maybe suggest to the king, that he name one son after himself…"

"Great…and easy, but…what of the other?"

"Well let her finish…my lord," roared Victoria.

"As I have said, one after the king, and the other after…what's his grandfathers name?"

"Oh Luis I believe," said Thomas.

"Then after his grandfather Luis, the queen's grandfather."

"You know Jeanine, I think you're going to be a fine nurse for our little princes'," remarked Thomas. Then proceeded to pat her on the shoulders.

"Why thank you sir. I shall do my best." Victoria joined in the praise. "I think the boys will grow to love you. Welcome to the royal household of Warwick. You will make a wonderful addition, I'm sure."

"Sorry to break this up, but I need to look in on his majesty." Graybourne tried to side step the cribs, but bumped into one of them. "Oops…don't want to wake them just yet do we? Good evening Ladies."

"Good evening, lord Thomas," said Jeanine.

"Yes goodbye Thomas." Victoria found herself sneaking to blow a kiss with her fingertips to her mouth. She did not want to be seen by either Thomas or Jeanine.

Thomas made good on his promise to check on the children, made his way back to the king's chambers.

On his way to the king, he saw the lady Kathryn strolling down the corridor.

"Good evening my lady," said Graybourne

"Good day sir," she replied, on her way to spy outside the kings' chambers.

"Where are you off to?" he asked. Remember the king is having a meeting now?"

"Well then I guess it's no point in a visit is there my lord?"

"No, I just thought I'd save you from going a step further," he added.

"Yes…" said Kathryn.

The guard standing at the king's door spied Graybourne rounding the corner. "Ah…good evening my lord Graybourne." Thomas acted as if caught off guard.

"Oh…hello there. His majesty is expecting me."

"Well then you are just in time for the party."

"Party?" said Graybourne.

"Why yes my lord. There is lord Guy and Henry Becket, the surgeon, and Ivan the seer."

"Hum…sounds serious enough, I'd better get in there."

"Yes sir, pardon me for saying so…but I think it wise."

All the while pushing the door open for him.

"Thanks Hollands, you're a good man."

"Good evening sire…gentlemen. All is well, your majesty."

"Lord Thomas, good…come, come. We're making a decision on the queen's burial."

Lord Thomas looked around at the others, while nodding his head, and then remarked.

"I understand the situation, so what did you come up with my king?"

"Lord guy here suggests that I send her body back to her grandfather, and let her family give her a burial in Spain. While Ivan felt I should allow England to mourn her properly with a Christian burial here. Now what do you think, lord Thomas?"

"And Henry…what does he think, my lord?" Then Henry ready with his answer said.

"I don't think either one matters much. Our loss is great, so where ever she is laid to rest, our queen will be mourned."

"Well said my friend…" said Lord Guy Well said."

"And you Thomas."

Thomas turned toward the king.

"Your majesty, it all sounds okay, but if you are not ready to travel to Spain for a month, I suggest a funeral in the court yard. Open it to the people."

The kings' eyes brightened, but he could not help but think of what Roger had told him earlier. He made up his mind to dismiss the thought, since Rosa was no longer around to defend herself. Then the king said.

"Wonderful, wonderful…I liked the idea of the people being involved. All right then that is the way we will handle the matter."

"All right your majesty," said lord Guy. I will send a courier to Spain at once…we must inform the royal family of the queens' death, as soon as possible."

Lyonus searched the room, and eyed each man.

"Are we all agreed?" Everyone spoke up almost together, "Agreed." The nodded their heads in one accord.

Lady Kathryn had been listening outside the Chamber door. She hurried away, but not without dropping a few pieces of gold behind her for the silence of the guard.

"Well it is time to dine now. Will you all join me?" said the king. Lord Guy, I do wish to discuss your trip this evening."

"Well your majesty…let me beg off right now, there is something I must attend before I dine this evening. Please my lords, accept my apologies."

"I understand lord Guy, it is allowed, but join me first thing in the morning, without fail."

"Thank you my king…and good night."

Guy backed away and bowed out of the room.

"Then shall we all adjourn to the dining hall?" said the king.

As the group walked down the corridor to the dining hall, the king tugged slightly at Graybourne's sleeve, then whispered. "My sons…are they okay?"

"Yes my king, the new nurse has arrived. She has come in and taken complete charge. She seemed to be quite capable of caring for them."

"Good…good to know. I'll go by as soon as we finish our meal."

"Sounds fine my king, whatever you desire…"

"All right Thomas, I know you…there is something wrong, you know I can tell."

Graybourne, with such a solemn look on his face said.

"I can't put my finger on it my lord…but something just doesn't feel right somehow…I can't explain it…It just feels wrong…"

"Well Thomas when you figure out what it is, I hope you will feel the need to share it."

"Yes your majesty…I shall."

After dining, the king and lord Graybourne walked to the nursery. When the guard opened the door, the king stepped in first, and found Jeanine and the twins cuddled up in a large quilt that was made for them. The quilt was very beautiful, and of many colors.

It was hand made by Rosa's grandmother in Spain. Now Jeanine was seated in a large oval chair with the quilt spread around her. She held a prince in one arm, and a prince in the other.

"Will you look…your majesty."? Said Graybourne. Jeanine motions for their silence.

"Sh…sh…please whisper, I just got them to sleep."

"Don't worry my dear Jeanine…" Just then Jeanine gasped, and groaned in a deep whisper, then looked up from the chair. "Oh…I…it's you your majesty. I did not mean…I did not know it was you, I'm sorry."

"Ah…don't worry, I'm not a monster. I will be careful not to wake them, I'm just so anxious to spend time with them. Now I have to get on with the business of giving them a name."

"Well my lord." announced Graybourne. Jeanine had a wonderful suggestion from earlier today."

"A suggestion? How so?"

"If I may Jeanine…?"

"Oh sure…please go right ahead," said Jeanine, with a huge grin on her face.

"Your majesty…she thought…Jeanine thought, that you could name one son after you, and one after queen Rosa's grandfather Luis," said Victoria.

"Ah…that's a great idea…I only need decide which one will be Lyonus II, and which Luis."

"I'm glad you have approved my king," said Jeanine. She rose up the blue-eyed son and handed him to the king.

"Your majesty!" she announced. Meet the prince of England, Lyonus II.

His eyes are pitched blue, just like yours my lord…if you don't mind my saying so sire?"

The king chuckled a little, and then replied.

"Oh…oh Jeanine, you are a spice to life right now…It's a pleasure to have you here."

Jeanine forgot to point out the special trait of Luis, called for the kings' attention, then said.

"Oh yes, and here is your other little prince, Luis, the first-born prince of England. He my lords, has dark brown eyes."

"Well my king, it seems, Jeanine Numero, has it all figured out."

"Indeed." smiled the king. Indeed she does."

Then he looked at his son lying so peaceful in his arms, and started to rock him gently back and forward. The king placed Lyonus II back in his crib. As he left he shared with Jeanine that he planned to spend lots of time with his sons. He also made it known, that he was satisfied that his boys were in good hands and being taken care of properly. He was now able to take care of his duties that had been neglected.

CHAPTER THREE
Twin Heirs

Many years had passed since the death of queen Rosa, and the little princes' had grown.

Daily the king would take little Lyonus II, out with him on long walks. He always found time to read, and teach him personally all the protocol of the court, especially the duties of the king. All the while leaving little Luis to the tutors and servants.

One very warm summer day, nurse Jeanine walked into their room, and found Luis snuggled in a corner crying his eyes out.

"Oh, dear Luis, what in the world is the matter?"

She began to wipe the tears from his eyes, and then said. "No prince should have to cry, not on a beautiful afternoon, like today. Come…sit here beside me." She moved over to make room for Luis along side her. But he climbed straightway into her lap. Jeanine began to calm him.

"Little one, be at ease…tell me what is wrong."

"Father…my father, has taken Lyon hunting with him, and he would not let me come along."

"What?…Do you mean he has taken him hunting again?"

"Yes…I wanted to hunt, but he said I should get busy with my studies."

"Well Luis, your father is the king after all, and he does know what is best for you…"

Luis cut her sharply.

"No…! He cares nothing for me! The only one who cares is Fredrick."

"Whom did you say?" questioned Jeanine, as she reared back to look him in the eye. Are you talking about lord Guy? Tell me child is that right...?"

"Well...and maybe you Jeanine..."

"Oh honey...listen, your father loves both of you equally...but I don't like you spending so much time with lord Guy."

"What do you mean? He cares for me, and he takes me with him everywhere. He takes me to meetings, and horseback riding...and lots of places."

"Yeah...and does the king know about those...lots of places? Your little travels?"

"You know Jeanine...once father told me I reminded him of Fredrick. Is that true? Jeanine, do I look like him?"

"Now Luis...for goodness sakes...don't be ridiculous, and you're being silly.

You're just upset. You have taken things too far Luis."

Before Jeanine could explain further, a knock at the door interrupts them. The door falls open.

"Fredrick...Fredrick it's you...!" The prince ran to meet him."

"Yes my little prince, it is I. Are you ready to do something adventurous today?"

"My lord Guy, I'm afraid Luis has strict rules today," said Jeanine. "The king ordered him to study."

Luis dragged his foot along the floor and hung his head, then said.

"But...he did not say how long...or what time I had to start."

"Luis...mined your manners! You must respect your fathers rules...Luis." Scolded Jeanine.

"Ha...ha...ha..." laughed Guy. "Come son, let us see what the world holds for us today."

"But my lord...you cannot defy the king!" said Jeanine.

"Well, you just let me handle the king..."

"Handle..." scoffed Jeanine

"I will take full responsibility...don't you worry your pretty little head about a thing. I'm sure you have other things to worry about...for instance cleaning this room."

Then Jeanine looked around the room to see what he spoke of, but he was merely trying to put her in her place. He then looked back at her and said to the prince.

"Come Luis, our horses are waiting."

Jeanine so angry, she muttered.

"Yeah…you better be careful your handling doesn't get your head cut off! I never liked that gent…no sir not at all. But Jeanine will keep her eyes on you…yes sir, both eyes on…you!"

Several hours later, Prince Lyonus and the king returned. Lyonus II came charging through the door.

"Hi Jeanine, where is Lou? I wanted him to know what I did today. Father and I went hunting, and he allowed me to help skin a deer…well, a part of it. But where is Luis?"

Before he could finish, the doors swung open, and John Myers walked in. "I'm sorry to intrude ma'am, your highness."

"Ma'am? My name is Jeanine Numero, the child's nurse. But everyone calls me Jeanine."

"Yes ma'am," said John. The king asked me to make sure the prince got changed properly for dinner…didn't know you were here."

"Thanks John, it's been great. The best day ever!"

"Good…I'll see you later little prince."

"Please tell father, that I'll see him at dinner."

"R…right you are there, little one. Good bye ma'am…ah…Jeanine."

"Goodbye," said Jeanine, as she walked around and picked up the dirty clothes Lyonus had flung around the room. She stopped to wipe the dirt from his face.

"Jeanine?" said the prince, while he squirmed about.

"Hold still Lyonus…put this shirt on!" The prince wiggled around anxious to meet his father.

"Jeanine, if father makes me king, will Luis and I still be brothers? Or will he be a servant and angry…sort of like today?"

"Lyonus, I don't know how your father will chose, I just know you should keep in mind, Luis is your brother, and your best friend…"

"But Jeanine one of us is to be king."

"Yes, and you are both wonderful sons, and you both deserve a chance to be happy, whether you are king or not."

Jeanine rubbed her head in deep thought, as she watched Lyonus.

"Oh no Jeanine, father says I'm to be king…I just don't want to lose Luis."

"Well, just remember, keep Luis as your best confidant, and he will always love you."

"Oh good." sighed the prince. I was beginning to worry a bit about that."

"Hum…" said Jeanine as she smirked at him. "Go and have your supper

Lyonus."

"All right Jeanine. And thank you."

"Ha...sure...now go."

Shortly after, Luis came back from his long afternoon with lord Guy.

"I'm back Jeanine!" said Luis, totally excited from his time with lord Guy. "We had a long ride. Fredrick...I mean lord Guy took me all around the countryside. He showed me all the land that I would one day rule."

Jeanine became upset, and immediately grabbed Luis.

"Stop Luis...just give me those dirty clothes. You must get dressed for dinner. Your father will have all our heads. Lyonus has been back and asked for you. He is already in the dining hall."

"Well great...now I can tell him all about my day as well."

"Oh...o, no you don't. If you go spouting your mouth off to your brother, what will your father think you were doing, instead of studying? That's right...and not only you, but I will be in trouble as well."

"I see...Well all right for now, but if he starts bragging about things, I might have to tell him a..."

"Oh, no! Luis, you'd better remember!"

"Just having a bit of fun with you Jeanine...don't worry, father will never know from me."

"All right hurry along now..."

Some time passed, and it was the thirteenth birthday of the Princes'. Everyone buzzed about in preparation for the night's celebration. Luis wanted to do something different.

"Lyon...Lyonus!" said Luis. Let's take some flowers to mothers grave, visit there for a while today."

"What...Luis?" said Lyonus.

"Well, we have not done that in so many years."

"No...no, Luis!"

"Why not Lyonus...?"

"Because I don't want to remember mother's death on my birthday...I don't want them together anymore...it makes me too sad Luis...no!"

"Lyonus...we have to remember her sometime you know. It's not right not to think of her."

No Lou...I don't even remember mother at all. Do you?"

"Well I feel that I do, because of all the things we've been told about her all these years."

"Look if you want to sadden your birthday, and waste the day standing over a stone plague, go right ahead, I have better things to do on my birthday. Besides, father has something special planned, so I shouldn't stray too far if I were you.

"Hum…as everyone keeps reminding me, I'm not you Lyonus…!" Luis mumbled under his breath.

Then Luis decided yet again to challenge the king. He burst into his meeting with his ministers.

"Father…father, please excuse my intrusion, but I need to get your permission!"

The king replied very annoyed.

"L…Luis, I have told you more than once about your brash interruptions…I've reached my limit with you!"

Lord Guy softly intrudes on the king's wrath.

"Pardon…your majesty," he said, with a whispery voice meant to calm the king. The lad…ha…our young prince here is full of excitement. It's his birthday today, becoming a man is a big thing my lord."

The king calmed down a little then turned to Luis.

"Son, say your thanks to our lord Guy today for reminding me what it is like to be a young boy full of impatience. Now…what is it that you desire of me?"

The king raised back into his chair, waiting to hear.

"Father, I want us to go and place flowers on mother's grave and visit for a while today."

The king shook his head back and forward, to indicate no, and then he said.

"Son…there is so much planned, I really can't make time to visit your mothers grave on today."

"Or…you won't try to make time…which is it father?"

"Luis…! Don't be impertinent! Now I have explained to you, in a way I thought you would be able to understand, but you take it too far…" The king tried to control himself and appease the prince and said.

"Luis…maybe we can visit say…next week. How about that?"

"Well father, I thought you were king…"

"What…what do you mean…?"

"When I am king…I will decide how I will spend my time…and with whom."

"I swear that boy is just as suborn as his mother," said the king.

Luis turned and jotted out of the door, and down the hallway. The king shouted for the guard, and Luis.

"L...Luis! You should come back here! Guard...! Somebody stop that child. Stop him at once do you here!"

"My lord he has disappeared," remarked lord Guy.

Then the king shrilled. "I swear I don't know what is to become of that boy."

"To be king perhaps..."said lord Guy sneering, as he watched the king from the corner of his eye.

"Ha...I think not, my lord. A king must be able to rule his own heart before he can rule the hearts of others."

The guard entered and announced. "The prince has vanished, your majesty."

"Ah...into thin air I'll wager," said the king, as he snarled a little.

"Yes my lord...I...I mean...no my lord..."

"Please. Just leave us."

"Yes you majesty."

Indeed, before anyone could catch him, Luis was out of sight. He had locked himself in his room. He flung himself on the bed, and picked up one of his books. Luis spoke aloud.

I don't want to spend the hold day in my room. I guess I'll wait for father to cool down some. I think I made him pretty angry." He was still spouting off.

Hum...He made me pretty angry too! Besides, he's not the only one with feelings,...hum.

Then he flung the large book clear across the room. It hit against a spot by the fireplace, and when it touched down, a door started to open. Luis, with much amazement, shouted.

"Oh boy! Look at that" He leaped from off the bed, and ran over to the fireplace. "Woo...look at that...I bet it leads somewhere in the castle." He felt around more, until he found a latch that made it open and close. "All right!" he shouted. Lyonus will be really surprised...I can't wait to show him this. Well I'd better investigate it first."

He slowly entered into the pathway. It took him directly to a room. Luis thought how strange the room looked. He had never seen anything like it before. It was filled with all kinds of bottles with colored liquid. The room contained tubes and cotton. It held dead insects and caldrons, and all kinds of books.

"What's this color powder for...I wonder?" He walked around a little more, and then spied a book of potions.

"This must be a sorcerers room!" He quickly pasted his palm over his mouth to stop himself from speaking aloud, and then watched to see if anyone heard him.

Luis fascinated, closed the opening and continued to look around. He found a book of spells, and his mothers' journal. The journal read;

"Queen Rosas' book of haunting secrets."

"Mothers journal…!" I wonder…"

Luis thought aloud. *Will this help me to know her? Lyonus was right; I've forgotten her too.*

Luis was steadily fascinated by what he found. He took the book and went back to his room. He crotched down in the old dusty corner by the fireplace, and started to read.

Suddenly Luis's name rang out through the halls. They found him at last.

"Luis…what is going on?"

"You have really made your father angry…but today is your birthday…and he will calm down. Luis…you're studying?" spouted Jeanine.

"Yes…I'm studying…you can tell my father that!"

"Oh…and rude you are, an insult to me and your father. I didn't teach you to be that way.

Luis."

"Jeanine, I love you as a mother I never had, but I am a prince of England. I won't take orders from servants."

"Luis…!" said Jeanine. You don't mean that!"

Luis stood up slammed his book and walked toward the door, then said. "So tell my father what you like…I'll handle him."

Jeanine eyes filled with tears…hurt that Luis has spoken to her in that manner. But she knew from whom he had been taught.

"Yes your highness," said Jeanine. Then she bowed out of the room. She was hurt, but knew none the less who had prompted his behavior. She thought of what might have sparked this change in him. Maybe Luis changed because his father ignored him; or maybe because of his brother, who never missed an opportunity to brag about his relationship with the king; maybe still, it was lord Fredrick Guy, who filled his head full of…only God knows what, half the time. Maybe it's just growing up. Whatever it happened to be there must surely be a middle ground, before it's too late…too late for this lonely boy."

Luis found another quiet spot, and continued to read his mother's journal.

Queen Rosa revealed how horrible King Lyonus had treated her. It went on to show how she had given Lyonus a potion made with Ossa powder, (dried ground poison adder).

The potion was only meant to make him love her, but it was not successful, at least not in time for her.

Of course this struck a nerve within Luis. He thought maybe he would try harder, and come up with a potion that would work.

As he lingered in thought a voice whispered through the crack of the door. "Luis…Luis are you ready?" called John Myers. Everyone is waiting for your presence. The king sent me to fetch you." John came in and looked around the room, and spied him in a corner. Your highness, did you not hear?"

"Yes I heard you. I'll be ready in a moment."

"Please hurry your highness."

Just then lord Guy entered the room.

"Happy birthday…little prince…Happy birthday my boy…! I have something really nice for you…Come on now and join the festivities."

"All right Fredrick…I'm on my way."

"Come lad…we'll walk together."

When Luis and lord Guy finally entered the dinning hall, everyone was seated. The King in good spirit, said.

"Ah…here is my other fine prince. Let everyone toast him this day. This is his thirteenth birthday. Let the festivities begin…!"

The party had all the makings of a royal wedding. There was a giant cake, with all the fancy trimmings. The party included fireworks, loud enough to wake the dead, and not to mention presents of gold and silver.

Now their gifts from the king, were rings with gold bands that encircled rubies, and a center that was a large pearl. Luis's pearl opened to reveal a secret compartment. Lyonus's ring also had a large pearl…the difference…His ring opened to reveal the seal of England. No one commented on the difference King Lyonus had made, but continued with their expressions of congratulations. Lord Guy pulled Luis to the side.

"Come with me my prince, I have your gift outside!"

Luis, and lord Guy went through the side door of the dining hall, and on to the garden wall.

"Open the gate guard!" said lord Guy. All right Luis, cover your eyes…Ready?"

"Yes…I'm ready!"

Lord Guy filled with excitement said. "Open your eyes now my prince!"

"Woo…woo, oh no! For me?"

"All for you…"answered Guy. His chest stuck out, because he knew he had topped the king's gift in the eyes of the prince.

"He's beautiful, I've never seen a horse as wonderful...and he's mine? When can I ride?" Luis so excited...he has always admired beautiful horses.

"Well...ha...ha...why don't we hold off on that until tomorrow, then we will go for a long ride across country...just you and I...Okay!"

"He is the best...and you're the best! Thank you for everything...I can't remember a better birthday my lord."

"Take him to the stables." Lord Guy ordered the guard.

"Wait!" said Luis. "I want just one touch more." He rubbed his hand across the back of the horse. "Look, blue black as ember, with a gray stripe. He's simply splendid! I just can't wait to ride him. I think I'll name him...um...Phantom. What do you think Fredrick?"

"Take him on guard," said Fredrick.

"I'm delighted you are so happy my prince. The name suits him I think, but we'd better get back. I don't want them to start searching for you...they'll be missing you."

"Hum...I suspect we should your grace, though I hardly think I shall ever be missed, at least...not by my father."

"Things have a way of righting themselves, remember that, my prince."

Guy grabbed Luis by the shoulder, then pulled him for a hug.

"When the tables turn...you will be the one person everyone is going to look to...remember that."

"I will...Oh by the way, what did you get for Lyonus?"

"Well...I found a Falcon not so well off, I thought he could spend time nursing it...ha, ha"

"Ha...ha..." They both laughed as they walked back to the great hall.

Meanwhile, everything began to wind down, as Luis and the lord Guy rejoined the festivities. Only Jeanine wondered where they had been. Everyone had been busy enjoying the wine, fine dainties, and fireworks.

"Your Highness..."said lord Guy to Lyonus II. I thought you might enjoy a Falcon. He will make a great pet and friend."

"Thank you lord Guy, I'm sure I will find pleasure in him."

What will you call him?" said Luis.

"I'm not sure, maybe I will call him Flacon."

"Well that's fine enough...I guess."

"A find gift for the boy..."said the king. He will learn to care for the heart of others."

Meanwhile, Jeanine spotted Luis.

"Luis, my dear, where have you been, I wanted to give you my gift." Jeanine handed over her gift, proud, thinking she had chosen the right thing.

"Oh…a music box shaped like a horse…Thanks Jeanine!"

"I hope you will glean much pleasure from it."

"I will…Look, lord Guy, it looks like Phantom."

"Come Luis." Luis looked back at Jeanine, while being prompted by lord Guy to move on.

"Let's go to your father, and show him your gifts."

"Fredrick?" asked prince Luis, in confusion. "Why don't you like Jeanine?"

"What a question…"

"If I could choose a mother now, and I were not a prince, I would pick Jeanine."

"My dear prince, when one is a noble, he does not look upon the servants except for what they are here to do…serve. Remember, my boy…one day you will rule, then will you want every servant to be your friend or family? Perhaps the cook could be your father, maybe your chamberlain could be your brother…Do you see what I mean?"

Lord Guy intent on teaching Luis that a person's station should be recognized.

"Well no…I guess not…but…"

"No…no buts your highness, you must learn early to know your station in life, and what it represents. When you are king, you will not care if you have a mother or not…because you will have the power to do whatever you wish…to whomever you wish."

"Yes your grace," said the prince. Saddened by his realities.

"Well now," said Guy. "What is this…your grace business?"

"As you have said, I must know the difference."

"Um…um…" Lord Guy groaned, while he rubbed his chin, and said his good nights.

The birthday party was over, and it was time to retire for the night.

A guard assisted the king and the princes' to their chambers.

"Good night Lyonus and Luis, my little princes'. Rest well tonight my sons, for tomorrow will bring a new challenge for you."

"Yes father," replied the boys in unison.

"Thank you for a wonderful celebration father," said Lyonus.

It seemed all to well that a big party like that would have been enough, especially with all the fine gifts, but not for Luis. As soon as he got to his room, he headed straight for the big book. He started reading more of his mothers' journal. Luis read well into the morning. He opened his hidden passageway door, went into the hidden room behind the fireplace, and picked up a bottle of powder that Rosa had already prepared. Luis knew exactly what powder to pick up. It was as if queen Rosa left explicit instructions on what to do. The more Luis read her journal, the more distant and hostile he became toward his father and others around him. Except of course for lord Guy, his constant companion.

Luis made a special trip to the kitchen each day just as queen Rosa had done, to make sure he placed just enough power in his fathers' food. He would sprinkle a little here and a little there.

Sometimes, he would go to the king's chambers, and shake a bit on his fruit bowl, that always dressed the table.

After a while, instead of the king becoming more loving toward Luis, He began to feel sick, more and more as each day passed. Luis had used so much of the potion; he needed to find a way to make more. He started rummaging around through the room, trying to find anything that looked like it was the Ossa powder. He added herbs, roots, and all the ingredients listed in Rosa's journal, hoping they would be the right ones. But Luis could not see what was really happening to his father. When Luis did not get the results he wanted, he went to lord Guy who directed him to the surgeon.

"My lord Guy, I have a situation…one of a very sensitive nature."

"Well…let's see, you have found a maiden you fancy. Ha…ha…just grab her boy…you are the prince, she can't refuse such a handsome lad…"

"No…hum…if it were that simple. No it's much more grave I'm afraid."

"So serious…your highness? Then by all means tell me."

"I have done something awful…I don't know why I thought it would work…"

"What is it son…just come out with it."

"It's father…"

"You're talking about the king?"

"Yes…I have done…well I found a room where mother used to mix potions and stuff, and I started reading her journal…It seemed the right thing to do at the time. But after a while instead of having gained father's love he grew mean and held even more distain for me. And so I gave him the potion to get rid of him…It's evil I know but."

"Your highness, you're telling me that you are responsible for poisoning the king? You…all alone?"

"Yes…I'm afraid it's gone too far, but I'm afraid he or Lyonus may find out…

"Ha…ha…my boy you are fit to be a king." Laughed Guy, while he reared back.

"No my lord! What shall I do?"

"All right I will talk to a couple of friends who will know just how to help. Tomorrow, go and speak with the surgeon, and do everything he tells you and it will be okay.

"Are you sure my lord?"

"Oh I'm more than sure, and your secret will be safe with me."

Falling right into lord Guy's hands, poor misguided Luis leaped in. Lord Guy was in control, one heir was better than two, and one heir under his control, was a way to the throne. Instead of the powder causing the king to become more loving, it slowly drove him into madness. One could not help but wonder if perhaps the prince himself did not go just a little bit mad too.

Now as things turn during the fall and winter, everything began to die, and so it was with King Lyonus I. The potion finally took its toll and the king alas was dead. Long lives the king.

Lord Guy, and Henry Becket, the surgeon, dismissed his death as a bad heart.

Since Rosa's death, the king had steadily decreased in his health. The surgeon produced documents that verified this fact, but what they could not change was the king's

Will.

Everyone gathered into the Great hall, Lord Thomas Graybourne who knew the king's choice, and Jeanine the nurse, who also knew the chosen prince. But all else thought it would be Luis, because he was the first born of the two. Lord Guy happy to make the announcement.

"Your royal highness'…my lords and Ladies…It is with great sadness, that I inform all of you King Lyonus the Merciful is dead…"

The crowd began to gasp in surprise and then sobbed…and so did the princes'.

He continued.

"Long live our next king, son and heir, Prince Luis De…"

Just then, lord Graybourne stood out of the crowd and said.

"I'm sorry to intrude, but before you make a grave mistake...I must stop you."

"What are you saying Graybourne?"

"I said, you have made a big mistake...The kings will, in which I have in my hand, states that Lyonus II...not Luis should be vested as king."

The court roared, which sounded something like a mob.

"I don't believe it...let me see those papers!"

Lord Westmoreland pushed to the front to see the documents.

"Well...these seem in order to me..."

"Westmoreland, you would not know in order if it bit you...! Give me those!" Guy insisted.

Lord Graybourne shouted with tears. "We have the last wishes of King Lyonus I..."

After all it was his very good friend who now lay dead.

Then he pulled Lyonus II from his seat and raised his hand to the court, then said...long live the king, Lyonus Warwick II, King of England."

Everyone cheered and shouted for Lyonus II. They sensed he would be a great king as was once his father.

Lyonus was taken on to the balcony, so that the people could see and cheer him.

The people remembered that king Lyonus I, was kind to them before the poison changed him into a tyrant.

Prince Luis, was heart broken...he did not think he would be bested once again by Lyonus.

At the funeral for the king, the people paid great respect. Lyonus II, now to be king, had his father's remains dressed and laid in the garden, so that the people could pay tribute. They came in droves. They threw all kinds of flowers, and rose peddles on his body as they passed him. They looked up at Lyonus II, and cheered him saying. "Great king Lyonus I is gone...Long live the King...!"

The lords' and ladies' all stood round about, showed their support for Lyonus II.

Lord Guy leaned over and whispered to Lord Biltfry.

"My lord...does this not remind you of queen Rosa' sad departure...hum...?"

Lord Biltfry with a look of confusion on his face replied.

"Lord Guy, I truly wonder if anything could make you...shall we say...remorseful..."

"My friend, I am not defeated, not by a long shot…I still have a plan!"

"Ha." scoffed Westmoreland. I don't know what I'd like seeing more, you defeated, or you remorseful…" Then he walked straight away from him, and left him with a look of defeat.

But Prince Luis stood at his window, and looked over the crowd. He had tears that seemed to choke all reason from him, when he yelled out to Lyonus II.

"This is all your fault Lyonus!…It's because of you, that father did not love me! He had to die…he had to die!"

Lord Guy called for the surgeon, and a guard to hurry to the room of Luis, and remove him from the window.

"Hurry! Stop him now!" said Guy.

When they arrived at Luis's room he was still yelling out the window. It was as if no one was listening. The people continued to cheer Lyonus II.

But someone did hear. Lord Guy was listening. He had to make sure that the prince would hold it together for a little while. Guy ordered the surgeon to give Luis a sedative. It was hard to hold him, while he kicked and screamed.

"He had to die! Don't you see he had to die! What have you given me…no I don't need any potions…no!"

Lyonus rushed to be with Luis, and there lord Guy steadily on the path to stop him.

They continued until they had administered the drugs. The surgeon had given an extra dose so that he would remain asleep for a while. That was a time that would not soon be forgotten.

Lord Guy seized the moment. He ran straight to young Lyonus with a gripping reality. "Your Highness…" he said, while he waved away the others. I need to speak with you in private." Almost pushing him through the door. It's a matter of great importance…"

"Lord Guy…what is it? I am mourning my father…and look at poor Luis. I've never seen him like this. The matters of the state can be handled later…Luis needs me."

"What he needs now like you my liege…is to rest, and spend some quiet time alone."

"Perhaps you are right…"

"But your majesty, this matter does concern your father and prince Luis," said Guy, as he looked around the room pleased with himself over what he had done.

"Very well then…leave us!" he commanded everyone. This will only take a moment."

Then Lord Guy began to sooth the emotions of Lyonus.

"My king, there are things that have gone on, that would make you doubt your sanity my lord...but I know of a way that will help us all..."

"What do you mean your grace...?"

"Well...for instance how your father died...for one thing...and your brothers bothersome attitude for another..."

"You dare speak that way of the Prince...?"

"No...my lord, I merely meant to say, he has not been himself. He has not been at all kind to you...you who have nursed him and tried to be his friend..."

"True...Luis has been a little...but what does that have to do with father?"

"He is responsible...!" said Guy.

"What...I thought, both you and surgeon Beckett...said he died of a very weak heart. As for Luis...the strain of loosing father."

"Oh certainly my liege, but...ah, there was a little more we failed to tell you about...that."

"All right then...what is it...?" inquired young Lyonus, so anxious to be trapped.

"I'm not one to spread rumors...but rumors will spread..."

"Please your grace, if it's that important..."

Lord Guy, so eager to win the confidence of the Lyonus, he could not wait to begin his tale.

"Your majesty, Prince Luis found your mothers hidden room, then he began to dabble a little with her potions."

"Potions you say...my mother was a witch...is that what you're saying?" The prince dropped to the chair. Then lord Guy continued.

"And, well...one day the prince came to me, with a notion that he could change your fathers feelings for him if...if he used it."

"Used it...what...on our father...?" Lyonus quickly sprang from the chair. "What!"

"Yes my prince."

"He gave father poison...!" Then dropped his head. "And mother, what of her...?"

"She practiced the art. Ivan taught her everything she knew, he could tell you, if...you wanted to inquire of him...my liege..."

"Horrible...no never...never about that. I can not believe this."

"I'm afraid so...my prince..." He bowed his head in homage.

"This can not be true...!" said prince Lyonus, with tears in his voice.

"Oh but it is true...an unless you want the ministers, even the whole of England to know."

"To know...?"

Lord Guy clinched his teeth, speeding every word to get it all in, not missing a beat.

"Yes...that your mother was a witch, and traitor to the king...and your brother who has gone mad, is a murderer...killed his father the king of England...you will sign this paper now...!"

Lyonus grabbed the paper and began to read.

It read something like this: *The here assigned, lord Fredrick Guy, will remain guiltless in any and all matters of interest to England, with total amnesty.*

"I don't understand...why...this says nothing of my father or brother."

"Because the crime of treason, is a death sentence, and I don't plan to die..."

"But..."

"Look at him...your brother." Guy with his arm wrapped around Lyonus, pointed to the bed. "The whole of England will cheer to have his head...murder, is not a pretty picture."

"No...!" said Lyonus.

"Then sign..."

"I can protect him...!"

"Then my prince..." said Guy as he spun around Lyonus to face him. "Who will protect you...?"

"I..."

"Just sign, it only means that your brother can not say that I helped him in any way, in his sickness...in the murder of the king..."

"What? I...I can not think..." Lyonus spun about the room in confusion.

"Sign...it's the only way to keep your family's secret...a secret. I assure you it's the best thing for everyone."

"No wait...perhaps I should talk with lord Graybourne..."

"For what purpose...my king. That meddlesome fool will just complicate things more.

"Look at your brother, how peaceful he seems just lying there...one would hate to think of him in a dungeon, or..."

"Stop!" shouted Lyonus

Lord Guy whispered close to Lyonus' ear.

"So far only you and I need know, these unfortunate events took place…and of course, I will quickly forget, the matter…once you have signed this…"

He held the document close to Lyonus' face. Lyonus walked with a steady pace to the desk that held a quill.

"Maybe this says I'm too young to be king…"

"Nonsense…who better to rule the land, than the son of Lyonus the great…! My lord."

"I…I guess, it has to be me. Poor Luis, he must be suffering."

"Go on my liege…sign…then it will all be over." Lyonus was drawn like a moth to a flame, drawn in to wait for the kill.

"There, now your grace…it is done," he said, while the prince wiped his eyes. "There is nothing else then…?"

Lord Guy looked over the papers, and then said.

"Your highness, you forgot your fathers seal…the ring, you must use the great seal. It keeps everything, as it should be, shows you will keep your word. Surely the king explained the importance of this…?"

"But of course he did…he taught me everything I know…" Then the prince began to sob.

"I'm sorry I had to come to you with this today of all days…come let us join the others."

All the while he stuffed his pockets with the paper. "Perhaps the others will bring you great comfort, your highness…they are waiting your return."

"Thank you your grace for being so discrete…"

"Of course my king…you will find me…shall we say, a most valuable confidant. I could be an even better ally certainly one who would keep your confidents…and your highness…"

Guy paused just a moment. "I hope you will keep this little matter between us." Patting on the papers in his jacket.

"Of course. Are we done here, I want to see my father now?"

"By all means…let me get the door…your highness…"

Lyonus turned to look at Luis asleep, then gazed back at lord Guy once more while he walked down the corridor, as if for sure, he had done the wrong thing. Wanting to take back the great seal he placed.

Now came the time to be vested king, it was quite and experience.

It became a trying time, for Lyonus, but lord Guy kept his word.

Everyone pledged his or her loyalties to the king, and prince Luis pulled himself together, long enough to give the new king his tribute.

"My brother and king…" he said, bowing before Lyonus. I need not tell you that you have my undying support,…as always."

Then Lyonus' eyes panned the room, then leaned over to Luis and said.

"Yes Luis…I do need you to tell me. Somehow, my brother…your eyes do betray you…"

"My eyes sire…?" Luis stepped back from his brother. "Is the king now a seer as well?" Then quickened his pace to leave the room.

"Luis…!" said the king. Please, wait…!"

"Shall I fetch him your majesty?" asked lord Guy.

"No…just let him go. He needs time to be alone…No…just leave him."

King Lyonus saddened by the display of the prince, called for lively entertainment.

While the musicians played, Lord Guy remained so entreating during the coronation ceremony. He was there at every biding of the king. No one even suspected that he had indeed used the prince, now king, except of course, lord Thomas Graybourne.

He feared leaving Lyonus in the clutches of lord Guy.

He remained watchful of the king until he married lady Claire, and moved from the castle. After that, it was more difficult to follow the steps of the king. So Lord Graybourne ordered John Meyers, to take his place as the new body guard for the king, in that way, he would be able to stay abreast of the happenings with Lyonus, and keep closer tabs on the dealings of lord Guy.

As time went on however, more and more hatred visited the heart of Prince Luis, till at last, there was darkness. The only thing that he could see through the eyes of his jealousy was blood. For him, there was nothing good, save the shrine he had built for his mother queen Rosa. And like the potions, it would remain inside the secret room, hid behind the fireplace. There was one other that could always melt his heart, Jeanine. Jeanine was the only person,—at least to Luis—which ever really loved him, and did not want to use him. He could never treat her as a servant, despite lord Guy's instructions. To Luis, she was in fact, his mother.

CHAPTER FOUR
Trap For a King

Now four years had passed, and Luis now seventeen, still blamed Lyonus for his father' distain for him. It was a difficult period for Lyonus II.

Luis plotted day in and day out, how he might rid himself of the only thing that stood between him and the love of his father.

Lord Graybourne, John Myers, Hollands and Lord Du'Voe, were constant companions to the king. They watched over him continually.

One day Prince Luis searched his mind. He paced back and forward. He stopped just short of the mirror on the wall that held two golden candlesticks. For something caught his eye. He turned, took a long stare, and said out loud. "With every part of my being, I will not rest day or night, until Lyonus II…joins his dear departed father in the grave.

Just then he spied, what look like a scroll tucked behind the mirror. Luis pulled open the scroll and began to read.

A magic spell placed on Lyonus, and Luis would not allow for any deadly harm to befall either of them, by the hand of the other until they both had a chance to rule England. If the scroll were found before both ruled, then let the stronger after time would need surrender to the weaker. Then Luis ranted.

"What sort of spell binds me to do no harm to my brother so he can rule? I shall look for a counter potion that will release me from this grievous bind. As lord Guy has said, I was meant to rule all England, and so I shall!"

Luis looked himself up and down in the mirror when suddenly he heard footsteps and voices in his room calling out.

"Prince Luis…your highness, where are you? The king requests your presence."

Shortly after the guard had left, prince Luis came out from his favorite place, stopped just at the door, for he heard a thump, and muffled voices that finally became clearer as they approached. He placed his ear to the chamber door.

"I insist, there is a threat of war, the king must be convinced…do you hear! And gentlemen…I want it convincing. Ivan, you will see to it, and Becket, you will verify it."

"And you…what will you do?" sounded another voice.

"Well…I will take care of everything else, naturally."

Then another voice added. "But of course my lord…but of course."

"Go now…before we are seen together, and I have to do a lot of explaining."

The men quickly departed the area, as instructed. Luis opened his door, thinking he would get a glimpse of at least one of them, though he was quite sure he knew the voice of a couple. Luis did not want anyone to spoil his plans for England, by creating an illusion of war. So he set out to find them.

Luis searched the corridor, no one but the guards were about, standing at their post.

He looked left and right until he reached the king's chambers. He pushed straight through the door and passed the guard. The guard tried to stop him, but he flung the door wide open.

"Luis…!" said the king. "Still the same old habits. Father could never break you of them! I sent for you earlier Luis, where have you been?"

"I know my brother, I was taking care of an important matter…" Lyonus marked with a look of distress, said.

"Oh…? Have you been…? Never mind, but what's more important than acknowledging your king?"

"Forgive me my king, I did not think it would displease you if I were not present."

"Luis…you are my brother…and you are important to me. Come closer. There is something amiss. I would like you to be my confidant, but Luis, if I can't trust that you'll be there for me…then what should I think?"

"Again…I say it could not be avoided. What would please my king?"

"I wanted you in our meeting to help make some decisions, my brother. Please, try and help…"

"Yes…my king…"

When Prince Luis raised his head and looked over, there stood, lord Guy, Henry Becket, Ivan the Seer, and Lord Westmoreland.

"Well...!" remarked the prince. What a pit of distinguished...men we have here."

"Luis...!" said Lyonus. Such a tone."

"Tell me my king, the king's surgeon and a fortune teller, what could it all mean...what could this spell for England...Perhaps war brewing...my liege?"

"Stop Luis please...these are curious times for the country."

"My lord Guy..."said Luis. When we are finished here, perhaps you and I can have a chat...it's been such a long time since we've taken time to really talk."

"I agree, my prince...it is as you wish."

"Good...good."

"Why...your highness." replied lord Guy. We...are about finished here, I believe...your majesty, are we not?"

"Yes, we are about done. But I want to take a minute to fill in my brother."

The king pointed at Luis to be seated, then said.

"Luis, I have decided to make the trip to France." Then Luis with an almost cynical look said.

"What...? You want to take a trip to France...? I don't know Lyonus...won't it be too dangerous for you now. I heard there is a threat of war."

"That's just it, I really don't think that there is."

"Where are you getting your confidence, my brother?"

"For one thing, I know of king Roswald, he is not a man of rash decisions...he would much rather come to a treatise, than open war."

"And for the next thing?'

"I have every confidence in Lord Graybourne...he has assured me, there is no threat."

"Lord Graybourne...lord Graybourne," shouted Luis. "He is only one man Lyonus, he is not God! Despite your desire to make him so."

"Luis...please, I need you to help me not fight."

"Ah...then why take the trip, your majesty...? Although Luis had calmed a little, and walked around a bit he then continued. "You said there is no threat?"

"Precisely, because there is none...Luis. But I need to flush out those who would make a mockery of..."

Luis with more questions interrupts.

"Then if the threats are real...How will you handle that?"

"Then I shall answer the treats against England, or...if rumors, dispel them...that nothing might affect any treatise we may make with France."

"Well my king...mighty one...when do we leave...?"

"You mock me my prince...?"

"You mock England by thinking you can solve the worlds problem just by showing up...when you have diplomats, trained to do just that."

"Since you feel that I'm not capable of diplomacy, then perhaps you should remain here, since you have had less training than I...and I shall have my first lesson...in France."

"Lyonus, I'm sorry. I didn't mean you were not ready. I just don't want you to get hurt."

"Well...I'm touched by your care, but I've decided."

"Lyonus...please, I want to go, I could use the trip."

"Then who will watch over England...if not you? King for a day, as it were?"

"I could be of help," pleaded Luis.

"No...I've decided this will be a trip best suited for lord Thomas, lord Biltfry, and myself. With a few guards of course."

"Oh...I see..."

"Luis, please don't be angry..."

"Your majesty," said Luis, while he bowed to the king.

"Oh, and my lord Graybourne will choose those guards who will be traveling."

Lord Guy showed his hostility and added.

"But your majesty, I have set up the meeting place and everything...if you change, it will spoil all my plains.

"My lord Guy...I do not mean to offend you..."

"But Your majesty..."

"No buts, lord Guy...am I not King?"

"Yes my lord..."

"Then it is my command..."

"Your wish is my will...my lord king. Will you need me for anything more tonight?"

"I will need to speak with lord Graybourne...make the arrangements!"

"Yes sire...right away..."

"I fail to see why lord Thomas was not here as I requested. Does everyone feel they can ignore their kings' commands?"

Henry Becket answered in response.

"Why your majesty, I thought you remembered, lord Thomas Graybourne, now lives in Hilton castle."

Oh…yes Becket…thank you for that, it had completely slipped my mind. He has always been so close."

"Yes sire," remarked Ivan. But time it seems has moved on…just a while ago, your father was king, God rest his soul…sire."

"Thank you Ivan. After next month, we will know what your visions really meant. My father trusted you Ivan…then so shall I…Take care not to be deceived."

"I am your humble servant…your majesty."

He bowed himself out of the room, while lord Guy was in a great huff.

"Well, your majesty…perhaps we all can be dismissed…?"

"But of course my lord's, I shall inform you of the rest of my plans, as soon as I have spoken with lord Thomas. For now good night to you all."

The kings summoned the guard, John Meyers.

"John, make sure lord Thomas gets my message tomorrow, I do not trust, that it will arrive by any other way…not tonight."

"My king…" John bowed in acceptance of the king's request, and started to close the door.

"Oh…one more thing!"

"Yes sire?"

"Let Thomas know that I have included you to accompany us as well."

"As you have commanded…your majesty…Rest well."

I shall…good night John."

Early the next morning, just as commanded, John Meyers took the king's message to Thomas Graybourne at his estate. Lady Claire answered the door. Her mouth fell wide open…She called for her husband.

"Thom…as, Thomas, please come here…quickly!"

"What is it my dear?"

"You won't believe it…!"

Thomas walked briskly to the door, fixed his shirt.

"Yes, what can…we…Yes son what is it."

Claire tugged at Thomas's shirtsleeve,

"Please dear…let us find out what the young man wants."

"Well sir," he said, while he looked back and forth between them, "it is a message from the king."

"All right…Claire, it is a message from the king."

"I heard that my lord…"

"Well son you just wait right outside a moment, and I'll be there."

"As you say sir."

Just as soon as John left out the doorway, Lady Claire buckled to the floor with a gasp.

"Ah…Thomas, my lord! He looks just as you did when you were younger your exact image Thomas. Will you not tell him my lord?"

"No Claire…I promised Victoria, I would not disrupt his life. He thinks he was orphaned as a baby…both parents dead."

"What of Victoria.?…She's his true mother. Does she not feel an obligation to him…don't you Thomas? It just doesn't seem fair somehow."

"What would be unfair, would be for me to show up now and proclaimed some type of lordship over him…never having rescued him from that rat hole he lived in so long…I think he should hate me more than the rats. I could not turn his life inside out again…in all fairness to him Claire."

"I see what you mean, but darling…what a shock when I looked at him…oh my!"

"I chose the boy as the kings body guard, so I could keep track of both him and the king.

But darling, we must keep it to ourselves…no one can know this."

"I understand…but will Victoria be okay with that?"

"I think she will know I have done what was best."

"Maybe you could drop her a note letting her know that we have seen him, and the secret is safe."

"What should it matter now, if you can't acknowledge him, you might as well let sleeping dogs sleep? But we must do whatever is right for the boy."

"Darling you know I am behind you any way you choose to go…you know that."

"I do my love…"

Thomas leaned over to kiss her.

"I love you Thomas."

"My life is made better Claire." Holding her hand gently between his palms. "Now that I have you in my life, and there is nothing better. Our child you carry, more than makes my life complete."

"I've decided Thomas, if it is all right with you, if it is a boy to name him after your father and a girl after you mother Melinda. I love the name."

"Lady Claire, you are perfection."

"No regrets?" she asked, as she looked toward the ground.

Lord Graybourne, raised her chin, and then replied. "Only that it did not happen sooner...I love you...lady Claire Graybourne.

With one more embrace, they parted. Claire waved good-bye from the doorway.

While John and lord Thomas rode back to the royal castle, it seemed a little awkward for Thomas.

"I wonder why the king needs me so urgently this morning...Have you an idea?

"Yes lord Thomas, His majesty has planned a trip to France."

"What!" said Thomas. "He knows this is not a good time...we've discussed it! What on earth has gotten into the king?"

"Lord Guy I would imagine," he muttered.

"What did you say John?"

"Oh, I simply said Lord Guy has made all the arrangements, but king Lyonus dismissed them, and said he would speak with you first."

"Well, at least he did that much right."

"Ha...ha..."

"What's so funny?"

"Ha...you should have seen the look on old Guys face when the king turned down his plan. He was outraged."

"Ah...my boy, don't toy too much with lord Guy. He doesn't like to lose."

"Neither do I..."

"Ah yes, but you don't have the power he has to make things happen," said Graybourne.

The ride was quiet for a second, as lord Graybourne thought to himself...you are your fathers' son. Then said.

"Are you sure, that the king ask me to plan the trip?"

"Well yes, my lord. I heard him tell prince Luis, that he would wait for your arrangements."

"I can understand why to be sure," John replied. Besides that, none of the people he chose to accompany the king was accepted. Oh I almost forgot, he said you should include me. You know, I think the king likes me."

"Ah...you are a fine lad to be sure...He does think of you highly. This is good, after all you are his bodyguard."

AWAKENED BY BETRAYAL

"He really upset that old fox...ha...ha...!'

"Well, this should prove to be an interesting meeting this morning, wouldn't you say son...?"
"I would indeed...my lord."

Now Lyonus and Graybourne met, and planned their trip to France.
But while they met, another meeting was taking place.
Lord Guy was steamed, because the king rejected his plans. He had to seek alternative means to finish his mission.
So he met with prince Luis, planted in his mind that the king did not trust his judgment.
"My prince, I wish the king had asked you, what you thought about the treatise with France. Doesn't he understand that you know as much about diplomacy, as Du'Voe?"
"Oh...I'm afraid my brother, thinks about no one but himself. He has always been selfish, and spoiled. Father always let him have his way about everything."
Guy added.
"...Left you all alone, with just your old friend lord Guy to comfort you."
"Yes...but one day, it all just might change!"
"Really my prince?" questioned lord Guy. Do you have a scheme you would like to share?"
"Ah...you'll just have to wait and see. It will be quite something, I assure you my lord."
Guy rubbed his hands together, like a fly over blotted bodies.
"My prince, I will leave things in your very capable hands."
Now it's the morning the ship sails for France. King Lyonus and his company are boarded.
Now Luis did not take too well being left out, yet again. So he set out to find another way to redeem his broken pride.
The king and his company traveled under a different name, so not to be discovered. When they arrived in France, they went the opposite way than directed by lord Guy. Bandits questioned them, who asked if king Lyonus was on board the ship, and how many men were with him. They were sure to need their wits about them.
On the wisdom of lord Graybourne, they were able to avoid most of the rabble, and go directly to Stockyard Inn, where they could refresh themselves.

John and the other guards mingled to find what information they could, that would be useful.

An audience with king Roswald was arranged for late that afternoon.

When they finally made their way to the royal castle of king Roswald. There they were stopped at the gate.

"Bonjour…Hello," said the guard, speaking in French. Where are your papers?" he asked them.

"I don't understand what…what are you saying? Do you mean this…our pass?"

"Oui oui…monsieur," replied the guard.

"Here…I have a letter from your king…Roswald."

The guard looked at the letter, and saw it was marked with the seal of France, and then said.

"I'm sorry for the delay…please come in."

"Thank you, my friend," said king Lyonus. Come let us go, allow John to take the lead."

It was time for king Lyonus to be announced. He threw back his cloak, and displayed a beautiful royal frock, fit for the king he was.

King Roswald bided Lyonus to come closer. They exchanged all the courtesies, that kings would give each other.

"Brother king," said Lyonus. A long life and good health to you and a prosperous kingdom…"

"…And to you my brother. I was told of your youth, but it has not interfered with your manners my lord. For you have been taught well in protocol."

"Why father, he looks the same age as I," said prince Michael.

"No doubt my son, he has had much tragedy, and it has forced him to grow up quickly.

"Thank you king Roswald. I still have much to learn. Perhaps, we will have a chance to talk more during my stay."

"We can agree, at least on that."

But suddenly, the ward of king Roswald entered the throne room, and just as slowly. She strolled as if the wind carried her. She sat down beside king Roswald, turned and dropped her head slightly, though her eyes never left king Lyonus. He could not remove his eyes from her. Almost immediately, he asked king Roswald, who she was.

"My lord king," he said. "One should be careful to display his best jewels, there could be thieves about. Perhaps, even one…unable to control his desire to have such a jewel. Would you not agree…my brother?"

"Ha…ha…ha. Quite so, king Lyonus. Let me introduce you to my son prince Michael, and my lovely ward…King Lyonus II of England, I would like to present Lady Miria Michelle De'Sheffield, ward of the king of France.

King Lyonus could hardly speak. She raised her head and looked deep into his eyes.

"My king," she remarked in a soft, sensuous voice. "I am delighted to meet you sire.

Will you be staying long on our fair shores?"

"You…my dear are most beautiful…my lady. I think, the blood that raced through my heart, has paused but for a moment…that I may catch my breath, while I gaze upon your loveliness."

"Why my lord Roswald, I believe he is a poet king," they all laughed.

Lord Graybourne and John stood close and nudged each other. Then Michael said.

"My lord, is there a reason for your visit…other than Miria of course.

"Your highness," said lord Thomas, while he prodded the king. Sire…the reason we have come…my lord." Lyonus seemed as though in a trance.

"Oh yes…yes," said Lyonus. The reason we are here, is of great importance to the people of England…well give him the papers Graybourne…please."

King Roswald read the notice. He shook his head the entire time, indicating a negative response. Then he remarked.

"I must say…my lord king, this is simply not our intentions at all. France is tired of war. For a time we would endeavor to enjoy the peace of this fair land. Have you noticed my lord king…our beautiful countryside…it's splendid. We are not a people of war anymore. We have struggled and compromised to keep our lands free from the savagery of war. It has been many years but we have accomplished a great deal.

I am afraid someone played you false my lord. Perhaps a cruel and senseless joke at your expense."

Then said Lyonus. "I do not think one could so falsely misunderstand their king, as to think this would amuse him. But I assure you; this deadly game…has a reward. I fear not many will escape its end."

"Well…since you have come all this way," said Roswald, as he rose from his seat. Let us not waste it. Accept our hospitality. Stay here in the castle…I insist. Together we will solve the mystery."

"Oh…of that you may rest assured," said king Lyonus. But I have another question that weighs on my mind rather heavily."

"Oh…and what is that, my lord?" king Roswald, asked knowingly.

"You are aware of the advantages involved…say if France and England were to join forces as brothers…a family if you will?

"I think I'm ahead of you brother king," said Roswald with a smile on his face. A treatise is a wonderful thing to have between two countries such as ours. But a union of marriage, well…it will thicken the bond…you agree brother?"

"Exactly my king," replied Lyonus.

Michael interrupted and said. "But my lord king, Miria is too young to marry."

"Nonsense Michael…But I must say now…I think it best to allow Lady Miria to make up her own mine about that. Her life is hers to choose, whom she will love, or marry. Ah…love it is a priceless commodity…Yet nothing can out weigh it…She will decide, my brother king."

"Michael…maybe you should take a lesson from our young king here."

Michael was angered and then ran from the room. Miria ran after him.

"I'm afraid my son has grown quite attached to Miria, they grew up together…family."

"Of course, that's understandable. I also have a brother, if he were to leave, I would be upset as well," remarked Lyonus.

Meanwhile Miria tried to console Michael.

"Michael…Michael airs," she whispered. Where are you."?

Suddenly he leaped from behind some drapes. "I am okay Miria. This foreigner may not take care of you."

"Ha," laughed Miria. He doesn't have to. I can take care of myself. And by the way, no one has asked me to marry them…at least not yet."

"Don't worry Mir…it won't take him long. I could see it in his eyes."

"In that case, I'd better hurry back."

"Wait!" Michael called out. But Miria without hesitation made her way back to see Lyonus.

King Roswald had already finished his business with Lyonus except to say. Leaning over to whisper.

"We however, would not want to see her hurt in any way."

"Thank you King Roswald. I appreciate your frankness."

"Great king, forgive my out burst," said Miria, when she walked back into the room. She stepped over to king Roswald and said. I would like to know what King Lyonus has said. Will you tell me then?"

"Ha...that...I will leave to my lord Lyonus to say...for now please let the king and his party freshen up my dear Miria...we'll speak of it at dinner."

When king Lyonus and Graybourne entered their apartment, the king exploded with anger.
"I dare they...I dare them make a fool out of England...out of me! No wonder I have a vision...war is upon the land...It really makes me suspect."
"Sire who do you suspect..."
Before Graybourne could finish his statement the king chide in.
"I suspect all, until I can prove otherwise...but when I prove it heads will roll."
"Well my lord for tonight at least, let it rest, and think on that fair lady that caught your eye."
"For tonight, we will place it to the side. I want to ask you my lord Thomas...what did you think of Lady Miria?"
"Well...sire..."
"My lord...tell me true. I really value your opinion."
"I know my king. I'll tell you this, a man would be a fool to turn away a real chance at happiness...especially when it comes so beautifully wrapped."
"...So, I'm making the right decision then?"
"Your majesty, you were struck by a bolt of lightening, and everyone could tell it. There's no changing that fact."
"Lord Graybourne?"
"That's right my king...just let your own heart guide you, it has not failed you yet. I fear we could not change it if we tried. Ha...ha...ha..."
"John...what of your answer?"
"Well sire..." John hesitated to reply.
"Out with it my friend."
"Your majesty...I strongly feel, you should let her dictate your moves...but more importantly sire...if I may speak so...?"
"Of course, that is why I asked that you were to be honest."
"Then be honest with her your majesty, and tell her what you are feeling...then let her show you the way to her heart."
"Well said my friend...well said."
Just then a knock came on the door to announce dinner.
"Good...I think I have built up rather a large appetite."
"Yes..." said Graybourne rubbing his stomach. "I could eat a small deer myself."

"Please come this way my lords," said the servant. "Come your majesty…your grace. We have prepared a great feast in your honor."

While they dined, King Lyonus was so distracted, that he could hardly eat for he watched lady Miria's every move.
Both kings talked business to resolve the matter of the treatise. King Roswald suggested that king Lyonus purpose to Miria.
"King Lyonus, you have finished…have you not?"
"I have dined sufficiently…Thank you king Roswald…"
"Then perhaps you would consider having our lady Miria, show you around our beautiful gardens."
"But of course…that is…if my lady does not mind. It would please me very much," said Lyonus.
"I would be delighted…to please you sire," replied Miria.
She could not wait to show Lyonus the gardens.
"There is nothing more breathtaking sire, than a view of our Southern hills, in the moonlight."
"Well…lead on, I can hardly wait to embrace them…see them, my dear."
Everyone began to laugh. Even Lyonus knew it was obvious at that point he had been captivated.
Lady Miria arose from the table, while the gents stood.
"Ha…ha…this way your majesty…" Directing his steps. Then John spoke up.
"Sire…should I accompany, you?" Graybourne looked at him with a frown, then said.
"My boy, the king can handle a short walk in he garden with a beautiful lady. "Ha…ha…ha. Let's finish our meal. This is a marvelous feast king Roswald…my compliments…wonderful company as well," he added, and then the ladies at the table smiled and blushed.
"Yes your grace thank you, however, I think maybe he stands a better chance as a diplomat…"
The entire table of guest looked around at each other in laughter. They knew king Lyonus could not resist the black haired beauty, lady Miria.

Once in the garden, silence took over for a moment. Miria and Lyonus took in the view. Finally, Lyonus said. "Miria…lady Miria that is…I can no longer hold my words."
"Sire,…your words? Have I restricted what you can or can not ask of me?"

"You are a treasure...most beautiful. More than I could ever imagine a woman to be."

"Then...are there not many women in England, or perhaps beauty, is all my lord looks for in a queen?"

"No. I would not presume that..." Before Lyonus could finish, Miria said.

"Do you see this rose? Take it in your hand. It is lovely to see, but tomorrow it will begin to wither. Then you can not see its beauty."

Then Lyonus said as he stared sharply at the rose.

"...But, I know that even though its beauty may fade...it does not take away my appreciation for the pleasure it brought to me as I looked upon it afresh...I would remember its' beauty."

"You are right my lord," said Miria, while she took a long whiff of yet another rose, and then said. "Just as the moonlight fades to reveal the daylight, so it is...with a woman's beauty my lord. But when I have passed the flower of my youth, I still expect to be the one wife, of the same husband...a husband who would still adore me and would know that my love was not to be bargained for. He would also know, there would be more to me than outward appearances."

"Then my lady," said Lyonus, as he searched her eyes. "How would one attain your love for a lifetime? And if he desired it much more, than the life time he could only imagine or hope for, how then could it be possessed?"

"You've spoken words that seemed to flow from your heart, I can not answer your every question my lord."

"Then answer the first my lady."

Miria turned slowly toward Lyonus, fastened on his eyes, and then said in jest.

"I believe you are a poet."

"No my dear, just one who's heart can not wait until our hearts beat as one."

"My king we've only met today."

"It matters not to me. Should I have crossed an ocean to find a wife? No, I crossed the ocean to find love."

"Michael says that you would want me only until you were home again and when you tire of me, all the young maidens would come out from behind the walls, and push me back from your sight, and there I would remain, alone and withered."

"Ha...ha did he really say all that...?"

"No...But he did warn me of your intentions."

"My intentions? I would think they were obvious my lady."

"It is not all ways easy to tell the thoughts of a man, especially if it is marked by power."

"Then look into my eyes and tell me now if you see a man who wants nothing, shallow and demanding…empty and wanton…if you do then he is correct to suspect"

Then he placed his hand tenderly on the small of her back and gently tugged her toward him and then said.

"…But if you see desire and a strange light that draws me to you as does a moth to a flame, but is never singed by the fire that burns, and continues to flutter about it. Then you may know my intentions are to fulfill that desire.

Mira stood a moment in silence, not able to breathe. Then she lead him away deeper into the garden while she gave herself a second to think making small talk as she pulled alone the vines.

"Oh Michael…he looks out after me, he always has. He and I have been together forever he means well."

"So I was told by your king. That is one part of your life that can remain a treasure…But now it is time for you to make a life with real love, like a man for a woman strong and complete." Lyonus fell to his knee, and held her hand. "Marry me Miria, become my queen…and I will love you forever."

"A king on his knees?…Please get up. I don't know what to say, I can hardly breathe!"

"Then say it to me with a kiss."

Said Lyonus, as he stood and held her by her bare shoulders and clinched her close.

"If for but a moment, I could feel this way, and freeze it in time…my king, then it would be enough for two lifetimes."

"Now who has become the poet?" Then he kissed her softly. She suddenly moved away again as though not sure of her feelings perhaps a little afraid.

"I feel as you my king. Though I don't know why I just can't be sure."

King Lyonus lead by Miria's response, said.

"…And if this night would stand the wait, I will hold it as a picture of you…and it will forever be in my heart from this night forward. Nothing…would ever change that image; for my heart wills it to be so…and my love will forever keep it from fading or growing old. Much like the rose that I am still remembering…"

A great silence swept through the night and another kiss. Then Miria said.

"If our hearts agree…I will be yours and you mine, and the only thing that will separate us is death."

AWAKENED BY BETRAYAL

"You speak of death before love my lady?"

"I speak as if it is possible to find love and then lose it just as suddenly."

"Ah...now you speak of someone who steals but not by force." They both laughed softly. Lyonus made light the moment.

"Yes...I believe you to be rather a thief, my liege," said Miria jokingly.

"Thief my dear? First a poet and now a thief?"

"For you have stolen my heart," said Miria Though I'm not sure how."

Then Lyonus could not help but say.

"Nay my lady, I am merely a man who has been driven madly in love. I wish not to steal your heart, but rather to be given it...forever."

"Ah...love...I must say my heart feels it too. It races as we speak...I can contain no longer, yes I will be your queen," said Mira.

Then Lyonus added.

"By all accounts, let your heart bear one more thing tonight, my future queen."

"If it must my lord."

"Let us further agree, that if death comes, and darkness takes hold over the night...let us search for a place where we could meet...if only in our dreams...to say a final goodbye."

"Then my king, let us seal it again with a kiss...a bond never to be broken."

They kissed deeply. It was evident, as Lyonus and Miria held each other underneath a blanket of stars, that king Lyonus received more than he bargained for by his trip to France.

A short while more, and they returned to the dining hall. King Roswald said with a wide grin.

"Oh...my king, I thought perhaps we should send the guards to rescue you..."

"Quite so, brother king. I've been made captive, and I've surrendered to my lady's charms."

"No...but it is I...who has been captured. Perhaps my lord, a prisoner for life," said Miria, as she recoiled and walked back out of the room.

Lyonus smiled and said. "She has consented to be my queen..."

Everyone stood and cheered. They raised their goblets, and made a toast to them.

Then King Roswald said.

"I shall arrange for your passage when you are ready to leave Lyonus."

"Wonderful king Roswald. Well my lord Thomas, we have much to plan for our home coming, so we will call it a night, and retire now.'

"I understand, brother. Rest well this night. Guard…escort our guess back to their apartments."

"Yes your majesty," said the guard.

"Graybourne?"

"Yes…sire"

"I have done it…!

"Done what sire?"

"I have made that giant step!"

"Yes your majesty, and you did it all by yourself…ha…ha…ha!"

King Lyonus laughed, while lord Graybourne took the lead.

John and Hollands walked together, and watched the king's folly.

"My king bid me speak?"

"Why of course, Hollands…what is it?"

"May I say you made a wonderful choice? I wish you every happiness!"

"Thank you Hollands, I truly believe, it will be so."

"I agree your majesty," said John. "There can be nothing more beautiful than to see you happy sire. Congratulations!"

"Yes congratulations sire…this is a trip I will not soon forget. I will be happy to return home, my king," said Graybourne.

"…So will I, especially now."

They all retired, and found the beds much more than comfortable.

King Lyonus was about to go to bed, when he spied a note passed underneath his door.

"What is this?"

At first, Lyonus thought it might be a letter from Miria. So he picked it up and read its contents. Through it he found that there was a plot, to have him assassinated on the trip to France. When lord Graybourne altered the travel plans, it removed the king from harms way. The letter also warned the king to be watchful, back home in England. There were still others, some with sight and some who prepared the sight…ready to usurp the throne. It named several who were involved in the assassination attempt.

There was no signature on the note, but it made Lyonus more eager to leave for England.

King Lyonus called John to fetch lord Graybourne.

"Yes, your ma…jesty," he answered, while he yawned with every word.

"This letter was slipped under my door, a bit ago. I was not sure quite what to make of it. What do you think?"

"I don't know sire...I can say, that the plot failed...For what ever reason, the author of this note wanted you to be aware. But for what purpose...and what connection would they have with England?"

"Maybe it would be best if Miria and I were wed here."

"In France sire?" questioned Graybourne. "Well...I suspect king Roswald would be more than happy to entreat that notion. Then what of your brother, the prince? He will not take it lightly."

"I know...he'll be a little upset at first...but when he sees Miria, she will help soften the shock. Something just says do it now."

"I don't see the problem," remarked Graybourne. "But...that aside...carry on with your plans...sire, I see no need to change them now."

"All right, I'll make my request known to king Roswald on tomorrow."

Well it took more than two weeks to make the wedding preparations.

King Roswald, and Miria were beside themselves, as they planned her wedding.

They decided to have the wedding in the Southern Gardens, where Lyonus asked for her hand.

The wedding was spectacular. All the French nobility attended, and the Southern Gardens were filled with flowers from all over the world. The gardens' fragrance was captured through the bride and groom's bedroom window, just above it

Lyonus and Miria gave gifts to each other.

Lyonus gave Miria a locket of silver, and gold, that could be separated. Each half represented a part of the union. The ring had a king of gold fashioned on one half and a queen of gold on the other. Where the hands met, was where it unlocked. When the piece was opened, it would reveal an inscription that read: Together forever, if only in our dreams.

Miria gave Lyonus a golden ring with silver fig leaves layered on top, with an inscription that read: Lyonus and Miria forever, in life and in death.

Now lord Graybourne sent a courier ahead, that prince Luis and the king's ministers might be informed of the wedding, and their expected arrival in England.

They had given them a more than gracious send off.

As they prepared to leave, Miria decided she would take along with her, Nichol L' Port, her lady in waiting, and Jacqueline Re'Mane her chambermaid.

King Roswald had prepared a wonderful honeymoon voyage for Lyonus and Miria aboard his private ship.

The moon filled nights and calm seas, helped to set the mood for a pleasant voyage.

When they finally arrived in England, there was awaiting them two coaches and six guards. They also brought, two extra horses.

John, Hollands and lord Graybourne, first walked down the plank followed by lady Nichol, and Jacqueline. Then slowly king Lyonus escorted queen Miria down the plank, to finally set her feet on English soil.

When the king stepped down he paused, then kneeled and kissed the earth beneath his feet.

"Thank God...my homeland!" said the king, for nothing with the exception of Miria, looked as good to him at that moment.

John walked over and reached to help Lyonus to his feet.

"My king we are also happy to be on English soil."

He turned to Miria, fell to his knees, and said. "Welcome home, my queen...I am your humble servant, and pledge my life to you."

Then Hollands being so moved by John's gesture joined him and repeated the vow."

Miria was overwhelmed by the sincerity of the guards that she began to cry.

"I am happy to be in the care of such true and noble men...my king has been honored."

"Indeed my queen, and there are no words needed for my lord and greatest friend Thomas Graybourne."

"Your majesty's...your will is my will, forever..."

Now when the coach approached the dock, lord Thomas became a little uneasy.

He looked inside each one, and examined the wheels and reigns. After his inspection, he asked all the guards questions, to see if they were truly the king's men.

They boarded the coaches and mounted their horses, and started on their way. One coach contained Nichol, Jacqueline and a guard. Then in the other coach were Lyonus, Miria, and the kings' chamberlain. John and Graybourne and Hollands, rode the extra horses.

All was going along smoothly, until suddenly lord Graybourne spotted a coach coming from the opposite direction.

"John…!" Lord Graybourne said, trying not to alarm the king. "Look…a coach approaches."

"Well…what have we here? How many coaches did they think we would need? Ah my lord?"

Graybourne ordered the drivers of the kings' carriage to speed up to go ahead of the first coach, and yield to the left. Lyonus sensing the change yelled out of the window.

"John…what is the mater?"

"Your majesty…we fear there may be a problem…"

"Find me a sword…I shall not be without one!"

"Yes sire…"

Lord Graybourne gave the king a sword, and told him to stay inside the coach.

The carriage that followed continued at a steady pace.

Thomas rode up beside the escorts and told each of them to encircle the two coaches.

So they pulled into an area that was thick with trees and the guards circled about the coaches. Then John hid in a tree, and lord Graybourne, hid behind some bushes. As soon as the carriage reached king Lyonus, the door opened and men leaped out in an all out attack. John jumped down onto one of the riders, and threw him from his horse, he then heard screaming coming from Nichol's coach. He dived from the horse onto two men who tugged at the door. King Lyonus fought off attackers at his coach. He pushed Miria to the floor, and rolled in front of her to protect her. The fighting was intense. Grayboune, in rare form, pierced and jabbed till he had killed many of the men. Hollands fought well but was slashed along the arm. They fought until there were left, three men. Two others had already retreated.

"Should we allow them to live?" asked John. "These are traitors to the king!" he exclaimed. Lord Graybourne answered while he panted for breath.

"Yes…and traitors always get the just end. Do you think for a moment, they will be allowed to live…if only by the ones who sent them? I'm afraid my friend…their fates are sealed, and our hands clean. We will not see them again. Let's go and check on our wounded and the coaches."

"King Lyonus…are you both all right, my lord?"

"We are John…what of you and Graybourne…the others?"

Graybourne rode up to the coach said.

"Your majesty, all are well. Hollands…he will recover. May God give us speed, to continue our journey in safety."

They looked up, and one of the guards dragged a body over to the coach.
"Who is this?" asked lord Graybourne. "Is he able to speak?"
"I found him over near the thicket…he is barely alive…but, alive still my lord."
"Let us find out who arranged this greeting," said John.
They stood him to his feet, so he could be questioned. Suddenly there was a sound as the wind whistling through the trees. It was an arrow that headed directly for the prisoners back. He fell to the ground. The king leaned over into the coach and asked Miria to stay inside. Hollands kneeled down looked him over and said.
"My lords…this one is dead." Lyonus walked over to the body, kicked him over to see his face. "Then," said the king. "God had indeed shown him mercy…for I have seen him with Henry Becket…He will answer for his treason!"
The guards took the remaining bodies, and piled them within the brush, so they would remain hidden from the road.
"Your Majesty…the queen and the others are quite shaken up. We must get off this road…before we are attacked again," said John.
Then the king looked at his bloody sword, and said.
"My lord Graybourne…is not your estate near to this turn in the road?"
"Yes your majesty…it is very near. Are your thoughts, to stop there for the night?"
"If it will not inconvenience the lady Claire…my lord."
"Why it would be her privilege…our privilege to have you both, sire," said Thomas.
They rode yet a ways till they entered the Graybourne estate, once known as Hilton castle.
"Fine land you have here, lord Graybourne," marked the king, as he noticed through he carriage window.
"Yes sire…your father gave me Hilton…many years ago. It was after a great victory that he rewarded me…Ah…we fought side by side, your father and I. He was a good, and a great man. Ah…now, I am getting too old for fighting."
"Oh my lord…you were great today. I am thankful for your skills," said Lyonus.
The coached stopped directly in front of the castle. "Whoa…whoa there," said the driver.
The driver stepped down and opened the doors for the king and queen to

step down, while Thomas went to the door of the house, and called for Claire. She was greatly surprised, when she saw the king and queen had arrived at their home.

"Thomas darling!" said the lady Claire, with a warm embrace. I've missed you."

'…And I, you my love…" Before Thomas could say another word, queen Miria stepped into the doorway.

"Oh…Claire…our new queen. Allow me to introduce, King Lyonus II, and Queen Miria, our majesties of all England…this my lovely wife, lady Claire Norwick Graybourne."

"Your majesties…!" said Claire, while making her point to bow. "We are more than honored at your presence. Please your majesties, come in and rest from your journey."

They all laughed a little, as they watched Claire scramble around the house.

"We are delighted to be here, Lady Claire," added the queen.

"Thomas," called Claire, as she whispered to him. She is exquisite…No wonder, look at her…the king could not have resisted I'm sure."

"Did not my lady…did not, ha…ha…ha…"

Then Claire and Thomas embraced again.

The kings' eye followed them, and then said.

"That is how I would have us, after fifty years, my queen."

"I love you Lyonus…"

"Remember, nothing within my power to control, would ever change my love!"

"Lyonus," said the bride, as she begun to blush.

Miria then turned her attention to Claire.

"My lady…you're with child. Would this be your first?"

"Yes, your majesty, we hope for a son, but whatever God grants us we will cherish."

Miria smiled at Lyonus. "I can't wait until we are feeling the same."

Now Claire, Thomas and the servants made dinner, and served the royal company a great meal. They were then ready to retire for the night. Lady Claire chose, the soft goose down mattress, for the queen, it was the most comfortable bed in the house. She offered them a huge room with a grand fireplace. The room had a large window to view the stars. It had two cushioned chairs, that would lean a little, and lots of soft pillows on the bed, with colors of purples and hues of blue. It offered a table with candles, and a beautiful arrangement of flowers.

"Thomas…will you please escort our guest to their rooms."
"Of course…please right this way," said Thomas.
We are more than thrilled you are here.
After a comfortable nights sleep, and a light breakfast, lord Graybourne loaded everyone that was in the kings' party aboard the carriages.
"King Lyonus, we must make way to the royal castle…I know they hoped we would have made it by now." Then John said with a frown.
"Oh my lord I think not…"
"What do you mean?"
"More like…thinking we aren't going to make it."
"Well, That's why I would like to make it there before dusk. I do so want to disappoint…them." Then closed the carriage doors.
Miria called out to lady Claire.
"Thank you for your hospitality."
"It is our pleasure to serve you…your majesties."
Lady Claire and all the servants waved goodbye to the king, and queen.

CHAPTER FIVE
A Great Judgment

Finally the king and queen arrived unharmed, at the Castle.

Lord Guy peered downward from his window. He was not happy that they had arrived no less for the wear. While he watched them withdraw from their carriage, he gritted his teeth.

From the first coach, came the kings' chamberlain, then Nichol and Jacqueline. Then Lyonus and Miria from the second. Lord Guy's mouth stood opened, he was floored to see the queen. A *vision, simply ravishing*, he thought while he hurried down to meet her.

Meanwhile, all the court assembled in the great hall and gave a formal greeting to the king and queen. Lord Graybourne whispered to the king.

"Sire, what is to be done with the traitors?"

"They will be dealt with, on the most serious of terms," he replied.

"My king, you can't let lord Guy just walk away…you can't mean that sire," exclaimed Hollands, standing on the kings' right hand side.

"I shall exact a punishment for him, otherwise anyone who wishes to attack me, will try over and over. Trust me, it may take a while. Guy has control of my army…It would be a mistake to do anything now."

"Sire?" said John, with a look of disappointment on his face.

"Be patient John, his deeds will not be disregarded."

"But your majesty!" Lord Graybourne added as he walked closer to the king.

"Lord Thomas Graybourne," said Lyonus, as he looked him in the eyes, waiting for a reply.

"My king," he answered

"Do you trust your king?"

"Without fail, your majesty…"

"Then trust me now about this…I swear on my fathers' grave to right the wrong he's done."

"As you have said…my lord," replied lord Thomas.

"…But we must speak your majesty," insisted Graybourne.

After everyone gathered in the great hall. The king and queen took their royal places.

The formal greeting was announced: Queen Miria De' Shefield, ward of his majesty Richard Roswald, king of France; wife of king Lyonus Warwick II, high protector of England.

Prince Luis was the first to speak.

"Your majesties…it is good to have you back…" Luis glanced over at Guy, then said.

"My brother…your queen is a vision of loveliness…I hope your journey was uneventful?"

"Uneventful Luis? What my trip has proven, is that, I know whom I can trust…"

The king looked over at Becket and Ivan, and then said. "…And whom I can not."

"Do you have a meaning behind your words…my brother?"

"I believe I have said it my…brother." The king also remembered the contract he signed leaving him helpless to act against Guy.

Miria reached over to grab Lyonus's hand.

"I am calm…my dear," he whispered with a smile.

"Let the Knights form their lines!" announced the king.

Each Knight made their pledge to the queen.

"My queen, I hereby promise to fulfill my obligation, to render service and protection to you, as a ruler of the realm of England."

Each knight gave the pledge, until all had sworn an oath. Then king Lyonus called for the sword of Evan, which stood next to him.

"Your blade…" Then he called John and Hollands to the stand in front of him.

He smiled at John and said.

"Kneel…" He looked out at the assembly, and said. For a valiant display of skills…courage above question, and saving your king and queen, from those who would commit murder…" The king looked around the great hall, as if searching for a familiar face then continued. "By the power invested in me as king of England, I dub thee a peer rise Sir knight." John looked up with eyes somewhat glazed, then whispered. "Thank you my lord king…"

"Hollands…keep kneeling," said the king, and smiled, then winked at lord Graybourne.

"I dub thee, a peer…Rise Sir Hollands, a true knight of England."

The king stood with John on one side, and Hollands on the other and announced.

"I have rewarded these two find champions of the crown…and accordingly, due punishment shall be rendered, to those who would commit treason."

The crowd gasped, as they looked around, having no idea. Then the king exclaimed.

"A list of names has been brought to my attention, regarding the assault against me and the queen, on our return home. Rest assured, there can be no escape!" charged the king. We shall retire now, for we are tired from our long journey. Thank you all for your warm welcome…and goodnight."

All the court bowed and kneeled, as Lyonus and Miria left the great hall.

Both John and Hollands could hardly contain themselves, as they escorted the king and queen to their chambers. When the door was opened, Nichol and Jacqueline were laying out fresh towels and water.

There could be seen a lavish array of flowers, and a basket of fruit. There was cheese and bread, along with a variety of wines. Their bed was scented with rose peddles, and strings of lilac hung from the window seal.

Queen Miria was very pleased with her reception, for the court made her feel very welcomed.

"Lyonus…this is far more than I could have expected…"

"What…do you think they would do less for my queen…?"

"…No, I just meant…I wasn't at all sure they would like me…you know, as their queen."

Lyonus took a deep breath, and walked over to Miria, then took her hand.

"Look at me," he said, while Miria glanced, with stars in her eyes. "This is your home now…our home. You, my dear are their queen…my queen. They serve you. There isn't a soul under God, who would disrespect you, or even pretend not to love you."

"That's what I mean…my lord, I want them to love me for me, not out of fear of you."

"Miria, I knew if I loved you, so would they…Remember they will see more of you than your outward beauty…then my dear, you will feel confident…just give them time…and give yourself time as well"

"You are right I know…"

"Ah…but what more is there?" asked Lyonus.

"Well…I was thinking of Michael just then."

"What about him?"

"I just wished I could tell him I was okay, and perfectly…so perfectly happy."

"Then write him, and send it by courier. It will take a while, but at least he will know, and you both can stop worrying."

Miria hugged Lyonus, then said. "No wonder I fell in love with you…you know, for such a young king, you are a wise one…"

"Thanks to my father…he taught me everything I needed to know, in order to rule a kingdom."

"Yes…and what about to rule a heart my king?"

"That lesson my love…I shall learn from you."

Miria and Lyonus walked over to the window together. "You miss him don't you Lyonus…your father?"

"Yes…especially during times like these…"

The king made a deep sigh, one of sadness, then said.

"Look Miria, our gardens are beautiful, but not as the gardens of your country."

"I've seen times such as these, in France…they make for awful dreams Lyonus…not knowing who to trust…It made me so afraid for the king, but he trusted his instincts Lyonus, and his closest friends, then he got to the bottom of things and now…he is still king. Do you understand Lyonus? She said putting both hands on his cheeks, and searching his very blue eyes. "You will handle it too my love I just know it."

"Yes…and that much I am sure of…but enough…let's not speak of these things now."

"All right then, what shall we speak of?" asked Mira, as she swirled around the king.

"Ah…let us speak of love," he replied, as he took her hand leading her toward the bed. "Then…where is the poet I married," asked Miria, as she rubbed her fingers through his hair, and touched the place of his heart. "I know he waits in there somewhere."

Then the king laid her across the bed and said. "Now, he is ready to fill the

night with love my flower. Love from a beautiful rose," spouted Lyonus.
"Hum…your wish is my will…great king…"

Now outside the king's chambers were John and Hollands.
"John, what was the king talking about earlier…some type of list?"
"Hollands do you recall, what the king said about camouflage?"
"No, I don't…I don't remember a thing about that."
Hollands you don't' listen…you haven't yet learned to listen closely to everything the king says…Well, do you know what he said or not?" questioned John.
"Yes…yes, I think he had reference to a ploy of Graybourne to catch a traitor," said Hollands, with a smile, perhaps teasing John. Look, they don't share everything with me, I just overheard them talking. But before it is all said and done, lord Graybourne will let us in on the plan."
"Ah…ha…! And when the traitors rear their ugly heads…the king will chop them off." John added.
"Well yes…it's just a matter of time."
"But I thought we all felt it was lord Guy…"
"The king wanted absolute proof…because of Guys' backing…and according to lord Graybourne, he will show his hand soon…he has too," said Hollands as he spied a figure in the corridor and then said. John, look…here he comes now!"
"Hollands…control…you must show control," cautioned John.
Lord Guy approached them smugly and said.
"Well…well…well, good evening sir knights…and congratulations. I'm sure it is in order. I see the king was feeling over generous. Ah, yes, that happens when a king feels threatened. Oh, not saying you aren't brave men of course…ha…ha…ha…"
Laughed Guy as he raised both his hands to wart off their anger.
"What do you mean…my lord?" asked Hollands.
"I meant no challenge to you, sir knights…but it's no secret, that there has been several attempts on the kings life. And now of course with a new bride…it just made since to secure loyalties," he said while he rubbed his chin.
John could barely swallow, but relied.
"Lord Guy…the hour is late, perhaps you need one of us to escort you to your room…after all, anyone loyal to the crown, might well have to watch his back…As you have suggested, my lord…secure localities."

Lord Guy paused for a moment, intending to comment with further details, but simply said.

"My friend, do not think for a second, that you are on equal footing with me…Take this tiny piece of advice…"

Guy walked closer to Hollands to whisper.

"One should be careful, where his allegiance is placed…it could be the difference between…say…a live knight, and a dead one."

"What!" John ragged toward Guy, just as Hollands held him back with his arm.

"Stop…John, it's not worth it…"

"You know, you are quite right, my friends," said lord Guy. "Let me bid you goodnight the hour is rather late."

Lord Guy laughed with a degree of sarcasm in his voice, while he walked away.

"I can't wait!" said John. "Surely king Lyonus will get great pleasure from his demise."

"Well if the king doesn't…everyone else will."

"Hum…come Hollands," remarked John, as he rubbed his hand across his sword. Let's get back to our post."

John and Hollands were somehow content as they reasoned that the king would take care of their enemy one day soon.

Time had passed all too quickly. It had been a little more than a year since the king and Miria, had returned from France.

The queen awakened early one morning, and spied a vase of flowers on the table.

"Good morning Nichol…"

"Good morning your majesty."

"Where is the king, Nichol?" Miria walked over, and picked up one of the roses.

"Um…the roses are beautiful!"

"They are beautiful indeed, my lady."

"Nichol, I asked you where is the king?"

"I'm sorry your majesty, he said to tell you, he would be in the great hall."

"Then, I'll ask you again, who brought the flowers?"

"Madam…it was brought in by…lord Guy…I did not ask him who they were from.

"Get rid of them…Do you hear!" then she said gently. "Please Nichol."

"Of course, your majesty...right now."

Nichol sensed the urgency and removed the vase, then headed down the corridor. While she searched for a place to rid them, Lady Kathryn saw her coming.

"Where are you going with those, my lady? They are lovely," asked Kathryn.

"The queen insists that I...throw them away...They are beautiful, in fact her favorite ones...I don't understand," said Nichol.

"Ha...ha." laughed Kathryn. I think I can guess. Wait till lord Guy hears that his small attempt failed. Ha...ha."

"My lord Guy...are you sure of that?" Nichol questioned.

"Why...I'd stake your life on it, my dear. Who else would have enough nerve to betray the king, and try to woo the queen right under our very noses?"

"But my lady Kathryn, what are you saying? I thought you and Lord Guy..."

"Well you thought wrong! There was something before...but. Never mind that, give them to me," said Kathryn, almost ordering her.

"You want to get rid of them for me?" said Nichol, as she slowly handed her the flowers.

"I would be more than happy to...just leave everything to me Nichol."

"Well thank you my lady...I must get back to her majesty...thank you."

"Sure," said Kathryn, as she sniffed the flowers. I do have wonderful taste," she whispered.

When Nichol returned to the queens chambers, and told her what lady Kathryn had said,

Miria wrapped her robe around her tightly, and then said.

"That...that...beast. I do not trust him...how did he come in without my knowing?"

"I can not say your majesty...perhaps the king, ma'am..."

"I don't like him so much...when he looks at me...I, it just doesn't feel right."

"I'm sorry your majesty, what can I do?"

"Just keep a close watch Nichol...He's not one to take lightly...and make sure to lock the doors," said the queen.

"Yes ma'am."

"By the way did you get rid of the flowers...they were beautiful?"

"As a matter of fact the lady Kathryn took them."

"Lady Kathryn?"

"Yes your majesty, she seemed to know what to do with them."

"Hum," sounded the queen. You may dress me now, I need to speak with the king."

"Yes your majesty."

King Lyonus decided to act upon the names of those who were accused of treason. This list was supposed to lead him to others, who had a hand in the treasonous act. The person who was to testify against lord Guy, was found dead just two days before. He was found hung in a room above Miles Tavern. But the king decided to go ahead with the charges against the others aimed at being a deterrent to future treasons.

So King Lyonus II called for lord Biltfry to reveal the names of those that had been charged.

"Today the good king Lyonus II, will pass forth judgment on the following:"

Ivan Fellows, court Seer; Lord Henry Becket, king's Surgeon; Miles Edwards, and Sir Richard Hopkins, members of the king's army. Step forward, and receive the kings justice."

"What say you Miles Edwards, and Richard Hopkins, knights of England?"

"Please your majesty...I made a mistake...I was tricked," said Miles who pleaded for his life. Then Richard spoke.

"I can only say, I am a patriot, and did what I thought was right for England," he stared blankly into space. Ivan Fellows made his statement next.

"My lord...I beg of you...please have mercy? Your majesty, I only reported what I had seen. It was misread and misused by others...by those who wanted to do you harm. I served your father for many years...served England my lord...All that time I remained faithful...even now my king unto you...please! Mercy..."

The king finally turned to Beckett. "What say you?"

Beckett looked at lord Guy, then finally remarked. "I have no words to say..."

"All right then...my judgment is this: Ivan Fellows, because you have served my father, and aided England in her many victories...and you have pleaded for mercy...Your life shall be spared. However, your sight shall not. In the same way in which your sight was misdirected, that an attempt on my life might be made; One eye shall be removed from your person...that your future visions, may be seen with more clarity.

Miles Edwards, you have served as a guard in my army, and know the penalty for treason, you have asked that I show mercy. I charge you as being a traitor to the crown. You will be banished for your lifetime from England, branded, that all who meet you may know you…as a traitor.

Richard Hopkins, as a knight, having pledged an oath…knowing the laws that bound you to loyalty to England…"

Then Richard blurted out. "I was loyal to England…my country!"

Then king Lyonus replied softly, in a whisper. "I am England." Then spoke aloud saying. "Your head shall fall this day…you will no longer suffer the trials of your patriotism. As for you Henry Becket…You were shared the secrets and the trust of the court, and failed them. You showed no mercy on the lives of my mother or my father…not even on the prince, so none will be given. For you no mercy shall be found, but a certain penalty of instant death.

The blood of the dead has called out for justice, from the grave. The sentence is clear.

This self-same afternoon, your head will be severed from your body, and placed in a separate grave. Pre adventure, you should pray for redemption in the next life…you will not be able to find your evil head, to once again plot against your king…Remove them!"

Then as the king stood to leave the great hall, he saw Miria who turned to leave. Then Henry called out to the king.

"Sire…please, I will…"

King Lyonus would not even turn to hear him.

He raised his hand in a wave, and made his way from the great hall to find Miria. Lord Guy followed Ivan and the others down the stairs toward the dungeon.

"Stop guard, just a moment," said Fredrick, to the guard that had Beckett and Richard.

"Guy…you said this could not happen…where was the proof?" shouted Beckett.

"Oh…proof ah? What were you going to tell the king, my friend?

"Listen…you can stop this…get me out of here…I can help you…Guy!" yelled Richard.

"You already have…now I'm afraid you have out lived your usefulness to me…"

With a smirk on his face called for the guards. "Take them away!"

Henry yelled and screamed, all the way to the chopping block.

"I'm more than sorry my friend, you heard the king…I can do nothing," shouting out to Becket. Their pleas became more and more faint, while lord Guy went directly to Ivan. When he walked in, Ivan was bleeding from his right eye. He was in much pain. He looked up to see lord Guy standing in the doorway. He began to scream at him.

"Get out…! You lied to me…to all of us! Even those men who followed your every order." Ivan sobbed sorely. Then Guy remarked. "They were, young fools…greedy. They could never have truly been loyal to England."

"Listen at what you are saying…those men were pleading for you. I can still here them. Yet you turned your back."

"You listen to me!" said Guy, with his teeth gritted together, as was his way. "I could do nothing! Nothing do you hear! Even if I could, the king would surely find me out, that would be a tragedy for many more of us."

"Yes…I know, you are worry for everyone else," said Ivan as he looked away.

"I tried to talk to the king earlier, and he would not give me audience…I was not going to try my hand. If it were not for a little assistance…I would be joining Beckett and the others."

"You know Guy, yours will come, and I'm sure when it does, there will be no mercy. The king rendered what he felt was justified, but you…yours is from pure evil and greed, to allow others to take the blame for your treachery. Now get out of my sight!"

Lord Guy walked to the door and peeped out to see if anyone was watching, then said. "Ivan, you just remember, keep your mouth shut…or you may miss your tongue as well!"

"It's to late for threats Guy…You don't frighten me any more…you dog! There is nothing else you can hold over my head…as I said you will receive yours."

"Yeah well…it won't be this day Ivan…or at the very least, you won't see it. Ha…ha…ha…" Then Guy left the dungeon watching behind him, being careful not to be seen.

Now the king had followed Miria back to her chambers, fearing she would be upset over his decisions.

"Miria, I'm sorry you had to witness that…I do not want you to think me harsh. I know it has been a while since those attempts happened."

"Has the king forgotten I was the ward of a king? I witnessed many such judgments, and I came to understand the penalty for treason…the cost of which is high. My king, I could never think of you as harsh, for trying to protect what you hold dear. I could not think that of you, without thinking that of me…for we are one. Whatever you desire, I desire. I know you wanted only justice…Remember what we discussed?"

"Thank you my love, I had hoped you'd understand. I could not bare it if, you were to feel anything but love for me."

"Grieve yourself no longer my lord…go then and rest your mind for a while, I have news I want to share…but at dinner…go please! At…dinner," she said nudging him on.

"All right, all right. I guess I'll have to get used to being ordered about…ha…ha…Ah John?" he said, as he watched Nichols' reaction.

"I'm afraid so sire." John replied.

Both John and Nichol chuckled to watch the king and queen so much in love.

As Lyonus left the queens chambers, Lord Graybourne met him in the corridor.

"Your majesty…we must speak…now!"

"My lord Graybourne you're in a huff. What seems to be the trouble?"

"This is what bothers me now…You said trust you, and I find this."

"What do you have there? Let me see it!"

It was the list baring the names of the traitors. With lord Guys name scratched through.

"Oh…you saw lord Guys name? And how did you get this?"

"Perhaps he wanted me to see it I don't know your majesty. But you stood there, and ask all of us to risk our lives for you, and to trust you, then you stand in judgment, and leave out the one…who out of all the men I have known, was the most worthy of dying."

They walked to the kings' room to further discuss the matter.

"I see you are not yourself. Please sit down my lord Graybourne…let me explain something to you."

Graybourne reluctantly sat himself down to listen.

"There has been a great secret shared by lord Guy and myself, since the death of my father," said king Lyonus.

"Secret?" questioned Graybourne.

"Yes…one that is dark and hideous. Lord Guy came to me at fathers' funeral…you remember; Luis had gone mad…just beside himself. I was pretty upset as well. Then he told me about my fathers death, and how it happened."

"What do you mean...how it happened? It was your fathers' heart."

"I was told Luis had dabbled in mothers potions and poisoned father as well."

Lord Thomas stood to his feet. Lyonus walked over to the window still holding the paper.

"Lord Thomas believe me if I had known...I was just so overtaken. It was the worst thing I have ever done. Then later, I found out, I signed and sealed his freedom to do whatever he willed. And there is nothing that can be done, because I approved it...stamped it with fathers ring. It became final."

"My lord...why did you not come to me for help? I was there for you..."

"As I said I wanted to protect Luis...It was a moment of weakness. Now I know the only way to stop lord Guy is to either retrieve that letter, or..."

Then Thomas interjected. "Or kill him...Sire!"

"Yes kill him...my lord"

"I can't believe he would take such a chance and do this to you...but I know it is what he's capable of."

"I can only apologize for being a young pitiful fool."

"You need not apologize to me my king, I'm sorry I doubted you. I knew it had to be something, I just didn't know what or why. What can we do now?" asked Thomas.

"Just wait...and tread softly my friend. I want him to think he is unnoticed."

Meanwhile, prince Luis, and lord Guy met secretly.

"My lord Guy, I don't want to be seen with you right now."

"You know why I'm here."

"Lord Guy, we'll have to do this after dinner, by then I'll know more. The queen has an announcement tonight. I believe I shall be able to make my move without a hitch."

"All right then...I'll come back later, and we'll discuss the particulars."

When everyone was assembled in the dinning hall. Lord Biltfry stood and asked all to raise their goblets in a toast to the king and queen. He then gestured for all to be seated.

"Quiet please...! Quiet. Her majesty the queen, has something to say. Your majesty..." he said, as he bowed to the queen.

"My lords and ladies, today we shall toast our lord king Lyonus II..."

Lyonus quite surprised at the toast, said.

"I do not need a toast."

"My king..."

Miria said to Lyonus, so he would not stop her. "King Lyonus II has sired an heir to the throne."

"What!" He shouted with such amazement.

"Yes my king…I am with child."

"How…when?"

The entire dinning hall rang with laughter.

"My king…I am pregnant."

"No, I mean when are you to have my son!"

"I'm only about two months."

The king almost forgot about his court, and then he asked, "How are you?"

"Lyonus, I am fine…I feel wonderful! Especially now!'

"Miria, I do not know what to say…"

"Are you pleased my king?"

King Lyonus leaped over and kissed the queen. It was as if they were the only two people in the world. Everyone loved to see them together…and so in love.

"My love…nothing could make me happier, except if there were two…ha…ha…!"

Then the king stood again and said.

"Raise your goblets once more! On such an occasion as this, it has been a tradition, to go to the hunt and make a feast. Sir Hollands!" he called. Make ready our things for the hunt! For tomorrow we will make way."

"Wonderful…!" shouted prince Luis. I would love to accompany you on the hunt."

"Why Luis…I didn't think you cared much for the hunt. You never came along when father and I would go."

"Well that's because, father would never allow me. I have always had to study. But now I've no more studying to, and I'd like to go, my king."

"Well, then…go you shall, my brother!"

"Sire…?" questioned John. "Would not it be better to postpone the hunting trip? Or maybe take lord Thomas and I along."

"Where is he tonight? No…this night I feel I can do without the plotting for once."

"But…begging the kings pardon…I only meant, because of the…a…attempts."

"Sir knight…it has been so long since anything like that has happened, and after today, perhaps we have discouraged…the notion."

"Your majesty…"

"Do you not agree, my friend?" said the king, with a firm look at Hollands

"It is as you wish, my king...I will make ready for the hunt."

"...And now that business is over, let us retire for the night."

"Go on ahead my lord...I need to speak with John for a moment," said Miria.

"Yes my dear, but don't be long."

Queen Miria pulled John closer to her as she tried to whisper. She waited for the others to leave the dinning hall.

"John, I'm afraid for my king. Can't you stop this foolish hunt?"

"Your majesty...it is not for me to stop...the king has expressed his will. I can not oppose it."

No...not even if it meant saving his life...you could point out the problems that exists with this tradition...especially for his safety, especially now!"

"My lady..." Bidding the queen to walk in front of him. "Did you not hear Hollands doing the exact same thing...the king is very...well...he will not budge your majesty..."?

Just then prince Luis came over to bid the queen goodnight.

"Queen Miria...I would like to congratulate you and my brother...I am truly happy for the both of you. You are looking particularly lovely tonight."

"Thank you prince Luis, and good night to you..."

When he had walked away, the queen turned immediately and started to shiver.

"What's the mater your majesty?" asked John. Are you okay? You look rather pale."

"No...I'm okay, it's just the way he looks at me...it's...um..."

"He is merely admiring your beauty, your majesty."

"No...it's much more than that...I can feel it."

"If my lady doesn't mind me saying...it was hard for King Lyonus to stop staring as well...remember?"

"All the same, I would feel more comfortable if he wasn't staring all the time."

"Let me walk you to your chambers...the king will be waiting."

"All right John...but promise me you and Hollands will keep your eyes and ears opened."

"You can depend on that, my queen."

John wasted no time getting the queen to her room. He wanted to talk with Hollands about the hunt. While John and Hollands mulled over the situation, prince Luis was mulling over something of his own.

Prince Luis had just finished making his last payment in gold, when at his door came a shove.

"Who is there?"

"It is I, lord Guy," he whispered.

Prince Luis dismissed Sir Evan, and asked Guy to come in.

"Go now Evan...and keep that gold out of sight...for pity's sake! And close the door you fool! Oh...It's so hard to find competent folk these days...would you not agree lord Guy?"

"That I do...my prince."

"All right on to unfinished business, and make it quick, I don't want to be seen with you tonight...there is too much at stake."

"I'll get on with it then. Do you have everything in order now?"

"Ha...you come here to ask me if I have things in order...after you and your guards made a royal mess...fiasco...almost lost all our heads."

"I thought I had it under control my prince," Guy mumbled. Then prince Luis said.

"Everything is going beautifully, I might add..."

"Well let's just hope it does...if not, it could be all our necks."

"Ha...I have no intentions of loosing anything, but rather gaining. I have a foolproof plan. I've completely thought it out, and it includes becoming...king..."

"Then perhaps, you should sleep longer on your fool proof plan...I have never seen a scheme, that could not be stalled because of one tiny detail that was over-looked...no matter how small Luis."

"Lord Guy, let us drink a toast to the hunt!"

"No...I never toast a victory before it is won. I found it to be bad luck...my friend."

"In any case." Boasted the prince. "I'm sure money buys enough favors, and I have made sure I've bought plenty...and to spare."

Both prince Luis and lord Guy begun to laugh in a low tone.

"To the hunt Luis?"

"The hunt...my lord Guy! I think it's quite brilliant..."

"Well...we shall see, what your gold has purchased," Guy remarked.

"By the way lord Guy..."

"Yes my prince."

"How do you think you escaped my brothers wrath today? Was it your wisdom that took away the proof, or my gold? Think on that tonight when you arrange your loyalties."

"I will indeed…I'm sure however, the answer to that question my prince, is sealed in black and white hidden away. Good night," replied lord Guy.

"Good night my skeptical friend," said Luis, as he turned with a frown.

As soon as lord Guy left the room, prince Luis mumbled aloud.

"…That fool, he's a strain upon my neck, these days. I shall be glad to be rid of him, and his scheming as well. Just a little while longer…and when I am king…I shall decide what should be done."

The next morning, everything was prepared just as the king had ordered.

He rose up early and woke Miria to say good-bye.

"It is time for us to leave Miria…awake my love, and see your king off to the hunt."

"Oh…Lyonus is it time already?" Yawning, as she sat up in bed.

"Yes dear…they are waiting for me."

"Have breakfast with me Lyonus?"

"My love the men are waiting…"

"Lyonus…let them wait. Her majesty requires a proper farewell." Reaching out to him meaning to be playful.

"I promise I shall return soon, and we will have a marvelous dinner," said the king.

Lyonus kissed her all the way to the door, while he was trying to talk. "Then we will make plans…and love…and talk…good bye, my love until tonight."

"…But Lyonus I don't want you to go…"

"Now Miria, we've gone over it, now…kiss your king. I shall return upon God's will."

"I pray that God indeed, will watch over you my love."

"John…Will you please take care of my queen?" said king Lyonus.

"With my life your majesty…"

"Wait…you're not going John?" asked Miria, as she wrapped her robe tightly.

"No my queen…"

"Oh no…!" cried queen Miria I love you Lyonus…forever and always…"

The king and Hollands went to the outer garden. The queen watched from her window, as they mounted their horses. She trembled, and flung her scarf with yellow roses out of the window, and down to the king.

"Come back to me Lyonus!" she shouted. But when she saw prince Luis, she trembled even more. "Return my love" she called out. Then King Lyonus waved his hand and blew her a kiss.

"John...?" she whimpered. We should have tried harder to stop him."
"Now your majesty...Hollands will give special care."
"I know John...I know."
The queen started to cry all the more.
"Please lady Nichol...take the queen and see to her needs..."
"Of course...come your majesty..."

King Lyonus, prince Luis, Hollands and Evan, along with five other guards headed for a spot that was great for hunting.

It lay deep in the woods of Brownstone forest, just off the highway of Fowlers row.

This was a favorite spot of Lyonus I., also for those who would rob and poach the king's deer. But somehow they seemed to have taken a road that veered more to the right.

"What is this?" questioned the king. "I don't remember this place."

They rode yet a ways, and then Evan spoke up and said.

"But your majesty...this is said to be where all the peasants were allowed to poach the royal deer."

"Allowed...sir Evan?"

"Pay no heed my brother...today is sure to be a perfect hunt."

"I am pleased you have come alone Luis...I have longed for the day you and I would share time together...I have been so overwhelmed since my return from France, that we have not really had any real time together."

"You are so right my brother...I am happy as well...Today, I feel everything will change."

"I saw that your eyes have fallen on Jacqueline..."

"What do you mean...that servant girl of the queen?"

"Well I thought I saw something I obviously did not...forgive me brother."

"I need not look below my station...I think we are coming upon our stop."

"I meant no harm Luis."

"...And none taken...my king..."

"I wanted to ask you Luis...do you still try and use mothers potions?"

"No.! I told you I have not even been in that room since well after fathers demise...his death."

"What a strange way of putting it...But I guess it would fit," said Lyonus.

"Oh look Lyonus...we are here I think!"

"Yes..." slurred Evan. "A perfect place for a kill."

"Um..." scoffed the king. Keep your eyes opened Hollands."

"Of course sire...I feel it too."

Four of the guards and the prince had lagged behind. They were to stop at a point between some trees. Then Prince Luis nodded his head, that they should start digging a shallow hole.

Meanwhile, king Lyonus and Hollands, kneeled down in the thickets. They knew it would be easier to spot the deer.

"Look sire..." whispered Hollands. "There...he's a huge stag...!"

"Sh...sh," whispered the king. "We don't want to frighten him away."

"Look at those antlers!" Holland terribly excited. "I've never seen this before."

"One would think you would have seen lots, since you hunted with father all the time."

"Your father always had me to guard the horses so I never really knew what it was like.

Ah...Look he'd make a fine trophy for the great hall."

"...To go along with all the others. Sh...I think he's spied us...be still," whispered Lyonus.

The king slowly raised his large bow, and pulled back on its string. When he released the arrow, it was dead center the mark. It was right in the deer's neck, down he went.

"Good shot, your majesty!" shouted Hollands.

"Ha...ha...ha...we bagged a beauty, Hollands..."

"No...you did sire...Look everyone!" yelled Hollands. "His majesty has landed a beauty."

Suddenly, the guards fell out from behind the trees. Prince Luis with a sheepish grin on his face said.

"Fine shot brother." With his head slightly turned.

"What is it Luis, are you afraid of a little blood? Ha...ha...!"

"Lyonus...perhaps father knew I had no stomach for this kind of thing...unless it was the blood of an enemy."

The king chuckled a little, and then said. "Luis...there is no dishonor in not wanting to spill blood...not of any kind. It makes you no less a prince."

"All the same...Maybe I'll wait by the clearing," said the prince.

Suddenly Luis signaled for his men to surround the king, and Hollands. One of the guards said.

"Get over here!" he said ordering Hollands and Lyonus as he pointed to the hole that was dug.

"What's the meaning of this?" spouted the king. "Are you all mad?"

"Luis...!" he shouted. "What have you done my brother? Don't do it...please don't. You won't get away with it...Luis!"

Evan drew his sword, and raised it. Then shouted

"Just mad enough to finish the job I started years ago!"

"What?" gasped the king as he reached for his sword that was then knocked away. One of the men raised the sword to jab the king. Hollands managed to push him away. As soon as he moved, another jumped at them. Hollands pulled Lyonus behind him. He used one hand to fight and kill one, and then another. The king reached for the knife Hollands kept in his boot. A guard hurled his sword at the king. Suddenly, Hollands leaped in front of Lyonus, and took the brunt of the blade. But the sword nevertheless, had gone clean through to the king's side. There they both fell into the opened grave.

"Go...go in there you fool, and get his ring," called the prince.

"What?"

"I told you to get his ring!"

Evan shouted to another guard. "Get his ring his highness needs it."

As soon as the guard jumped in but before he could remove the ring, Evan stabbed him with his sword.

Then Luis stepped out from behind a tree, and said.

"Now there are three more...we started this trip with nine...um..."

"Yes my lord." Evan agreed then said. "It is four of us that remain...should there be three my lord? Should we cover the grave?"

"No...leave as much blood in the air as possible. The wolves shall find it easier to dine tonight...but..."

Luis reached for Evans sword, and then killed one other guard.

"My lord?" questioned Evan. Won't we need these men?"

"Well Evan...how many men would it take to let the kingdom know it's king is dead...?"

When the last guard saw and heard what was happening he jumped on his horse and then shouted, "No...no...please!" He rode as fast as he could, intending to get away. But Evan pulled his bow, and struck him down from his horse.

"Now," remarked Luis. How many, will it take to spend a fortune in gold? Ha...ha...ha!" The prince laughed as if he had gone insane, and then finally Evan asked.

"Your highness, do you plan to kill me as well?" Then Evans' hands shook just a little.

"Evan, a question like that coming from a trusted companion really hurts.

Unlike my lord Biltfry, my pay off is in gold. Ha…ha…ha…! Evan, I trust you with my life, I always have. Oh…and your secret is safe with me. Besides, I'll need you by my side when I am vested king. And I really don't care what your preference is. Now go on…we've got business to finish."

"Yes my lord…we need to make some wounds of our on…hate to mention it but we didn't get the ring…"

"It's too late to worry about that now. All right hit me…make it good!"

Evan struck the prince so hard, it knocked him to the ground. The entire side of his face began to swell, and his chin opened up and blood poured out.

Then prince Luis grabbed Evans sword and swiped it across his chest. Blood streamed from his chest like a fountain. The prince managed to tuck a torn piece of his cloak into Evan's shirt to stop some of the bleeding.

"I think these wounds will suffice," said Luis, grunting from pain.

"Yes, maybe enough to convince the people at that old farm house we passed."

"Convinced or not," said Luis. I'd just as soon try to make it to the castle tonight."

"Impossible, your highness," replied Evan. We'd never make it passed the wolves, the way we're bleeding…we will need help ourselves…pretty soon."

"Maybe you're right Evan…we should go on to find help before the late hour falls upon us."

So prince Luis, and Evan, left the bodies as they had fallen. They wanted the attack to seem real. Then they rounded up the horses, and attempted to make it to the Lansing's. Their farm was at least six miles away. Riding hard and fast, till arriving, the two of them were barely able to stay on the horses.

Robert Lancing and his wife Abbey were more than happy to accommodate the prince. It was difficult, however, to hear the story they spun about the king. They were truly shocked to find that the prince and Evan were the only ones who survived the attack.

Evan explained how the band of men came suddenly upon them, and added how bravely the king fought for his life before he was cut down. Then the Lansing's said almost together.

"King Lyonus will be sorely missed in the land." They bowed at the feet of prince Luis, and said. "Long lives' the king."

"Thank you, my loyal subjects, my brother would have been proud to know, he was so well thought of by the people of England."

"Abbey you should tend their wounds…I'll get water and bandages," said Robert.

"Your wounds are pretty deep sire, but I think you will be all right."

"Thank you my lady for that fine bit of surgery."

"Rest now, my lords…then come and sup," said Abbey.

"Yes…you must be exhausted from your ordeal…and famished," remarked Mr. Lancing.

"Thank you," said Evan. It is a delight to find such folks willing to help a stranger."

"Indeed," said the prince. We would require a morsel or two, if you please."

Then Evan added. "Perhaps, my lady…some wine."

Mr. And Mrs. Lancing glanced at each other. Mrs. Lancing angled her head, and eyes toward the kitchen. She motioned for Robert to join her there.

"Dear…does it seem as if they're celebrating, to you? Ordering wine…they don't seem a bit sad to me Robert."

"Don't be silly, Abbey, that's just how royalty act when someone dies…When a person dies, they drink wine and eat great feasts…you know sort of like a send off."

"Yes Robert, I know about royalty. I'm not royal but I know dying and being murdered, are two different things."

"Don't talk like that. Come on…we'd better get back in there."

"All right," said Abbey. But I don't like this one bit."

"Just maybe the prince will reward us with some gold or something."

"Maybe…for my part…I'd settle for them gone. I don't like being in the middle of such trappings."

Prince Luis, and Evan, had made themselves welcomed in the Lansing's home for the night. The prince sent word, by one of Robert and Abbeys' friends, that the king had been attacked.

CHAPTER SIX
The Taking of a Throne

Meanwhile as king Lyonus lie in a shallow grave presumed dead.

The king began to come to consciousness, when he felt the wolves tugging at Hollands' body on top of him. They snarled and jerked, trying to make a meal of Hollands. If something wasn't done quickly, the king knew he would be next. Luckily his body shielded the king from the wolves. But Lyonus held on to the knife with the golden handle he pulled from Hollands' boot, during the attack. He began jabbing the wolves.

"Get away…you…filthy beast…you'll not touch him!" shouted the king.

He stabbed at their paws, and faces, until they whimpered from their wounds, and backed away. But the other bodies were fair game for them. By the time the king had lifted himself out of the grave, the wolves were gone. They left very little flesh on the other bodies. He wrapped his head with Miria's scarf and instinctively pushed dirt over the hole where poor Hollands would now rest.

Surely the wolves intended to return, perhaps this time with more of the pack, but they would not use Holland's body in which to make a meal.

The king was badly hurt. He had deep stab wounds in his side, and gashes in his forehead. Lyonus had all types of cuts and bruises on his face. The loss of so much blood left him dizzy and disoriented. He could barely stand after he covered the grave. But staggering, and falling, he walked to the edge of the highway, before his legs finally buckled underneath him. Then he lost all consciousness.

It appeared that fortune would smile down on king Lyonus that day. For shortly after he passed out, a wagon came barreling down the dirt road. It was the wine maker, Jacob Corley accompanied by his friend, Roland "Skunk" Peters.

Well, he was called skunk, let's just say…he was not the bravest of fellows. A skunk branded him years ago. But it was old Roland, who discovered the body of Lyonus. He was laying quite still along side the road. The glitter of the kings' ring caught old Skunk's attention.

"Woo…ho…slow down a minute Jacob…"

"What is the matter Skunk?"

"Well, it looks like something shiny there…oh and a man, just laying there."

"What shiny?"

"Jacob…just stop and pull over."

Both men got down from the wagon, and walked slowly over to king Lyonus.

"I thought it was a man," whispered Skunk

"I see it is…a man who's been badly hurt."

"Jacob, I'm not sure I want to get myself involved with it…no, not at all."

"Well Skunk, its just a little bit too late for that, now isn't it?"

"We could just…oh…take the rings and pretend we didn't see him."

"Now that's just great Skunk! If it were you, wouldn't you want some kind soul to attend you?"

"Of course I would…I suppose…yes." Jacob took a closer look at the body.

"Move back Skunk…Let me take a look at him…I can't tell a thing, except if we don't get him some help, he's going to die."

"Oh no…"Replied Skunk "It nothing but trouble."

"Hush Roland…and help me. Do you want him to bleed to death?"

Jacob stared at him for a minute more, and recognized him as Lyonus, the king.

"Ha…oh my Lord…!" Jacob stood up, and put his hand over his lips.

"What…what is it?" questioned Skunk.

"I've seen that face…Roland, do you know this face, who we have here? It's the king of old England."

"What…No…way…Do you know what this means?" asked Roland.

"Oh yeah…somebody didn't want the king found. At least not alive."

"Jacob, if we're found helping him…or even knowing anything about this, it could mean death."

"If I sense this situation right Skunk…it would."

"Situation…the man is dead. What situation?"

"No he's not. But I think somebody didn't plan on the king being found…not for a long time."

"But Jacob…Who would dare…?"

"I don't know Skunk. Maybe someone who wanted to be king, or would benefit from his death somehow…"

"Okay all right, but shouldn't we just let them have their way after all, if they went far enough to kill the king, they would not hesitate…"

"Exactly…!" interrupted Jacob. "Now do you see what I meant, when I said…would kill us?"

"Come on Skunk…help me get him in the wagon."

So the two men struggled to lift the body and place it in the wagon.

"Hey…pile straw over it," said Jacob

"Will you stop saying it…Sounds like we're dealing with a dead man."

"Well as far as they're concerned, he is dead. We will put him in the hands of a friend who will care for him until he heals."

"Or dies…and just who might that be?" asked Skunk.

"You'll see. But first we have to go to Flowers Row to the Tavern there."

"Flowers Row? Won't they recognize him there?"

"Not the way he looks now. His own mother, rest her soul…wouldn't know him now."

"I don't know Jacob…more people are murdered on Fowlers Row, than die from drinking your ale. Ha…ha."

"Very funny Skunk. But it's the only place I know, where no questions would be asked. If you have the right price that is."

"Okay…but where are you going to get the right price?"

"Skunk…look at him. He is the king. He is wearing gold rings on several fingers…a medallion around his neck…solid gold."

"Yeah…and I bet those shoes would fetch a nice price…and look, the knife with a gold handle…It must be worth a kings ransom!"

"So don't tell me…all that gold won't keep him safe until he can heal."

"Well, whether it does, or doesn't…I say we drop him off, and leave him…and Jacob, we won't…look back."

"Then my friend…that is exactly what we will do."

"Just a few more miles and we will arrive old boy," Skunk said, as he leaned over to talk to king Lyonus. "Then maybe you'll learn who your friends are."

"Skunk...we have rounded the corner now...let's get him ready."
"All right."
Finally, they arrived at Miles Tavern. Jacob took his wagon around behind the building.
"That pretty little Constance should be working. I'll tell her about our small problem."
"Let's just get him in already." Insisted Skunk. Jacob tried to lift him, then said.
"Help me Skunk...He's dead weight!"
"Make it quick Jacob, I don't want to be seen with him."
"We will leave him in the corner here. You bring the wagon around front, and I'll come out that way..."
"Okay...but don't be long."
When Jacob went inside to deliver his barrels of ale, he spied Constance in the corner, clearing one of the tables.
"Pssst...pssst...Constance, come here," whispered Jacob. I have a small problem."
"Well can your small problem wait a minute? I have a job to do Jacob."
"Yeah...okay..."
"Then...go and wait at the back door. Go on..." Constance almost nudged him on.
After Constance had finished cleaning off tables, and getting a few drinks, she made her way to the back door.
"All right Jacob, what can I do for you...and just what is this problem you're talking about?"
"Get a load of this...just look!" Jacob pointed to the king lying beside the Tavern door.
"Oh! Who in the world is he? He looks like he's been hurt really bad. Is he a friend of yours?"
"Constance...take a closer look...give it a good stare. Tell us what you see."
"Why he looks just...or...no, that couldn't be the..."
"That's it exactly. But listen, you can't breath a word of this, not to any creature. We dare not..."
"Jacob...! What have you gotten me involved in? Oh boy...he looks bad."
"Yes...but I figure your dad, being a surgeon and all..."
"How in heavens name, am I supposed to keep him...take care of a king...especially without money? That's another thing I haven't seen my father for years. Well...does he have anything on him?"

"Settle down Constance…that he does, this should ease your doubt some…"

"My…goodness," said Constance. He really is the king. Have you seen all that gold?

"Sh…sh…! If anyone heard you, and found us they might well finish the job they started."

"I'm sorry," whispered Constance. What do I do now?

"Keep him upstairs in your room. There's no telling if they're searching for his body, even now. Got it?"

"Oh…he is so helpless…well, don't just stand there…let's get him upstairs. Hum…where's Roland?"

Oh Skunk…I told him to meet me around front."

"Well get him…his body is too heavy just the two of us…Go, I'll wait with him."

Now that the problem of caring of the king was solved, Jacob and Roland decided to rid themselves of anything dealing with their find. This of course included the ring with the seal of England that Skunk had held back. So a few minutes after they had helped get the king to Constance room, a knock was heard at the door.

"Who's there…?" said Constance.

"It's me…Jacob, open up."

She cracked the door just a little, to see his face.

"Constance, here are the things we found on him. The gold handled knife should bring a pretty penny, I'll wager. Here is a solid gold ring…I'm sure could be traded. There's some other stuff here, just do what you need to do."

"Thanks Jacob, I'll do what I can…but don't expect too much…he's lost a lot of blood.

Then she looked in the bag, and saw g gold ring with the seal of England engraved on it.

"Jacob it's true…he really is the king," she whispered.

"I told you…this proves who he is…what were you going to do with this?"

"Well, I suppose I'll…you know put it away for safe keeping. I know I can't sell this one. This scarf is no good now filled with blood. I wonder if it belonged to the queen?"

"All right Constance…I hope you can pull it off. I'll check on you every now and again."

Constance gave Jacob a pat on the shoulder, nodded her head, and then said.

"Jacob...you are a good friend...don't worry, you have done the right thing."

"I felt sure of it Constance," he said. Something, good will come out of it, I just know it. Good luck, my friend...You are a godsend."

Constance closed the door, then walked over to survey. She took a deep breath, as she tried to clean the kings' wounds, and said to herself in a shallow voice.

"Oh...I'm a godsend all right. It's probably the most idiotic thing I've done in a long time...putting my life on the line this way...all because they thought he looked like the king" Then she said to herself. What if he stole all those things?

Hum...well; I'm stuck now aren't I?

Constance took another deep breath, then looked at the damage Lyonus sustained.

"Okay...but if you're not the king...so be it, I will try and help you. Hum..."

Now the next day at the Lancing farm, prince Luis and Evan awaited the convoy of soldiers coming to meet them.

They finally came late that afternoon. The soldiers surrounded the place, and a few of them went inside. John Myers was the first to speak up.

"Ah...your highness." John rushed over to greet the prince. "It's good to see that you are okay. Evan..." John nodded his head in greeting. "Where is his majesty...is he up stairs?"

"No John..." said the prince. "I'm saddened to say, my brother and king is dead."

"No!!" shouted John, as the other soldiers gasped. "And what of Hollands, my...friend?

Evan spoke out, with his head lowered.

"Just like the others sir John, Hollands fought well defending the king, but the attackers was too many to oppose.

John chimed right in with sarcasm, pointing at Evan in a hostile manner. "Yet...you survived. No doubt, you must have fought harder than them all!"

"I recent your implications!" yelled Evan. "It sounds like a challenge to me!"

"So be it!" John said, and reached for his sword. "I'll tell you this Evan, you won't find me…so easy to defeat!" Then prince Luis stepped in.

"Stop! Stop this at once!!" Hammering on the table. Then stood up and said. "Have you lost your thinking? Did you come here to accuse us? Are you thinking perhaps we have dishonored the Crown! This is a sad time for me, as well as England. I dare you barge in here, with unfounded accusations, when we all were attacked. Evan fought hard to save me, just as Hollands fought hard to save poor Lyonus. Maybe…I should have you hung for such an offence to me!"

At that point John realized what he had done, and began to clam down a little, then apologized to the prince.

"Your highness…pardon. I meant no disrespect to you. I…only…meant."

Then prince Luis gave John no chance to finish his statement, when he said.

"I know full well what you meant…and I'll hear no more of it! Have you given any information to queen Miria?"

"No…your highness, we did not have all the details, so we thought it best to wait until we did. Are we to find and bring back the kings' body for burial?"

"I insist you look today, then by tonight, finish the matter! By then I want to be ready to leave…to give my brother a burial. Now is that quite clear?"

"Yes your highness…I think I understand…perfectly."

"Good! Now Mr. And Mrs. Lancing…has been very kind to help their prince. I want them to be given ten pieces of gold. They have greatly aided us, and a reward is in order."

"Yes my lord, we should be leaving now, to look for the king…"

"All right…go then, do what you can, till tonight."

John and several soldiers rode out to search for the body of king Lyonus.

They found themselves, off the path that the king would usually hunt. They were surprised that the king would have gone that deep into Brownstone forest.

King Lyonus knew the reputation of that part of the forest. The soldiers were reluctant to give up the search, but John called for an end of it.

Suddenly as they made a turn through some brush, they spotted a lot of bones, and skulls near what seemed to be where wolves had eaten.

Once they had examined the area, they realized it was a shallow grave. All around the grave was evidence of a small scrimmage. The soldiers found pieces of clothing, and body parts that remained, most of which were filled with blood. There was no sign of what could be the kings' remains.

So the hour was getting late, and according to the orders of prince Luis, they were to return and start for the castle.

John and the other knights came back to the Lancings, and accompanied the prince and Evan back to the royal castle. When they all arrived, every member of the court was gathered. There they anxiously waited to hear the news of their ordeal. Queen Miria was the last to enter the great hall. Lord Guy stood gapping at prince Luis, and then said.

"We've awaited your news your highness…"

Prince Luis backed up to the kings' chair and stood next to Miria. He then made the announcement.

"Your majesty…lords and ladies…our good king Lyonus II, my brother…is dead. Murdered by a pack of robbers. Right in front of our eyes, in the thicket of Brownstone Forest…Our men fought as best they could but against so many…we could do nothing…"

Queen Miria stood to her feet, and then let out a scream that would wake the dead…cold and shrilling, until atlas no sound came from her. Her mouth hung open, and her eyes were filled with tears. She wagged her head back and forward, not accepting what she was told. John who stood beside the queen, and in a tone meant only for her ears said.

"My lady…your majesty…it is true, our king is dead. Everyone is dead."

Finally the queen watched the eyes of prince Luis, as he panned the room, then she replied.

"Not all of them are dead! I want to know all the details…why did you not protect him? He was king! I cannot believe, that he could so easily be destroyed. There must be more to the story…Lyonus would not leave me…not like that!"

"Please your majesty…"Sighed prince Luis. "You must take hold of yourself…"

Then John, with an accusation in his eye, signaled for lady Nichol to assist the queen.

"Fetch the surgeon…the queen is in need of calming," spouted lord Guy then said.

My queen, and my prince, I too share your pain, and deep sorrow."

Lord Guy, already kneeling at the feet of the prince, rose up and lamented.

"I somehow feel, I should have been there, to better protect my king…and you. Maybe if more of us had gone along, we could have warded off the attack…"

John shifted his shoulders a little, to get a better glimpse of lord Guy, to show his indignation as lord Guy continued.

"…But on my word your majesty, and your highness…we will not rest day or night, until the dogs that did this terrible act, have been caught and brought to the queens justice." Queen Miria, strained to regain her composure, then motioned for help to be seated.

"I thank each of you for your tribute to my husband. I am grateful for your loyalty, love and support. No one will know how deeply I will continue to grieve. But as for his son…he will never share the pleasure you've had of knowing him…But…I am his queen, and as such, I must maintain a certain amount of dignity before you…while in my private chambers you will be aware, that my heart breaks. Prince Luis, I am sorry you were injured, and had to watch Lyonus killed. I am glad however; you were able to subdue your attackers. My only hope is…that if not now, one day I will look into the eyes of my husbands killer, and pass down to him, with the same amount of rage…a judgment…that will send him to the deepest part of hell, where there I feel sure, not even an angel has dared to look into. Moreover, I am happy to know, and this is to you knights…that the hunt for Lyonus's killers will not stop! Never…until justice is done!"

The knights gathered around her cheered, after she made her remarks. They raised their swords to her in salute of her bravery. Then she added.

"I must retire to my room now…"

Lord Graybourne charged into the room, fell to his knees before queen Miria and roared with a voice that resounded throughout the great hall.

"My queen…my…queen…! It cannot be. My king and friend…I have just received word!"

"Lord Graybourne, I feel you are deeply grieved, and saddened by the report. The news is a shock to me, and I need to be alone. I will forever be grateful to you as your queen, but as a woman, I will forever remember your great love and deep devotion toward my husband, as his friend and consort…I can say no more, please…Good night."

The queen stood and departed the great hall. Lord Guy watched the prince while he took charge, finding himself a seat in the chair of king Lyonus. He signaled for his attention.

"Thank you all. It was quite an experience, but we are grateful to be home alive. I am also thankful to Evan for his bravery…without which, I would not be standing before you now. He must be rewarded. Evan and I both need the attention of the surgeon, so please come to my chambers. For now I bid you good night."

Now prince Luis had barely gotten into his room, before lord Guy had

AWAKENED BY BETRAYAL

followed him. He entered right in behind Luis.

"Lord Guy, I really must say good night, I am exhausted and I'm waiting for the surgeon…"

"I say…that was quite a performance you gave out there." Guy encircled the prince like a vulture." Ignoring what the prince had said. "Even I begun to believe your story…your…grief stricken expressions…very good…very good indeed!"

"…Careful, my lord Guy…A sharp wit is not always appreciated, at the expense of others."

"Can I assume everything went along as you planned?"

"Quiet…! Sh…you! What are you trying to do? The last thing we need is for someone to hear us talking. Now then…there is one more person between me and the Crown…"

Guy railing with his sarcasm said. "Oh…and whom might that be?" Lord Guy silent for a moment, then both Luis and lord Guy said in unison. "Miria…"

"My brother left Lord Du'Voe reagent in his absence…what of him?"

"Ah…it was done. We need only wait. Our dear lord Du'Voe has met with an unfortunate situation…a little accident if you will, this morning. It looks as though poor England now stands without a king, or reagent. Only a prince and a grieving widow…Great prince whatever shall we do?" As they both began to laugh.

Both Luis and lord Guy, laughed over their victory.

Consequently their plans up to this point had all been realized.

"Finally," said the prince. "The crown is within an arms length from me. I can almost feel it on my head…ha…ha…"

"May I say your majesty…it fits perfectly…ha…ha…ha…!"?

"Now…" said Luis. Tell me about the queen…"

"The queen?" he said, annoyed by the question. "Miria will do as she is advised to do remember, right now she is the grief-stricken widow…and I…the helpful consort. You see she listened to John Myers and lord Graybourne and the kings' closest friends…that only got him killed. I on the other hand, tried my hardest to persuade him to stay. I think she will listen to me now."

"Well let us hope she listens, at least for the next few weeks…instead of that meddling Graybourne."

"Never mind him…I have the Duke working on something…I think it will surprise you."

"Who…Westmoreland, I wouldn't be surprised if he didn't trip and cut his own throat, the way he bungled those last arrangement in France."

"Now, now my prince…you shouldn't be so hard on old Westmoreland. He still may prove to be of great help in the coming months."
"That my lord…I should like to see."
"Listen Luis…Since Miria is pregnant, the last thing she will probably want, is to deal with a lot of State affairs. This…is where we take control, and as for Graybourne, he has his own problems. He also grieves, so I will play the good friend and sympathizer…he will confide in me…We also have an ace Kathryn as the queens consort. You know…she has always been one you could depend on for a roust…she's perfect for the part…and beautiful too."
"Well…sounds much to my liking, lord Guy…We can finish what we started low those many years…with the great Lyonus I."
"My prince the army is in our control…we need fear nothing!"
"Great…I will wait for Biltfry's report as well."
"You trust Biltfry?"
"Of course not…but he's working up a document for me…and I need his talents, but when that's over…well you know…no loose ends"
"Yes but can he prove Miria's to deliver a bastard son?"
"Oh…oh…Ho, my lord Guy, that's very good…wonderful in fact. You can see through anything…"
"I told you…it was already in our hands…your…majesty!'
Guy took his bows and made his reasons to leave. "I'd better go now, there is still much I need to do…good night my lord."
"Good night, and sleep well."
"Oh…I shall!" Insisted lord Guy.
He could not wait to get to the kings chambers. He headed straight there.
Fredrick entered the kings' chambers, creped about, and then consequently found the wooden chest. He hastened to open it, anxious to search its contents. When he opened it, he became white, as if he was drained of all his blood. The chest was completely empty.
Lord Guy flung the chest to the wall, and turned over the table where it sat. He stomped from the run. He left grumbling, and mumbling down the corridor. But as soon as he came out of the chambers, he stumbled right into lady Kathryn.
"Lord Guy…" she said, with a smirk on her face. "How are you tonight?"
"Wonderful…of course."

"Oh? Even with the death of the king?" Turning her head slightly to the side.

"Come Kathryn, you and I have history…understandings…don't we?"

"Fredrick…you play too much with my affections. It is true, there is no love lost between the king and I. Fredrick, I won't become one of your little strumpets or pawns…not in this game. There is far too much to loose, if you don't win…and I like to win…"

"Now mi lady, a creature as lovely as you…it takes a strong man to resist your wiles."

"I see what you're trying to accomplish," said Kathryn, scoffing at him.

"You can see nothing, if not the desire in my eyes. Too many nights, I've had to fight against myself…just so I would not try to enter your chambers."

"Now Fredrick…you're still teasing me…what a liar!"

"My lady…you cut me to the quick! Here I am pouring out my heart to you…"

"Yes…in a drafty corridor no less."

Then allow me to escort you to your door, that we may continue this."

"By all means," said Kathryn, as she looked over the hallway. "Let's finish this in my chambers." But when they arrived at her chambers, she held her hand up for him to stop.

"I think this far enough, my lord…I don't see myself taking the chance."

"Sometimes my dear, things must be said, and the consequences be damned."

"Who do you think you're fooling? That's a pretty sad attempt to get me to play your little game…"

Fredrick watched her with a measure of surprise, and then said.

"Kathryn…now you hurt me deeply. Yes from time to time, I have done some pretty scurvy things, just as you, but I have no motive now, except to spend some time with you. What could be the harm in that…my lady?"

"Fredrick, you should see yourself through my eyes right now, because if you did, you would run to get away…"

"Hum…but you are not running my love."

"That's because, I know you and I do not fear you."

"From your tone, it would be far better for me, not to know what you see."

"Well my lord, up until now, I'll admit I had not taken your advances seriously for what they might be…but I know, treason is a hanging offense, one I can't take lightly."

"I see then! Have I emptied my heart in vain? Then let me say good night, before I'm further rejected."

Lord Guy grabbed Kathryn's hand and kissed it gently, bowed...then said.

"My dear, if you can not think me serious, and return the sentiments, then don't expect me to continue to try and love you...I have no choice, I will say good night now."

Fredrick rubbed her hand as he let it go to walk away, then suddenly Kathryn pulled him back.

"Wait, wait Fredrick. I am sorry, I really didn't think, well if I could speak openly, I really did not think you cared. But I have always thought you were a brilliant, and remarkably handsome. I can't leave out...a pretty good liar."

"Well I'm not lying about how I feel about you now! Can't you feel when something is real?"

"Yes I guess I do feel something...I can't say exactly what it is."

"Then be with me Kathryn!'

"I guess there is no reason why I shouldn't."

"What of the queen?" questioned lord Guy. "Will she allow you to leave tonight?"

"I am the queens lady...her consort, but she is not my life. I will make time to enjoy the pleasures of love...She above all people will understand that...besides she has been given a sedative, and won't awaken for hours."

"Then my lady Kathryn meet me in an hour, for a carriage ride, and take in the view of the beautiful countryside."

"Sounds wonderful Fredrick...I think I'll play your game...there is something I must add."

"Until then, my sweet...?"

"Yes, until then Fredrick."

Now Fredrick and Kathryn have gone their separate ways for a while, each one biding for their part, of the crown of England.

At this time however, Fredrick feels he has mastered the game.

Meanwhile Kathryn decided to play along with ideas of her own. She too wants to see where it would lead. Both however, are predicting the outcome of a deadly game that they might well become lost in. While they toy with each other's feelings, they have forgotten prince Luis in the middle. Who could become victorious, in such a triangle? Where then could it lead?

It's the next morning, and the queen has had time to absorb the news of Lyonus's death.

She and Luis must come together to make arrangements for the kings' funeral.

AWAKENED BY BETRAYAL

Lyonus of course is alive, and resting in miles Tavern. He was caught in a web of somewhat strange circumstances. Lyonus is unable to remember who he is or where he came from, and certainly not, that he was king of England.

CHAPTER SEVEN
Lyonus Is Saved by Love

Now it was Constance Devereux, the daughter of Simon Devereux, surgeon—the second Earl of Bisland—who took especially good care of Lyonus.

Constance left home at an early age of ten. She even refused to accept money from her father. She made her way to Fowlers Row, the worst place possible for a young child to wander, but from there she went on to Miles Tavern. Two drunks raped her when she first came to that place. One day the men returned, but this time Old Mr. Bennett, a master sword maker, was waiting. He told them to leave and never come back to Miles Tavern, but they insisted on drawing their swords. So Mr. Bennett took on both men, utterly destroyed them. He felt so sorry for Constance that he took her under his wing. She lived with him in his broken down farmhouse, but he always saw to it, that she never went hungry. He taught her the sword, and self-defense. Mr. Bennett gave her all the tools she needed, so that no other man would dare hurt her again.

Now about six years later, Mr. Bennett died. Constance had turned sixteen, and became quite the young lady. Mr. Bennett had no other relatives to put a claim on his property, so he left Constance his sword collection, and five gold handle knives. He also left the deed to his place, and a horse named Romania. It was difficult for her to loose him, for he was the father she had longed for. From that point on, Constance was determined to make it by herself. She began working as a barmaid at Miles Tavern, and took a room just above the bar. There she practiced everyday, and became more and more skilled in the art of the sword.

When Constance was about ten years old, men broke into their home. She was able to recognize one of the men before she hid under her bed. Constance's mother Amy was murdered in her sleep that night, while Simon, lay in bed next to her left unharmed.

Constance always felt, that her father was behind the murder. She never understood how Simon, being a man of medicine, could do such a thing. Consequently she never forgave her father, thou Mr. Bennett tried to convince her to go back.

Each night for many years, all she could see in her dreams, was a man that wore a patch over one eye. He would always walk closer and closer to her, and then disappear in the dark. Constance would wake up screaming, and Mr. Bennett would try to console her.

When Constance encountered King Lyonus, his misfortune, somehow sparked the memory of her personal loss. She had no desire to identify with the tragedy of murder, and of betrayal. Nevertheless, Constance saw that Lyonus needed a surgeon, and decided to make the trip back to her fathers home that night, to seek his help.

Constance looked at Lyonus, then shook her head, seeing that he was unconscious, said.

"Oh…just look at you…laying here all bloody. Why would anyone one do this to you?" Speaking into the kings' ear. Then she wrapped pieces of cloth around his head and side, trying to make bandages tight hoping to stop some of the blood.

There were so many areas that needed attention, she decided to bend the rule she made so many years ago, never to return to the place where her mother died.

So Constance called on her father's home late that night. She got down off Romania, and slowly walked to the door, not knowing what to say or what to expect. She could see in her minds eye, the horror that accompanied that dreadful night. But, determined to save king Lyonus, she swallowed her pain, pushed aside her hate, and knocked on the door.

One of Simon's servants, Hannah, answered the door.

Hannah's sight was a little dull, but when she looked directly into the eyes of Constance, she fell back a little to brace herself on the door.

"Oh…my…! Is it you child, my little Connie? Could it be…ha?"

Constance with the biggest grin, leaped toward her, and then said.

"Hannah, it is I…How good it is to see you!"

"Where have you been…all…these years? First, I looked for you, and then I prayed you would stay away to spare yourself further pain watching your father go through his madness. The doctor went crazy when you left, he could not work, could not eat…Connie, my little one all grown up…standing here."

Hannah's eyes filled with tears, grabbed Constance,—her little Connie, as she called her—and brought her into the parlor.

"Just wait here, wait right there…I'll be back with your father…he will be both shocked, and pleased…Connie…" Hannah muttered as she left the room. "Oh lord…oh my goodness!"

As Hannah approached the sitting room, she stopped to gain some self-control. Then entered and said.

"Lord Devereux…my lord. Are you asleep?"

Mister Devereux, turned his body around in the chair, and then replied.

"No Hannah, I just nodded off for a bit. It's been a long day…but what is it Hannah…Hum?

I thought I heard someone knocking at the door."

He said, as he squirmed around on the seat, and stretched his arms in the air.

"Is it someone in need of my services?"

"Well…yes there is sir…but, I must tell you something about that before you go in…!"

Simon groaned as he arose from the chair.

"Oh…these old bones, Hannah…could definitely use a long rest."

"I know sir…but your guest…!"

Oh yes…I'm on my way."

"…But wait…it's going to be a shock…"

"What are you saying, Hannah…?" he asked, while he continued to walk away.

"It's Connie! She has come home…Connie has come back!"

"Who…Constance…my little girl…?"

Simon charged toward the parlor. Then stopped just short of the doorway, peered in and then slowly started to speak.

"Constance! My dear Constance I have missed you. How long I've waited to see you. I needed to explain what happened to us…your mother, my Amy…"

"I'm not here for me…and I'm certainly not here for you to explain anything…but I have a friend that needs a surgeon…the last thing I remembered was…you were!"

"Daughter, please listen to me!"

Just then Hannah stood with her fists clinched over her mouth so not to gasp, while Simon reached to touch Constance.

"You are all I have Constance. Before I agree to help you, you must listen to what I have to say…"

"If I must…then make it quick, before he bleeds to death, and I promise you…it won't change a thing!"

"All right, the night your mother was taken from us…"

"Hum…you mean murdered by you!"

"Constance…!"

"Go on then…"

"I don't recall much of that night…but I heard your voice calling for your mother. I told her to go back to sleep. I didn't rise up just then, but I heard you again, a moment later…a bit louder than before, as if you were crying. When I tried to get up, I could not move…I could not lift my head or neck. My head was turned toward Amy…I could see her face as she sleep. All of a sudden, everything went dim, I could not tell what was happening, though I could see shadows moving about. When I could see and move again…Amy, was lying in a pool of blood. I could only think they thought I was already dead, or someone stopped them."

Simon began to weep, as he tried to tell Constance what had occurred.

"I loved your mother, more than anything…and when I saw what they had done to her…I lost my mind. You could not imagine the pain and horror I felt that night, I lost her too!"

"Connie! Do you understand that? You must believe him, he tells the truth," said Hannah, with her eyes full of tears. "Listen…!" Hannah pleaded.

"When I found you…you were hiding underneath your bed. You were just staring into space…I called your name over and over, but you would not answer. Then your father could not respond to me, he could not tell me what to do, I was so lost. When I came back in your room to take you away with me, you were gone; you had piled some things in a bag, and climbed out of the window. Your poor father…he has only a few patients now…you know, just to keep busy…but nothing too strenuous."

Then Simon spoke up and said.

"I'm sorry you had to suffer. I'm sorry you had the wrong notion, all those years…six years of wasted time.

"Please Connie…your father is no liar, he speaks the truth about this."

"Constance…say something…anything!"

"…Well…I find it hard to believe, but I guess it could have happened the way you say. I was just so young, and…well, so hurt. I didn't know what else to think or do. The man I saw with the patch on his eye…haunts my dreams. I remember calling for mother, it seemed like over and over again, until I heard a noise…a strange sound. I got very quiet, and started to your room. When I came to the doorway, I saw the man with the patch on his eye. I thought he was coming toward me…I don't know what happened, but I ran and hid under my bed.

Then I heard mother scream…I knew she was dead, but I never heard you scream, so I thought, they must have let you live. I don't know what I must have thought, I just know I was afraid you were trying to have me killed too…so frightened, I ran. I took your horse from the barn, and rode and rode…"

"But where have you been all this time. I have gone out of my mind trying to find you. After six years and then nothing, no clue nothing…I just gave up…and now, now you're here!"

Simon and Constance embraced deeply, as if making up for the time they missed.

"Father, it was awful…I didn't know what to do or where to go. I found myself on Fowlers Row, headed for Miles tavern."

Simon interrupted.

"Fowlers row? That is a terrible place! Miles tavern…how did you manage to eat or…who clothed you? After all you were only a child."

"I don't know, when people saw that I was helpless they did what they could. At first I was very frightened, then a wonderful man named Mr. Bennett, saved me. He kept me with him at his farm until he died. Then I found work at Miles tavern, and a room just above the bar, I've been there ever since. Now I'm here…which brings me to, why I have come."

"Go on my dear…I'm waiting."

"You must promise…that what I tell you now, will be kept in your heart. I mean in strict confidence. Our lives may depend on it."

"What have you gotten yourself into, Constance?"

"No…it's nothing I've done…well…I…"

"Okay take one step at a time." Then looking over at Hannah said. "Please bring us something to drink Hannah…"

"Of course sir…I'll be right back."

Hannah brought in some tea to drink, handed me a cup, then said.

"Go on now child tell us the rest."

"There were two friends of mine…their names aren't important right now. They found a body laying along side the road."

"What!! A dead body or something?"

"Please father…Remember the story about the king going hunting, then was attacked and killed?"

"Of course I do…but what does that have to do with you?"

"Well those friends I told you about, brought him to me…he's staying in my room, at the tavern…there…I've gotten it out…"

"Now let me see if I have this straight Constance! "Your friends brought the king of England to your room above Miles tavern Inn, and your keeping him there…Wait!"

Holding up his hand for her not to speak, then continued. "People who tried to kill him are now trying to find him. You've managed to keep him hidden and safe so far, but now he needs to have medical treatment, so you brought him here. Is that it Constance?"

"Well…in a not shell…I guess that about sums it up father."

Just then Hannah spoke up.

"Constance Devereux…What have you been doing? What made you do something like that? Those people, who tried to kill their king, won't hesitate to kill you, or any of us. It may not take them very long to find out who helped him either. Have you thought this out?"

"Yes…yes I have."

"Listen…" said Simon, as he panted for breath. "It's not too late. We could take him away from here…far away, and leave him…"

"No! Father…Hannah…I can't do that. He needs help, he needs it right now, and there is no time to loose. I would feel awful, if he died because we stood by and watched him bleed to death, afraid for our own lives…like cowards…"

Simon and Hannah looked at each other with a long pause, and then Hannah said.

"My Connie…you have fallen in love with this king of England, Ah?"

"What a question…I'm merely trying to be a good citizen, and save our king. There is such a thing as loyalty…you know."

"Oh…silence Constance, just let me think…we're in a mess now!"

"No…not we. I only need for you to bind him, fix his wounds or whatever it is you do. Then you can go back to being afraid."

"Wait just a moment young lady! Don't you dare!! You don't know the kind of people you'd be dealing with."

"Yes I do! They're the same men whom I served ale and food everyday.

They are the same men who pawed, pinched and pulled. Those I've had to fight off…How about those that raped me with a knife at my throat…a child I was…the stench of wine on their breath, whose foul odor made me vomit. I could not wash away the dirt; no matter how hard I tried. Maybe they're the same ones who killed mother! Are you talking about them…are they the ones you want to be saved from, father?"

Simon gasped and then held his hand over his heart. He staggered backward a little, and then said.

"My Child…how they have hurt you…child."

They all began to weep aloud, and held each other tight. Then Constance stepped back, looked at both Simon and Hannah, and asked.

"Will you help us father? I've never asked you for anything…and father, I won't ask again…"

Simon, after pondering the risk for a moment, opened the closet, grabbed his bag and said with such commitment.

"Where is he? Lead me to him."

"Ah…oh thank you father! I won't forget this…not ever."

Constance jumped up and down, as if she received a birthday gift. Simon looked surprised. He could only say.

"Well…where did you say he was?"

"He's in my room at the tavern…hopefully he's still alive…I think he's asleep, last I attended him."

"Well, I'll get the carriage…meet me out front."

"Oh no father, I've brought horses, they're faster…"

Simon then turned his back, and gave a look of confusion, and said.

"Please Hannah, where is my bag? Will you get it…and hurry."

"You've certainly thought of everything," she remarked, as she raced to pack the doctors things. "Do you need me as well?"

Constance leaned over and kissed her, then said.

"Thank you…I've missed you too." And then in a voice for only her ears, confirmed.

"…And to answer your question…I do love him."

"Ha…ha…ah…I knew it. Good luck child, and go with God…my little Connie…"

"Considering the hour Hannah, don't wait up for me…I'll see you in the morning."

"All right my lord Devereux."

Good bye and take special care."

Simon and Constance rode quite a ways in silence. With only the sound of the horses' hoofs, that kicked the small pebbles across the dusty road, for company, Simon finally asked.

"How much further is this Miles tavern, any way?"

"Now father...it's my home."

"No...we just left your home..."

"Hum..." Constance all ways letting out a breath, and raising a brow to show she's thinking.

All was silent again, until they reached the tavern.

"Is this the place...Constance?"

"Yes. Let's take the horses around back. I can go up to my room from there, without going into the bar itself."

"...Oh..." scoffed Simon. "That must make it really convenient."

"Let's just not have this conversation father."

"What? What did I say?" asked Simon, while he hunched his shoulders.

"Hum..." said Constance, cutting her eyes back at him. "Come on...my room is just here, a couple of doors down."

Constance slowly opened the creaking door. She hoped Lyonus would still be there, alive.

Both Constance and Simon went inside the room. Simon walked over to the bed where Lyonus was laying. He looked back at Constance then smiled and said.

"Well daughter...it looks to me as if he's still breathing." Simon took his bag, stood and took a longer look, paused then said.

"Ha...Constance, this really does look like the king...it is him...!"

"Yes...father I know."

"I mean really..."

"Hum...father..."

"Oh I'm sorry dear..."

"Oh boy," said Constance. "Father is he going to make it?"

"Just let me take a closer look at him here...he's lost a lot of blood. It doesn't look good right now. I'll sew these open wounds, and bandage him...perhaps, in the morning we'll know more."

"I understand...just do your best, he'll make it I'm sure. Besides, he's held on this far."

"You are right of course, my dear...he is relatively young and strong..."

"And handsome father...I can tell."

"Give him time to heal Constance...we'll see..."

"Most definitely…"

"Constance…"

"I mean, the quicker he's better, the quicker he can leave my room…" Constance sending her eyes around the room. Hum…"

"Well…" groaned Simon, as he raised that one brow. "I'll need for you to get a room for the night dear…"

"But father…I already have a room…"

"Yes well, I'll stay with the king tonight." Simon pushed her toward the door. "He may awaken during the night, and need me dear."

"Oh…"

"Yes, Constance…so I'll say goodnight."

"Hum…" said Constance, backing out slowly. "Ah…If you need me just give a yell."

"I will…"

"I won't be far away father…"

"I know, Constance…you'll be down the hall," said Simon who dragged out his words in an attempt at being sarcastic. "See you in the morning, and we'll discuss other arrangements…now good…night!" Simon pushed against the door to close it.

"Good-night father…and thank you."

Simon spent most of the night, with a watchful eye. He made sure Lyonus would not loose any more blood, and on his way toward healing. He washed him, and heaped wood on the fire to keep him warm, though Simon was quite warm enough.

The light from the torn curtain at Constance's window alarmed Mr. Devereux that it was morning. He stood, yawned, and then walked over to Lyonus. He stretched then scratched his beard. He had bandaged the king so well, that no one could see his face for all the wrappings. This may have indeed been a blessing in disguise. Simon swore with an oath, not to reveal Lyonus's identity to anyone. He agreed to keep him safe, but he had an even better idea. A knock at the door, it was Constance, bright and cheery.

"Good-morning Father…"

"Good-morning Constance, did you sleep well?"

"Very well father, and how did our patient fare?"

"Oh I think he'll be all right. But it's going to take a little time."

Constance still peering through the door, made a giant leap inside the room to hug Simon.

"All right…okay now. It's fine. Listen, how about you and the king coming to stay with me at the estate…Hannah and I would be more than happy to take care of your friend."

"You would consider doing something like that? It's so risky…"

"What is a little risk, when it comes to having my daughter home with me…where she belongs."

"I just don't know what to say…father…I don't."

"Well just say yes, and it's done."

"Then…yes we will. We will be happy to come…that is if, you're sure?"

"My darling daughter, I've never been more certain of anything in a long time, as I am of this right now…this very moment…"

"Okay then…as soon a Lyonus is ready for travel, we will be home…I guess."

They both laughed a bit, as if they two shared a great secret. The next day, Simon left for home shortly after eating breakfast.

"Father," said Constance. "Please ask Hannah to get my old room ready!"

"That I will do, my dear. Now don't forget to hurry. Oh and leave the bandages on."

"I will…good-bye."

Constance spent more and more time with the king. He was in and out of consciousness for sometime, until one day Constance dressed the wound to his side, and began to talk to him.

"I know you can hear me," she said, with her lips close to his ears. "…And if you can, please open your eyes and speak." At no time in the first week, did the king open his eyes or speak. It was though being unconscious was a retreat for his battered soul.

"Rest then, my king, for when you awaken, a new life will await you. I pray I can be apart of that life."

Constance continued to allow Lyonus to sleep on the bed in her room, while she slept on the floor. Whenever Lyonus would become feverish, she would climb onto the bed, and use her body heat to keep him warm from the chills.

Constance was caught off guard one afternoon. The king was having a nightmare of sorts. He began to toss and turn, and call out the names of people and places. It seemed to be a dream from which he could not awaken.

Constance became a little frightened. She heard him speak while he dreamed, and then she said.

"I don't know what you're talking about." Then she thought. It was as if he watched some scene played over and over in his mind. But. I'll bet it has to do with the people who tried to have him killed…He probably knows who they are."

Finally about two weeks later, Lyonus sat up in the bed, and looked around.

"Well…How are we today?" said Constance, while she pulled back the curtains to let in still more sunlight.

"Who are you…and…where am I?" he replied, as he covered his eyes from the glare of the sun.

"You are in Miles tavern…in my room…in Miles tavern to be exact…don't you know who you are?"

"I…I'm not sure just who I am but, I'm pretty sure I don't know you." The rays of the sun shown through the window even more as Lyonus starred at her.

"Come closer…" he said, holding out his hand to her.

"My name is Constance Devereux, I prefer to be called Constance…" Laughing to bring a little levity.

"Well hello Constance, can you tell me how I came to be here?" Lyonus raised the covers to find he had on no clothing, and then asked. "…And where in God's name are my clothes, surely I had some on."

"I can assure you God does not have them. But to answer your first question, some friends brought you here to me, for help…well to help you."

"What happened to me?"

"The surgeon, my father, was here to attend you. He said that you would need plenty of rest and care for the next few months, in order to completely recover. To answer your next question…I took your clothes, washed and mended them." Constance pointed to the chair by the fireplace. "Your things are over there. They were covered with blood. It was difficult to get them clean."

"Oh…may I have them please?"

"Do you feel well enough to get out of bed today?"

"I…can try…By the way, how long have I been asleep?"

"Um…off and on for about a month, I guess."

"A month!" Yelled Lyonus. "I don't understand!"

"Please…calm yourself…I will tell you all that I can."

"But…"

"No buts, just lay still."

Constance went over and sat down on the bed next to Lyonus, took a deep breath, and started to tell him everything about his misfortune.

"One day you were found badly wounded…near death really. You lay on the side of the road…unconscious. None of us knew how you had gotten there. We recognized you, and knew whoever had done this evil thing—if they were to find you still alive—would finish the job, and we would be included, for assisting you. There are people still looking for your remains as we speak, those that are not so kind, I might add. If by chance they were to spot you and me together now, they would surely take care of the both of us."

"Hum…"

"Queen Maria had knights that searched for you for weeks, then latter we heard that the king was attacked on a hunting trip, and killed. In fact they had the funeral two weeks ago."

"Well, what on earth does that have to do with me? Did I kill the king or something?"

Constance looked bewildered, then said.

"Oh…my, you really don't know who you are!"

Constance reached on the table and got him a mug, then Lyonus tried to stand up again, but was so weak, he fell right back down on the bed.

"Listen…I promised I would take good care of you, until you were able to do it yourself, that is…Are you?"

"I don't suppose I am, at least not today."

"I didn't think so…but here…" Constance, gave him a cup of soup. "Drink this, it will make you feel better, you must gain strength."

"Um…" said Lyonus, as he sipped from the mug. "This is quite tasty, what is it called?"

"I know one thing…you are full of questions."

"I'm sorry if questions annoy you."

"No they don't, it's just that…I was hoping…"

"What were you hoping?"

"Never mind!! It's beef broth, with herbs and small potatoes. Drink up…and not so much talking!"

Lyonus peered over the top of the mug, as he watched Constance do her chores around the room.

"You're quiet…should I say something now?"

"What? I can understand…you're not used to giving apologies, don't read too much into my attitude. I'm not that offended."

"Oh…did I say this broth was delicious?"

"Yes, twice already…ha…ha, .ha."

They both began to laugh at each other, in hopes of finding some middle ground for what certainly—at least for Constance—had become a delicate situation.

"As soon as you are better, I'll take you to my father's house. You can finish your recovery there."

"Does your farther share his kindness with all wounded strangers?"

"Of course not! Only those of whom I feel especially close to, come home to fathers…"

"Oh…I see."

"Oh, you see nothing…just lie back there."

Constance laid him back on the bed. Lyonus clutched her hands and gave a gentle squeeze. They glanced into each other's eyes, and then Lyonus said.

"I may not know how to be apologetic…but I do know how to say thank you…!"

He lifted his finger under her chin, raised it to his lips, and kissed her. Constance became carried away. She put her arms around him and started to squeeze him.

"Aw…oh…" yelled the king, as he pulled away in pain. "Are you trying to kill me?"

"Kill? I'm sorry…I…I simply forgot your tender condition."

"It's all right…I guess I will survive."

Lyonus put up his hands for space.

"Hum…" scoffed Constance. "Really, will you…?"

"Really…it's okay."

"Then if it's really okay…" smirked Constance. "Why…you can kiss me again, and I'll promise not to hurt you."

"What…?" smiled Lyonus. "You'll not hurt me?"

"…Not used to women who know what they want hum…?"

"Aren't you the bold one?" said Lyonus, with his brow lifted.

"Well how about that kiss?"

"What is this a game you're playing?" Constance teased him and said.

"You're…stall…ing lover. Are you afraid of a little pain?"

"Ha…ha. You are a challenge…aren't you?"

"The question is…" said Constance, when she turned and sat down on the bed. "Can you handle the challenge…?"

Now Lyonus was determined he would not be out done, as he replied.

"If the second kiss is as the first…" All the while, moving closer to her.

"Yes…" Constance whispered.

"I think sometimes without suffering pain...we miss out on the true design of pleasure."

They leaned into a kiss, but this time, Lyonus wrapped his arms around her. He did not pull away, or yell in pain. Afterward, they did not speak a word for a moment, just looked deep into each other's eyes. Then Lyonus said.

"You see my dear...the pleasure of your kiss, was worth a little pain!"

They kissed again. Constance could not help but say.

"Oh yeah...you'll be just fine my lord!"

Then he blurted out. "You...you remind me..."

Constance would not let him finish, and said. "If you say, I remind you of someone you knew, I will yank off your bandages...!"

Lyonus kissed her again. Then she swooned even more in his arms.

"Hum...I really think you'll be fine."

Now a few more days passed, and Constance and the king were ready to make their trip to Simon Devereux's home. She borrowed a wagon from Wayne the bar keep, and loaded their things on board. She made sure Lyonus was wrapped in blankets on the wagon, so he would not be detected. Constance got down from the wagon.

"Hey...where are you going?"

"Sh...I'll be right back, I need to get something."

She remembered her bag, hidden under a floorboard in her room. It contained Lyonus's things, along with the property Mr. Bennett had left her. When she returned to the wagon, she threw the bag under the seat and grabbed the reigns.

"Hey...hee...come girls, let's go!" Then made a clicking sound with her teeth.

"No...!" Moaned Lyonus, as he peeped from under the blanket.

"No? What do you mean...no?"

"I mean...look! I don't think these horses are females."

Constance with a strange expression on her face, said.

"Hum...well if it will get us there faster...maybe they should be..."

"No...Constance..."

"...Hum..."

A silence covered the air for a moment, when Constance noticed a few men on horseback. It seemed they had been following for a while.

"Lyonus listen...there may be trouble. Be perfectly still and quiet."

"What's going on?"

"Some men...just let me handle it. Give me the bag."

"This one?" He handed her the bag with the rings.

"No...the bag with the swords!"

"If you think we need to fight, then I'll take one as well."

"Lyonus please...if they discover you...there will be no more help I can give. So just be quiet."

"Constance...?"

"What?" Whispering to each other.

"Why do you continue to call me Lyonus? Is that really my name?"

"You just can't remember anything can you?"

"It's beginning to drive me insane...I just can't remember my life."

"I'll make a deal with you. You relax and recover, and let things happen naturally, and everything will fall into place for you."

"Well that won't happen with that clicking sound you keep making."

Constance glared with one eye. "...Hum...yeah, you're going to make it."

Now the riders came nearer to the wagon, Constance turned and looked back to judge the distance.

"They are too close for comfort...if I go to Mr. Bennett's old place...just near here, I'll have the upper hand. Then I'll know if they have followed us or if minding their own business."

"Hi...ya..." shouted Constance, as she rode the horses a little harder. "It's only a few miles more. Go girls. Go...!"

"No!"

Finally they reached the Bennett farm. The riders were still following them. So Constance circled the wagon in close to the barn. She leaned over to Lyonus.

"Sh...stay quiet now...I'll be right back."

She got down, and ducked behind the wagon, as she watched the men ride in.

"Here...they...come."

Constance tucked her knives in her belt, and put both hands on her sword. One of the men called out.

"Hey...Norris...check around the barn. Their wagon is here, they couldn't have disappeared."

Then the tall man said in a low voice. "Let's split up...this shouldn't take us long."

He walked around the barn, and called for Constance. "Come out little girl," he said, his voice coarse as the dead. "I won't hurt you...much. Ha...ha...not much."

As he approached the wagon, Constance gave a swing of her sword, to his midriff.

"Whoa..." She slurred, and wiped her forehead. "That was close."

Suddenly the man who gave the orders came barreling around the corner. Constance started to run inside the barn. Once inside she climbed into the hayloft. The rider called out to her.

"Where are you...?" he said, in a voice that let her know he was angry. "I know you're in here...so no need to hide."

"I'm not hiding." Constance stood to her feet, and looked down over the loft.

"Why are you following me?"

"We just wanted to talk to you...ask you a few questions...that's all."

"I think you should have told your partner that..."

"You have killed my partner, and I'm not going to let that slid...!"

"What do you want with me?"

"If you come down...we can talk about it."

"I think you smell better from here."

"You'll die, from there!" he said, as he charged up the ladder, foaming at the mouth, swatting his sword. Then Constance made her way around to the other side and climbed down. Then she stopped and looked up, with her hands on her hips then shouted.

"Hey there...! Still want to talk, then come down?"

"Why you...you little winch," he shouted, as he slid down from the ladder. "Come here you..."

Constance stood toe to toe with him. I don't know..."

"You don't know what?"

"If I should cut your great fat belly, or slit your throat...maybe you can help me."

Constance really provoked his anger, by laughing at him.

"I'll...help you all right...!"

He began to swing and lunge toward her. She moved around trying to tire him out, till atlas she struck with a twist and thrust. He stared at her for a moment before he reached for her. Constance stepped back away from him, as he continued to fall. It all happened so quickly.

With two of them gone, the only one that remained was Norris, as he was called. She knew that he was still hiding out behind the barn. Constance eased out the front door of the barn, while she watched for him. Then she thought perhaps he was near the wagon. When she went around the building to see, she spied him with the blankets raised. She had to do something fast. So she spring out toward him to take his attention from looking further.

"Ha...ready to join your friends...?"

"If you think me easy...?"

"Well come on...Norris..."

"How do you know my name little girl?"

"I asked your friends...just before I slit their throats."

"What!"

"...Hum...My name is Constance. I guess there's no harm in telling you before you die."

"Well it doesn't matter...when I'm threw...ha...ha...I'll kill you, then I'm going to take you, and rape you time and time again, and after that, I'll feed you to my horse..."

"But Norris, you can not do any of that...if you are dead."

Both Norris and Constance circled each other; around they went, each one waiting for the other to strike, until finally Constance began to swing her sword.

Back and forward they went. He was the best of them all, she thought. Then Norris was able to knock the sword from her hand. Constance picked up a small log from the ground. First swung at his head then his chest. He started cutting at it with his sword. At that point Norris, wanted nothing more that to strangle her, so he slung his sword to the ground, and reached for her neck.

They wrestled for a while, till Constance was up against the wagon. Norris had a good hold on her. Constance reached for the knife in her belt, when suddenly, Lyonus reared up from underneath the blanket, with a knife in his hand. They both stuck Norris, one in the chest, and one in the neck. He continued to hold on to Constance, until she pushed him to the ground. Then she rubbed her throat, and leaped onto the wagon, then hugged Lyonus with tears in her voice.

"Thanks...thanks Lyonus..."

Constance got down from the wagon.

"Where are you going now?"

"I'm going to finish him."

So she picked up her sword and drove it into his heart. Making sure he was dead. Then she tied his body to the wagon, dragged him to the haystack, and covered it with straw.

"How did you learn to do all of that...? Why do all of that?"

"Well, I don't want the body to be in open view...someone might think, they found what they were looking for...and from Mr. Bennett..."

"Come on..." said Lyonus. "Let's get out of here, it's getting dark."

"Right...and father will be waiting."

"This time I'm riding up there."

So Lyonus determined to sit next to Constance, pulled himself upon the seat.

"You fought quite well back there. Have you had formal training?"

"Well...yes and no. I told you."

"How so?"

"I left my home when I was really...why is not important, and this man named Bennett..."

"Oh...the place we just came from?"

"Yes, he took me in and taught me everything I know."

"Sounds like a wonderful person."

"He was a great man...I shall miss him terribly...enough of reminiscing, how are you feeling now?"

"One area is starting to bleed a little, but I think I can hold on till we get to your fathers."

"Then we need to hurry...! Hi...ya...!"

Constance guided the horses with all speed; she knew time was important to Lyonus.

They rode for several miles when Lyonus spotted something shining from, underneath the seat.

"Hey...what's this?"

Lyonus pulled out a gold handled knife that belonged to Hollands.

"Oh...that...? It was among your things, when they brought you to me."

"There is a name engraved on it...I can hardly make it out...Let's see...says: To Sir Hollands from Sir John Meyers friends forever. There...that's it then, my name must be Hollands."

"No...I don't think so..."

"Why do you say that?"

"For one thing, that's not an English name..."

"What? And the other?"

"For the other...you don't look like a Hollands."

"Oh I see...is that also like that clicking thing you do?"

Rounding the road they approached the estate.

"...Hum...looks as though we're here..."

"It's a beautiful place, Constance," said Lyonus.

Then she allowed her eyes to wonder, as she searched to remember.

"Wait Lyonus, let me help you down."

Just then, Simon and Hannah, and the other servants rushed out to greet the wagon.

"Hello Hannah…father!" said Constance.

"What in the world happened to you?" asked Simon

"Um…we ran into a little trouble along the way, but it has been removed."

"Here, take my arm son," said Simon to Lyonus.

"Oh I'm sorry everyone, this is Jonathan, the friend I told you about…Jonathan, my father Simon Devereux, and Hannah, his house keeper."

"Constance, you look lovely my dear…" said Simon, trying to lift her ego. Then Hannah chide in. "Oh yes…like a spring blossom, doesn't she Jonathan?"

Lyonus (Jonathan) pulled back his head with eyebrows raised, replied with sarcasm.

"Oh, yes…a fresh bouquet of wild flowers…" Smirking at Constance.

"Ah…father, maybe we should go inside now?"

"Certainly my dear, I'll have your things brought to your rooms."

"Rooms?" squawked Constance.

Her father sent a bellowing replied as he walked in front of them. "One for each one of you!"

"…Hum…"

"Come Jonathan," said Simon. "Let's take a look at those wounds, my friend."

"Sure. I feel a lot better; except for the headaches…I can't remember who I am or what happened to me. It feels so strange, as if there were a void that can not be filled."

"That is not an uncommon feeling Jonathan…especially with headaches, and the type of injuries you incurred. But it's possible your memory could return within days of the injury, or in some cases, like yours for example…it could take months, even years."

"Years?" said Lyonus (Jonathan), as he dropped his head. "Has there ever been a time when a person…say…never regained there past?"

Just when Simon would have answered, Constance, listening outside the door walked in.

"Father…I hope you are putting his mind to rest. He's had a rough morning."

"...And just what about this morning? You never told us."

"Not now father...please."

"Well...I've said all I need say for now. By the way your wounds are healing nicely..."

"What a relief..." remarked Constance. Then Lyonus (Jonathan) spoke up.

"I believe he was speaking to me...Constance."

"Quite...hum..."

Then Simon turned while leaving and said. "Jonathan, I shall take off your bandages in a few days."

"Wonderful...and I thank you for everything...I mean it, not many people would open their homes to an injured stranger."

"I see...well, if you are a friend of my daughters, whom I trust...then you are welcomed in our home..."

Constance looked over at Simon and mouthed the words, thank you father, and blew him a kiss.

"All right...I'll see you both at dinner...which should be in about and hour from now...Coming Constance?"

"...Hum...Oh, right behind you father...!" Rolling her eyes upward, and closing the door behind her, then said. "I know...my own room...hum..." Simon laughed and shook his head.

King Lyonus, or as he's called at this point Jonathan, has made great strides in his recovery thus far.

Time continued to move, always steadily forward, until the puzzles that demanded attention, no longer took priority.

CHAPTER EIGHT
The Heirs Are Born

The king left a will for his heirs whom now, it seems is just about ready to be born. After the funeral of the king, the queen would stay for the most part, in the company of Jacqueline, lady Nichol, and lady Kathryn

Queen Miria has found it more difficult to rule and survive the vipers at court. She had only a few friends in which she could trust.

About now, Queen Miria has been called to an urgent meeting, to discuss violations of the treatise with Spain. Lord Du'Voe, the appointed Reagent for Lyonus, had been arrested and imprisoned somewhere in Spain. The king of Spain, at this time, had refused all ambassadors representing England. King Emanuel has insisted he will only negotiate with the queen. Consequently, with Miria's somewhat delicate condition, the question is if she should go.

A courier arrived in the Great hall, with a letter for the queen. Everyone kneeled, as Miria walked through the doorway. The shape of mother hood had replaced her shapely figure. She was within two months of her delivery, but wore it well. Queen Miria was simply a treasure, in any form.

"Read the message!" commanded Miria.

"Yes your majesty..."

"Due to the sensitive nature of our treatise, it is imperative, that an envoy be sent to hear and respond to the conditions set fourth in the treaty, between our two countries. There has been a breach, in the agreement, and a breakdown in communications. Your minister, lord Du'Voe, has been held until we retrieve the documents that placed our country in great peril. If you do not respond, we will treat it as a sign of war. We will await your reply in person. Signed the Sovereign of Spain, King Phillip Montego Emanuel II."

"That is it your majesty."

"Thank you for the reading…Well, my lords, I'm opened for comments, and suggestions. I don't see England at war, however, we must find the person who has continually made dissension a way of life for us…I know how Lyonus would have handled the past events…He would have cut off the heads of his advisors…and started all over afresh! If it were possible…I would send my child to Spain!"

"What are you saying…your majesty?" asked lord Guy, as he walked closer to the queen. "Is it…you think we are incapable?"

She then gave lord Guy and empty stare, and said, rather upset to be sure.

"Incapable. Mon Dieu! My God! I'm saying lord Guy…that a baby…could better negotiate to stop this war, than the lot of you!"

"Your majesty…!" said duke Westmoreland. "We…as you know…" Pointing at each one of them. "Have had our hands tied, since King Lyonus declared Du'Voe Reagent."

Then lord Biltfry added.

"Yes my queen, we have had reports, that the king made certain agreements, and secretly retrieved documents…while he gathered alliances against Spain."

"I can tell you this…King Lyonus, never made any such alliances with any country against Spain, or any other treatise…and you know it!"

Lord Bilfry spoke out again.

"Your majesty…these are difficult times…what can we do against such charges?"

"Oh Monsieur please…" Turning her head in disgust. "It's a, matter of diplomacy…And it appears England is seriously lacking in that department!!"

"Why your majesty!" said lord Guy, while they all gasped. Queen Miria harped in.

"I mean it lord Guy! Now you…all of you, England's trusted diplomats and advisors, have placed your own queen in an awkward position, even life threatening! And you think I should take this with just a whimper, and politely commend you, for doing a wonderful job!"

Just then, prince Luis stepped in to ease the queens' wrath.

"My queen…your majesty, may I speak?"

"Yes…maybe you can say something…venal…to save all your necks!"

"My queen, you are quite right. Our diplomacy has indeed placed you in a dilemma of sorts…" Prince Luis looked around the room, and then said, "England has no choice…She needs her queen. A service that only you can do, your majesty…leaves the rest of us, bowed in humility."

"Oh…hog wash, Luis. I don't need my ego stroked right now, I need answers!"

"Please…your majesty let me finish…"

"Go ahead…"

"Perhaps if you were to send ahead some small token…say…some gold, and maybe a promise to protect their northern gates…then it would help to soften the negotiations. Maybe your stay would not have to be as tedious. It is said…the king likes his gold, and his beauties…Moreover, it might save my lord Du'Voe…in the process."

"Prince Luis, that I guess…is a modest idea, but at least it is and idea. However, I cannot say if our high Reagent, Monsieur Du'Voe, even deserves being saved…but I must consider every angle. The ladies…ah?" Thinking of his idea. "Perhaps if England were in the slave trade, it just might work…"

"Yes your majesty…"

Lord Thomas charged through the crowd, after he heard the prince.

"Wonderful…Lord Thomas, your arrival is rather timely!" said Miria.

"Your majesty…lords Belfry…Westmoreland…Guy. My queen, greetings!" Then he made a long bow, and then stepped toward the throne.

"…And to you my lord Graybourne, I trust the meeting was successful?"

"Much more than imagined, your majesty."

"Good…good, come to my chambers later, we shall speak of it. But my lord the dilemma at hand…has left us at awe. Can you shed some productive light on the subject…Thomas?"

The scribe handed the letter to lord Graybourne, and he began to read its contents.

"Well let's see…now. I must say…you're left with very little choice. I think it was planned quite well…your majesty."

"I understand your meaning…my lord. If Spain wants war…and I'm not convinced they do…then I say off to battle we go. You should not have to risk anything. I don't know

exactly what lord Du'Voe has gotten into, but England should not have to go to war to solve it. Furthermore, King Emanuel, is all too familiar with our terms for war. He could have talked with us before making such a strong demand.

The treaty has not yet been broken, and this letter does not fully explain what crisis draws England's queen away."

Lord Graybourne looked at lord Guy, and then said, "What documents does he speak of?

"In your condition, my queen, it would be a strenuous voyage. My advise then…is to stay here…and if need be, I will go and talk to king Emanuel and challenge this document."

Lord Biltfry spoke up and said.

"That was well said, my lord Graybourne, but we are all aware that king Emanuel speaks out of both sides of his mouth." Then queen Miria interjected

"Yes…as do some others…"

"Begging your majesty's pardon…As far as we know, he could have already forged our allies to his sympathies. If he wants the queen, then that is what we should do, to prevent all out war…after all we can not stand against the world."

Then queen Miria stood and asked.

"Does he then own the world? What then of our friends?"

"Are we at all sure we have any, since the death of king Lyonus?" asked Biltfry.

"Your majesty," said lord Thomas. "You know we have France…"

"Do we lord Thomas?"

"You asked my feelings on the matter, and I have responded based on what I know of treaties and war. You must now decide if it is worth the chance…but I say, stay and allow me to try, and reconcile the issues."

"Thank you, my lord…I do value your assessment of the situation, however, we can not afford to offend Emanuel unnecessarily. We do not know where our allies lie. Well…I suspect if I must go, then I must."

"My lady, you're so close to delivery, could not this be a way to avoid travel…make it the excuse?" asked duke Westmoreland.

"Thank you for mentioning my delicate condition again. But king Emanuel has in fact made it quite clear…his terms specific. It's either risk travel to save England, or risk war. I have after all, an obligation to the people of England, which makes my decision difficult. The question is…does England's finest have a stomach for war? You know, this situation reminds me of and incident several years ago, when I met my husband…perhaps the fates have something special in store…I'm sure; all will be well, if not certainly revealed…Well…is there any other business to cover, or anyone to which I need give audience, before I retire...?"

"Yes! Your majesty." Shouted lord Biltfry. "There is the matter of the documents that the king placed in his chest...for safe keeping..."

"Well...what about them Biltfry?"

"I simply felt those papers could bare some importance to your trip...I thought I should look them over before you leave...my lady."

"All right...ah...though I haven't seen any such papers..." Miria glanced over at Thomas. "I will allow you to look through the chest on the morrow."

"Rest well...great lady..." said lord Graybourne, as he nodded with a smile.

"Good night all...Nichol, come..."

All kneeled and curtsied, as queen Miria rose and left the great hall.

While Miria and Nichol walked to her chambers, there was a steady stream of questions.

"My lady...how long do you think we will be away?"

"Well Nichol, if all goes as planned, and king Emanuel accepts the gifts of gold and the like, then it could be less than two months."

"Oh not good your majesty...It won't do at all to have your child in Spain!"

"I agree...some concessions must be made alone the way. My child will be born in England...I promise you that, if I have to take a bit of England's soil with me, and remain on the ship."

"Yes your majesty." Replied Nichol, as she shouted out orders and motioned for the guard to open the door, and then said.

"Jacqueline, make sure the queens' bed has been turned down...please."

"It is already done my lady..." scoffed Jacqueline. "It was done before the queen left."

"Oh well...thank you." Jacqueline addressed the queen.

"Will there be anything else...your majesty?'

"Why as a matter of fact there is. We're making ready for a trip to Spain. You can surely began getting our things ready."

"To Spain my lady?"

"It's nothing...I just need enough things for a month or two...ah, have Jeanine pack some things for the baby, just in case..."

"Oh ma'am...you don't think you'll have your baby in Spain do you?"

"I'm sure that won't be the case...Jacqueline!"

Nichol fed up with her questions said.

"I suppose it's getting rather late, and her majesty needs her rest."

AWAKENED BY BETRAYAL

"You're so right...my lady, perhaps we should be leaving."

It seemed as if both were vying for the queens' attention.

Many weeks had passed, and the queen was made ready for her departure to Spain.

Sir John Myers was of great help, when he assisted her into the coach.

"Your majesty, do you think you'll be comfortable here?"

"I think I could be comfortable, as much as possible John...thank you. Kathryn could you get me one of those pillows there...my back...?"

"I'll get it madam!" said Jacqueline, as she rushed to put the pillow behind Miria.

"Well, this goose down pillow is much better...thanks."

"Your majesty, I really wish you would take my lord Graybourne's advise, and hold off going."

"It is settled John."

"Remember my queen...when your pleas went unheeded?"

"How well my friend...I only know now...I must do what I must."

"As you have said...great lady! Let's move!"

So off they rode; John, lady Kathryn and lady Nichol; Jacqueline, a guard named Atwood, and four others.

The coaches moved with great speed down the open road.

The cobbles on the road made a crunching sound, as the wheels rolled over them. However, with each roll, it was to the queen, as if she were being bounced upon her fathers knee.

"Oh my goodness!" said the queen. "If you keep that up, I'll probably have this child in the coach!"

"Sorry...your majesty." Shouted the driver. "The roads are not good for you."

"But you know ladies...this reminds me of the way Lyonus and I would ride across the countryside...I really miss him..."

"It's nice to have memories like that...hum..." replied Kathryn, with eyes that starred in a day dream-like gaze.

"Kathryn, what about you and lord Guy...Isn't there something special between the two of you?"

"Well...it seemed to be just physical...nothing deep or lasting, I'm afraid. He now seems to be drawn toward Nichol."

"Me!" said Nichol, in a voice that lifted above and whisper. "I can not stomach lord Guy...begging your pardon, your majesty...I will have nothing to do with that one. He's not to be trusted...no ma'am."

"I think you'll know love when it comes to you, and nothing you can do will change that feeling."

"Are you sure, my lady? I do so want to fine true love" Remarked Jacqueline.

"My dears…you can not choose your love…love chooses you. Then it seems you're stuck with the choice forever…or so it would appear."

"You are so wise my lady."

"Lyonus and I knew right away. He would not let me give an excuse not to marry him. I would not have wanted him to."

"A match perfect…would you say?" added Nichol.

"I would indeed. It's strange, Lyonus and I promised each other, on the night we were wed…that even if one of us should die, the one that remained would dream them back, and in that dream, say I love you and good-bye…but of course it was just foolishness."

"It's a wonderful sentiment, your majesty," said Nichol.

"It is that and more…that is why it was hard for me to accept his death. Not once have I dreamed…

"Why do you say it was foolishness…my lady?"

"Because, it just is…I have not once dreamed of my king since his demise."

Then Jacqueline spoke up with such enthusiasm. "Well maybe that means he's not at all dead…maybe he's hiding, sick or something, I don't know!"

"Absurd!" remarked Kathryn, "You don't know our king very well."

"No I don't…but I know sometimes people get caught up in things, situations they can't always escape from…that doesn't mean their dead."

"Je ne sa pas…Jacqueline, I just don't understand it, Lyonus and I were still brand new."

"The fates have a way of toying with our lives madam…and sometimes it leaves us wondering why." Added Kathryn.

"I don't believe in fate, and neither did Lyonus. He believed so strongly, that if love was strong enough, that though one be dead, for a brief moment, oh so brief, the other living, could carry that love into a dream…just long enough to say good-bye."

"I would savor just having a piece of that love…I don't think I will ever find that," said Kathryn.

"I don't know, but Lyonus and I did…we had something rare…and I refused to give it up…not to lords of the court, or even to death."

"If you saw him now in a dream my lady, what would you say?"

"Um…I would say…come back to me…and I want him to wait for me. If he couldn't, we would decide on where to meet in death, so we could always be together…This I know, he will find a way to get to me…as long as I am alive."

"My queen…" said Kathryn. "I feel I know you a little bit better now. You are so open about your relationship with the king."

"It's so easy to be open about Lyonus…"

"Yes, but…it's more…I don't know, I somehow feel different…closer."

"That's wonderful to know Kathryn, It's good to have someone you can trust and share your concerns. Nichol, and Jacqueline up till now, have been my greatest consorts. You and I shall speak again, and perhaps…I will hear of your love and that special someone."

"Perhaps…your majesty." The lady Kathryn replied.

Lady's Kathryn and Nichol, along with Jacqueline, sat and watched Miria with great awe. Somehow Miria made an impression on the ladies; a sort of bonding took place.

They found in the queen, a type of closeness. At least for the moment, a bond, that would make for a lasting friendship…for the house of Warwick.

Just then the carriage started thumbing and wobbling. The queen was being jerked about.

"Kathryn?"

"Are you all right, my lady?"

"No…! Find out from that driver what is going on!"

Kathryn yelled from the window of the coach, through it's blowing curtains.

"What's happening?"

John who was close by the carriage said.

"Are you ladies all right?"

"You're shaking us up in here, maybe you should stop for a moment. The queen is in great discomfort."

"I'm sorry…" he said as he rode steadily to keep up. "…But I fear we're being followed, and I need to make sure we are not."

Then queen Miria shouted back.

"I would also like to make it there in one piece John…now stop…this…coach!"

"I'm afraid, I must disobey, my queen, for your own good."

"John Myers!"

"Hold on, we are almost at lord Graybourne."

"Lord who? John you'd better start explaining right now! Are we using lord Thomas' house for a half way point or a hiding place for every situation?"

Queen Miria began to hold her stomach, and crouched over in discomfort. She was bent over on the seat moaning in pain. Then Kathryn tried to comfort the queen.

"Your majesty…just a moment longer, John has tried to care for you…"

Queen Miria looked over at Kathryn and smiled, then replied.

"I know…why do you think he still has his head."

"Yes your majesty…but it appears by the looks of you, going to Graybournes home, wouldn't be a bad idea."

"Nope…not bad at all…woo!" screamed the queen.

"Your majesty?"

"I think I'm ready to have this baby…!"

"Not yet my queen…"

"Oh…yes!!…"

"Just don't push…don't push…!"

"John!!" screamed Nichol. "The queen is ready to have the baby…we should get the midwife…hurry!"

"Hurry driver!" shouted Jacqueline. "We can't have this child in the coach…!"

"We?" the queen said with a snide remark. "If it were we, you'd be sharing the pain, oh…!"

Both the guard and the coach driver rode with all speed to their destinations. Queen Miria began to moan and groan even more.

"Do something Kathryn…!" called the queen.

"Please your majesty…hang on, we have arrived as we speak." She stuck her head out the window. "How much longer? The queen can't wait."

John riding up to the coach, said.

"We are here…arriving through the gates now. I'm going on to alert lord Thomas."

John immediately called back to the coach.

"Good fortune…the midwife is already her visiting."

Now the servants of lord Thomas had already alerted him, that the royal coach had approached the gate. Lady Claire awaited the queen. She had just put their daughter Melinda to bed. Finally the coach pulled up to the front door.

"I'm sorry Lady Claire for the inconveniences," said John. "But her majesty, is ready to deliver, and is in need of a midwife, soft pillow, and a bed."

"Yes…but her majesty is in need of those things now!" replied Nichol

"Well…" said lady Claire, the bed I can surely deliver…and the midwife already here." With her eyes stretched, glanced over at John.

"Speaking of delivery…" said the queen, smiling at lady Claire. "Where is the midwife…oh…ah…?"

"Yes madam, she is bringing hot water right now," said Kathryn.

Lady Claire, pulled back the covers, and laid her on the bed.

"Help me get her up! Sit down the hot water for Victoria please, Margarete!"

"Yes ma'am…"

"Here is Madam Victoria, your majesty…"Margarete very nervous.

"Wonderful Margarete…" said lady Claire…now go!"

"Hello my queen…how good it is to see you."

"Oh!" said the queen in a grunt. Then Claire remarked.

"A delight Victoria…I'm sure, but the queen is in great pain…I think it may be turned wrong."

"Well, let me see what I can do."

"Hello your majesty…how often is your pain?"

"What a question…constant and right now…I'm in pain!" she squawked.

"No…not pressure but pain…"

"How about this then…get this child out of me…now!!"

"All right…try to push now…"

"Grrr…I've been trying to…but I…"

"Wait, I'll need to turn him a little more."

"Oh…ah…oh!" Screamed the queen. It seemed the pain was too much to bear. "Will you people make up your minds? First, then you say don't push…oh…oh…get him out!"

"Oh finally…the head."

"Where's that water…Margarete?"

"Look Claire, I see the head…"

"All right…push more…"

"Here it comes…It's a girl!!!"

"Oh…a girl…oh…"

"Wait, Claire…another head…hold it, look! It's a boy!"

"Oh…twins…ah…ha…!" shouted Claire.

"Your Majesty you have two beautiful babies…" said Victoria.

"Ha...um...two of them...and one a son...perfect!"

Then queen Miria, passed out from exhaustion.

"Is she alright, Victoria?" asked Claire.

"Oh yes...she seems to be okay for now. We should get her and the children cleaned up."

"Right...We need John to get her some things from the coach...Margarete!"

"Right away ma'am..."

Then Victoria looked over at her and said.

The best thing for her now, is to let her sleep."

"Yes..." She is really worn out...It was tough going there for a moment."

"I know," said Kathryn. "I was afraid she would not make it."

"Me too," said Jacqueline.

"By the way Victoria...you did a fine job..."

"Come Claire, let's get a little wine."

"I do agree...ha...ah..."

Margarete entered with the queens' bags.

"Thank you. Will you sit the bag down over there?" Pointing at a small wooden chest near the bed. "We can use some blankets from that old chest."

"My lady, there is lady Melinda's old crib in the barn...should I fetch it?"

"Yes excellent...Margarete, get Royce to help, it's quite a bit heavy dear..."

After they got the children all cleaned up, they began working on Miria.

"Your majesty, we have the children all cleaned up."

"Yes, my queen, and all ready to greet you..." said Victoria. "Sit up dear..."

Then Jacqueline chimed in. "What will you name them, your majesty?"

"Ha...ah...ha..." laughed Victoria. "I think we may need to give her a little time, Jacqueline."

"All right, but I have some names in mind for the beautiful princess."

"I wanted to name my son after his father. I thought to call him Lyonus III. But now, I think it best to stay away from that name. I didn't plan for twins either...I don't know...I need to think."

Both babies began to cry.

"It looks as if it's feeding time...your majesty..."

"Of course...bring them to me please." Miria with her arms out stretched. "Oh he looks just like Lyonus..."

Victoria and Claire could not hold their laughter.

"Why your majesty...Laughed Victoria. "That is the girl you're holding..."

"Well a girl with no hair, makes it hard to tell…"

"I remember Melinda…born without a stitch of hair…bald as a cooked chicken…ha…ha."

"I know lady Claire," said Victoria. "Now she is even more a beautiful little girl."

"Victoria…" said queen Miria. "What is your mothers name?"

"Why…her name is Jessica…your majesty."

"Then Jessica it will be! That's a good name."

"I'm more than flattered, your majesty…but are you sure?"

"Definitely…I am more than grateful. If Lyonus were here, he would probably start throwing about gold coins…and clanking goblets of wine. In fact, John," she called, motioning for him to hurry along. "Come in here please."

"Yes…your majesty."

"Get for me a bag of gold from the coach."

"At once, my queen…and might I say my lady, king Lyonus would be more than proud. I feel his joy."

Miria nodded her head, overwhelmed with excitement and happiness, but also grief.

"My queen…" said Victoria. "Gold is not necessary, I am the midwife."

"Yes, yes…and there is nothing that says you can not be rewarded for what you do."

"Here you are your majesty," announced John. "Where shall I put it?"

"Give Mrs. Jeffers ten pieces, for each child…no make it twenty."

"On your command, great lady," remarked John.

"But your majesty…I don't deserve all of this…please."

"Silence! Obey your queen…take the gold…I command it."

They all laughed and laughed. Then Miria said.

"Well…do see that Jessica? That's the first time I've ever had to force someone to take gold…she is a remarkable woman. That's the type of character I want for you little princess."

"Thank you…I'm certain I can put it to good use."

Then Miria turned to Claire, and said.

"Claire, I will leave the rest of the gold for you. We have intruded upon your home, and we are more than grateful."

"No my queen…Thomas would take away the roof, if I were to accept any payment."

"Well…just tell him I've ordered you…and you had no choice."

"You may tell him yourself, your majesty…here he is now."

Thomas, rushed into the room with his arms opened wide.

He could not wait to greet the queen.

"I heard...my queen...twins. You have done well. Lyonus would be more than proud. I can almost see him, strutting around the room...with his chest stuck out...bragging to every lord and lady. One of each...he'd say, one for me one for her...my beloved king Lyonus."

"Yes Thomas...I miss him too."

Claire handed Thomas the little girl.

"My lord this is Jessica...queen Miria named her for Victoria's mother."

Lord Graytbourne took Jessica in his arms very gently, then said.

"You are as beautiful a vision, as is your mother...and where is that fine little prince?"

"The prince is waiting to see the lord of the manor. Take him sir."

"He truly is his fathers son, my queen. Now what have you named him?"

"I shall name him Orin, after my grandfather. It is a French name, and it means...born out of grief...I thought it would be appropriate."

"But now I have news..." announced Graybourne. "We must make ready to leave."

Lady Claire spoke right up and said.

"Oh no Thomas! She can not be moved right now...not after all she's been through."

"Your majesty, no one understands needing to rest any more than I, but it is imperative that we take you to a safe place."

"Now wait Thomas, I thought we were safe here."

"There are spies everywhere...watching, waiting and reporting our every move. I have to safeguard you and the children, your majesty...not to mention these documents."

"What! Lord Graybourne, are those...?"

"Yes my queen. These are the papers Biltfry and Guy were hoping to find...drooling to get their hands on."

"When...how did you get them?"

"Remember, my queen, I told you I found papers in King Lyonus's chambers before I left for my trip?"

"Yes I do remember. What...are these the?"

"I found them shortly after the so called accident of the king's. I felt they would be safer in my keeping. I also have his other ring..."

"Oh tell me it has the seal..."

"It does indeed, my lady, wrapped up tight for you and your heirs...I knew it would be better to keep them hidden."

The queen looked at Claire and said.

"Thank you my lord Thomas…and you thought your deeds not worthy of a little gold…you are both worth your weight in it! Now let me see those things…"

"Here they are."

"Look at these…I thought you might enjoy."

"The blackmail papers lord Guy exacted from the king!"

"Yes! I had Kathryn steal them…let's say at a more intimate moment."

"Ha…" laughed lord Thomas. "You are a very wise woman, your majesty."

"Just a little something I learned from France."

"No wonder lord Guy was so upset before we left…"

"Right you are…my lord."

Queen Miria, looked over the papers carefully, and then shared.

"Lyonus trusted both of us…didn't he Thomas?"

"Yes he did, your majesty…but there are others…"

"Oh yes…and some he would not trust at arms length…Ha…ah…ha…"

"My queen," he called. "Please hurry!"

"Lord Graybourne. Claire, Kathryn…all of you…Do you know what this means to me and the children? These documents, declare my children rightful heirs to the throne of England…It cannot be disputed. King Lyonus himself has proclaimed it. I see why those thieves wanted to get their hands on them. Not to mention being free to go after lord Guy."

"We shall keep them safe…"

"I'm afraid they won't be of any use to us, if we are dead…"

"Listen…" said Thomas. "The king knew there would be those who would try and usurp the throne, that's why he wanted this will safeguarded. The king was quite aware of prince Luis' instability. But now your majesty, we must go. I've made special arrangements."

Lord Graybourne called for a servant.

"Royce…would you bring to the back door, a wagon please…Make sure there are plenty of blankets."

"Yes my lord."

"I also would like for you Kathryn to go back to the royal castle."

"Am I not going with her majesty?" asked Kathryn.

"Well, there has been a small change in the plans…for now try and go along, without too much protest. Langly and Royce will bring horses to the front door. Langly will escort you back to the castle."

"Well what should I say if they ask me any questions?"

"Oh they will definitely ask you questions…you will say…the queen and two guards are waiting at Longshaw Castle, till the next ship should sail for Spain. Do you understand?"

"Of course, I hear you, I just don't understand why all the pretense."

"Then perhaps, lady Kathryn we should just say, the queen has sworn you to secrecy."

"Certainly not…they would threaten to cut out my tongue if I did not tell them."

"Exactly…this way you will have something to tell, and they will be none the wiser."

"All right then, I guess I'll be on my way your majesty."

"Good Kathryn, you're a good friend. We shall see each other again. Goodbye."

"Goodbye everyone."

Lady Claire was not too pleased with lord Graybournes decision to move the queen.

"My lord…the queen has been through enough for one day, it is quite an ordeal…this giving birth. Could this move not wait until the morning?"

"That is precisely why I can't wait until morning…I need for them to think we've waited, to give the queen a chance to get aboard the ship. If we wait she will indeed miss it. Remember here, the queen is on a mission of peace, or at least to try and salvage it."

"Well what about the children? Are they to be left to chance as well?"

"At least one heir must go…"

"Why only one…there should be at least one heir left to take the throne. We dare not take the chance that they would not discover the heirs and have them killed as well."

"I guess you are right, Thomas, but I don't think she should take the children."

Queen Miria interrupts lady Claire and Thomas.

"Now, I hate to be spoken of, as if I'm not here lord Graybourne. May I speak now…?"

"Of course your majesty…we were just trying to…"

"I know…I have heard your words Thomas, and I appreciate everything you're trying to do for us…but I must be on that ship, that I may answer king Emanuel in a timely manner. This is too delicate a matter, and war…my lord Thomas, is not an option."

"No…you misunderstood my reasons, your majesty…I don't feel the threat from king Emanuel was real. I think it was just another ploy in which to leave England without a ruler seated on the throne."

"You're saying, just as was the case with Lyonus and the trip to France."

"Exactly, my queen. Around the corner will wait men with bows and axes, to cut you down!"

"Frankly, their threats of war have become a little tiresome…can they not think of anything else?"

"Perhaps…the more idol the threat, the easier it would be to lure one away."

"…And if it is not an idol threat…what then, my lord? Who will pay the price for the delay? Is it the kings' brave knights, the families of the farmers who have gone off to fight…or maybe, the children, who will never see or know their fathers? Even still mothers who stand and wait to mourn their sons, whose bodies can not be found…Or is it the house of Warwick whose line is destroyed because of greed. Tell me my lord Graybourne…what is left to do? Except a certain looking forward to death."

"All right your majesty…I have given Kathryn enough information to hold them up, at least long enough for you to board the ship safely, if they buy it. Beyond that…I don't know. I cannot know what dangers await you on your journey. There may be no way in which to communicate with you. That leaves me sickened. But if you are to go, then we must leave now."

"Then ready my things, and the children…" said Miria. "No! Get Orin ready, not Jessica."

Both lady Claire and Jacqueline said in unison.

"…But your majesty!!"

"No, buts…I will take Orin! He will one day be king. He should fill his fathers shoes."

"…And what of Jessica, your majesty, does she not also deserve a chance?"

"You question my motive? Of course you do…" The queen bowed her head in tears. "It pains me that I must choose…but I know, if they do not suspect two children, the female would be the likely one to go unnoticed. At least she would have a semblance of a life…I know at the very least, you'll love her as your own."

"Our own?"

"If you would…find someone…for England…"

"Well then…it is settled. We will send a servant along with you to assist you further…Margarete…"

"Yes my lady"

"Are you ready to fulfill your duty to the Crown?"

"It is my solemn pleasure to give my life for England...whatever I must do, I will do for king Lyonus and his queen and heirs."

Margarete packed the rest of her things and lord Graybourne helped her load them.

"You really don't know what this means to England and the queen. I can't leave out lady Claire and myself. We are so very proud of your courage...and indeed honored to have known you," said lord Thomas.

"I'm ready to do what I can, my lord."

He reached over, took her hand and gently kissed it, and said.

"You are every bit a lady...and this deed will not be forgotten."

Then Margarete replied, with a smile on her face.

"Don't write me off just yet...I have plans of returning home..."

"Farewell, dear Margarete...and God speed."

"Good bye my lord."

While lord Thomas said his good-byes to Margarete. Claire, Victoria, and Jacqueline, loaded the queen in another wagon. Claire still unsure, said.

"I'm afraid for you, your majesty. You are so weak. To have to handle such a small child under those circumstances...I just don't feel right."

Then the queen grabbed Claire's hand, and gave a big smile, then said in a very low voice, so that only she could hear.

"Claire...I...like king Lyonus, have learned to trust my lord Graybourne...even with our very lives. I know, if Lyonus had listened to him...he would still be with us today, to see his children born. I will not hold him accountable for what is sure to be fall us."

"Yes, I must admit, I too have learned to trust his judgment...but he too fears for you now...both you and Orin. .I suppose this is no time to waiver...well..." said Claire, as she pulled and folded blanket after blanket. "Let's get you wrapped up your majesty."

"We are ready, my lord." Called Victoria. "Be gentle with the queen..."

"I shall. What about the child?"

"For tonight, my dear, she will remain with me. We will take Jessica to Victoria's home in the morning...She will be fine, until the queen is ready to emerge. My prince is ready for travel."

"I wonder just how long that might be, lord Graybourne?" asked queen Miria. "I don't want to be gone long, from my home or my child."

"I honestly don't know...that would depend solely on your skill as a diplomat your majesty...and whatever you may encounter in Spain."

Lady Claire and Miria began to cry. Miria of course, was sad at the thought of leaving her newborn baby daughter behind.

"I know you will treat her as the little princess that she is."

"Oh yes, my queen. When the time is right, we will tell her about both you and the king. But it is our prayer, that you will not be away that long."

"Who can really know, with Luis, and Fredrick Guy plotting? Once we've left England, there is no telling what they will try. I'm almost afraid for you who are left behind as well."

"Oh…" said Miria. "That reminds me, look in my bag Graybourne…" She pointed at the gray cloth bag. "Yes…that's it…give it to me…"The queen pulled out a necklace with a beautiful charm, then explained.

"I wanted Jessica to have this, and the other things here in this pouch. She will know from these things, where she truly came from" They all took in a breath, and then Claire said.

"Why…it is simply breathtaking! Beautiful…I've never seen anything quite so stunning!"

"Well…" sighed the queen. "I know there would be nothing I could ever do or say, that would make up for ever having left her."

"It's only for a little space in time…My queen," said Victoria.

"Just until king Emanuel frees Du'Voe." Added the lady Claire.

Victoria and Jacqueline brought the prince and princess to Miria. She introduced them to each other, while she held them in her arms.

"Orin…this is your sister, princess Jessica…and Jessica, this…" Queen Miria could not hold back the tears, and then continued and said, "This is your brother prince Orin. He and I will leave you now, but don't fret, we will always love you…don't ever forget hearing those words from me. If your father could see you now, he would think you a treasure indeed…"

Claire held Jessica as the queen kissed her for the last time. She placed a necklace within her blanket. Miria took and extra sniff of her blanket, for it smelled of rose peddles which was her favorite fragrance.

The queen gave her thanks to the household, handed Claire some gold. Then took her place in the wagon.

"No…your majesty…you will need your gold for your trip. We need nothing…please! It is more than a pleasure to serve you…Thomas and I adore you, and the king."

Then Victoria added. "There is nothing we wouldn't do."

"Then…accept my love, gratitude and my undying faith in you. Take care of the princess."

They continued to cry…while they waved goodbye.

"Goodbye your majesty!"

"My friends call me Miria…" she shouted out to them.

"Godspeed…Miria and Orin.

Lord Graybourne gathered the men to ride, and then said his farewells.

"Good-bye Claire…my love…Take care of everything. Oh and…James, you and Olivia, help my lady while I am away."

"Certainly…as always, my lord Graybourne." They both announced.

Now Graybourne, left in the queens coach, and the queen left in a broken down wagon.

She was tucked inside the wagon filled with folded blankets, and barrels, as they headed for their destination.

Lord Thomas hoped for a distraction that would enable the queen a clean escape.

Nichol, Margarete and Jacqueline also rode with the queen.

Graybourne and John rode as far a Longshaw road. Then they stopped and watched the queen's wagon as it headed for the seashore. There they would board the ship Ferdinand.

Finally they were out of the sight of John and Graybourne, and ready to load the ship that had been waiting.

The two guards, Atwood and Hudson, helped Margarete and Jacqueline load their things aboard the Ferdinand. Nichol was busy with the queen and Orin. When Margarete went up the plank carrying her last bag, she noticed that the ship had pulled anchor. She yelled for Atwood and Hudson to stop, but they were in a scrimmage with some other men. The anchor was lifted, and the ship would not stop. She immediately told the queen.

"Your majesty…they are fighting, attacked…"

"Sh…sh." Jacqueline motioned. "You will wake the baby."

"…But your majesty, we are moving, sailing away. The guards are fighting, disabled!"

"What are you talking about…Margarete?"

"They have been attacked…just look."

The queen walked over to the port bow, and saw that the dock had become a small island to her eyes. Watching the ship pull further and further away, she said.

"I don't know what this means…I've got a mind to make them turn this ship around!"

"You can't do that…or we will never reach Spain," said Nichol.

"Very well…thank you for reminding me of my realities."

"At least our accommodations are in order," remarked Nichol.

"Okay…any last request before we die…?" said Jacqueline. "This all seems different than what lord Graybourne described."

"Perhaps it is…" said the queen. "But we will get to the bottom of things once in Spain…Of that I feel sure."

CHAPTER NINE
Banished

When the ship Ferdinand, finally arrived in Spain, met at port by a driver with a small wagon. Queen Miria was more than ready to comply with terms of king Emanuel. So she insisted on going directly to the royal castle. The driver made it known that he had other orders.

"Look ma'am, I have my orders…and they say, take you and your company to the Regale cottage, in La Vega."

"…And by whose orders were these?!…" questioned Miria, right now steaming mad.

"All I know…is that they came from king Emanuel."

Everyone took a deep breath and looked at each other. Not a word was uttered for a moment. Then Orin started to cry.

"Look! I understand you have your orders, and I respect that…but I am the queen of England. My company and I are here at the request of your king…so tell me then…why would he not want to see me?"

"I can not answer your questions. I was told to say, what I have said…and no more. Now…I'll take you to your place.

"Ma'am…" Looking at Jacqueline. "Is this the last of your bags?" Trying to avoid talking to the queen.

"Yes, I believe it is…but…"

"Hey! Monsieur…se IL vous plas…if you please! We are in a foreign land…I am here to discuss the treatise between Spain and England…can't you just take me there. I know if I can see the king, he will accept me."

AWAKENED BY BETRAYAL

But for some reason unknown to the queen, king Emanuel refused to have audience with her. He gave order that no one welcome her.

"Very well then, take us to the Regale cottage. Perhaps we can sort it all out there."

So the driver took them on to the cottage, and even helped them unload their things. He collected firewood for them, and stored it on the side of the house.

"Thanks very much for your help."

"No thanks needed Senora, just doing what I was told."

"Well..." said Jacqueline. "...Mind telling me who you work for. Did you understand what I meant, between servants and all? I know it's hard when people try to boss you around. I has really made me angry, how they have treated the common folk, like me and you...By the way my name is Jacqueline...What is yours?"

"Me? Why my name is Ricardo..."

"Oh, I like that name Monsieur Ricardo, it is a pleasure to meet you. Do you work around here...I mean anywhere close?"

"No...I work in the royal castle. I was sent by a Senior Ochoa, to meet your ship and give you the message...I was only suppose to drop you off here and come immediately back."

"Oh...I thought maybe you lived near here...then we could...maybe become friends."

"I would like that a lot..."

"Is there a Senora, about?"

"Oh no, my wife died five years ago...fell off a horse and broke her neck...terrible accident. It has taken me a while to get myself going again, until I started working for Senior Ochoa. He helped me so much...I owe him my life."

"I see...well perhaps you can come back for dinner some night."

"It would be a pleasure...Senorita."

"Please, by all means call me Jacqueline...I insist..."

"Se' Senorita Jacqueline...I will come back in a couple of days and check on you."

"That would be great...Ricardo...thank you."

So Jacqueline returned to the house...gloating of her accomplishment.

"He'll be back..."

Margarete started asking all kinds of questions.

"Well did he tell you where he lived and all?"

153

"Yes he did. Do you know he lives in or near the palace?"
Then queen Miria said.
"Oh...he refused to talk with me because I am royalty...is that it Jacqueline?"
"Yes ma'am...He is just a servant, like me. We have a few things in common."
Then Margarete said.
"Did he give you any details about king Emanuel?"
Well...no...apparently he works for someone quite powerful in the castle...a Monsieur Ochoa...I think he said."
"You mean Senior Ochoa..." Nichol added. "In Spanish it is Senior."
"Okay...does not matter..." said the queen. "I need to find out all I can about what is going on with king Emanuel."
"I invited him to come and have dinner with us."
"That's good Jacqueline..." said Nichol. "Then we can question him further."
"He said in a couple of days...I hope."
"We'll see then. Meanwhile, I'm writing my lord Graybourne, and then, the king a letter requesting audience again...Maybe I can have Monsieur Ricardo deliver it for me..."
"Perhaps your majesty...we will see."

The ladies looked to see what sort of food there was in the house. They found lots of fruits and vegetables. There was also a side of beef already prepared, with several loaves of warm fresh baked bread. Someone had prepared a welcomed feast. This was indeed a fortunate find for them.

When they walked around the property, they saw that it had several fruit bearing trees, and a few chickens and a horse, in a coral of sorts. Something at least for a time, would aid in their survival.

All did not seem lost, but merely a miscommunication of some kind. So the queen continued to write messages for the king.

Now everything was being prepared for Senior Ricardo's return for dinner. Jacqueline searched the seller for wine. She came across a room well stocked with all types of fruit wine and ale, and cheese. All the ladies felt a little better, just knowing that someone was looking out for them.

Meanwhile Ricardo was back at the royal castle. He explained the response made by the queen of England. Senior Ochoa was more than delighted, to know that the queen did not bring any guards with her to make trouble. Truly this afforded them a way to keep her from the castle. Senior

Ochoa had received communication from England days before they arrived. This was just another way in which someone would try and take control.

Atlas two days had gone by, and Jacqueline was ready to receive Senior Ricardo. He arrived right on schedule, but he brought an extra horse with him. Jacqueline ran out to meet him, when he said.

"Senorita Jacqueline…I must apologize…"

"Apologize? Apologize for what Monsieur? You are on time…"

"No, I can not stay…Senior Ochoa, wants me there today…right now, and I can not turn him down."

"Oh I see…" replied Jacqueline, somewhat disappointed in his response. "If it is what you must do…However, I was looking forward to having supper together."

"Maybe another time Senorita…please try and understand."

"Maybe…"

"…But I am leaving the wagon and another horse with you…so you can get around. Just go north and it will take you to a tavern…a surgeon and several farms. Any other direction may mean trouble. If you need food just go to one of the farms and they will sell you items you need."

Wait Ricardo…we don't plan to live here for ever…it's just until the queen can see and speak with your king."

"What ever you say…I'm telling you, it will not happen, something is wrong. I've never seen the king so mad…He has been in a terrible mood lately."

"I'm sorry, but he should not take it out on the queen…after all, he's the reason she has come here."

"Well…I must go now. Don't let anyone know where you got the wagon…I don't know when I'll be back again Jacqueline…but it was nice meeting you. La Vega is a nice village, you will make a few friends here I'm sure…Good-bye, Senorita."

"Good-bye."

Jacqueline slowly opened the door to the cottage, with a long face, she advised the queen of what Ricardo had told her. Queen Miria was sick at heart.

"If this is the way it will be, I guess we should book our trip back to England."

"Yes your majesty," said Nichol. "It's the only way to straighten this hold mess out."

"The way he talked your majesty…was as if we would not be leaving the country."

"That's absurd…they have no authority to hold us here. Anyway, why should they?"

"It could be your rivals back in England. Remember what lord Graybourne said before we left?"

"I just didn't think they would have enough nerve to try a stunt like that…"

"My lady…" said Nichol. "It was really difficult not to suspect them…they seemed too anxious for you to leave. And that letter they had…why was it sent after the king just happened to have been attacked?"

"Yes your majesty…" said Margarete. "…And the prince comes back virtually unharmed. It all added up to strange happenings to me."

"Oui…Jacqueline…I see what you mean…we will try tomorrow to find a way home."

The queen never found a way to board any ship leaving Spain. Every merchant ship refused her as well.

The effort seemed futile. But she tried continually to get messages to lord Graybourne in England.

Meanwhile, back in England, lord Graybourne was saddened that the queen decided to take the trip to Spain. He never trusted what the advisors would attempt in her absence. Graybourne never really trusted Kathryn not to reveal trusted information about the queen. Besides, Kathryn was close to Fredrick Guy, and would probably reveal anything to him if he used his gentle persuasion.

Lord Graybourne and queen Miria hoped that the documents left by king Lyonus II would be enough to protect the birthright of their children, Jessica and Orin. But before lord Graybourne could figure out what to do, he received news and was called before the royal court at the castle. Thomas waited before he left, in order to attend his wife, and make final provisions for the princess Jessica.

Graybourne, and Claire, called upon their friends the Jeffers. Victoria of course, delivered the queens' babies, and her husband John who was a good friend of lord Thomas. They were the perfect couple to rear Jessica. They would never reveal her true identity, and would keep her safe, until the queen's return.

Mixed information was given to the usurpers, but news quickly spread throughout the realm, that twins were born to queen Miria that night.

It was Victoria Jeffers that recalled the queens' desperation, for her children. She was more than happy to assists the Graybourne's.

In the beginning John Jeffers was a little skeptical, because of the reputation of prince Luis, and Fredrick Guy. But after they heard what had happened to the queen, and the throne, he was quite ready to protect the princess.

Finally a week later, lord Graybourne made his way to the great hall, as summoned by Prince Luis. He was acting as king in the absence of Miria, and Reagent lord Du'Voe.

After Thomas arrived, he first encountered lord Guy, who was fresh, waiting to accuse Graybourne of treason. But lord Graybourne, sharp as he was witty said.

"Ah…your Royal Highness," he said, as he bowed to prince Luis. "I have made way, as you requested. And I bring news about her majesty the queen."

"News?" asked lord Guy.

"Oh…greetings. Lord Guy, I did not notice you there." Acting as if he did not see him. He turned to look at Guy, and then back to the prince, and then said. "The queen wanted you to know, she has begun her journey and all is well. She does not foresee any problems, and is expecting to return to England within a month, or two."

"Really…" scoffed Luis. "Just what are go getting at, my lord?"

"Why, the will of her majesty…of course."

"Well…I have a letter here, that shows the will…of her majesty, as you call it…Her will is both questionable, and unacceptable…as the queen of England."

"Oh…how so?" Graybourne questioned.

"For openers, the letter states she has not been seen or heard from since she set sail. And that she was in the company of a strange man…aboard the Ferdinand. This man was said to be the true father of the child she called my brothers, and heir to the throne…!"

"What…that can't possibly be true! Who had bought such lies?"

"Bought…my lord…?" said Luis, raising his hand. "What are you suggesting?"

"Lies are easily enough to defend…where did they come from?"

"Lies…? This comes directly from the king himself. His further reports were quite disturbing. The reason I summoned you, was to inform you that I have assumed kingship over the land, in the absence of lord Du'Voe."

"Well...that's no great mystery to me!"

"Hold your tongue!" shouted lord Guy, while he took a step forward.

"The tongues that should be silenced are those who would spread such rumors about the queen of England, and soil her reputation...!"

"Please...please, my lords!" Luis tried to call to order the disruption.

"Well...what of the queen then, your highness...?"

"Her misconduct, and unacceptable behavior...Treason!"

"Your highness...?" questioned Thomas.

"Well...one can only imagine the shame brought upon the good name of Warwick, not to mention the entire country of England. We believed in her loyalty to us, and in return, she has destroyed our faith..."

"Your highness...such character does not ring true for queen Miria. She grieved more than any of us for the king...and I believe she grieves still."

"Well..." lord Guy remarked. "That would be easy enough to fake."

"Then perhaps you gave good lessons my lord," said Graybourne.

"Why you...!" said Guy while holding the handle of his sword.

"Stop!" insisted Luis. "Nevertheless...I'll get right to the point lord Graybourne, I have here, papers that denounce the queens good behavior, and accuses her of adultery."

"A ridiculous Claim!" exclaimed Graybourne

"Let me finish sir! There is also the claim that the children born to Miria, are not those of king Lyonus..."

"I should like to see the man who would slander the name of the queen with such filth! I would put his tongue to rest permanently!!"

"Perhaps you should put my lord on a short leash...my prince..." said lord Guy as he leered at Thomas.

"Maybe then, it is your tongue we are discussing...Guy!"

"Stop! This is getting us nowhere...!" said prince Luis.

"Your highness, this is absurd...and you know it. Why, there's nothing more than a note...no seal, no signatures...and for that...a pack of lies...you usurp the throne and denounce the queen. You would steal her children's birthright, as heirs to the throne!! That in itself is treason...treason I say!!"

That statement brought the now king Luis to his feet in protest.

"My lord king...!" shouted lord Guy. "Send him to the gallows and be rid of him!"

"Silence...silence...I say! Lord Graybourne, if I did not know of your feelings...or did not think you too upset...I would have...your head! But I am aware of your closeness with both my brother and Miria. So therefore that is why I...despite my lord Guy's council...have allowed you to spout on...this one time…understood?"

"Yes…I understand quite well. I have been in the royal service, since the time of your father, and my dear friend and king, Lyonus the great. I also served your brother and king, Lyonus II, a true king of England."

"Now…careful…" Luis cut Graybourne short, showing his impatience.

"Yes, yes, and queen Miria yes, yes…" he said waving his hands about.

"That's right…I, alas…I see that the great kings have ended for England…It's time for me to retire my sword."

Grayboune then turned to walk away with his head hung low, dragging his sword in his hand.

Then lord Guy tried even more to anger lord Graybourne, he had hoped to provoke him, and then said.

"Don't be ridiculous Graybourne, it seems to be a bit dramatic even for you, and a tad bit overdone."

"Dramatic Guy? Over done…? You say!"

Graybourne moved in closer to lord Guy, stepping fast.

"I can give you dramatic Guy. If I stood here…right here…" Graybourne pointed directly at the floor. "Yes here…I can see, one who would bargain with the grieving boy king to do whatever evil he would, that England's laws could not touch him…then I'd stand and accuse you of treasonous acts against the crown! Over done? I would render the proof of these things you offer against queen Miria, as a pack of willful and spiteful lies…that by your own evil will and greed, has labeled you unworthy to judge. That, my lord Guy…would indeed be dramatic, whose end I am sure, would be that of the hang mans noose!!"

Lord Guy furious, charged. "My lord prince, let me have him drawn and quartered…this traitor to you and the crown. I have had enough of his insolence!"

"Not…till you have sufficiently tasted my blade…!" said Graybourne.

"Enough!" shouted the usurper.

"King Luis! Bid him give you the ring of Lyonus and the papers he stole…!'

"My lords…put away your swords…I command it!" said Luis. "This is not a time for hot headedness. It's a time for thinking things through with levelness. We must decide my lords what to do about this dilemma."

"Oh…" said lord Graybourne, with such sarcasm. "Am I to be included on the decision made here today…this, dilemma as you call it? I thought sure, it had already been decided."

"Of course not…just why do you think I have asked all of you here today.

No one means to hurt dear queen Miria, but we have to do what is right for the people. If we have facts...we must act on them. Everyone here will agree...that is how king Lyonus would handle the situation. We can not allow the willful actions of one, to be placed above the law."

"All right...as you say, then allow me to peek at the other documents you have."

"Certainly...I have nothing to hide from you my lord." Prince Luis nodded his head at Guy, and then said. "Ah...the noble one moves closer. Listen lord Thomas; I have always thought highly of Miria...you know that. I thought she was a wonderful wife to my brother...But this I can not abide...traitor to Lyonus!'

"Your highness...my lords, I've read nothing that gives valued proof of Miria's unfaithfulness or any improprieties...Words, that's all, just words! From this alone you would choose to exile the queen?" said Graybourne.

"Better than death..." Lord Guy murmured, while he turned his face away.

"You...poison adder!" yelled lord Thomas. I should...!"

Once again, prince Luis frustrated, stood to his feet, and shouted.

"Yes...and her bastard child as well! Yes!"

At this time lord Thomas saw lady Kathryn, as she stepped back into the shadows. Lord Guy then spoke.

"No my king...I was informed that there were two of them...two such children!"

Luis held up two of his fingers.

"What did you say? Two children?"

"Yes my king..." Guy replied, smirking the hold time. "But only one was reported to have traveled with the queen to Spain."

"Well! What have you to say of that little interesting fact, my fine advisors?" said Luis.

Both Biltfry and Westmoreland kept silent through the entire confrontation with Thomas. But when asked, lord Biltrfry spoke out, wearing his tight bottoms and low cut shirt, fidgeting about his collar.

"Lord Thomas Graybourne...can you tell us then, where we might discover the where-abouts of king Lyonus's will...I know he wrote one, you see...I aided him in it's writing.

When I looked for it before the queen left, it was nowhere to be found...but you however, were in Lyonus's chambers searching for something...were you not? Can you help us my lord?"

Just then, Duke Westmoreland started to speak.

"Well I'd like to know, my lord…as I'm sure we all would, where is the other child? Is it a boy…or girl? That's my question…"

"Now do you really think such things are entrusted to me?" answered Thomas.

"Come…come now Graybourne, we understand…we know the queen entrusted you with documents before. We know she trusted you with her life…though I must say from here, you have bungled the job old man…" said lord Guy.

"Having said that, then do you think if I had the will…which I don't…that I would turn it over to a pack of wolves, or be a part of an innocent child's murder?"

"No…! But as your king, I demand you tell me what you do know!" said the prince.

Lord Guy leaned over and whispered to Luis.

"Just take his head your majesty…we really have no need of him…"

"Come now lord Guy…don't be hasty. We are neither rash, nor are we barbaric men. I have no desire to harm lord Graybourne…I merely want him to trust that I will do the right things for England."

Lord Thomas slowly glanced around the great hall. He was remembering the times of Lyonus the great, and of Lyonus II with Miria. It was a time of wonderful love, and full of pleasant memories. Then lord Thomas said.

"Your highness…my lords…I can only say, it saddens my heart to find what the letter implies. Also, that you've chosen to exile the royal family…"

Lord Biltfry was ready to interrupt Thomas, when Luis motioned and then said.

"Let him finish his speaking…lord Biltfry…"

"I must follow my own heart, I can not agree to this…furthermore, I request your permission to leave this audience…"

"Well said then, Graybourne…well said indeed! You may be released from your pledge. I have no choice, but to accept your resignation…I bid you farewell!"

Graybourne took his time, as he walked away from the throne, when Luis shouted his last command for him.

"Graybourne…remember, you are no longer welcomed in the castle…or on the grounds…from this day forward…"

Then Graybourne turned to look back with distain…drew his sword, flung it to the floor, and replied.

"Just as you have said…from this day…forward."

Prince Luis sat himself to the edge of his seat.

"Never mind, my king…let him go. We're better off without his self-righteous indignations any way." Scoffed Guy.

Then lord Graybourne turned and shouted, "If ever you are at Hilton lord Guy…do stop by…!"

"Did you hear his empty threats…my prince?"

The prince staring, as if in awe of lord Thomas, said.

"I've all ways admired his courage…his daring. But let him ramble on, that men will think he's mad."

"Oh…" Lord Guy not satisfied with Luis' response.

"But, are we really better off…?" asked Luis. "The things he knows…it could be…"

Guy not giving Luis time to finish interrupted.

"There are always methods of getting what you want, or getting want we need without him…but he'll help us more than he knows…"

"Well…did you really think he was just going to lay it all in our hands?" asked Westmoreland.

Then Biltfry added.

"If I may speak…I truly think we could have handled it better…"

Lord Guy charged over to Biltfry's face, and said.

"That's precisely why you don't do any thinking Biltfry…No one just handles a man like Graybourne, he's too smart for that."

Then Luis replied.

"Well handle or not, it makes no difference…I will have my way. I want a search for this…child…and it will continue. No one eats or sleeps until it is found…understood!"

"How long must we have the search go on, my king?"

"Until…I am…dead Westmoreland! I will not lose the crown to Lyonus again. That, I swear on his grave…or yours! Wine!" shouting for the steward. "Bring more wine. My lords we have all done well. We have accomplished a great deal today."

Luis motioned for Guy to come closer, and then whispered.

"I know…I can depend on you to finish it…"

"Yes…your majesty."

Lord Biltfry remarked in a voice that trembled.

"We sent a letter to king Emanuel of Spain, sire."

"All right…let me hear this letter," said Luis, sitting so proudly in the kings' chair.

So the proclamation read:

Let it be known, that on the fifth day of May, in the year of our Lord 1549,

A court found Miria Michelle De'Sheffield Warwick, to be guilty of adultery. Mira Michelle De'Sheffield Warwick, henceforth and forever is stripped of all rights and privileges, and titles under the laws of the sovereign of England. Any and all children born to the union of Lyonus Warwick II and Miria are thereby included.

As undesirables, are hereby removed and banished from all England, exiled, for as long as they should live. By order of Prince Luis Warwick, Protector of the Realm.

All advisors, except lord Thomas Graybourne, signed the proclamation. It was never stamped with the seal of England.

Now when word reached the ears of king Emanuel, he sent out a command throughout the country of Spain, that no one was to aid an exile from England, named Mira De'Sheffield. Banished and dethroned, she must live in disgrace. There was never a letter regarding a treatise.

CHAPTER TEN
In Spain

By the time Miria and the other ladies found out what had happened, it was too late to try and change King Emanuel's heart. Miria was now forced to live far beneath her station.

Miria tried many times to seek an audience with the king, but each time he continued to reject her.

The letters she sent to lord Graybourne, and to France, never returned an answer.

"My lady…what shall we do?" cried Margarete.

"I don't know Margarete…We have no lord Graybourne to protect us now…"

"Wait!" spouted the queen. "I have an idea…I'm not sure the good it will do, but I want to try it."

"All right my lady, tell me…" said Nichol

Then the others insisted on knowing right away.

"Jacqueline…"

"Yes your majesty…"

"Bring me one of your dresses…"

"Your majesty…!" Wearing a great frown on her face. "You want a dress of mine…to wear?" she asked.

"Yes…I thought if I dressed as a servant, then took the wagon into the court yard, I could find out why the king has denied me audience."

Nichol added with a tearful eye.

"My lady, you would be taking a grave chance wondering about the city.

They don't want us here...you can't change that...wearing Jacqueline's silly old clothes."

"Silly...I was going to choose my best taffeta dress...thank you...a blue one..."

"Ladies, please...we must now put our heads together...it is no time for petty strife."

"You are right, your majesty...but I would like to be the one to go."

"Why...you wouldn't know what to say or do to pass the guards...do you speak any Spanish?" asked the queen.

"No...but I could wing it...maybe I could fine Ricardo, he would help me..."

"That seems a little risky to me..." said Margarete. "But maybe it's worth the risk we need some answers."

"Do you want me to give it a try or not? What other choices are there? Stay in Spain?"

"I don't think so," said Margarete. "I'm English through and through..."

"Do we try then...your majesty...everyone?" asked Jacqueline.

"We do indeed..." sighed Nichol, shaking her head no...at Jacqueline's blue taffeta dress.

"Let her go on your majesty...you are certainly in no condition to be riding about the country side. Besides Orin will need you when he awakens," said Margarete.

"All right then...Jacqueline do it...it's decided, but take some gold along...you may need to buy some information."

"Then what will you do for money to buy food?"

"We still have several more bags...remember the gold I was bringing for the king. I guess...I can use it to get to him after all."

"Okay...let's get her ready, Margarete," said Nichol...

"Right behind you..." replied Margarete.

So the ladies prepared Jacqueline for her tour of the city. Margarete took special care to fix her hair just so. Nichol helped fasten her, in her best blue taffeta dress. The queen walked in, and marveled at how beautiful Jacqueline's hair looked.

"Jacqueline, your hair looks wonderful...you ladies have done well."

Then she pulled her arms from behind her back, to show a stunning gown.

"But this...might well suit your purpose..."

"Ah...ah." They gasped, while they gazed upon a lavish gown of purple and gold.

"It's too much…my lady. They might mistake me for a queen in that dress," said Jacqueline.

"She's right, my queen…as much as I hate to admit she's right…" replied Nichol.

"Wait…perhaps instead of just being a servant of some sort…maybe one of those ladies of the court…you know that sit around all day watching the prince, waiting to be courted."

"Good thinking Margarete…" said Miria. "You see, when we put our heads together,

We can to anything."

"Yes, but can we teach her Spanish in a day?" asked Nichol. "I don't think so…"

"You've got to think of something else…"

"No, no, just wait…Give me half and hour…I'll be back…just wait," said Jacqueline.

Jacqueline went outside and got the horse and wagon ready. She took some gold along in her pocket, and headed north, as Ricardo had advised. She continued riding until she saw and old farm that seemed abandoned. When she approached the gate, a young girl ran out to meet her.

"Hello there!" said Jacqueline. "Do you speak any English?"

For a moment or two the girl said nothing, but looked Jacqueline over, up and down. Then she said.

"I speak some…but where did you come from?"

"Well…" answered Jacqueline, "I am a friend of Senior Ricardo. Do you know him?"

"Si…Ricardo? Sure, I know him. He comes here to buy chickens from my mother…but he has not been here in a while."

"Oh I see…"

"Are you looking for him…Senorita?"

"Actually…I'm looking for you."

"Me…Senorita…?"

"Si…My name is Jacqueline," she announced while she held out her hand.

"Oh…my name is Consuella Juanita Garcia…"

"Consuella…uh. That's a pretty."

"Si…I like it."

"Yes, well…I wonder if your mother wouldn't mind. You could ride with me and show me around your village…ah…I will pay you of course."

Jacqueline threw down three pieces of gold, and then stepped down off of the wagon.

"My mother will not mind she died over six years ago."

"You...you just told me your mother sold chickens too..."

Consuella cut her off saying.

"I'm sorry Senorita, but my brother said to tell every stranger the same thing, so they will not bother me while he is away."

"Your brother? What is his name...and where is he now? Jacqueline still puzzled.

"I don't know when he well return Senorita, but his name is Emil."

"Emil...that's a nice name too."

"Se, Emil...Ricardo Garcia.

"Your, Ricardo's sister?"

"I am Senorita..."

"Oh...I could kiss him!"

"I can not look, if you do that Senorita...just by a chicken instead."

"You wouldn't understand...but listen, how would you like to help me find your brother, and bring him some of these chickens to sell?"

"I don't know Senorita...Ricardo does not like me to leave the farm."

"He is my friend and I need to talk to him, so do you think you can be my friend too? I really need your help."

"Buenos...Senorita...ah..." Consuella, held out her hand, then said, "But first the gold, three pieces...you promised."

Jacqueline laughed, and then replied.

"I really look forward to our friendship...ha...ha...ha."

Consuella and Jacqueline loaded themselves onto the wagon, and headed to the cottage.

Once they got to the house, Jacqueline brought in her surprise. She opened the door, and then stepped away to reveal her new friend Consuella.

"Hello there!" said Jacqueline as she spun about the room. "Here is my idea."

"Well hello there," said Miria. "Where do you come from?"

Consuella was not at all sure of what to say, since she was not used to so many foreigners. She paced herself, and then replied.

"My name is Consuella...Senora...I am the sister of Ricardo."

Then Margarete said.

Oh yes...he was the one that backed out on dinner...right Jacqueline?"

"He had to be at the royal castle...something rather urgent, he said..."

"Oh I see…" said Nichol.

"Never mind him…my idea was to find someone who could speak Spanish, show me the way around the village. The reason I brought Consuella was just that. They own a chicken farm; they sometimes take them around for selling. Sometimes they go to the royal castle."

"Right…" marveled Miria. "That's a great idea…Do you think it will work?"

"I think it's got to be worth a try," said Nichol. "Don't you Margarete?"

"I'm ready to do what ever it takes to get back home."

So Jacqueline took down her hair, and put on a simpler dress. Miria gave her more gold to buy information. Then they headed for the city.

Consuella, stopped at a few places where she normally sold her chickens, and introduced Jacqueline, as a family friend. Consuella did not want Jacqueline to be looked upon as an outsider. They continued on their way, till they arrived at the gates. Soldiers guarded, while others they paced back and forth.

"Are they watching us…?" asked Jacqueline. "I mean…look at them."

"No Senorita…they stare into space like that to keep their concentration."

"Concentration…on what?"

"On…just standing still, I guess."

"Will they allow us go come in?"

"Let's try it," said Consuella. "Give me one of those chickens."

Consuella, got down off the wagon, and approached the guard holding a chicken in her hands.

"Hola, Senor…I am here to sell your cook a chicken for the king today…"

Then the guard glanced at the chicken, and back at Consuella. Then said.

"Is that the only thing you have for sell?"

"Well…no, I have some vegetables and some eggs as well…may we pass…my friend and I?"

"I really shouldn't Senorita…we have orders not to let the peasant through."

"Oh but Senor…we have these beautiful chickens that want to be used to please the king."

Then Jacqueline stepped down and started moving around the wagon, allowing the guard to get a better look at her. Then she asked Consuella.

"Consuella, are we to sell anything here today? The sun is hot…perhaps we should take our wagon elsewhere…"

"I don't know…this nice guard has not made up his mind."

"All right, all right," said the guard. "But hurry with your business, don't linger too long…I'll be waiting for you to come out."

"Si, Senor…we will hurry."

Once inside the gates, Jacqueline could not wait to start asking questions. But Consuella had to show her how to go about it.

"Wait…Senorita, Jacqueline…we must first go to the kitchen, there, no one will care about our business. If you show the people here your gold, they will think you are a spy. These people are used to plenty of gold…they might as soon have you arrested or something much worst. What do you want do know?"

"I want to know if they have heard anything about the Queen of England, or, of the negotiations with them. We were turned away from an audience with king Emanuel. I would like to know why."

"Okay, here…just follow me, and do not speak."

Jacqueline was willing to follow Consuella. She watched and listened, as Consuella talked to the servants. First, she brought the chickens to the cook…wagging them in her hand said.

"Hola…amigos. I have some beautiful vegetables and these lovely chickens for your king…"

"Oh!" said the cook "Hola…they look mucho Buenos…very good, I would like them very much my friend…"

"Buenos…they are very cheap…only one piece of silver."

"One piece for the two chickens Senorita?"

"Se…for them both Senor."

"Oh, then in that case I'll take them…ha…ah. The king will enjoy his meal tonight. I have a special recipe to prepare."

"Buenos, Senor…I heard he was having visitors from England…Have they arrived yet?"

The cook pulled Consuella to the side, and whispered in her ear.

"Don't speak so loudly, Senorita…the king has commanded no one help this queen, who was a traitor to her country. If anyone should be caught helping her…"

"Why…what would be so wrong in helping her. Did they have proof of this?"

"The cook looked around to see if anyone was listening, and then whispered.

"They say, that the queen had an affair with someone and became pregnant. Then she stole some documents, and sold them to the enemy…it was a very big deal here. But no one speaks of it now. They have to stay away from their country forever, and never return to their home again."

Just then Jacqueline spoke up and said.

"No! How can they do that…?"

"Who is your friend, Senorita? I am afraid she does not understand things around here."

"Oh no…" replied Consuella. "This is her first time out to sell the chickens…we always leave her at home…you know," said Consuella, while she pointed at the side of her head, and then added. "Just a little…"

"Oh I see…well maybe you should go now, and take your friend from the heat. Surely she will bring lots of trouble for you. Take your silver and go…"

"Thank you…thank you for your business…"

Then both Consuella, and Jacqueline paced themselves, as they moved out of the castle kitchen. Guards were everywhere, and no one was allowed to move freely about the place.

Jacqueline could not help but say just as soon as they were outside.

"Did you just tell that cook, that I was out of my head?"

"Sh…sh. Not so loud."

"Well…did you?"

"Yes…yes."

"Why…I…!"

"Listen, I only said you were a little loco…you know with the heat. Senorita…I told you not to speak. I did not want you to give us away."

"Well…I didn't think that was very nice."

"I am sorry Jacqueline…I only tried to help."

"You did fine my friend…I guess I got a bit upset when I heard the news. I can't believe someone would do a thing like that to the queen."

"You love your queen, yes…?"

"Of course, she is a wonderful person to serve."

"Si…she is very beautiful too…who would do this thing to her?"

"I can only guess…I have a pretty good idea who is behind the whole thing."

"It is a difficult thing to have happen…to be banished from your home."

"Let's get back to the cottage Consuella, I want to tell the queen as soon as possible."

"Si…Yo Comprendo Senorita…I understand"

When they arrived at the cottage, Jacqueline could not wait to tell the queen all that had happened. While Jacqueline was telling her story, Nichol began to cry.

The queen tried to reassure them that somehow they would get back to England. They all seemed to have felt it was hopeless.

The next week, Jacqueline contacted Ricardo. She wanted him to introduce her to Jon Bolene, one who trafficked in the black market. Jon Bolene would be able to book passage back to England for them on his ship the Tempest.

Ricardo took his time finding Mr. Bolene. It was defeated in the effort, for Bolene was willing to take only one person as passenger to England. He was filled up for months.

When Jacqueline heard this, she was dismayed. The problem would be, if only one person could go, queen Miria would have to leave Orin, and the rest of behind. Who then, would be the likely choice?

Now Jacqueline arrived back at the cottage very late that evening. She was anxious to share the information with Miria and the others. There was no doubt that any news would be welcomed news to the queen.

"Hello, Jacqueline," said Nichol. "We thought you had gotten lost or something."

"No. I went to see this man to get tickets for the voyage to England. He told me, he could take only one of us. I tried to impress upon him the importance of four going…but he simply shook his head no."

"Well…" said Miria, as she looked around the room. "I don't know who the one person would be…I mean, either one of you is worthy of going, and I don't want you to have to stay. I certainly cannot leave Orin…so that leaves me out. I just don't know"

"Well my lady…" said Margarete. "Let's just sleep on it…maybe we can come to a decision then."

"I don't see how…" added Nichol.

"Getting some rest…" yawned Jacqueline. "Sounds like a wonderful idea to me."

Then Margarete inquired.

"Where did this man say he would meet you? This person who is to sail?"

"Why?" asked Jacqueline. "I mean it's not like we're really going to be leaving."

"Oh…oh, I know…I was just wondering if it was close. You know whether you had to ride a great ways to get there…since you're so tired and all."

"Well it's not so far, if you know where you are going…but as you say, you were just curious."

"Yes…Right…"

The rooster crowed, and the sun rose high above the little village in La Vega Spain.

Miria called all the ladies together for breakfast.

"Ladies..." she said, smiling and holding Orin in her arms. "I thought long and hard about our plight last night. I know I could not take Orin...so we are out..."

"Are you thinking...my lady...one of us should go alone?"

"I was indeed...Nichol. Maybe the one who goes can contact lord Graybourne, and he in turn can send help somehow."

"Well," said Margarete. "Since it's just you and Orin being exiled, then we are all free to go back home...aren't we?"

"As your queen...you are still in my service."

"But my lady...you are no longer queen."

"Then let me say it this way Margarete. You were a servant to lord Graybourne, who was a servant of mine...He then imparted you to me to serve. So as it were, you are still a servant until such time as I release you from your servitude...Understood?"

"But of course your majesty...I only meant, it would be less trouble for you to have to worry about four, when it wasn't necessary. Besides I worked for lord Graybourne, and would be expected in his household."

"Then by all means Margarete...try your luck returning home...I release you from your obligation to me. In fact I release all of you...I do not want to make you stay in a land that you can not make your home."

"Your majesty..." said Nichol. "I have pledged my undying loyalty to you...And can not leave you now."

"Thank you Nichol...It is rare to find such loyalty...Now what of you Jacqueline?"

"I am leaning toward staying...I have plans of my own. But until they are complete, I would like to remain here with you, and Nichol."

"Hoping for a future with Ricardo...are we?"

"Yes, as a matter of fact, I do hope he and I can come together."

"Well...there you are Margarete...There stands no one in objection...so go..."

"Your majesty, are you upset with me?"

"Not at all Margatete...I realize you were trying to be loyal when you came along with me. I know you didn't sign on to leave all you knew in England to become exiled with me."

"I'm happy you understand your majesty..."

"The formality is no longer needed. You were correct...I am no longer queen."

"I know, my lady."

"Jacqueline...!" shouted Miria.

"Oui Madame..."

"Will you give me the half bag of gold please...?"

"But of course Madam."

"All right...Margarete...just take these gold pieces. Use them for your travel home. I would also like for you to take a letter to lord Graybourne if you don't mind."

"Sure...is it ready, my lady?"

"Yes...I hope you impress upon him the need we have to hear from him soon."

"Pardon, your majesty," said Jacqueline.

"What is it dear...?"

"Have him send it under an assumed name."

"What...?"

"If he sends it that way...no one would be the wiser."

"Wonderful thinking! What name then should I use?"

"How about using Consuella's name. She wouldn't mind. I know she will make sure you get the letter.

The next morning Jacqueline and Margarete set out for the ship. Jacqueline helped by driving the wagon. They drove for quite a ways, before spying some men standing next to their horses, in the middle of the road. They yelled out.

"Woo...ooh there...!" One of the men jumped in from of the wagon, and bided it to stop.

Then he said with a coarse voice.

"Buenos Dias Senoritas...my name is Raphael, and this scurvy gentleman is...Pablo. We are here to take you to meet Senor Romano..."

Without hesitating Jacqueline spoke up and shouted.

"Aren't you the men from the black market? I mean...the ones' who should have taken me to England...Monsieur?"

Then the men looked at each other and began to laugh. Then Raphael said.

"Senoritas...we must hurry. Senor Romano is waiting for us."

"Oh...and who is Senor Romano?" asked Jacqueline. "I have never heard of him."

"Why he is a famous desperado in all Spain, se...ha...ha...ha..." Their great fat bellies giggled as they all laughed and laughed. The three men found it so funny, that we did not know who Senor Romano was.

Then Margarete spoke out and said.

"So...you expect us to go with you quietly...to see someone named Romano. Someone of whom we have never met?"

Jacqueline tried to get the wagon moving, but the men had a good grip on the reigns.

"Please...let us go, we don't know anyone named Romano, nor do we want to go with you...!" yelled Jacqueline.

The men grabbed them, as they squirmed. The more the ladies moved, the tighter the men held on to them. Suddenly Jacqueline broke free, them jumped on the back of the man who held Margarete. She was then able to get a loose.

"Run...run Margarete!" Jacqueline screamed. "Run as fast as you can!"

"What about you...?" said Margarete, as she pulled up her dress and took flight.

"Just keep running north...Margarete."

"North? Where are you? Please hurry Jacqueline...!"

"I'm right behind you..." answered Jacqueline. "But I'm going to get our wagon...they'll have to kill me to keep it.

The other two men ran steadily behind Margarete, while Raphael slapped Jacqueline to the ground.

"Is this how you Spaniards treat your women...?" said Jacqueline, while she rubbed her face. "To slap a women is a sign of weakness Monsieur..."

"Just get up...and close your mouth...!"

"Sure..." she said, while she held out her hand for his assistance. "I'll be happy to get up...!"

Then she kneed him in the groan, picked up a rock from the ground on which she fell, and hit him on the head. Raphael drew up into a big ball, he did not know what to grab first. He backed a way from her, and fell toward the ground. That was her perfect opportunity. She jumped aboard the wagon and took off, heading straight for Margarete.

Jacqueline drove the wagon hard. She tried to run down the men chasing Margarete.

"Help!" shouted Margarete. "Get them off me...!"

Jacqueline pulled a big stick from one of the nearby tree branches, and started hitting the men.

"Stop! Get off her you idiots...!" Jacqueline continued to hit them, then said.

"Margarete…go on…get on the wagon…hurry, they won't stay down long…go!"

Margarete stopped kicking long enough to get on the wagon.

Then they saw Raphael running toward them.

"Let's get away from here…Hi…ye…" Pulling the reigns to turn the horses. She began to drive the horses. Then a voice echoed out.

"I'll see to it, you'll never leave Spain alive…mark what I say…!"

He shouted still running to catch the wagon. Jacqueline in such a panic drove the horses so hard she did not take care to see the direction she took. As it began to darken, Jacqueline did not recognize where they were.

Margarete watched to make sure they were not being followed.

"What…Do you still see them Margarete?"

"No…I think we've lost them for now…"

"Judging by your expression, Jacqueline…maybe we're lost…ah?"

"I'm not sure…I thought when I passed that row of large oak trees…we were headed north…"

"Yes…" said Margarete. "…But if we left the cottage heading north, then to get back we should…" Before she could finish Jacqueline joined in unison.

"…Be going south."

They stared at their surroundings, and then Margarete said.

"I'm afraid…what did those men want with us."

"Well…My guess would be to rob, rape, trade or kill. Take your pick…neither is something I'd find fitting. I'm just glad we were able to fight them off," said Jacqueline.

"Yes…this time. I don't think I had time back there to say thank you…for your help."

"Forget it…you would have done the same for me…I'm sure…"

Suddenly they fell upon a row of mature trees, and then Jacqueline stopped the wagon again.

"Hold the reigns Margarete…"

"What are you trying to do…?"

"I…am…going to climb the tree here…"

"What! No Jacqueline…"

"I need to take a look, and see if I can tell what direction we're going."

"Like what, for pity's sake?"

"Well…like the palace for one thing…some sign I can recognize."

"The palace…you've seen the palace?"

"Yes…If I see some sign of it…I'll know what direction we will need to take."

"Be careful Jacqueline..."

"If I spot the palace...I know that direction is north, and I'll go the opposite."

"Just hold it steady Margarete..."

"Do you see anything familiar...yet?"

"I...I don't see anything just yet..."

"Keep looking Jacqueline, you're bound to see something, but hurry before those men decide to follow."

"Right...Wait...I think I see..."

"What? Do you see it Jacqueline?"

"Yes...yes...!" said Margarete. "Now we can leave this awful place."

"Yes...I see the tip of the flag."

"Great...now hurry and get down..."

"All right...hold the horses still...now let's get out of here, and go that way."

Jacqueline found the direction and proceeded south. When she had gone yet a ways, she realized she was close to Consuella's farm. It seemed they were lost forever, to have been so close to a friend. When she stopped the wagon, she got down and knocked on the door.

"Consuella...Consuella...Are you there?"

"Maybe she's asleep..."

"No this time of the day...Usually she's tending her chickens."

Jacqueline walked about the farm, looked all around, and then went to a window and peered in.

"I know something is wrong. She's always about."

"Well...maybe today she left...for some reason."

But Jacqueline continued to call out.

"Consuella...It's me...Senorita Jacqueline...Do you hear me?"

"I don't think she does..." remarked Margarete.

"I'll just go in..." growled Jacqueline, and then forced her way through the front door.

"Wait...!" said Margarete. "You just can't go barging into someone's home like that..."

"Sh...quiet Margarete...I want to think..." Then she braced herself against the door. "Oh...no!" she screamed, while she looked down on Consuella, who lie there, by the side of the table, on the cold hard wooden floor.

"I wonder how long she's been laying there...like this?" said Margarete.

Jacqueline pushed over a chair, trying to get to Consuella.

"My goodness!" said Margarete. "What has happened to the poor girl?"

"I don't know…" Jacqueline answered, with a look of pain on her face.

"Who would have done this…?" She raised Consuella's head in her arms. "Can you hear me…? Consuella…please open your eyes…"

"I'll get a cloth and some water…poor girl. I wonder how long she's been laying here?"

"Hurry…Margarete!"

Margarete rushed to get the things they needed, and back again. She noticed that Consuella was holding something.

"Take a peek Jacqueline. She's holding some paper or something in her hand…"

"I see…we'll get to that. Let's just see if she'll breath…Consuella, just breath."

"It doesn't look as if she's going to…"

"No…she is breathing…its just very shallow, that's all."

Then Margarete wiped Consuella's face and hands with cold water, it, began her revival. She slowly started turning her head, moaning and groaning.

"Consuella…" she called out. "It is I…Senorita Jacqueline…can you hear me…See me now?"

Consuella nodded her head. Then closed her eyes again.

"Consuela…please!" said Jacqueline. "Can you tell us what happened…?"

"No…n…o," she replied in a whispery voice, as if her voice had left her. "Give me a moment please."

"Good…Maybe the water is helping…"

"I'm sure Margarete…She has begun to stir a little."

"You know Jacqueline…I haven't thanked you for the help you gave me…you saved my life back there in the woods…I will always be grateful."

"It's no big deal. Besides, you did thank me. We both were running and fighting for our lives…who knows, you may have saved me by just running. Let's just call it even."

"I don't want to make too much of it, but I feel quite strongly about it."

Consuella spoke up, as the two of them were talking.

"I wasn't so lucky…they broke in on me early this morning…"

"Consuella, who did this?" Margarete asked. "What did they look like?"

"One of them was called Raphael…he's the one that hurt me, the others stole the food."

"That rotten…! He's going to pay someday!" said Jacqueline.

"I managed to pull this letter from his pocket, when I tried to fight him off. I just clung to it as if it would give me life…"

"Con…suella…" said Jacqueline, dragging out her name.

"Funny…I don't even know what it says…"

"Take it Margarete…"

"Mademoiselle, I have a thought, since Consuella is recovering, why don't I just stay here with her until she is better…sort of help out around here."

"Well Consuella…what do you think about that…?"

"I think I would like that very much Senorita," said Consuella. "I could use the company right now…thank the both of you…"

"Now…let me see what is in the letter."

"Take it, I want to know as well…"

Jacqueline read the letter silently.

"Jacqueline…come on now tell us what it says." Shouted Margarete.

"Oh…it says something about a Prince visiting Spain next week…I can't tell anymore."

"Well, that nothing that concerns us," said Margarete.

"Are you not aware…prince Michael and queen Miria grew up together…I mean in the same household. What if it's him?"

"What will that do for her now?" Consuella asked.

"For one thing. He will recognize her, and maybe help her get to France."

"I don't see anyone helping an exiled…oh no…"

"…And for another," said Jacqueline, with a frown on her face. "He could also get word to lord Graybourne…or even give her money to help with Orin…I don't know…"

"Then, Senorita, how will she get to him…so he can do all this helping…?"

"Well…that's a good question, but I'm certain we will find a way to make it happen."

"Then let's go show her the note…" yelled Margarete.

"No…remember, you're to stay with Consuella…I'll come back and let you know what had been concluded…Margarete…just stay close, and lock the doors for now…"

"Do you think those men will return…?" asked Consuella, while Margarete looked rather strained, shrugging her shoulders.

"No, dear…I think they are long gone…Oh, I don't think they would dare return here again. You should have seen the way Mademoiselle Jacqueline, handled those men. She gave that Raphael a run for his money…and a little pain to boot. I don't think he will be beating anyone else for a while…at least not this day," said Margarete, with a big smile on her face. "She gave him a big pain in his little brain…ha…ha…"

"I was lucky…we were lucky to have gotten away with just a few bruises…I thank God it was not worst. No telling what they would have done, if we did not have our wits about us…And it was a great advantage to be out side, it gave us space to run…"

"Well…I'm just glad it's over…"

"Do you think that they were the same men who came here?"

"It makes me think yes…Mademoiselle…when you said you heard them call him Raphael. That is the same name as the man who attacked us."

"I'm glad…Senorita Jacqueline, you gave him the big boot…"

"So am I Consuella…" Jacqueline replied, "So am I…"

"How soon before you leave for the cottage?"

"I guess I should leave now…and make my way before midnight."

"Be very careful…it's no telling what's out there," said Margarete. "Tell my lady I'll see her tomorrow."

"Yes…I'll let her know where you are…just take care of my little friend here…and I'll see you both tomorrow.

Jacqueline took the wagon and headed straight for the cottage. She was certain that the message would aid the queen.

She busted through the doors.

"Where is the queen…?"

Nichol tried to silence her.

"Listen…you'll wake Orin…sh, sh…"

"Where is she…it's important, she will want to know this."?

"Yes…but does she have to know it now…? And so loudly…?"

"I think this will make her afternoon a little bit brighter." Smiled Jacqueline.

Miria walked into the room as they started talking, and then asked.

"What is all the commotion about…?"

"Your majesty…I have news…"

"What is it Jacqueline…did Margarete get off safely?"

"Oh…no, I'll tell you about that in a moment…your majesty…look. You must read this!" Jacqueline, much to excited, could not wait to see Miria's reaction.

"What is this, Jacqueline…?" While the queen was reading the letter,

Jacqueline started clapping her hands, and spinning around.

"Oh...Michael airs...maybe it's him...prince Michael!!!" said Miria, bursting at the seams with joy.

"I can't believe this...what fortune...the prince and I played together as children!"

"Yes, my lady...!" answered Nichol. "...But how will we get to him your majesty?"

Then just as suddenly, the happiness, faded. Miria responded and said.

"We will go to the palace, and stand with the crowd...Then when he comes passed us, I will yell out his name."

"But won't there be...too much shouting to even hear?" asked Nichol.

"Oh...it brings back such memories..."

"Did the two of you play games together?" asked Jacqueline.

"Why yes...this one game, where we would hide from each other. I'd say Michael...Michael airs, and then he'd say he's caught up in the devils snare. Then he would try his best to find me...ha...ha. I always bet him at that game."

"That sounds like such fun."

"It was indeed, Michael always had a hard time finding me."

Then the queen seemed to have faded into a deep thought for a moment.

"My lady, are you alright?" asked Nichol.

"I was just thinking, Michael never got over my marriage to Lyonus. He never acknowledged me after that."

"Well..." said Jacqueline. "I hope he'll spot you this time...if it is him."

"So do I...my friend...So do I."

"Oh, my lady, Margarete stayed with Consuella tonight. She was attacked by some hombres today..."

"Hombres?" said Nichol.

"Yes, as a matter of fact so were we...but Margarete and I were pretty much

Unharmed, but poor Consuella was beaten..."

"No...what kind of man does something like that?" said Nichol. "I knew something wasn't right when you came in the door...I could tell."

"I'm all right, I just hope Consuella will be okay."

"Um...Margarete has done a good thing, having stayed to care for her...I feel better about her now," said Miria, as she shook her head at the whole thing.

"I think it will be okay...I just wish I had gotten there before they did…maybe I could have done something to help her."

"Now you can't blame yourself…" said the queen. "Men like that are born for one purpose…"

"…And what is that my lady?"

"Well…to help create better ways to hang them, of course…"

"Ha…I guess you have a point there, my lady."

Jacqueline checked on Margarete and Consuella everyday, to make sure they were okay.

Ricardo was quite pleased that she had shown such love and interest toward his sister.

One day Ricardo confided in Jacqueline.

"My dear Senorita…" said Ricardo. "I find much pleasure in the things you do for me and Consuella."

"Do you Monsieur?"

"I feel somehow, I should repay your kindness…"

"Oh no Monsieur…Senor. No payment is necessary. Consuella and I are good friends now…there is no need to repay an act of friendship…that is what friends do. Can you not agree?"

"I agree Senorita…"

Jacqueline, smiled at Ricardo, and then said.

"Please call me Jacqueline…I would like that."

"Well Jacqueline…perhaps we could…it would be easier for us to get to know each other, if you moved closer to the palace."

"Oh…I'm afraid that would be impossible right now."

"Impossible for a wife…?"

"Wife…Senor?"

"Yes Jacqueline…I want you to be my wife."

Jacqueline gasped, and blushed till her cheeks turned apple red.

"Ricardo…we barely know each other…I'm not sure about this…"

"What is it to know…I think you care for me…no?"

"Of course…I mean I don't even know what you do at the palace…or anything. Ricardo, my feelings are because of the way you have run off into the night. I'm not at all sure what that means."

"Listen…I have much work to do each day. Sometimes, I don't get home to check on Consuella but once a week. My duties keep me constantly at the palace."

"You see…that's what I mean. I know you're at the palace but doing what?"

"All right...I am Senor Ochoa's right hand man. He is the Governor of Spain. Senor Ochoa travels a lot, and I am by his side everywhere he goes."

"Oh like a body guard then...you are a soldier?"

"I am..."

"Then why did you not just say? I would have understood."

"I have been working to leave the service of Senor Ochoa...He promised me if I found someone he could trust...someone as good as I was, that he would release me, and give me an estate that I have been admiring for a while...That is if I wed."

"Do you honestly believe he will allow you to leave his service, knowing all that you know about him?"

"He gave his word...if I found the right man."

"If you can not find such a person...then what of your wife to be?"

"I will find a way to do this...if she would consent."

"I will find it difficult to leave my friends...the queen, and Nichol."

"No...my dear...do not speak of her aloud...it is far too dangerous."

"I am not asking you to leave them...only that you join with me."

"Just...I'm not so convinced, Ricardo."

"Believe me Senorita...I am trying very hard to express my feelings for you. I am not often in a situation with Senoritas, where I am free to speak my thoughts...but with you I feel very comfortable to do so."

"That's very flattering Ricardo. I...I'll need to think about it for a few days."

Understandable my dear...It will give me time to choose another soldier for Senor Ochoa...and you time to convince your friends, that I am the right man for you...ha...ha."

A week had passed, and the arrival of prince Michael was at hand.

Miria, and Orin Nichol and Jacqueline, prepared themselves to go to the royal courtyard.

They were dressed to meet a king, but in hopes of meeting a prince.

When they arrived at the courtyard, it was filled with all the neighboring villagers. People gathered from all over to get a glimpse of the prince. Miria and the others were unable to move in closer because of the press. As prince Michael approached trotting on his steed, the crowd cheered loudly. The roar was so loud it started Orin to cry. Miria made her way closer into the crowd, to see if she could make him hear.

She began to call out. "Michael...Michael airs..."

The Prince seemed to have heard something for he paused to see if he could hear his name. When he stopped, the crowd yelled all the more. They drowned out poor Miria.

She continued to shout out his name, but each time it was swallowed by deepening voices. However the prince still looked as if he heard his name. For his eyes searched the crowd, as if he was searched for a priceless object that would never be found. Finally the group gave up. The prince had made it into the palace itself, a place neither of them was permitted. Saddened by the course of events, Miria took Orin and the ladies back to the cottage.

"Well…you tried my lady…you really did."

"Yes…well it didn't do any good now did it?"

"No…your majesty…"

"I told you Nichol, you don't have to continue calling me that!" Miria was more than a little upset when she shouted. "I'm no longer queen…not of anything…so just don't…please."

"Yes…my lady." Replied Nichol. "I did not mean to upset you further."

"Oh…I'm sorry…it's not at all your fault…it was that…lord Guy and those advisors I trusted. They are the ones I suppose I'm truly angry with…I'm sorry"

When they returned to the cottage, Jacqueline broke the news of her marriage to Ricardo

"Well…finally a note of cheer…" said Miria. "Bring in some wine then Nichol…let's celebrate."

"I haven't given my answer as of yet my lady."

"Why not? She asked while she paused to pour a drink, and then said. "It's not everyday a girl meets a fine gentleman like that."

"Ho…oh…well, let's see now…" said Nichol. "I bet he's just dying to hear your answer."

"He said I had time to decide…I really think I would be happy with him…my lady."

"Then by all means…go, go…I will not be accused of standing in the way of true love."

"My lady…" Jacqueline blushed like a little girl.

"Remember what I said to you on the carriage ride, back home in England…about when true love comes?"

"Yes…I think I do…"

"Well, it has found you…and you can not turn your back on love…for if you do…it may leave, and who knows if it will ever find it's way again."

"I will tell him yes…Yes…!"

"Good! Now let's drink to happy days ahead for true love."

"To happy days..." They cheered, as they clanked their goblets together in a final toast to Jacqueline.

It had become quite clear to Miria at this time, that Louise and lord Guy, had finally gotten their wish, they were now rid of the only people that could destroy their chances to rule England.

Miria and Nichol were destined to struggle. They tried as best they could, to raise Orin.

All that was left of her fortune was a few bags of gold and a few jewels that she wore.

Miria found herself wondering if Orin would be loving, and caring, or vindictive in spirit as lord Guy and the other buffoons at England's court. Five years had passed, since they were exiled to La Vega Spain. Miria sold everything she could to send Orin to school. Her desire for him was that he be educated in the protocol with the Spanish courts.

They sought the help of black marketers, to purchase papers and a new name that could not be traced by the people of Spain. Under his assumed name of William Lancaster III, grandson of the second Earl of Somerset, he would enter school.

CHAPTER ELEVEN
Luis Finds True Love

Meanwhile back in England, the now-king Luis, felt in total control. And why shouldn't he? After all, he plotted to kill his brother, the true king. Then he accused the queen of adultery, and treason, then exiled her along with her son and heir. All, while having the ministers buy into it. Consequently, Luis took measures to remove anyone who opposed his will.

Finally, he called together the fairest maidens in the land to a mask. Luis thought he might find a wife, and in his attempt, the servant girl. Kira caught his fancy.

During the mask Kira, began to pour wine for the king. He started to kiss and whisper in her ear.

"My sweet, you are a tiny morsel, and a cool sip of drink…I should like to sip of your cup this night."

"What? Why your majesty…I am but a servant, there could be nothing fine in me for my lord." Kira tried to remove herself from Luis, but he remained persistent.

"My dear…" said the king, with his goblet held high. "Pour the wine my dear, and we shall drink together of the wine of love tonight…"

"No my lord! Please…I can not do such a thing…!"

"Why…don't worry my sweet, you shall come back…let us say…a bit less wanting."

"Can my lord not see…what is truly in front of him?"

"And what is that my dear?"

"Why…it's the fair ladies in the land, they long to spend just one night with you…to measure their lust."
"…And what about you?"
"I am waiting for the man who desires me for life, not merely for lust."
"Ha…ha…ha." Laughed Luis. "You think there is such a man in England…in the world?"
"I think there is a man somewhere for me, who would care enough to take me from this life."
"Do you think a life here in the palace is a life unworthy of you?"
"I think to share a bed with a man that does not love me is a sin before God…"
"Ah…I see you are a religious beauty. Is that how you hide yourself…?"
"What do you mean sire?"
"You protect yourself from love, hiding behind God…?"
"Perhaps my lord can not understand the meaning of real love, nor God."
"You speak to your king in this manner?"
"Forgive me your majesty…I merely wanted you to understand why I…"
Before Kira finished, the king asked.
"Could you teach me?"
Kira turned to look in the eyes of the king.
"What…you want me to teach you love?"
"No my dear…but how to love."
"…But sire, I can not teach such a thing…I would not know where to begin."
"We could start from the beginning…could we not…?"
"My lord…this thing you ask…it is, impossible…love comes from the heart sire!"
"Not if I were to give you this…?"
The king handed Kira a silver chain he wore around his neck, with a pendent of leaves layered in gold, and surrounded by rubies.
"It's beautiful…but I could not take it…"
"No I insist you take it. It is my payment to you."
"Now…do you see sire, that is your first mistake."
"Mistake…?"
"Yes…you can not purchase love, it is not for sale…and if you find your self selling such a commodity, it was not really true and you were not worthy of it. Do you understand?"
"I think I see your meaning. Then will you consider it a gift from a friend?" asked Luis.

"I tell you what...look carefully at the maiden in the purple gown. Do you see her, the beauty that is smiling at you now...?"

"Ah yes...I see her quite clearly, she is lovely."

"Good! She is not right for you, she does not love you, and she lusts. She is here only to seek comfort for her old age, or what trinket you might impart to her."

"Are you quite sure..."?

"I would wager your necklace sire, that her heart would not be true. Watch how she also stares at Lord Biltfry."

"I see your meaning. Kira, come to me tonight, and teach me more about the subject..."

The king took back his hand from her, and then said. "On my oath, I will not demand from you anything you are not willing to give...agreed?" Kira reasoned within herself for a moment and then said. "Agreed...I will trust you my lord."

"Very well then, I shall expect you after the masque."

So king Luis and Kira, shared many days of afternoon horseback riding, and moonlit strolls. Luis was indeed leaning about love between two people.

Kira said to Luis, as they stood and watched the sun come up.

"My king..."

"Hum...?"

"Have you ever wondered about the power of the sun, and how...just as the moon, our eyes are drawn to it...?"

"Right here, and now...I am captivated by your beauty. The only power I want to see now is the power of your kiss."

The king spun her around and kissed her, and she returned his kiss.

Now, Kira has taught Luis the value of shared love. He understands now that there is more to being a man that simply having power to be king.

"Luis..." she whispered. "I should like to see that again." Then they both shared a smile. King Luis had finally found someone who could return his love.

Kira showed Luis what being in love could mean. The king had decided to ask Kira to be his queen when he returned from his trip.

Then on that day, while the king was away, lord Guy paid a visit to her chambers, as she bathed.

"Young lady..." he remarked, as he pushed himself in the door. "I'm sorry to intrude on your bath."

"Then why do you sir?" she exclaimed. Kira's attendants gasped.

"Well...what are you waiting for?" yelled lord Guy. Leave us."

"Sir…?" questioned one servant.

"I need to speak with my lady privately." Then Kira became outraged and replied.

"Go…get out!" she shrilled, pointing to the heavy wooden door and shouted to her attendants. "I…said…out! Everybody out!"

"I hope you didn't include me in your little tantrum."

"I beg your pardon sir!" said Kira, still trembling.

"Oh…you beg my pardon do you…? Ha…" Lord Guy smirked. "I see the king has taught you proper manners. And what else has my lord taught…ah?"

"Can you not see sir, I am trying to bathe…?"

"Oh…that I can see quite well, my dear. You are rather lovely…but nothing I haven't seen before."

"Well…" She stuttered, trying to cover herself. "What is it you want of me?"

"Ha…what a question my dear…why the same thing as any other man…" Stepping closer to stroke her hair.

"My lord king should be returning shortly. Perhaps you should leave, the king does not have to know you were here."

"Then…do you think I fear your king?"

"My lord. I know nothing of you, or your wants."

"Oh…but you do know what I want?"

"…And that is sir…?" she asked, and then turned her body while she tried to move closer to the door.

Lord Guy reached to grab her then said.

"Why…to be taught of love. Ha…ha…ha…I hear you are a great teacher…so teach!" Then placed his hand over her mouth, and flung her to the bed.

"My lord please…no!!" Then she jumped up, and started for the door.

"Come back here winch…! I will not have you interfere with my plans! I will however see you dead first…!"

Kira gave a chase around the room. She turned over lamp stands and chairs to block his path. Subsequently she was subdued.

Lord Guy leaped on top of her and pulled her arms over her head. Suddenly Kira, raised her knees, and gave him a blow to the groin. She rolled over and tried to run for the door, all the while screaming for help. But no one dared interfere. Then Lord Guy stood her up, and slapped her several times, so hard in fact, that she fell and hit her head on the tub. He shook her for a moment, and then realized she was not moving. Then he said aloud. "What is the death of one servant, to me…?"

He wrapped her in a sheet, and called for the guard Evan.
"Yes, my lord..."
"Evan, I need you to take care of our problem..."
"Our problem sir...?"
"Come in my friend. There is too much at stake here, for me to call on just any one. I know I can trust you," he said, as he wiped his face with his sleeve.
"Why...certainly sir," said Evan, who looked somewhat confused.
"Good..." said Guy, looking over at the silver chain. "Here...a little something for your silence."
"My lord Guy, that belongs to the king, I'd rather not be caught with it..."
"Ah...a smart man. I knew I chose the right person for the job," said lord Guy as he threw the chain to the floor.
"What would you have me do?"
"Take the body, and bury it where neither man, nor beast can find it. Do you get my meaning?"
"Perfectly."
"Then take this..." Guy reached into his pocket and handed him a bag of coins. "Just for your trouble...as a friend...of course."
"Thank you my lord." Evan picked up the body, and then lord Guy held his arm and said. "Your word of silence...or it will be the last you shall ever say."
"I understand...my lord, on my word."
"Good...now go, and for God sakes keep quiet."
Evan grunted, as if the body was too heavy for him to carry.
Lord guy stayed behind, to clean up the mess. Then he called in her attendants and said.
"If the king should inquire...and he will...you will say, our mistress...left with a stranger, but left a note.
When the king returned, he headed straight for Kira' room.
"Open the door, my love. It is your king. I have a great present for you...please don't make a beggar of me."
Finally, the king just opened the door. Both her attendants stood shivering.
"Why did you not answer the door...are you deaf as well as dumb?"
The king looked around a second then asked. "Where is she...Kira? Is she here?"
"No sire..." replied one. "She has gone, and left you this note."
"A note...left me, the king...a note!"
Then the king read the letter.
My lord, I can no longer stand this prison, royal or otherwise. I have

sought my freedom. Please do not try and find me, I should not want to be found, Kira."

Luis shouted. "No! She can not mean this...!" Then looked over at the attendants, with pity in their eyes...and dropped the letter to the floor, then commanded with a fury. "Burn everything that remains, I should not see these things again..."

Then slowly hung his head, and closed the door.

Then lord Guy presented his amends. He found a woman named Elaine. She resembled Kira in some ways; lord Guy thought she could replace her.

"Your majesty...there is a winch outside your door, just waiting to warm your bed."

"Oh..." remarked Luis. "And what is that to me?"

"My king, you can not punish yourself, because of the actions of one servant."

"Kira was more than a servant..."

"Your majesty...surely you don't suggest that you would have married that girl?"

"I most certainly do! What do you know of it? For years I've watched lady Kathryn's rejection of you, and not once have you made an attempt to marry anyone."

"Sire...you would make a whore a queen...you can't mean that...my liege...!

"I mean to...if I should find her..."

"This is ridiculous...!"

"Silence...I want to hear no more of her."

"Certainly sire, that is why I have asked the beautiful Elaine to comfort you tonight." Lord Guy beckoned her to enter.

"Come in my dear. The king needs cheering up."

Luis looked up at her, thought for a second it was Kira. Then lord Guy closed the door, supposing he was successful.

"Kira...?" called the king. "By all accounts, you resemble her." Then she spoke. And her voice, brash and coarse, was neither soft, nor comforting, as was Kira'

Then Elaine found herself in a tight.

"No, leave me!" the king commanded. "Guard, take her away!"

"Your majesty?" the guard questioned. "To the dungeon, until she rots...I care not."

She was imprisoned, and left to rot, according to the king.

Not long after, king Luis began to have dreams of Lyonus and Kira. They were sometimes so frightening; he would go days without sleep. It seemed he was being driven a little more insane, with each sunset.

So to help him forget, the ministers found another course of action, the Lady Anne Rochelle.

Ann was the daughter of an Italian noble. Of course, Luis forced the hand of Nathan Rochelle, to become an alley, and took the hand of Anne.

After a few years, Anne announced a royal heir to the throne.

This, however was not, nor ever could be in the plan for lord Guy. He was determined to stop this birth in any way possible.

"This will never be!" said Guy.

"Oh please my lord, you have been trying for years to sit on the throne…Frankly I've grown tired of your scheming. Can you not now just resign yourself to being a nobleman…a very rich nobleman I might add…my lord?"

Then he said to lord Westmoreland.

"Now you listen to me!" Moving closer to Westmoreland, pointing his finger. "No other heirs will deprive me of my opportunity again. I'm tired of waiting for what is due me.

"Then if you are determined…perhaps, we can find a way."

"…As I have always said my friend, the man who controls the army…should be king."

"Hum…" remarked Westmoreland, with a grin on his face.

CHAPTER TWELVE
The Truth Discovered

During the years that ford ahead, king Luis thought himself free. But Lyonus II had found himself still a captive of the past. For Lyonus, the days had become weeks, and the week's years. Finally he was forced to make a move.

As he became closer to Constance, Simon and Hannah, it became apparent who the loves of his future would be. It was the lost loves of the past that still haunted him.

He thought his memory would never fully return, until he tested the waters, sort-to-speak.

As the years continued to pass, Lyonus (Jonathan) had begun to see images and places in his dreams. He thought of names, but could not sort them out, shadows of faces that he could not recognize.

Yet one more thing unknowing to Lyonus, that would soon became a stumbling block. Ann and Luis were now expecting a child, another heir to the throne.

So one day in this world wind of thoughts and dreams, Constance found his things all packed.

"Jonathan…what are you doing?"

"Now Constance…it is a little difficult to explain."

"No!" shouted Constance. "There's no reason for this…no!"

"Wait now…listen Constance…I owe you and your father everything. I owe you my life…my very soul. You saved me from only God knows what."

"…But…"

"No, no my love, you've sheltered me here for so many years. During that time, I've only taken from you all. If there is to be a future for you and I...I must find some answers to my past."

Constance continued to cry sorely.

Lyonus tried hard to break it gently.

"You said that Jacob would help me when it was time...and now it's time."

"You can't..."

"Constance, I know you like the back of my hand...and I feel this is the only way that I can keep from loosing you too. Please don't cry...Am I worth your tears?"

"Oh? Hum...what makes you think my tears are for you...I cry now for having meet you."

"My love, if I say I care as much for you now as anyone, it would not be a lie."

"Then why...why now?"

"Because I'm a prisoner of my own past."

"But Jonathan...you can not say I'm the only one you love!"

"You have said it...this very moment I can not say but don't you see, that is precisely why I have to go."

"All right then, let me help! I can...I can help you, just don't leave."

"Listen my love, remember when you said we were in mortal danger from the people who tried to kill me?"

"Of course..."

"...And that the rest of your family were in danger as well."

"Yes, and if you start asking questions, that will only resurface the killers."

"So?"

"I plan to disguise myself, and maybe work with Jacob a while...He can help me get around here and there to pick up bits and pieces. By mingling, maybe something would click, or someone would draw a picture for me, I don't know..."

Constance had heard enough. She went barreling out the room and onto the porch, straight into the arms of Hannah.

"Connie...What...why are you crying?"

Constance crying so hard she could not see. She only shook her head.

"Oh, I see. Our somewhat restless friend must be ready to leave."

Constance slowly stopped the fierce tears that flowed from her eyes, and then Hannah continued.

"Here me my child." Hannah placed her hand at Constance's face, and with a gentle smile said. "If your love is strong enough, and it is meant to be, there is no power on earth that can keep him away. You need not seek for it, he shall return...and find you.

Do you hear me Connie...?"

"I do Hannah, and I believe what you say, because I love him so much. It just has to be true."

Now as Jonathan (Lyonus) said his goodbye to Simon, they walked out onto the grounds.

There stood both Constance and Hannah, who had finished their talk.

"Good-bye Hannah. I'll never forget what you have done for me..."

"Oh...! Are you sure? Everyone laughed. That was Hannah's way of breaking the tension. She gave him a hug and kiss goodbye.

"That's right..." added Constance, and laughed harder.

"Well you've forgotten things before you know..."

Then Jonathan grabbed Constance and kissed her lips with a sense of urgency, then said.

"Farewell...till next we meet...if it is right that we should do so..."

Jonathan walked away with his head wagging. Just then Constance yelled out to him.

"Wait a moment!" Then with a voice as if she needed to swallow, said.

"I can't let you go like that."

"No Constance we're not going through that again..."

"What?"

"Well what do you mean...?"

Constance walked over to the stable, and brought out her favorite horse.

"Here you are, take my horse Romania. Oh, and Jonathan, your real name is Lyonus II, true king of England. That is the name that almost got you killed, so don't go spreading that about..."

Lyonus walked closer to Constance, and said in a voice that was very shallow, as if just for the two of them.

"I treasure the time we've spent together. If I am king again, I should like for you to sit by my side as my queen. There, I am certain would never be a tedious moment."

Constance placed her fingers over his lips to hush him, then said.

"Don't Lyonus...it's okay. I feel all right about this. You'll return to me someday, I know it. You'll come back, and when you do, you will know who you are, and what you want...and it will be me."

"I'm loving you now, this very second Constance, and that is what I know."

Then grabbing up his bag said.

"Jonathan (Lyonus), take your bag with you, it's important. Jacob Corley, will help explain the things inside."

"All right, and thank you."

Simon walked up and slapped Romania on the rear to move her along, then said.

"God speed…Lyonus king of England…safe journey!"

They all waved farewell to Jonathan, until they could see, only his lean silhouette against the tall shade filled trees. The trees themselves seemed, to wave a long farewell to him.

"Father…" called Constance, as she dropped her head and wiped her tears away.

"It is for you as well, that he leaves my dear…"

"You mean instead of staying on, and never trying to relive those days, when he had the world at his feet, and be with just me, with only dirt at his feet…?"

"It is for you, because he truly loves you, not the king, but the man. He needs to sort out that love, to accept it. He must return to the past, to remove anything that will spoil once again his chance of happiness. Surely Constance, you above all people, can understand that. My dear Constance…you should believe in his return."

"Finding his way will be difficult, father."

"Let's just hope for now, he stays alive long enough to realize who he is. That boy is king…!"

"…Hum…I suppose you're right father, and remarkable he is, as well as king…"

"Surely my dear, you have chosen well…well indeed."

Jonathan (Lyonus) rode steadily onward toward Jacob Corley's farm. Jacob, who would keep him, and help him find his way back to the throne, would have no clue, of what was about to change his life forever.

He rode until dark and finally approached the house of Jacob. He surveyed the land a moment, and then dismounted Romania. She began to whine a little. Then Lyonus still held her reigns while he walked up to her, looked into her eyes, and said.

"Woo…woo girl. You are a lot like your mistress ah? I will find you a place to rest in a moment…okay? But for now, be absolutely quiet, until I can find our new master…"

Romania calmed herself, as if she understood everything Lyonus had said to her.

He smiled and rubbed her head, rapped her reign about a bush, and then walked to the porch. He looked through the side window, but found no light, then remarked.

"Well…no light ah…then let's just knock a bit, and see if we can rouse my lord Jacob."

Lyonus knocked and knocked.

"Hello there…!" he called. "Is there anyone home?"

Finally a dim light approached the door. It seemed to send sprays of light through the cracks. It opened back slowly, as if it's hinges needed much oil.

Then a shadow appeared, that stood wagging his body to and fro, as in a stupor.

"Good evening sir…" said Lyonus, squinting his eyes to see clearly. "Good evening."

There appeared at the door, a short stocky man with a beard, wearing a stocking cap.

"Evening…sir? It is late! No proper gentleman would disturb anyone at this hour…!" said Skunk. By that time Jacob was awake, and headed for the door, carrying a large candle and spouted.

"Skunk…who is it at this hour? I'm not making a trip for more ale, I don't care if it's the king of England himself…!"

When Jacob brought the light closer to the door, both he and Skunk stood with their mouths open. Then Skunk said.

"As I live and breathe…Jacob look here!" Standing with his opened wide, then continued. "It's that fellow we found bleeding to death on the side of the road…!"

"What…! My lord…king!" said Jacob.

Both he and Skunk fell to their knees.

"No…no, ah…lord Jacob please…Mr. Skunk. Rise…please. I am here for your help."

"…But you are king, my lord," said Skunk.

"They say…but for now, I am merely a man in search of his past. I can only recall bits and pieces…but please may I enter in? What about my horse?"

"Oh…Skunk please, put the horse in the stable. Please my lord come in…sit."

Jacob directed Lyonus to a chair by the fire.

"You are truly I say…a man whose life is for a great purpose," said Jacob.

"Why do you say this my friend…?"

"I have seen many men hurt such as you, and they never made it a week, with all the injuries they received…but you survived it all, and now ready to regain your throne."

"Hold on now! Wait! I am not yet ready…I cannot remember even still, my life as king. It was told to me but…"

"My lord, then why are you here?"

Skunk entered the room.

"That's a beautiful horse you have there. Where did you steal it?"

"Ha…ha…ha," laughed Lyonus. "I think I will like it here."

Then Jacob added.

"Skunk…sometimes you say some crazy things…just…sit there, please. You were saying my lord…"

"Yes…I am here that you may guide me into my memory…Constance said you could help…"

"But I know nothing of your life before…how can I help you regain that?"

"No…you see, you can take me to places, and see people who might be able to help me recall facts and faces…things I have forgotten."

"…But my lord…"

Then Lyonus said with a rather stern voice, almost as a command.

"Then is this too much to ask…by your king…that you come to his aid?"

"I'm sorry…whatever I…we can do to assist you my lord, it is our pleasure to do so…but be warned. There are still those rambling about, searching for your heir. They will kill you on sight, if they suspect you are…you."

Jacob pointed at Lyonus from his head to toe.

"But then you don't really look like you…I mean the king…Does he Skunk?"

Skunk replied.

"Not as he did the day we found him. He has more hair or something…"

"Yes," said Lyonus. "I have allowed my hair to grow out long. Constance said I wore it neat and trimmed as king. Do you recall much of what I looked like…I mean at the castle?"

Jacob pondered, then rubbed his chin and said.

"Ah…I remember how you sat on the throne with your beautiful queen

Miria. Rubies and gold encircled you both...it was stunning. You wore your hair to your shoulders, only cut...trimmed neatly and you were shaven."

"Rather handsome fellow..." added Skunk "But rich..."

"Skunk..." cautioned Jacob. "Let us not offend our guest."

"Pardon, my lord."

"Oh...*I am not offended,*" said Lyonus. "*His feelings can be understood. I've wandered in, and invaded your peace. It is not so uncommon to feel a little apprehensive.*"

"You are more than kind, sire," said Jacob.

"Listen, the first thing you must remember is to call me Jonathan. That is the name Constance gave me...I will answer to it naturally."

"Fine then...Jonathan it is. I have learned one thing...as long as a man is dirty or unshaven, he will never be suspected as royalty...so you sire, are safe..."

"Then I guess it is well with me that I stay this way for a time. I have many questions of you...is it possible you can tell me about the contents of this bag?"

Jonathan (Lyonus) shook out everything that was included in the pouch.

"Well..." said Jacob, as he looked at the contents, then at Skunk. "You'd best get us some ale, it's going to be a while."

Skunk brought both of them drinks, as they sat down by the fire, and Lyonus proceeded to touch each item.

"All right, this ring for example...it has a seal..."

"This seal is the seal of England...anyone baring this, can make any piece of paper law, and binding."

"You seem to know a lot about things at court sir."

"I suppose it's from having been around them all of my life...working there you know."

"Oh..."

"Your father the great king Lyonus I, was a wonderful man. He never looked down his nose at me...but gave me much respect, even though I was his servant."

"You knew my father?"

"I knew him well...He said I was the best wine maker in the world..."

"Tell me...was I a good son to him?"

"I tell you, you were his favorite son, and the only one he recognized. Your brother Luis, who is now king, was rather ill treated as a child. I really felt it drove him quite mad."

"Then, was it he who wanted my life?"

"Yes…and that of your heirs…but not him alone…"

"My children…I have children?"

"Yes my lord…a sad story to tell."

"I will hear this sad tale…leave out nothing."

"Your queen was pregnant when they tried to have you killed. They did not know for a while, that she delivered twins…but treachery…left its mark…"

"Twins?"

"Correct my lord. One of the children the queen took with her to Spain, where she was exiled, banished from England…"

"Banished? Not allowed to return to her own country?"

"My lord…your queen was from France…She was the ward of the king. You married her on a trip there. The two of you were something to see. The whole country was excited to see you both together."

"Then why have her exiled…?" asked Lyonus, like a child filled with curiosity.

"Because treachery ruled England after you left…and greed still…"

"Who…? Tell me."

"Your brother for sure. But there is also, Fredrick Guy…called himself a nobleman. But I say a cheat and a swindler. More taxes each year higher taxes, meant to fill his lust for more. It is more than the people can bear."

Then Skunk chide in.

"A rat in a sinking ship he is my lord. It would be better to trust a viper, than to turn your back on that one."

"Then he is the one I should seek?"

"No…he is not the one you should seek…He is a vicious man, and if he knew you were here, the entire army would be hunting you down, and Skunk and I along with you. I say anyone who helped you. It is not yet time to reveal yourself…it will take planning, great timing, money and many soldiers."

"I think I understand…I have been patient thus far, I suppose I can wait a bit longer."

"Good…good. Now you are talking," said Jacob. "We will perhaps take a number of years to accomplish this…but we must start with your memory and go from there."

"Well…can it not wait until tomorrow my lords?" asked Skunk. "We began our morning early…picking grapes for the wine…It is a hard job."

"Good night…" said Skunk.

"Sounds like a good idea to me, it's been a long day for us all, I'm sure."

Answered Lyonus. "…And many thanks to both you and Skunk for all you have risked for me."

"We are happy you want to regain your throne sire. I can't stomach that lord Guy; somebody needs to run him through. You will get a glimpse of him tomorrow…at the castle…I hope…"

"We are going there tomorrow…why so soon?"

"Oh…I had forgotten, I had some barrels of wine to deliver…it won't take long. However, it will give you a chance to look around and familiarize yourself with things."

"Is that…when I should run him through?"

"No…ha…I don't think you are any match for him just yet, although my lord Thomas of the Blade taught you well. Guy would kill you before you took a step…"

"Do I know this Thomas? Where then was he, when my queen and my children were being banished?"

"He, like the rest of us, were not in a position to object to your brother and his so called advisors…namely Fredrick Guy…"

"Perhaps, in the end…Guy will get what he deserves."

"I think then it shall be me…I will send him to his end…" said Jonathan.

Then Skunk spoke up and added. "In spades I hope…" Then blew out his candle.

"Let me show you to your room…Jonathan," said Jacob.

"Very good…you remembered to call me Jonathan…" said Lyonus while he patted Jacob on his shoulder.

"Indeed my lord, we can't waste any more time."

"Good-night and thank you."

The next morning came with sounds of horses neighing and barrels thumping. Jacob was busy stocking his ale. He loaded his wine onto his wagon.

Jonathan (Lyonus) rose ill tempered.

"Hey there, can you keep it a little quiet? I am not yet ready to rise…"

"Yes, my lord you are ready…we must tend our business…remember?"

"Oh…yes, that business…"

"Exactly…So rise and shine…" said Jacob. "Here is a little breakfast, gobble up and let's ride."

"I wonder sir," said Lyonus to Skunk. "What kind of a name is Skunk?"

"I was branded years ago…but it is of no consequence now."

"Yes…but what is your true name?"

Skunk turned and stared at Jacob for a moment. Then Jacob nodded his okay.

"My name is Roland Peters…my father was a soldier in your grandfathers army. But that is another story…for another day. For now…it is enough to know my name is Roland."

"Sounds like a find name to me…Perhaps one day you will come to trust me, then you will share your story with me…" said Lyonus.

"Maybe. Let's get started Jacob…" said Skunk, as he grabbed the last barrel of wine.

"We're all loaded Jonathan…hop aboard…"

Skunk came trotting out holding a plate of food to be eaten on the run. But Jacob yelled.

"Skunk…put away those things…you're staying. "We should be back before lunch."

So, off they went Jacob and Lyonus headed for the royal castle. Jacob was not one for small talk, but Jonathan had tons of questions about the castle.

Now when they arrived at the castle, the guards signaled for Jacob to bring his wagon around back. Once there, they proceeded to unload the barrels. Jonathan almost dropped one of the barrels, and then Jacob winked at him and said.

"Hey you…be careful with those barrels…! It is hard to find good help these days…"

And then he shook his head at the guard.

"Ah…you've hired a new man have you Jacob?" asked one of the guards while he looked him up and down.

"Yes…a sorry day it is too, my lords."

"Hurry and get them unloaded…I haven't got all day…"

"Yes my lord…sorry…sorry…"

The guards laughed at Lyonus's clumsiness. They began to mock him.

"Why…it seems he's most likely been busy drinking the wine himself…ha…ha…" They laughed, and laughed, as they reared back their heads.

Jonathan hung his, and adjusted the barrel on his shoulders.

Once inside, Jacob cautioned him to be careful, not to look anyone in the eyes. He also instructed him that his head should remain lowered, and not to speak to anyone.

When they had finished bringing in the wine, they stacked the barrels in the wine seller. That gave them a few more minutes to look around the castle.

Lyonus could not help but ask Jacob to show him around the court.

Perhaps he had hoped for some small recollection.

Then Jacob showed him a long dark corridor, then whispered in his ear while he pointed at the room. "There…just down the hall…is what was once your room."

"How do you know such things?"

"I observed the goings on of the people at court. I recalled you trotted off to your room many times."

"Do you think there is anyone in there now?" Lyonus asked in a whisper.

"I could not presume to know that…it would not be safe to try and find out, I'm afraid."

"Then let's ask someone…maybe one of the cooks would know."

"Jonathan…! Don't bring anymore attention to yourself, than you already have…Let's just go…"

"Oh all right…but what of lord Guy…?"

"He's to be saved for another day…let's go…"

Just then Lyonus spotted a bust of his father Lyonus I. Then he asked.

"Wait…is that a statue of my father there…at the corner?"

"It is…and there is one of you and your brother around the corner outside the dining hall."

"Can we take a closer look?"

"Jonathan…make it quick…we can't afford to get caught."

So they peered around corners and hurried to find the sculptures Lyonus longed to see.

He saw a tall dark-haired man that stood a few feet away from the bust.

"Look there…" said Jacob. "It's Guy. "Look at him…so smug and confident."

"So that's him…"

"No doubt he's planning some evil thing now…as is his way…" said Jacob, and then paused, while he pulled Jonathan out of sight.

"Get back Jonathan. He almost saw you there…I've told you, now is not the time…"

"Then let's just go Jacob…I'm sorry. I don't want you to get caught."

"Yes…besides, the guards will make their rounds and if they catch us away from the seller, we may not get a chance to discover anything but a noose."

On there way out, Jonathan looked up at the wall in front of the great hall. There he spied the great seal of England.

"Look Jacob...!" said Lyonus, as he pointed at the seal. "It's just as the ring...you were right...!"

"Yes...hurry Jonathan...hurry along now."

Once Jacob and Jonathan (Lyonus), had made it back to the wagon and out of the castle gates, they felt safe in discussing the things in which Jonathan had seen.

"I really felt something there today Jacob...I really did."

"Felt something sire...?"

"I mean...as if I belonged there."

"Well...you do belong there sire...It was taken from you...You just have to try and get it back, starting with the day you went hunting."

"I only remember...a tall dark man, that stood in the shadows, then a woman talked with me...pointed to a window. That is what I see in my minds eye. My dreams are dark...and filled with shapes of people, but they have no faces. It is not clear who or what this woman should represent, or where the people are from. It is so strange..."

"We will make a visit to a place where people do a lot of talking, perhaps...they too, will spark a feeling..."

So Jonathan and Jacob parked the empty wine wagon at a near by tavern. When they went in, Jacob nudged Jonathan for his attention.

"Listen we'll sit here..." he said, as he moved toward a table by the window. "This is a good spot."

"I guess..." replied Jonathan. "There are not many people here."

"That's because it is still early yet...give it a little time, and you won't be able to move about."

"What shall we drink Jacob?"

"We shall have a small mug of ale..."

Then the barmaid finally addressed the table.

"Good day kind gents, what will you have?"

Jonathan spoke right up and said.

"Bring us ale...!" As if giving an order, which made the barmaid frown.

Then Jacob spoke out in a voice of calm, and said.

"My dear...I've heard your service is the best in the valley, and your drink to match...Now..." As his eyes traveled to meet Jonathan, and back to the barmaid. "We'll have two small mugs of your finest ale, please..."

"I will come back directly with your drink my lord," answered the barmaid.

Then Jonathan asked...after being scolded by Jacobs' look.

"What was that about, was she not to take my order...?"

"Of course, but servants aren't to be talked down to because it is their station."

"If I am king then..." he said, whispering very low to Jacob. "Do I not give commands to my subjects?"

"If you were...you and I would not be sitting here ordering ale together...so no, at this point you are just as I...a customer paying for a drink, and the barmaid is the one who brings it. Here, if you want good service, you must treat the servers with respect. That my lord is your first lesson in regaining your throne."

"How so...my lord Jacob...?"

"The same vagabonds you see here, are most likely soldiers long forgotten, but would gladly lift their swords to fight for England's causes."

"Oh...I see. Well...it is a lesson I must take to heart...Thank you Jacob."

"It is my pleasure...the more you learn about being a peasant, the better it will be for peasants when you are king again..."

The barmaid brought over the ale to their table, while she starred at Jonathan.

"Here you are sirs...two mugs of our finest...!"

"And we thank you..." replied Jonathan, and tossed three gold coins on her tray.

The barmaid eyes fell from her head in surprise.

"What...this is way too much my lords...please sir take it back."

"I insist..." said Jonathan. "You are a great barmaid..."

"What...?" she scoffed, as she turned and left the table stuffing the gold in her apron.

"Why did you give her that much gold Jonathan...?" asked Jacob, cutting his eyes upward.

"Didn't you say I should treat her as my equal...? Well I thought if I gave her more than the ale was worth, she would be happy."

"Oh..." sighed Jacob. "I said peasants should be treated with respect, not over paid for serving ale...I...I see we have a long way to go..."

"Maybe I'll do better on the next test."

"Test!" said Jacob, with a firm voice. "There are no tests here...this is real life. It's about learning to live with people. You may come in contact with some of them, the rest of your life. There is no remedy for having been spoiled all your life Jonathan...even if you can't remember being so...except to go about living the peasants life, and perhaps that will shake up your compassion, and sensibilities..."

"Well...this I can say...as Jonathan, I will allow you to scold me...for my learning. But as king of England, I can not allow it to be so."

"True…But as Jonathan, you are as a son to me…learning the real meaning of humanity. But as king, you will once again assume your place with great power…manipulating humanity."

"Oh…?" questioned Jonathan, with a slight frown. "Is than how you view your king?"

"I will say this, you were a far better king than your brother Luis. He burdens the people with taxes, and allows that Frederick Guy to drain the people dry…soon, there will be no loyalty for the House of Warwick."

"Then I must hurry and learn all the quicker…if I am to resume my rank."

"Yes, my lord…but it will not be that easy…first you must be taught the sword."

"Great…! Who do you have in mind?"

"Ah…" said Jacob. "Good question, but do you see that fellow over there?"

"Do you mean that one in the vest there…with his head on the table…drunk…?"

"I do indeed."

"Wait…what can a drunk teach anyone…?"

"Lesson number three, my lord…never judge what is on the inside, by what you see on the outside…"

"So…he has great skills then?"

"More than great…he makes swords…and his brother taught the kings men, your men the art of the sword as well…He comes from a long line of fighting men."

"His brother you say…who then is he? Shouldn't I know him then?"

"You do indeed…his name is lord Thomas Hendly Graybourne, he was a captain of your army. Everyone called him Sir Thomas of the Blade…a great man."

"Is he there still…I mean my captain, in the castle?"

"He was made an advisor. I'm afraid, he's retired they said it was due to your death, and the queens exile…but I don't know all the details."

"What is this fellows name?"

"Oh, his name is Richard Orin Graybourne. His father Orin Hendsly Graybourne made swords for your father, Lyonus I. When he died, Richard took over."

"What about his wife…what became of her?"

"His wife Diana was so upset. She thought it was beneath their station to make swords, and left him for some Earl or something or other…then later it was said, she was killed late one night driving away from Miles Tavern...The details were sketchy."

"Then he began to drink?" asked Lyonus.

"With a vengeance, and for a long time too. He had a few sons...I think about three. He took stock of them, and stopped drinking as much, but every now and then, I would find him like this, in a tavern where I'd deliver wine."

"If he's like this, how can he teach me the art?"

"It doesn't seem now that he is able to do anything, but when he sobers up, he will give you a run for your money. Make no mistake about it, he is strong and well versed..."

"Shall we ask him about it now...?"

"You go and get in the wagon...I'll talk to Richard."

"Shouldn't I ask him...you know to help?"

"Just go out Jonathan...let me handle this for now..."

"All right, but don't be too long."

So Jacob approached Richard Graybourne, about teaching Jonathan the art of the sword.

At first, Richard was reluctant to do it. But he was soon persuaded, when Jacob told him that Jonathan was an important diplomat in disguise.

"Richard..." said Jacob. "How soon can we start...?"

"Ha...ha...as soon as I sober up...my friend."

Richard held his mug up high and took yet a final drink from it, dropped his body on the stool, then said.

"Why don't we just say tomorrow...about noon."

"Sounds fine to me..." stuttered Jacob. "We'll see you there."

"I'll drink to that...!" said Richard, raising his mug again to drink.

Then Jacob put his hand over Richard's mug, and said.

"Listen Richard...we really need you, for England man...!"

Richard dropped his mug and wiped his mouth, stood up, then said.

"I would do anything for England...She's a good old girl."

"Great, England will reward you well...then we shall see you on tomorrow..."

"Tomorrow it is...!"

After Jacob made arrangements for Jonathan, he walked outside, and got onto the wagon.

"Everything is all set for tomorrow..." said Jacob. "He seemed more than willing."

"I'm looking forward to the challenge...but wait..." said Jonathan

(Lyonus). "Did I not know the art of the sword from my days as king?"

"You certainly did indeed my liege. However, I thought…since your memory loss, you would be in need of a refresher course…you know, to reacquaint yourself. It won't take much for you to regain your skill I'm sure…"

"Oh…I suppose you're right…what can it hurt…? This will be good…I'm ready…"

Jacob looked at Jonathan (Lyonus) with a smile, and then said.

"I hope you never forget the times we've had thus far."

"I've come to know you a little…my lord Jacob. I trust it will be a lasting relationship…even when I am king again…"

Jacob, with a long look of sadness that came directly over his face as a shadow, replied.

"As king my lord, I am sure you will not give thought to the small part I've played here."

"Well…" said Lyonus, as he placed his hand on Jacob's shoulder. "I can not forget the things that would restore me to my rightful place as king…it would be an insult to that which England stands for. You have been a true and loyal confidant. I only wish to reward you well, for all you have done for me. And as king, I will be in a position to do just that…"

Jacob urged the horses forward, and then said.

"I do understand this…before this tale is done, there will be others to reward. Your journey back to your throne will be long and hard. Many will die that you may live."

"What do you mean…many may die?"

"Look Jonathan…you are not dealing with a lovable person in your brother Luis. He is mad, and deals with a viscous, evil man…that loves inflicting pain."

"No…you mean…murder…?"

"I mean your brother has maimed, blinded, even cut out the tongues of some. Everything you could imagine to get his way, and keep the throne. And with that lord Guy as his closest advisor, the evil never sleeps."

"What about the army…can't they just take the throne?"

"Oh yes…like he took it from you…is that what you mean?"

Lyonus dropped his head and conceded to the idea of Jacob.

"I think I understand…but I'm not at all sure, why this lord Guy is allowed to live."

"Listen son…the man who controls the army, is the man who should be king…But remember, you once said, you yourself would bring him to justice…so I guess it will be you…that will free England from his heavy hand."

"Indeed…" said Jonathan (Lyonus), as he shook his head in despair.

So they rode on to the estate, and prepared themselves for an even longer journey together.

Once they arrived, Jonathan immediately found his bag of trinkets given to him by Constance. He asked Jacob to tell him all about the things he found there. But Jacob, a man of business stalled again, then said.

"It has gotten late, my lord, I have a busy day tomorrow…work you know. Those things will need to wait for the right time, then you will understand each of them."

"Yes but shouldn't I know what these things mean?"

"Please Jonathan…you've asked me the same question, in a different manner. Tomorrow my friend…tomorrow there will be enough time to answer your questions. But for now…let us retire, and meditate over the day."

"I see…I will be patient Jacob. There is one thing I must say though…"

Jacob shrugged his shoulders and made a loud sigh, turned to Jonathan (Lyonus), then said.

"I give up, what is it…?"

"No…this is important…"

"All right then…what is it?"

"I think I remembered something today…"

Jacob's eyes grew larger than a gold coin.

"What…you remembered something…?"

"Yes…I thought of a room in the castle, that had a hidden passage. It was dark and cold, but when I tried hard to recall more…the memory faded."

"Well…that's a start…Ha ha, ha…that's a great start my boy. It seems we're on our way to recovery."

"Then I feel much better…"

"Good night, sire. God spared you for a reason…maybe together, we can find out his design."

"Let us hope my lord Jacob…Goodnight."

When Jacob, Jonathan and Skunk heard the sounds of the morning. They found themselves wondering about the fields with baskets, picking grapes for the winepress. It was important to Jacob that they were picked at exactly the proper time. This allowed his wines and ales to yield the best flavor. Jacobs' wines of course, were accepted all over the land. King Luis especially loved the taste of them.

He took more satisfaction from the taste of the almond wine.

This was an opportunity that could not be missed. The delivery wine, gave Lyonus the chance to visit the castle in disguise once again, and familiarize himself with the goings on there.

"Everything looked great here...I'm pleased with the harvest," said Jacob.

"I'm glad," replied Skunk. Then he said to Jonathan, in a crash voice. "There's no living with him, if his crop is not just so..."

"I wouldn't say that Skunk...It's just important that the wine tastes it's best."

"Well if you ask me...a drink is a drink...just ask old Richard Graybourne..."

Then Skunk said under his breath, in a whisper.

"This one knows all there is to know about the drink..."

"Go...help take in the crop Skunk...I think you've said quite enough..."

As Richard fell from his horse, Jonathan (Lyonus) did not seem to be impressed.

"Are you all right...?" questioned Jacob. "You hit the ground pretty hard there..."

"I'm fine...let's get started. Where is your sword?"

"I don't think I have a sword sir."

"I like this one Jacob...he has manners...and good looks too."

"Sir?" said Jonathan, who stood with such a confused look on his face.

"Can you handle a sword, as good as you look...?"

"What...?"

"Never mind son, I took the liberty of bringing a few swords. You can choose from these."

Richard pulled two beautiful swords that belonged to his father.

"This one..." he said, holding the black handled sword. "This belonged to my father. He was a great swordsman. He made only the best."

"Oh..." said Jonathan. "Are there any better around here?"

"There are none better in all the world...Choose your weapon...! On guard!"

"Wait...wait!" yelled Jonathan. "Aren't you going to show me how to hold the sword?"

"I wanted to see what you had boy..."

"Oh…"

"Now…you're standing all wrong…no…no…no!" shouted Richard.

"Oh gentlemen…" announced Jacob. "I say farewell, and will leave you to your work…it seems you have it cut out for you…Richard…"

"Indeed!" shouted Richard.

So the day wore on, until at last, Richard was pleased with Jonathan's efforts.

This would become the beginning of the rebirth of Lyonus II.

"Ah…Jonathan, you have shown great progress, in a matter of hours…"

"Thank you, I have set my sight on a great prize…"

"Well it has certainly caused you to focus…"

"Yes…but there is much I must re-learn for myself and my country."

"Well…" said Richard, as he took a gasp of breath. "I fear the country shall have to wait a spell for your help."

"You mock me sir?" scoffed Lyonus.

"I do no such thing. I merely meant to point out, that kingdoms are won with many swords, and for now," he said while he flicked at Lyonus' blade and then continued. "Your sword my friend…would seem to be a bit rusty…and alone."

"I trust then that all your efforts will be placed at the tip of my blade, that I may retain the skill I need to regain my throne."

Richard fell to his knees.

"Your majesty…! I thought Jacob the liar when he said you were actually the king of England…When he told me I must keep silent, I thought him in jest…A thousand pardons my lord."

Lyonus helped Richard to his feet then said.

"Sir, it is most important that no one, I mean no one know that I am here, or who I am. My life has been threatened and that of my family. I've spent many, many years without a memory. There are a few things I can recall, but for the most part it is a blank. There is no telling what would happen to the person who could tell that I was alive…I wager not a warm welcome, and certainly a quicker death…Do you understand my meaning?"

"Do not fear your majesty…I can not bear your brother, and that fool he calls his minister. There is very little we can do without a true leader. But perhaps now God has answered the prayers of the country, that Luis be removed from power, and lord Guy his just reward."

"All right then, teach me what I should know, and leave Luis and Guy to me…"

Richard took a bow and a hearty stance. "On guard…your majesty…"

Lyonus and Richard worked for hours on technique and gained quite a fondness for each other. They talked about ways to get control of the kingdom. Richard told him of the one person he knew, that could help restore his memory.

"Richard...this fellow you spoke of, is he near?"

"He is in fact at the tavern nearly everyday, your majesty."

Lyonus cut him off.

"Richard you must remember to call me Jonathan...It is vital."

"Yes...yes...I forgot my self a for a moment. It won't happen again."

"All right...Now then what were you saying?"

"His name is Ivan. Jacob knows him as well."

"Yes, I believe he has mentioned him to me once before."

"Then my...lo...Jonathan, he is the one."

"Will you go with me to see him?"

"Yes. But we must hurry, we want to make sure he does not leave."

"I'll get the horses," said Lyonus.

"I'll put away the swords," said Richard, as if they were comrades at arms.

"Tell me sir, can you not remember anything of your past?"

"Only as I told you bits and pieces, a little of my life as king, but I...I just can't..."

"It's all right Jonathan, it will all come back. Sometimes it just needs a little shock."

"What kind of shock? What do you mean...?"

"Well as I said, Ivan will be able to help."

"Just who is this Ivan fellow anyway...I mean what does he do?"

"He worked for your father, the great king of England and he also worked for you, until..."

"Until what?

"Jonathan, maybe it is best if you allow these things to come back naturally."

"Richard, I am hanging by a thread here. I need all the help I can get if I am to win back my crown and save my family...Please. Now tell me."

"Ivan Fellows was the court seer. He helped in times of war, but after your mother died..."

"Yes go on...after my mother died..."

"He paired up with the kings surgeon, and some terrible things happened..."

"Yes...go on."

"Well years past and when you became king, Ivan being afraid of lord

Guy, did his bidding and you punished him with a terrible punishment..."

"I...with a terrible punishment. What could that have been?"

"Jonathan you had one of his eyes plucked out."

Jonathan gasped and covered his mouth.

"What! I did that to the poor man? I must have been a harsh ruler." Lyonus turned his face away.

"No listen to me. You were more than fair. He did something unthinkable against the crown, a penalty that could only have been death, but you my lord showed him mercy. You gave him his life...and for that he is eternally grateful."

"You know this...that he is grateful?"

"My lord, he hopes you can forgive him."

"Perhaps I have much more to learn about myself before I try to regain the country."

"You are the country, my lord Jonathan," said Richard, as he handed Jonathan the reigns of his horse. "Now let us ride quickly to see Ivan."

They rode steadily without conversation, only short glances at one another until at last they reached the tavern.

"We have arrived my lord Jonathan. I'll tie down the horses. Go ahead on in."

"Who...how will I find him?"

"Oh he'll be the one with one patch over his eye."

CHAPTER THIRTEEN
A Vision Within a Dream

Lyonus finally arrived at the tavern. Once inside, he looked around and then spied a man sitting far to the rear. He was dressed in rags, and had a patch over one eye.

He must be the one thought Lyonus, and proceeded to talk to him.

"Kind sir," he said, leaning over the table. "Would it be possible for me to speak with you for a moment?"

"Look! What do you need of me?" asked Ivan, bringing down his goblet, and wiping his mouth with his sleeve. "Go away…I just want to be left alone…!"

"Please sir…" pleaded Lyonus. "It will just take a minute of your time. Will this help?"

Showing Ivan a little gold. Then He looked up at Lyonus, and saw something that made his blood run cold. "No…! Shouted Ivan and jumped from the table and out the door.

"What!!" shouted Lyonus. "Please…I just want to ask you some questions!"

So Lyonus followed Ivan to his wagon, calling for him to stop. Then Ivan stopped and turned to Lyonus. "My lord you gave a merry chase…" said Lyonus, trying to catch his breath.

"It was not the chase I had intended sir. I could see there was trouble."

Lyonus stood with a frown, and said.

"Sir, I bring you no trouble. I am one in search of my memory, and was told…you were the one to speak to. By the way, why did you run back there…are you wanted by the crown or something?"

Ivan stood and looked Lyonus in the eye.

"I know those eyes, and I know who you are. When I looked into them, they reminded me of hell. One I should not like to relive."

"I don't understand. You know me? I can not remember…not very much anyway."

"Follow me," said Ivan. "…And I will reveal to you some of your past…if you have the stomach for it."

"I'm not sure what you mean, but if it is mine, I should like to remember, what kind of king I was, if indeed I was king."

"Oh you were king alright, there's no denying that, I have the scares to prove it. Come on then…" So he followed Ivan to his house. When they reached the broken down shack, Lyonus asked. "Is this where you must live now?"

"No…" said Ivan. "This is where I choose to live. You see here, bandits don't bother to call on me, for from the outside appearance, they think there is nothing worth stealing. And of course, those of privilege would not be caught dead asking for a cool drink from my well, let alone for a nights lodging, so…I am, as I choose to be…"

"…And just what is that my friend?"

"Alone…left alone." Replied Ivan, with a voice that was deep and icy.

Once inside, Lyonus was amazed, there were all the comforts of a great court.

"I see what you mean sir," he remarked, as he touched the precious gold vases sitting about. "The place is magnificent!"

"I'm glad it pleases your royal senses, my lord."

"Indeed…this reminds me of someplace…" he added.

"Now take a seat, I will make us a drink," said Ivan.

"That would be wonderful."

Ivan began to warm over some tea, and then added a purple powder to it, at least two spoons.

"Tea? You offer me tea…?"

"Tea, my lord, is a soothing remedy," coached Ivan. "Relax and drink, you will find it quite calming."

"I could find a good ale calming as well…" said Lyonus looking into his cup.

Ivan sat down across the table, and began to drink.

"Please drink all of it. This will help you to see your past."

"Very well," said Lyonus. "If I must."

"Now…" said Ivan let me tell you a story.

"A story…?" asked Lyonus with great sarcasm, looking over his cup at Ivan.

"Yes. And it is as true as it gets. Once there was one with the sight. He became greedy, and arrogant. So one day he opened himself up to be used by an evil power thirsty devil, and was tricked into revealing a vision. But gave the king the wrong interpretation of that vision. This almost cost the king his life, and that of his queen. So as a punishment, the king took away an eye. {That my visions may be seen more clearly}…he said."

"So that is what happened…? To your eye I mean…"

"And you my lord, are that king."

Lyonus dropped his cup, and became a little dizzy. The room started to spin, and he was ready to pass out, when Ivan grabbed hold of his hands and called his name.

"Lyonus…look into my eyes. Look deep into my eyes…"

Lyonus raised his eyes and starred at Ivan, then closed his eyes to dream.

"Look with me…" said Ivan. "See your past."

Lyonus' body seemed to be suspended, almost limp while Ivan spoke.

"There you sit on your throne, and your queen also, the beautiful Miria who is with child. The both of you are so much in love. There is Luis your brother and now king, along with his consort lord Guy. Now you see Hollands on your hunting trip. The guards that attacked and killed him are all dead except for one. The wolves found him as their meal. Your brother Luis then leaves you to your fate. Now Jacob found you, and a young lady named Constance nursed you back to health.

Now Lyonus…when you open your eyes, you will remember your past, and remember…to forgive an old fool his err. Open your eyes Lyonus.

He opened his eyes, then starred at Ivan a moment and said.

"Ivan Fellows…court seer to Lyonus I, and court seer to Lyonus II. Punished for his deeds…by me the king of England."

"Yes your majesty…" cried Ivan, then fell to his knees, and kissed the kings hand.

"Rise up Ivan, you have done me a great service. I remember now, this thing done to me. Poor Hollands, my friend, and knight."

"My lord, I have done nothing now, but I beg you to forgive me a grave fault of the past."

"Consider yourself forgiven, the deed you have done today, makes us even. You gave me back my memory, that is something I shall never forget."

"Now what of my queen?" asked Lyonus. "She must be beside herself by now. Just how long have I been away?"

"Oh my king, it has been at least ten years."

"What…then where is my queen now?"

"I'm sorry to tell you this my lord, but the queen was banished in exile to Spain, alone with your heir."

"Heir…?" gasped Lyonus. "You mean I have a son?"

"Indeed my lord…and also a daughter."

"This is more than a man's heart can bear in one sitting sir."

"Yes, but it gets worst."

"No!" shouted Lyonus. "I can not bear it. The fact that my family in exiled is enough."

"My lord…with the regent imprisoned in Spain, you dead, and the queen banished, Luis and that old fox lord Guy now rule England. Together, they have laden heavy taxes, and if you do not pay, they maim and lame, until tax is gathered. One either pays, or signs over property, or their daughters. One way or another they get their way…and all the richer for it."

"Enough." Sighed Lyonus, heartbroken from all he had heard. "How could I have been so weak…?"

"You were only a boy, but you can show strength now, my king. Take back that which belongs to you!"

"…But how?" cried Lyonus. "I have no gold, or land. I have no army, or weapons. What can a man do under these circumstances?"

"He can become ruthless. Then he relies on friends and builds relationships. He does what it takes to succeed!"

"This will take some doing…"

"Yes…and we start by becoming thieves."

"What! I'm no thief sir…"

"Listen to yourself. You want to be king, but you don't want to fight the battle. You want to steal back your kingdom, but not get your hands dirty. How do you think your brother now has the throne? Do you think he played fair when he had you attacked? I suppose you think he will just give it all up because you walk up to him and demand it. Well think again my lord. It takes nerve, and a lot of savvy, to win a battle, but you my lord need to win a war, and that takes loyalty…Loyalty from people like me."

"Well my friend…I suppose you have cleared up for me what it takes, I guess now I must find the way."

They walked over to the door, and Lyonus stopped.

"Ivan, you never answered my question about my queen."

Ivan dropped his eyes for a moment, and then answered.

"She will die in Spain."

"…And my son?" Lyonus questioned.

"He will rise, make himself known in royal circles, then he will know of you."

"Then…I will see my children?"

"Yes, my lord…you will see them."

"Then, the way is clear…I haven't a moment to waste. I must begin to build an army."

"No, my lord. You must start to build friends."

"Listen my lord, there will be a great banquet at the castle in a month or so for the visiting king. Luis will also use the banquet to celebrate prince Edwards seventh birthday. He has himself sired an heir."

"There is no time to loose."

"No your majesty, do not trouble yourself in that, for my lord Guy will never allow that child to live. He plots now, even as we speak, to rid himself of the child as soon as he is allowed to move freely to and from the castle."

"…And queen Anne?"

"I'm afraid she too has no future."

"Then, I must find a way to punish him. I will not be weak again."

"What is it my lord, you look strange?"

"I was reminded of my lord Thomas Graybourne, trusted friend. He was as much a Warwick if ever there was one. Maybe he could help?"

"Ah…sire, there is another sad tale, the house of Warwick still suffers much death, and bloodshed.

"Explain yourself Ivan."

Ivan began by sitting down and folding his hands across the table.

"It was only a few years ago that he was murdered, along with his lovely wife Claire, and all their servants. Their daughter Melinda was the only one to escape the madness."

"Please tell me of it…" entreated Lyonus. "There should be someone to mourn my friends, and England's great loss."

"The story is long, my lord."

"…And," said Lyonus, sitting himself down. "I have time, and no place to go. There will not be any men at the taverns until nightfall. Please continue."

"Well," said Ivan. "Lord Thomas Hendley Graybourne had resigned from the court of king Luis, and left them with a rather bad taste in their mouths. The way they treated the queen, angered him sorely, so much that he threatened to kill lord Guy. The king told him never to return to the castle again, not even on the grounds.

It was okay for a time, for Luis had his marriage, and affairs of state to attend. Lord Guy grew impatient. He ordered a greater search for your children, and documents. When the search for your heirs and your will proved empty, lord Guy turned to my lord Thomas, whom he believed the queen had entrusted with the papers. Graybourne swore an oath to protect them.

As time went on, lord Guy also missed the letter you had signed with the seal of England which gave him card blanche to do his evil."

"How could I have been so blind? Said Lyonus. "I should have been able to see through him."

"Do not blame yourself my lord, he is a very powerful and persuasive man."

Forgive me Ivan, please continue."

Desperate he was, he naturally turned to my lord Graybourne, and sent his henchmen to collect."

"Yes." Interrupted Lyonus. "Tell me everything…please."

"Now I see, it was a few years ago, on their daughter Melinda's eighteenth birthday, that Lord Graybourne and lady Claire, prepared a surprise party for her. While they worked all day getting everything ready, the lady Claire heard the noise outside. I hear her voice."

"Oh goodness," she said. "What are horses doing at Hilton manor? We're not expecting anyone four hours."

Lord Graybourne paused from shining Melinda's present, quickly wrapped it, and hid it behind a wall. Then he went outside to talk to the men. There was so much dust from the horses, that my lord could barely see the faces of the men. Lady Claire asked from the doorway.

"Who are they my dear?"

"I don't know for sure, perhaps strangers who have lost their way."

Thomas pulled up the door, till just a little light would show through.

When the dust cleared, Graybourne could recognize one of the men, and then said to Claire.

"My dear, hurry and bolt the door…do it quickly!"

"No! What is it? Come inside Thomas…!"

"There is no time Claire, now do as I say!"

Finally they got down from their horses, and Thomas asked the men to state their business.

"What is it you seek…? We have already paid our taxes…what more could you want from us?"

"Step aside…" said one of them. "I want to go inside."

"No!" said Thomas. "Well, you will tell me what it is you seek or you will regret coming."

"Look old man," said another. "Maybe we got off on the wrong foot. Let's start over. My name is Hawk…" Thomas cut him short then said.

"I know who you are, you're scum, and I want you to leave."

"Then if you know me, you also know I work for the king."

"The king!" replied Thomas. "I know you work for that dog Fredrick Guy, whom I just as soon kill with my bare hands."

"It is all the same to me…" Looking around at the rabble, then said. "The king has sent us here to retrieve papers, and information."

"For the King you say…?" questioned Thomas. "Then where are your papers?"

"Papers…ha, ha, ha." Laughed Hawk, which started all the others to laughing. "Why, you have them, that's why we've come, remember?"

"I know nothing of any papers save my own affairs, none of which would serve any purpose to your king.

"Let's go in…you know how it is, sometimes our wives remember things we sometimes forget," said Hawk.

They pushed lord Thomas in, and made their way through the door.

"Ah…there she is, the lovely lady Claire I presume," said Hawk.

Looking around the room, then asked, "…And where is your daughter? I was told there were three of you…?" Then closed the door behind them, and said.

"Come over here and join the party…" he ordered the servants.

"Looks like we're just in time for a celebration boys." The men began to mumble.

"I say again…we have nothing. I know of no papers," said lord Graybourne, as he starred at Claire.

"I should like to know, where the heir to the throne is…?" sounded another from the back of the room.

"Heir…? I don't have any idea what you're talking about," answered Thomas.

"Do you see that servant there? Pointing to the one closest. "What is his name?"

They all shook at the sound of his voice, and then he yelled, and walked toward him.

"What's his name...?" He pulled him over closer, then drew a dagger from his belt, and began to bargain.

"His name is James..." shouted Claire. "Please don't hurt him..." she pleaded.

"I tell you what..." said Hawk, as he lowered his knife a little. "If you would give me what I want, I would allow James to live. Sounds good to you, doesn't it James...?"

All of his men laughed, and encircled the others. Just then lord Graybourne reached for his sword.

"Old man...I wouldn't try that if I were you...!" said another of the men. He gently pulled the sword from Graybourne' sheath. Then Hawk added.

"I know you were called Thomas of the blade. But that was a long time ago. And your reputation won't help you now. Besides...you and I...have a lot in common."

The lord Thomas shouted. "We are...nothing alike." Turning his head in disgust.

"Well I beg to differ, my lord. We both work for the king, we both get paid for it."

He moved around the room a little, looking at Claire then said. "We both love the pretty winches."

"Oh...you...!" said Claire disturbed by his insult.

Then he smiled and continued. "...And we both have a reputation with the sword."

"You're a liar...!" charged Thomas.

"Oh...does the lady Claire not know of your little escapades with the ladies my lord?" he said, using an evil grin.

"Don't believe him Claire...he lies through his rotten teeth!"

"Ha...ha! Never mind that. What have you to say about my proposal? I want an answer now, or James, will die now!" He raised the blade to his throat, waiting for a response.

"...And I've told you before...I have no...!"

Before Thomas could finish, Hawk slit the throat of the servant, then pulled another.

"What about this pretty winch...is her life perhaps worth more than poor James?" He held her close to him, almost fondling. "Hum...she smells pretty, like...lilacs I think..."

He spun her around then said. "Maybe this is your daughter? He placed the knife at her throat, and then yelled. Now tell me...!"

"Wait!" said Claire, "Thomas...give them what they want...please! Not Olivia too...your own daughter!"

Claire quickly thought of a way she might save Melinda, who was due home any moment.

"My darling..." said Thomas. "It wouldn't matter whether I gave them everything or nothing...I know these men, they would simply kill us any way."

"But Thomas, not Oliver, our only child. Can't you at least think of her that she may live?"

"If I give them anything, I will become worse than they...a traitor to God, England and the queen. Claire...becoming a traitor to all I hold dear? As sad as it is...that I can not do."

Claire ran over to lord Graybourne, and cried. "Oh hold me my darling...I love you."

"With all my being Claire...I love you."

Then Hawk reared back with his sword and said.

"This is all quite touching, but I will have my way! Now for the last time...!" He paused for a moment, then stabbed Oliver, and slash into Thomas. The men dragged lady Claire to the table. She kicked and screamed all the way, then they slung her on the table, while Hawk commanded them saying. "If you do not give me what I want." Pointing around the room at each member, then asked. "You see these men, do you not? I will give each one of them a taste of you...my lady."

Then Claire screamed out, with great swelling tears. "You will surely be damned for what it is you do sir...! I know nothing!"

"Then my lady," he replied, walking around to look her in the eyes. "We might as well go a bit further do you agree? We will take you...over and over, until you have been sufficiently ravaged but not quite dead. Then we will feed what is let of you to the wolves and the vultures. Does that sound damned enough for you? Ha...ha...ha, ha." They all continued to laugh.

Then Claire turned and spat in his face, as her final way of retaliation.

The men began to attack her. Hawk assigned some of them to thoroughly search the house and find what they could. When they were finished, Hawk gave orders to burn it all down. However, they rode off empty handed. For my lord Graybourne had indeed hidden the papers well.

Now by the time the fire went out, and it was smoldering, Melinda came riding down the road. She could see smoke from a great distance away. She leaped from the wagon. When she neared the gate, she ran head on to the house.

"Oh no!!" she screamed. "Father…where are you?" Trying to find her lord Graybourne through the ash and smoke. But when she looked toward the table, she saw her mother, laid across it. Her clothes were gone, and body singed from the fire. Melinda ran in a fit of rage from the ruins. Her uncle could barley hold her.

After a while, they buried the both of them, near her mothers' favorite shade tree. They placed lord Thomas' old sword as a headstone for them both. Melinda swore to revenge the murder of her parents."

"Well…!" gasped Lyonus What a fantastic tale you've spun…"

"Tale?" he replied this story is more than true."

"Where is the daughter now…?"

"Melinda stayed with her uncle for a while. I know he worked with her in her training, but I can't say for sure now just where she is."

"Poor Graybourne, what a brave man you were. I should have had a small amount of your courage. If that were true, maybe you would still be alive, and I would still be king."

"You can not dwell on the past, you must now focus on the future. There are men still that want to see the throne returned to the rightful heir. They would risk all to accomplish this goal, with the right man to lead."

"Then that man shall be me!"

"Well said your majesty."

CHAPTER FOURTEEN
Miria and Nichol's Desperation

Meanwhile back in Spain, Miria and Nichol found it more and more difficult to survive.

Orin grew so fast, and looked more and more like his father Lyonus.

It had now been ten years since they were exiled to La Vega Spain. Orin began to ask questions about his father, and why they could not go home to England.

Miria found herself trying desperately to fill in the missing pieces for him.

"Mother..." said Orin, as he walked close to her and looked at her with a wide-eyed glance. "Why are you no longer queen? He asked can people just move a queen from her country...?"

"Oh Orin..." she said staring over at Nichol, as if begging for help. It's more complicated than that. There is so much I need to tell you, I hardly know where to begin."

"Well perhaps my lady..." said Nichol as she starred straight out the window "It is better to begin from the beginning. It will leave fewer questions my lady to be sure."

"Maybe you are right Nichol..."

Orin settled himself down at a comfortable spot on the bed. He sat, as if waiting to hear some bedtime story told over and over. Miria, cleared her throat, and raised her eyes, while she thought of just how to begin the tale.

"Orin, years ago in France," she said while he drew closer to her, I was found by the king, and lived with him in his castle. He treated me as if I were his very own daughter. So I grew up knowing only him and his son Michael. I grew up knowing their great love for me; they were the only men I had ever loved." Orin interrupted. "Except for me…mother?"

"Ha…ha, darling you came a lot later, now where was I? Oh yes…until one day…this wonderfully handsome dashing knight in armor came to claim me for his own."

Orin then interrupted her.

"Was he really a knight mother…really?"

"Oh my son…he was more…much more than that, he was the king of England.

When he came to us, he was in search of a traitor, but it was among his own advisors."

"Did he kill them my mother…?"

"Please…let me finish the story dear, without anymore questions…okay?"

"All right mother, I'm listening with both ears."

"All right then…your father Lyonus II, king of England, was nobodies puppet. Lyonus demanded respect, and had a very commanding presence. There was no one that did not bow before him. I fell head long in love with him. When your father first saw me, he could not keep his eyes from me. I was just as mesmerized by him."

"What does mesmerize mean mother…?" asked Orin.

Miria laughed a little, and began to explain.

"We looked at each other and saw no one else. We were totally in love. I never looked at another man like that anymore. Your father's brother, named Luis—now king of England—was very jealous of your father. He wanted him dead, and plotted with your fathers advisors to have it done."

"So…my uncle killed my father, then sent us here to live…?"

"Well not exactly. They never found Lyonus' body, and I never really believed he died, not my Lyonus. But now Fredrick Guy…it seems would need a lot of help. To exile a queen is too elaborate for just one person, though I feel he is the man I should hold to blame for Lyonus."

"Is he the man you think killed father…?"

"I think Orin, something happened to your father…something so bad that it would keep him from us. I don't know what, I just know that Guy had a great hand in it's completion. I feel he made it so that Lyonus could not find his way to return home."

Orin began to cry a little.

"Oh don't cry dear, oh my darling. It is hard to understand, but you must survive this. You must, in order to go back to England some day…after all you are her rightful king now that Lyonus is gone."

"Well what about king Luis…will he let me just take it back…?"

"Never! That swine…He will try and kill you as well…but you must find a way to defeat him and take back what belonged to your father, and now belongs to you and yours. There is one more thing I must add to the story Orin…"

"Yes mother." Orin sat up against his pillow, ready to hear.

"I must tell you. You have a sister, a twin sister named Jessica."

"I do? Where is she now, mother? Did king Luis do something to her as well…?"

"I pray each night that he has no knowledge of her where a bouts, and that she has grown well, and happy…and safe. The little princess remained in England."

"Does she know about me too mother?"

"No, she knows nothing of either of us yet. But the people I left her with swore, they would let her know about her family, once she was old enough. I hope one day, the two of you will meet and find a life around each other. That…right this very moment, is my wish. Now enough, my love, it is time for you to sleep…"

"Yes mother, goodnight Nichol…"

Orin rolled himself over into his covers, and snuggled in, more than ready to dream.

"Good night young prince…" said Nichol, in a quiet whisper.

"Sweet dreams little one," said Miria, as she wiped the tears from her cheek.

"My lady, what shall we do for Orin? We must see to it that he survives here…I worry for both of you. This certainly is not England," said Nichol.

"No Nichol, it isn't France…but we will survive it to help Orin. We will do all that we can. What then do you suggest Nichol, we are almost out of gold…?"

"Well I've heard people talk about ladies that do odd jobs around the village…"

"Odd jobs, like what dear…?" asked Miria, not understanding Nichol at all.

"Well for example washing…"

"Washing…? You mean someone's dirty clothing…?"

"Well my lady, if I can do it for you and Orin, I think I can for others. I could get real money and supplies for us…"

"Yes but…you've always taken care of me and Orin…I…"

"Look ma'am…if I don't mind doing it…that should be the most important thing, and I don't mind doing for you or the prince."

"Then I should take on a job too…"

"My lady…" chuckled Nichol "You have never done a days work, you would not know how to wash a shirt."

"But I could learn how…" said Miria.

"Suppose you could, then who would be left to take care of Orin?"

"Well…I guess you've settled that argument smoothly. Are you sure you're not a diplomat?"

So, Nichol took in wash from the villagers at La Vega, to help support their needs.

With the little gold that remained, Miria purchased papers for Orin that served to hide his true identity. In that way, he was able to move around the country without hindrance.

One day Nichol decided to be brave.

"Where are you going Nichol?"

"I am going to find Mr.Bolene…you know the man Margarete bought the ticket from."

"Oh…" said Miria "You mean the one who took our gold and refused to let her sail…?"

"The one and the same…he owes us for her ticket, and I plan to make a fuss until he returns the gold."

"But what if he tries something rough with you?"

"Then I will be just as rough…don't worry, it will be okay. I will be back later…"

"Be careful Nichol…" sighed Miria. "I don't want to lose you too…"

"I will see you later…trust me."

"Oh it's not you I don't trust…"

Now Nichol left in search on Jon Paul Bolene, and found him in a tavern at the end of the town.

When Nichol walked in Jon Bolene rose up from his table. He seemed to have recognized her, or least wanted to know her.

"Good afternoon…lovely Senorita, is it…?" he asked, with a simple grin on his face. "Haven't we met before?"

"Oh yes…we have in a way," she replied.

"Then what brings you here?"

"Do you see the bag I am holding…Monsieur?"

"Of course…" he said, as he waved his men from the table. "What of it…?"

"This bag held gold, that was paid to you for a ticket to England, which was never received."

"What are you calling me a thief…?"

"Why no…you made yourself the thief, when you did not live up to your deal."

"Now I know where I've seen you. You came off a ship with another women trying to get to the king. Ah and your friend wanted a ticket to England."

"Yes…" said Nichol. "And it never happened…you kept the gold my friend…"

"I waited for the young lady to show up…"

Nichol interrupted his statement.

"Yes, and while she was conveniently being attacked, you sailed off into the sunset with her gold and the ticket."

"Well I'll tell you what I'll do…I don't want you to think badly of me, I will give you another ticket or passage. How about that."

"Oh…ho, that's not good enough," said Nichol, as she stood to her feet. I don't want a trip to England."

"Well then what do you want from me…?"

Then Nichol sat back down, leaned in to Bolene, and said.

"I am in search of papers."

"Papers…?" He said what forged papers? What kind of person do you think I am…?"

"Well, I don't think you really want me to answer that question monsieur."

"Oh but I do…I do want you to answer, but I warn you…be careful."

"Hum…you are a man with great influence…an a greater number of associates.

You sometimes get things done with a little persuasion."

Jon Paul cleared his throat, and then said.

"Continue…my dear."

"Well…you have a way with the ladies, and you don't mince words. A man of means…a man of muscle…a man of resources. One I need right now."

Nichol looked at Jon Paul with a glare in her eyes and then asked. "Did you get my meaning?"

"I don't know it all depends on you. Did you get my meaning?" he replied while he eyed her chest.

"I need the papers in a week."

"What exactly are your terms Jon Paul? Oh…I can call you Jon Paul, can't I?"

"My dear you may call me what you like, but I don't know if I can meet with your price. To find the things you seek, might take more than a little gold. The price of a ticket, is nothing compared to what you have asked…"

"I have no doubt…you of all men, would be able to get me exactly what I need…and in a week…"

"I'm touched by your confidence, but I prefer to see the gold."

"Look Jon Paul, I have told you, you have already been paid…"

"Yes…" he answered and I told you it would not be enough for what you ask…"

"You see, I know people, they will say one thing and do another." Jon Paul starred into space, and then said.

"Like that fellow, a scurvy one, if ever I've seen…came here long time ago, about twenty years ago, bought himself a name…I believe it was Guy…He wanted to be a Duke or Earl or something. That fellow never did return and pay me my do. From then on, I started helping men get on their feet after they come out of prison and all. I knew they wouldn't fine a life here in Spain. Most of them wanted to leave and go to another country, but the fare was always a little to high. I would take them, and let them work off their debts and such. The favor turned into what you see, a tavern and a ship."

"Then how much more will I need to accomplish this thing?"

"First tell me what it is…I mean everything."

"Well first, I will need a family name, that would be difficult to trace back to. Then, I need the ancestral papers to match the new name, for a male child about thirteen."

"Hum…to do this would take me a little time…I have to search very hard."

"You have a week Bolene…to make it happen."

"What is your rush, my dear…? Is this boy in some sort of trouble?"

"Just the opposite…I'm trying to keep him out of trouble. It's complicated Jon Paul. I need to know that you can do it…"

"I will give it my best…but I require a payment in advance…"

"What kind of payment?" asked Nichol, as she began to shiver.

"Oh…I think you know what I mean…"

"I'm not quite sure I can go that route Monsieur…I hardly know you…"

"No…I was just kidding about with you…I tell you what I'll do. I will get the papers for you…and if they are okay, then you will consider having diner with me here…How about that…?"

"I tell you what, get the papers, and I will not let the patrols know you are allowing criminals to escape on your ship. Or that you are selling passage then having the people assaulted, so they can not take advantage of the ride."

"You would not do such a thing…"

"I told you Jon Paul, we've done business with you before, and came out on the losing end. That's just how serious I am about getting what I need."

"I tell you truthfully, I had nothing to do with those ladies being attacked."

"I did not say who or what happened. How did you know they were attacked, if you had nothing to do with it?"

"Being who I am, I get wind of all sorts of information. For example, the lady you spoke of was traveling with a queen that had been exiled from England…no one was supposed to help her. Miria was her name. Is she still alive?"

"Very much alive…and I plan that she stay that way. We wasted years seeking an audience with your king. At first it was all seemed to be hopeless, until we heard about you and your ship. It was the ray of sunshine we needed."

"Yet you trust me now Senorita?"

"I trust no one. As I have said, you kept the gold. I haven't given up on the deal."

"All right…I will make a deal. If I can get what it is you ask, you will only need give me…hum…say, twenty gold…oh all right, fifteen gold pieces…"

Nichol looked at Jon Paul with such fierce eyes, then said.

"How about you get the papers, and I give you ten pieces of gold, that would make it even."

"All right…all right, you drive a hard bargain Senorita, for such a pretty one…"

"Thanks Bolene…I'll be back in a week, with the gold."

"Let me ask you…if I may, Senorita…What made you think I would allow you to leave when you threatened to bring the patrol…?"

"I figured you among other things, a man of his word…"

"You showed much courage coming here, this is good. I like you Senorita."

"Well monsieur, I thought I could trust you, once I looked into your eyes."

"Oh?"

"Yes, I could always tell a lot about a person, by their eyes."

"Thank you Senorita...I will get what you need..."

Then it was settled. Nichol had made an impression on Jon Paul Bolene. He truly fancied her and not only got the papers she requested, but the name of the best school in Spain.

He also got a letter through to the castle to King Emanuel, from Miria.

Though too late to save the time lost for Miria, he was in plenty of time however, to help Orin.

Jon Bolene turned out to be a special friend to Nichol.

Miria and Nichol, found the best school possible for him.

Mira wanted Orin to receive the best training in the Spanish courts, and acquaint him with the ways of royalty.

Jacqueline and Ricardo were a great help of course, when Ricardo who had introduced Jon Bolene in the first place, helped to find the necessary people to forge the papers needed. Ricardo took the letter to the king. But it was not in time to turn things around. Miria had not received any response from king Emanuel.

This served as little comfort for her.

Now with his new name, Orin was ready to move in the circle of royalty.

While under the assumed name of William Lancaster III, the grandson of the second Earl of Somerset, he would enter school. There he met Miguel the son of a count, and thereby his sister, Teresa.

Teresa fell madly in love with William (Orin).

After a while he wooed her, and took advantage of her position in the Spanish court, but later, learned the value of being loved. Orin was able at last, to love in return.

Miguel, and Teresa finally introduced Orin at court. Tall dark and handsome, he swept the ladies off their feet. But Teresa kept hold of him.

This is the thing Miria had hoped for, while in La Vega. That Orin would one day move in position to return to England, and claim his rightful place.

After many more years in La Vega, Nichol took ill with scarlet fever and died. This was one more point of devastation for Miria.

She stopped communications with Margarete and Consuela, not one word from them.

She became quite ill herself. While she tried to nurse Nichol, she contracted some of the symptoms.

With no one to help or hold on to, Miria felt forsaken. She had very little emotional strength that remained. As she looked out her window upon the parched land, it reminded her, she would never see home again. While the thought of never seeing Orin continued to haunt her, it was all too much to bear.

The letter that was supposed to have reached the king was never acknowledged.

Then in her last attempts to keep her sanity, she called out for Lyonus, but no one heard her voice. Alone and forgotten, she tied two bed sheets together and stood upon a stool that always sat by the fireplace.

Then with a long glance at Orin's old crib, she planned to leap.

Miria realized that was a coward's way out. All the years she spent priding herself on staying strong would have been a lie. So as she weakened, she gave way to her bed that seemed at the time the only place of comfort. Miria knew that death was a short time away. So she lie quietly on her bed, and rubbed her face alone Orin's blanket.

As her life began to drain, she could only see the sight of her and Lyonus together. While their children, Orin and Jessica played happily before them; they were united as a family.

While the life slowly seeped out from her thin sleek body, riddled with fever, she took one long gasp and her body went limp. Her long graying hair covered her broken face. Miria, once ward of a King, and Queen of a country, lay in poverty, and died in despair. Mocked by the very thing she had grown to hate, loneliness.

Jacqueline finally returned to visit Miria, a short time later, bringing with her the news, that king Emanuel had determined to see her. But instead of a warm welcome, she received a sight that drew her to the floor.

She opened the door, and found Miria dead. Her corpse had already started to rot.

At first, Jacqueline could only scream, until atlas, she could no longer make a sound.

When she looked closer, there, within Miria's fingers, was the locket given to her by Lyonus on their wedding day. It seemed Miria had sold everything, except the locket. But now, Jacqueline would use it to buy a plot for her body, and a headstone. However, Jacqueline could not find one person in La Vega, Spain that would make a headstone for Miria. So, she and Ricardo buried her body on an abandoned estate near the village graveyard.

Later the people of the town put up a stone that read, "Here lays Miria De'Sheffield, an exile of England."

Now William (Orin) was sent word of his mothers' death. He returned home too late to see her, but visited the place where she was buried. There was a simple flat rock for a headstone that was wedged into the ground. Just who carved the writing, no one knew exactly.

He was appalled by what he saw carved in the rock. Orin was so upset at what the marker read, that he pulled it from around the grave—flung it as far as he could—and mashed it against a tree.

He cried sorely on his knees, and swore on Miria's grave, that he would avenge her death on the life of king Luis's heirs, even if it took the rest of his life.

By this time Orin, known in royal circles as Edward Lancaster III, had acquired a great deal of money. This was mainly due to his marriage to the Countess Teresa Christina Fernando.

The marriage brought him great prestige and nobility.

He was ready, to make his move back to his homeland of England. But first, he had Miria a stone newly fashioned, and placed at the head of her grave. It read. "Here lies Miria Michelle De' Sheffield: Beloved Mother, Daughter of France, and former Queen of England."

Now Orin was ready to celebrate his eighteenth birthday, he looked much older, as if the years of struggle with revenge had hardened the lines on his face. So much so, it was as if he had become a man overnight. But it was his marriage to Teresa, which eased his thirst for vengeance.

While in town, Orin had overheard some of the men talking about Jon Paul Bolene. Orin asked the men to set up a meeting with him, and so they did.

Meeting Mr. Bolene was quite enlightening for Orin. He was able to touch elbows of many shady fellows.

Those, who could not freely pass from any port of call, primarily used the services of Jon Paul. It would include men who sought flight from the king's justice, or thieves and murderers, and those who had served time in prison.

For a few bags of gold, or the right price, he would smuggle a person anywhere they wanted to go. He also forged passports and papers.

In this area, he was well acquainted.

Orin talked at length with Jon Bolene, and found out much information about the royal court of England.

"Mr. Bolene…I seek passage aboard your ship sir…" said Orin.

"Oh…?" said Bolene, as he looked Orin up and down. "What is your name…? You don't seem to be like the scurvy sort of fellows that I'm used to looking after."

"What do you mean?"

"I mean you seem like an aristocrat or something. One who could pay with much gold…why would a person of your statue require passage on my ship? Are you in some sort of trouble?"

"No, I'm not in any trouble. I just want to surprise some friends of mine. My name is William. William Lancaster III. Sir…" said Orin.

"Yes, I'm quite familiar with that name."

"What do you mean, familiar?" questioned Orin.

"It is of little consequence, Senior. What is your pleasure?"

"I want to return to England."

"Wouldn't happen to know a gent in the royal court by the name of Fredrick Guy would you?" asked Jon. "Lord Fredrick Guy he calls himself now…He owes me big money…I haven't been able to catch up to him."

He did not give Orin a chance to answer, before he spouted off all the more.

"If I offered you a seat on the Tempest, would you promise to deliver my message to that swine, Guy?"

"This lord Guy in which you speak, the same advisor to the king there in England?"

"Why yes…then you do know him?"

"Oh, I've heard a little about him. I heard he was not one to trust, very ruthless."

"Well I don't know all the details, but I do know his entire family was killed mysteriously. Then just as suddenly, he found himself on board my ship, claiming to be something special. But he never gave me all my money."

"Do you think he will even remember owing you any thing?"

"Why don't you allow his memory to be refreshed, with the things I have told you."

"Hum…that might be one way of getting to met this man of high standing in the royal court."

"Or get yourself killed," said Bolene.

"Let me worry about that."

"So you will meet with him then?"

"Of that my friend, I can assure you…"

"Why don't we meet soon, at the old Cantina, just above the grave yard? Do you know the place?"

"Oh, I think I can find it."

"It's the only one in the village, and away from the prying eyes of soldiers…"

"I will let you know when I am ready to go…" said Orin.

"I will be at your service…"

So Orin, determined to leave for England, decided to tell Teresa the truth about his name, and his life.

He found Teresa outside in the garden.

"Teresa…I need you to listen to me now…and please, don't interrupt until I have finished…please."

"All right, my love…what seems to trouble you?"

"I must tell you the truth, I have lied to you from the beginning."

"Lied…my dear?"

"Yes. Teresa, you did not marry the grandson of the earl of Somerset as I had told you…but instead, the son of Lyonus II, king of England—prince, and the son of Miria Michelle De'Sheffield—daughter of France and queen of England…exiled in shame. There I have said it, I can only hope your love will not turn to hate for me. If it does…I will leave quietly, and never bother you again…"

"Now, don't be ridiculous. Let me tell you something my husband. I have no intentions of letting you go anywhere quietly, or any other way. I love you very much now and always, and there is nothing you can do that can change this, my husband. Besides, I have always known who you were…" Orin's' eyes grew large in surprise.

"What?" He shouted with a gasp, "You mean you knew before we were married?"

"Yes…long before. When your mother sent you to school, the papers you presented, were a little strange to my father, so he had them traced to the black market. He also knew the Earl of Somerset, and it was not your grandfather…but because you were Miguel's friend, and I loved you…we persuaded him to allow you to stay.

He became quite fond of you and knew exactly what had happened to you and your mother."

"But…how…?"

"Lord Graybourne contacted Prince Michael of France about your mother. He came to visit King Emanuel, and told him of your mothers' plight. At first the king would not give in to the prince, but later my father talked to him and he was ready to speak with her. Some of her friends helped to get the message through. The king wanted to give her a chance to tell her side of the story. When they tried to find her, it was too late, the fever had all ready found her a way out."

"I can not believe you let me continue with this charade, all this time…"

"What choice did I have? It was you who did not trust that I could love you without judging you, even as you were. You held back the truth from us…I had to wait until you were ready my love. We all had to wait…"

"What about Miguel…?"

"Yes…Orin, we both love you. He was waiting for you as well. There is no shame in this my husband, It was awful what they did to your family. We will help in any way we can of course…"

Teresa's father stood in the doorway, as he listened to the conversation added.

"My son, we truly want to help you…"

Orin turned to look at him, and said in such sadness.

"Senor…I am so ashamed…it is very difficult to face you now…"

"Nonsense, there are worse things than having lied to save yourself…you felt you had no choice…"

"But…Miguel…?"

"Don't worry about him, he is on your side as we all are."

"I can't tell you what this means to me…"

"Oh my son even king Emanuel has offered his help…"

"What? How can he help now? He would not even give mother a chance to explain."

"He asked me to give you his apology in the form of…this way my son…"

Senor Fernando pointed to a room, and lead Orin there. He opened the door to reveal piles of gold.

"What? Is this for me?"

"As much as it takes to redeem yourself to your country…"

"With so much…one could buy a city…" said Orin.

"Or an army…" replied Senor Fernando.

"I…I don't know what to say…thank you sir…!"

"Thank my Teressa…she is the one who always knew your worth. She loves you more than life my boy…don't hurt her…"

"I love her as well sir. But for now I must do something she won't think is best."

"…And what is that…?"

"I must return to England, and clear my mothers name, and find out what happened to my father, king Lyonus."

"Not to mention reclaim your throne. Well, I think that can be understood…she knows about such things…"

"I'm not at all sure myself, just how to go about this! " said Orin, his eyes searched for help.

"This will take a little planning."

"Yes…we can not go there with an army, for the English, it would surely be taken as a sign of a broken treaty. War is not our goal."

"No…but a small scrimmage would not be too much to handle."

"What do you suggest Senor?" said Orin, as his hand ran through the loose gold.

"I think we should acquire the assistance of some of your caballeros in England. We need those of the shady sort, who would fight for money…then buy some land…perhaps and estate there, to establish ourselves as wealthy. Wealth has always attracted the attention of the nobles especially a rat like Senor Guy…"

"You know him…how…?"

"Not personally, but he is the one who sent papers of your mothers guilt to king Emanuel. The king admitted, it seemed strange, but he was afraid of war…"

"But now he is not…?" questioned Orin.

"Listen, don't look at this gift with contempt, and throw away your chance to get back some of what you have lost. Understand…the king has tried to make amends…he does not have to. He could just allow you to stay as you are here with us, or return you to your state as an exile…"

"You are right after all Senor…I am…just so angry, it is hard to think straight."

"That is all right my son…why do you think we are here…?" said Senor Fernando, with a smile. "It is my job to protect you and my daughter…Come, let us plan what we should do together."

CHAPTER FIFTEEN
Melinda Finds a Friend

Melinda Graybourne, who after the Graybourne's murder, lived with her uncle Morgan. They lived in a small Province off the outer shores of England. She continued to exact her skills as a woman of the sword. Much like her father Thomas, Melinda became well versed enough, so she could take her revenge. Then one day, she decided it was time to find the people responsible for the death of her parents.

Now Melinda used one of her fathers' favorite horses. She brought him with her after the fire. She loved that horse, mainly because it was her lord Thomas' favorite. He was named Graymere, because of his gray shine.

As Melinda said goodbye to her uncle, she remembered leaving some things at the old homestead, and dropped by to see if things were as she had left them.

So as she rode upon the estate, she saw that weeds had grown up over her parents' graves. But the sword was still stood as a headstone. She slowly dismounted Graymere, and walked to where the entrance to the house once stood. There, she looked around a bit, reliving what she had seen lo, those many years ago. After a moment, she went in. Melinda walked around and looked for anything that was usable. Then she remembered her old hiding place. She ran over to the slit in the wall, and pushed the corner, out popped a long bag. Melinda could not wait to see its contents. She took the bag outside, to have better light, and then opened it. Inside she found several bags of gold.

She also found a sword wrapped, a beautiful sword, with a note attached that read: To my beautiful daughter on your eighteenth birthday. May you enjoy this special gift, my grandfather gave it to me, and it should remain in the family. We love...

The letter was incomplete. But Melinda could only imagine the next line.

So she looked further into the bag and caught hold of a stack of letters, or at least it seemed so. She started to open and read one, it said: I, Lyonus II, King of England, hereby leave to my heirs...Melinda sat for a moment with her mouth open, then opened another, skimmed across the writing, that read: Here the assigned Frederick Guy,...amnesty...laws of England...will remain guiltless. Signed Lyonus II.

"Oh my goodness!" she shouted, and then said. "What was father into? These must mean something to England. I wonder if these letters were why my family was murdered....And...what is this?" she questioned, as she opened the next letter.

"Oh...this answers a lot of questions." Then she pulled the last one apart, then said. "She gave away the heir to the throne. How could she do it?"

Then Melinda continued to read the letter that revealed the plot to seek out and kill the heirs to the throne. Then she shouted.

"This has to be why they killed them, they would not give up these letters. Hum...but they will wish they had never come to Hilton!" said Melinda, steaming as she mangled the paper in her hand, then reread the letters. As she read about the heir, she continued to think of her, and call her name. "Jessica, hum...Jessica, I wonder if she is beautiful. She should be about my age by now. I wonder if she is even alive. Oh well," said Melinda. "I'd better get these things packed, and be on my way, it will be a long ride."

Then on her way out she stopped at the gravesite and said.

"Father, mother, you were the bravest two people in the whole world. I shall always remember you, and I shall try to do things that would have made you proud. Though I don't think my revenge would be among them." Then rearing up on old Graymere, bade them a grand farewell.

Melinda was indeed a beautiful girl. Her baggy pants, old ruffled hat and vest that belonged to her uncle, kept hidden her more feminine features. She did not want to appear and easy mark along the road, in fact she did not want to appear to be a woman at all.

Now approached dusk, by the time Melinda and old Gray finally arrived at an Inn. They needed somewhere to rest for the night. She tied old Gray to some bushes, and pulled off a bag from her saddle. She opened the doors that squeaked just a little, and peered inside. The tavern was filled with both men and women, eating and drinking. They all seemed to be having a grand time, getting drunk and falling all over themselves. So Melinda finally went inside and stopped at the bar.

"Hum, um, um," she muttered, clearing her throat to get the bar maids attention.

"Just a minute!" she yelled you are not the only customer I have don't you see? You'll just have to wait your turn."

"All right," said Melinda, in a quiet tone. She was trying not to bring attention to herself. Then the barmaid asked.

"Well...you mister, what will you have?" she said, pointing at Melinda. But Melinda was looking around the tavern, and did not know the bar maid was speaking to her. I say there you with the funny looking hat...do you want a drink or not? I don't have all night!"

Suddenly a woman nudged Melinda then said. "I think she's talking to you my lord," As she turned away to take a sip of her cup.

Then Melinda realized she was dressed as a man and would be treated like one. "Oh, yes." With a stutter, then said. "I would like some beef, and some bread...and a little cheese please. Oh and a small goblet of wine, if you don't mine. You can bring it over to my table."

Then the bar maid seemed to get a little upset, and mocked, her. "...Bring it to the table, if you don't mind." And then she asked. "Well...would there be anything else for my lord?" Snapping her voice at Melinda.

Melinda paused for a moment, then said. "Yes, I'm afraid so." All the while, she tried to deepen her voice. "I will need some accommodations for the night."

"Yeah?" said the barmaid. "Well Alice, can help you there. Alice!" she yelled, then finished some ale in a goblet she held. "There's a fellow here wanting a room."

Then she turned to Melinda with a curious look, then remarked. "All right, she'll be with you in a moment...sir?" The barmaid took a closer look at Melinda, shrugged her shoulders in doubt, and then walked away. She glanced at Alice, and shook her head, as they passed in the hallway.

So Alice escorted Melinda to a room that over looked the stables.

"Hello there. Said Alice, as she watched Melinda's stride. "Here you are sir. This is a very comfortable room."

Melinda walked over to the window then said.

"Is this the best view you have, a bunch of stables? Don't you have something, maybe with a view of the stars?"

Then Alice said with a frown.

"I'm sorry sir," said Alice. "No we don't! Besides, none of the other men have ever complained about the view before."

With a grin on her face, Alice hurried down the stairs; she could not wait to tell the others, about her conversation with Melinda.

"Guess what?" she said. "That fellow wanted to have a view of the stars, instead of the stables. What do you men think of that?"

They all started to laugh, and starred up at Melinda. She came down the stairs in time to hear Jessica speak out.

"Well, I don't see the problem. I wouldn't want to open my window to some smelly stables either, unless of course, I already enjoyed the smell of a horse."

Then they stopped laughing just as suddenly, and went about their business.

Melinda walked over to Jessica, and then asked. "What is your name? You have intervened for a second time."

Jessica, made her way to a table, and then answered. "My name is Jessica, Jessica Jeffers to be exact." She held out her hand. They shook hands, and then Melinda replied.

"All right Jessica, my name is Melinda, Melinda Graybourne to be exact," she responded so smug and proud.

"Good to meet you my lady," said Jessica.

"My lady?" she said in a whisper, as she leaned closer to Jessica. How did you know, I was a woman that is?" Stuttering, with such surprise.

"Please Melinda, I've not seen a man yet, with as tiny a waste or skin as smooth as yours, in all my days, and I've seen a lot of men."

Then Melinda even more curious, asked. "Then how can I hide it, I don't want to be pawed on, and treated as a winch in here."

"Well never mind that, the way you are dressed, that will keep away most men I know."

"What do you mean!" said Melinda, with a scoff.

"Well, I thought you liked to look like this," she said, when she pointed to her baggy pants and vest.

"Well I do when I'm traveling so far from home, but I didn't think I looked that badly."

"Let's put it this way, you are not going to cause the men in this room to fight over you. Okay? Look at it as if you got what you wanted."

Jessica finally sat down at the table, and then said. "Look, do you see that woman there?" Jessica pointed to a lady in a red, very low v cut dress. You see Melinda, they would fight all night to bed her."

"Oh, yes, I see what you mean. In that case, I guess I understand what you have said."

Now the food Melinda ordered has arrived at her table. Then barmaid gave a little wink.

"Here you are sir." The maid smiled, then said. "I hope everything is to your liking." Melinda glanced over at Jessica, and back to the maid. "I'm sure it will be fine. Thank you." Then she turned to Jessica, and asked. "Have you eaten today?"

Jessica shook her head no; all the while she watched the food on the table.

"Then please," said Melinda. "Stay, have some food with me. After all, there is plenty, and it's the least I can do for your kindness today."

"All right then, I think I will. It does look delicious."

Melinda, and Jessica hit it off nicely.

Then Melinda thought back to the letters she found at the old estate, and then began to ask Jessica all kind of questions.

"Jessica, do you have family around here. What does your father do?"

Jessica, looked very sad, then answered. "My family is dead, all murdered, and right before my eyes. But I don't want to talk about it now."

"Oh it's okay," said Melinda, as she reached for Jessica's hand. "I fear we have more in common, than you might have guessed."

"Really?" said Jessica.

"We'd better eat now," said Melinda, as she took her hand away from Jessica. "Your sarcasm has shown its face."

"Oh?" Jessica grunted when it's about my family, you have no idea."

"Well. Maybe I have found out more about you, than even you could know." Melinda replied, while she put food in her mouth, to avoid another word.

A silence took over for a moment, then Jessica asked.

"You mentioned a bit ago, you knew some things about me, that we had things in common."

"That's correct. "Said Melinda, while she leered at Jessica, as if she held some grave secret.

"So then, besides the obvious, what did you mean?"

"You said that both your parents were dead, or murdered."

"Yes I did."

"Well that's what I meant. Both my parents were murdered as well."

"Oh. I see," said Jessica, and then looked away from Melinda.

"But hey!" remarked Melinda, with a determinant voice. "You could wager on this one thing however."

"...And, what is that?" Jessica questioned, as she watched Melinda' lips move.

"I will find those who killed my father and mother."

"Then maybe I could join you in your quest. You never know what we could turn up," said Jessica.

"I've traveled alone thus far, I'm not at all sure it would work out Jessica."

"I'm pretty good with staves." Then she paused then added oh, and a sword, I could prove useful. No matter, we could be going the same way, after all."

"I'd rather it be done alone, then, I will have no regrets, except for myself."

"Oh, you didn't have a thought I might need protection did you? Jessica asked as if her pride were wounded, then replied, "Well...if you feel that way about it, I won't interfere."

"Thanks Jessica for understanding."

"You also mentioned something about, you knew about me. What was that all about?" Now Jessica was filled with questions, she had not given Melinda a chance to answer one before she had asked another. "What did you say your name was again, your last name?"

"I said it was Graybourne to be exact." Melinda answered, while she pushed her plate away.

Just then Jessica took notice of the men that sat at the table in front of them. Their ears were glued to the seats. Each time Melinda spoke, Jessica saw that they drew their heads closer to the table.

"Tell me again what happen to your father, this time just whisper." Jessica wanted to see what the men would do.

"I've already told you."

"Then tell me again." Jessica said, while she tried to motion for Melinda's attention on the men's table.

"All right," said Melinda, as she watched the men from the corner of her eye.

"Some men came to the estate one afternoon. They looked for some documents or papers, something like that, and my father refused them."

"Just what was your fathers name?" said Jessica.

"His name was lord Thomas Hendly Graybourne. He was called Thomas of the blade."

"I think I have heard of him." Then Jessica motioned for Melinda to take note of the men.

"Why don't we leave now, our talk could be finished on the road." Jessica hurried Melinda from her seat.

"Wait, I need to get my bag I left upstairs."

"Well get it and hurry, I think we've got trouble," cautioned Jessica.

"Right," said Melinda, as she ran up the stairs.

While Jessica stood waiting for Melinda to come down, the men went out. They waited for Jessica and Melinda to get outside, and on to their horses. Then the men proceeded to follow them.

"Listen, did you understand what I meant back their?" Jessica asked, with a worried expression on her face.

"What did I say that would cause them to...? Oh!" said Melinda. My father."

"Exactly," said Jessica. They heard you say Grayborne, and they sat up to hear more."

"I know...I saw," said Melinda, as she held tight to Graymere's reigns.

"Let's just keep riding, follow me. I know a place where our business can be handled."

"Alright, lead on."

So Jessica and Melinda rode steadily, until they reached a place, where Jessica felt, was right.

"We are still followed." marked Melinda.

"Then let them come!" said Jessica, as she dismounted her horse.

"Wait!" whispered Melinda. "Shouldn't we continue on?"

"No! This is the best place to find out what they know. Now get down, and ready your sword."

"Al right! Here they come!"

The men rode over to Melinda and Jessica. Then the men swung their swords. They hoped to have struck Melinda, but quick as could be, she ducked away. Jessica caught one of them, as he got off his horse. She threw her stave into his coat, and fastened him against a tree. He struggled all the while, trying to get free. Then Melinda, fought one of the men, and injured him badly. While Jessica kept busy, Melinda talked to the one who seemed to be the leader.

"Hey, I don't want to kill you, but I do want to know why you are following, and trying to kill us?"

"I don't worry about a winch, and a boy. You said you were a Grayborne, and that's why you must die."

Then Melinda pulled off her hat to show that she was a girl, and then said.

"I'm no boy you idiot. No wonder they couldn't get the job done…they sent you."

"We finished off poor old Thomas didn't we, ha…and that pretty little wife of his, ha ha."

"Well you forgot one, the one that is going to kill you now!"

That comment angered the man, and he plunged violently at Melinda, and she struck him down.

"You fool, you could have lived, if you had just told me what I wanted to know."

Then she turned straightway to Jessica.

"Hey Jess, is everything under control?"

"I think so, but I'm becoming rather tired of this game."

Just as Melinda caught his attention, Jessica stabbed him in the heart.

"That should take some of the wind out of him."

"Well," said Jessica, while she walked over to the man caught on the tree. "What should we do with this one?"

"I'm not sure," Melinda replied. "Maybe if he's cooperative, we will let him crawl back to his friends."

"Or, maybe not!" said Jessica, starring him in the eyes.

"Who are you, and what do you want? Tell me quickly," said Melinda I am very tired. It's been a really long day, and as you can see, I'm not in a great mood."

Then Jessica placed her blade at his throat, and then said.

"Maybe a little gentle persuasion will help his memory."

"Wait!" said the man.

"All right, I'm waiting," said Melinda, "tell us!"

"I was sent a while back…to the Hilton Estate, to retrieve some papers."

"…And did you get them?"

"We left empty handed."

"Liar!" shouted Jessica, "You did not leave empty handed. I thought I recognized you."

"No Jessica wait, I want to hear more. Well go on man." Motioning for Jessica to move away,

"Well we had been looking for the heir to the throne, and the documents for years, it was like no end to it. So we were ordered to kill any one who resisted."

"…And were you also ordered to rape, beat and leave for dead, any girl who resisted."

Then Melinda saw that Jessica had gotten out of control, and said.
"Look sir, what is your name?"
"My name is Martin," he stuttered, in fear of the girls.
"Well Martin," said Melinda you should have stayed at home today."
"You raped and beat me. I will never forget that awful smell as long as I live," said Jessica.
"Ha…ha!" chuckled Martin then replied. "I'll never forget the taste of you, though I've forgotten your name."
"No Jessica!" said Melinda, while he continued to taunt her.
"The way you wiggled and screamed. And your father poor old man, just wasn't quick enough. You all are dead!"
Then Jessica took both her staves, as quick as could be, and drew them across his throat, and said.
"Then tell it to my father when you see him…it's your turn to join the dead!"
"Oh Jessica."
"What is it?"
"Don't you see…he taunted us because he wanted us to kill him?"
"Then I am happy. I felt as a genie would today."
"A genie, what do you mean?"
"I was able to grant him his last wish." Melinda kicked him over, and then said.
"I wish he hadn't wanted to die so badly, we could have found out who he was working for."
"Yes well, that chance is gone, they are all dead. We'd better find something to do with them, before someone comes along."
"Right. Let's get their horses, they can help us take them into the woods."
"Woods? Aren't their wolves in there?" said Melinda.
"Now you're getting the point. Help me tie them to the reigns. We will let the horses pull them in, and then cut them lose."
"Okay, that sounds like a plan."
Late that night, they stopped near a lake to rest for the night.
"Look, I need to stop. I'm exhausted, and poor old Gray, is ready to pass out too," said Melinda.
"All right, I tired myself. Let's make this the place. There's plenty of water, it will do."
So they made a small fire, and started to pull their bags from the horses.
"You showed great skill back there," said Jessica. Did your father teach you?"

"Yes, and my uncles. All of them were sword makers. I've been around them all my life."

"What about you? You were no slouch back there yourself, very good in fact."

"Thanks, but I learned from everyone."

"What do you mean?"

"Well, there was always a knight coming around the place to speak with my father, and offered me a lesson or two. Then after a while they would not challenge me any more. So, I practiced with my father. He was a great swordsman."

"Let's sleep on it tonight, and talk more tomorrow over breakfast, okay?"

"Sure," said Jessica. I'm in no hurry to tell my story. Good night Melinda."

"Good night Jessica."

All of a sudden, Melinda rose up then said, "Jessica!"

Jessica turned over moaning a little. "Jessica!" she shouted. You are the one!"

"What? What do you mean? Go back to sleep, you've been dreaming."

"No, I'm have not Jessica, it's you in the letters."

"Oh Melinda, what letters?" Jessica dragged herself to sit up. "All right, I got it, we're not going to sleep now."

"Listen, I have the letters, those people have searched for all those years!"

"You?" said Jessica. "…And what made you think you had that kind of information Melinda?"

"Take a look at this!" she said, as she waved them around in front of Jessica' face.

"What? Let me see that?" she said, and snatched them from Melinda' hand.

She read the letter that said she was to be left in the care of the Jeffers. Her mouth stood opened. Then she dropped the letters to the ground.

"What's the matter?" asked Melinda, while she touched her shoulder. "You are a princess, you can trust that."

"I heard my parents talk at night when they thought I was asleep. I just never knew what to say. I couldn't question them because; I didn't want them to know I eavesdropped. But I am surprised to learn there is a document to prove they were right."

"No Jess, not that they were right, but that you are the heir to the throne of England…royalty my friend."

Then Jessica cried great swelling tears.

"I can't be a princess...until I've found the people that killed my family."

"Well, since we're up for the night," said Melinda. You might as well tell me what happened to you."

Jessica began her story.

"Hum..." she said, Just where to begin...my mother could never stand it when I wore pants, she would always make me put on a dress, then say. {Now you look like a proper little princess}. I miss them both. So...one day I decided to make papa's favorite apple pie.

You see we had a huge apple tree at the very edge of the farm, near the cobble stone road. When the tree was full, the apples would sometimes fall onto the road.

Then one day I put on my mothers favorite blue dress. I climbed that tree, to fetch some green baking apples. I could hardly climb that old tree, with that blamed dress that drew itself up between my legs. So I took it off and used it as an apron. I threw apples down into the dress, as many as would have made a few pies. While I continued to pull off apples, there came a sound of thunder that barreled down the old road. When they rode closer to me, I tried to act brave. What do you want here I asked them?

One of the men spoke up, said his name was Hawk. He asked if they might water their horses at our well, and perhaps get a drink for themselves. Not knowing what to do, I gave permission. As I watched them ride passed the well to the house, I became frightened, and lost my balance. I fell right out of the tree, and smashed most of the apple. I put on my dress, and limped as fast as I could to the house. When I finally got there, the men had sat down around the table, and started to eat. Then my father said in such a clam voice, {Jessica, go get my bed roll from the barn please}. Then I knew there was something wrong. My father had asked me to get the bedroll that held his staves, and sword. He told me, they were his prize things, and would never let me touch them before. I really became frightened, at what that meant. When I returned with the bedroll, the man I killed here tonight was there, standing at the table. He talked to my mother and told her what an excellent meal she had prepared. He said they were looking for children who had escaped the king. Then demanded my parents tell where the children were. {The heirs to the throne, I want them), he shouted. My father insisted he knew of no such children, and then asked them to leave. I could not move from my spot at the doorway. I don't know, I seemed paralyzed by my fathers' words, I guess.

Then the one they called Hawk reached over with his sword, and cut father down. My father was dead, and that same man took my mother in his arms, and asked her the same question. She slapped him so hard, that it turned his face so that he looked at me. Then, he stabbed her in the chest, right there in front of me. I pulled out a stave, from the bag and flung it at him, but it only sliced off his ear. Then, I turned and ran to the horse that was outside. I heard him say as he screamed from the pain, that I should be stopped. I remember…I thought at that moment…good, that's for my father. Then I tried to ride away, when several of the men followed me, and attacked me. I was able to kill one of them, but the others that followed subdued me. They raped, and then they beat me with fists, and sticks until they thought I was dead. I guess, to all I had known, I was dead."

"Oh Jess," cried Melinda. I'm so sorry." Jessica continued her story and said.

"The next thing I remembered was Mr. Hawkins, a friend of my fathers, standing over me. He carried me to his wagon. He and his wife helped clean me up. My nose was broken and I had all kind of cuts and bruises. I had a broken arm and ribs too. I can no longer have any children from what the Surgeon said they did to me. Mr. Hawkins buried my parents, behind the barn. I won't forget their kindness, not ever. But I could only stay with them for as long as it took for me to heal. I had to search for the murderers of my parents."

"Jessica…just, how many men have you killed?" Melinda asked, being quite careful to choose her words.

"More than my share," she answered….And any man who touches me without my permission, will join that number!"

"Do you understand what is happening here?" said Melinda. "We are bound together this night, by the things that have happened to us years ago. Don't you see Jessica, we are fated to be together, to find the people who killed our families, they are one and the same."

"Well then…there's one down, and, as many as need be to go." Then she searched through the rest of Melinda's letters, and said. "Let's see what else you have here of interest."

"Ah, yes." replied Melinda, as her voice seemed to have faded away.

"You don't think the letter spoke about you then, is that right Jess?"

"I've told you before, I don't quite know what's to be made of it. I do know that if I am of the house of Warwick, then the people out there who were searching for me are searching for me still. And now, I would like to know more about my royal family. If a Warwick now sits on the throne, what is he to me?"

Melinda spoke as if she had the perfect words, answered. "Jessica, your father Lyonus II was king, and your uncle Luis now king, had him killed to get the crown."

"You know this for sure Melinda?" Jessica asked her, with a brow raised.

"Everyone knew the reason Luis had your father murdered Jessica. Not to mention, he had your mother Miria banished from England."

"You know so much!" exclaimed Jessica, very upset at the idea.

"Well I'm sorry Jess, it was a matter of record. King Luis made it known to everyone, so he would be justified."

"Justified in what Melinda?"

"Usurping the throne of course."

"Then I must work harder to get it back from him."

"Oh Jessica, that is a very difficult task you seek. Finding the men who killed your parents is one thing, but overturning the throne, that's quite something else."

"No matter!" she spouted. "I will find the men, and regain the throne, because I now see they both are the same. Now are you with me or not?"

"Of course Jessica, but we must use restraint."

"Are you with me?" she yelled.

"I said yes Jessica, you know that I am."

"Then that is all I needed to hear, from now on we fight for the crown."

"Jessica just what do you have in mind? It will take a great army to defeat king Luis."

"There is an old soldier, well not that old. Well a soldier that was banished along with many others around here. His name is John Myers. He could join our quest."

"How do you know of such a man?"

"I've heard talk between the men while I sat around the taverns. They loved to tell tales of their glory days. But his tale was one not so happy. He loved my mother, the queen he'd say. He'd tell of her beauty, and wit. Anyway, I bet he would be willing to take on the task of leading banished and fallen men to victory against king Luis."

"I hope you know what it is you do Jessica, because I'm following right behind you."

"For now let us rest. We should head out in the morning for a little town and ask a certain dressmaker, to help with our problem."

"Oh, and what can a dressmaker know of this?"

"Ha, ha." laughed Jessica. You will see…but later in the morning. Good night Melinda, and thanks for everything."

"I don't quite get it, but you are welcome, and goodnight."

From that point on, Melinda and Jessica shared everything, which included the things they had in common, the men who shattered their lives.

CHAPTER SIXTEEN
The Black Market in Spain

Meanwhile back in Spain, Orin, made plans to meet with Jon Bolene.

With the help of Senior Fernando, they would embark upon a journey set, for England. Orin hoped to follow through with his determination to win back the throne stolen from his father, and avenge his mother's death.

"Senior Fernando," said Orin. "While we are waiting for Jon Bolene, let me ask you. Will I be able to get men from Spain, to accompany me to England? I don't want to go there, without any type of support."

"Why certainly. You will have as many men as you need. There are also men here, who would fight for payment in gold, just as in England. But the men waiting outside, are special friends of mine." Fernando replied.

"Then tell me Senior, what should I do?"

"There are six men waiting outside to go with you, as we speak my son," said Senior Fernando, while he bided the men to enter. "Come in, my friends. Meet the man you will be protecting in England. You of course know Miguel."

Orin said to the men with a big grin.

"Hello Miguel, my friend." Then proceeded to greet the other men. "I am Orin Warwick, of the royal House of Warwick. I am a prince of England. But I have lived here under a different name. I assume Senior Fernando, has told you about my situation?"

"Yes," said the men, as they nodded in unison.

"Then just let me say, that there is plenty to be made and plenty to be paid, for your loyalty to me."

Then one of the men named Alberto spoke up.

"Senior, please, excuse my words, they are not so good. It is not hard to do this thing for you. Senior Fernando…he has done so many good things for out families. He told us all about your mother and you. What happened to her was very, very sad to me. The men and I would feel only to glad if we helped you get rid of this lord Guy fellow. He is very, stupid."

"Well," said Orin. At least on that point, we are all clear, but we can never under estimate how wide spread his power is. Now then let's formulate our plan." He then motioned for the men to sit down around the table.

Suddenly Jon Bolene entered the room. "Well, I see all the kings men are here." Laughing because he knew them all. "Hello Alberto, Mateo!" Waiving about his hand.

"Si Buenos dias, Senior." they replied. Are you to go with us?" Mateo asked.

"My job is to supply the way there," he said.

"Then come in and sit. We have been waiting for you," said Senior Fernando.

"Si, Senior, I have planned to be ready in a week to leave for England. Can you be ready?"

"If Senior Fernando thinks we have enough men, then, I don't see why we could not be ready to sail. Senior Fernando, what do you think? Orin turned to look at him.

"Yes Orin, I don't see any reason why we should not sail. Are you satisfied with the men here?" Orin looked around at the men as if trying to search their hearts, then said.

"I think I could trust these great men with my life." Then the men stuck out their chest with pride.

"Well said there Orin, for they very well may be doing just that," said Bolene.

"All right then my friends, let's say when you get to England, you will go to an inn close to the shore."

"Why close to the shore?" asked Orin.

"Well, it will enable you to enter the country, without drawing a lot of attention to yourself, and us."

"Yes." Bolene added. It may be necessary to acquire some assistance from someone of statue. You won't be able to just waltz into England and join the elite without first being recommended by one of its own."

"Like who for example?" asked Senior Fernando.

"Well, like our infamous lord Guy, of course."

"Of course..." replied Fernando, understanding more clearly.

"All well and good," spouted Orin. But how do we get his attention in the first place?"

"Ha, my boy," laughed Bolene. The same way you get the attention of any man, with money."

"Yes, I'm beginning to see," said Orin, waiting eagerly to hear the rest.

"You seem to know this lord Guy quite well, do you not?" asked Fernando.

"I know enough of him to say, it would not be impossible to buy his mother from him, if he had not already killed her."

"Well I just know he was behind my mothers death. She spoke of him when I was little."

"Well when he was a very young man, trying to make a name for himself in France. He was drawn by the wars in England. His mother kept getting in his way. He did not won't any one to know his mother was a whore, selling herself on the streets of Paris to support the two of them, so he arranged for her to have an accident, a very fatal one. When the governor threatened to take his life, he came to me for forged papers, and a way out of France. To my regret and everlasting shame, I helped him. That is how I know Monsieur Guy. I have not laid eyes on him since, and he still owes me money."

"Then, tell us Monsieur Bolene, how have you managed not to be caught in all these years?"

"I never said I was never been caught. I said, one could buy just about anything, if they offer the right price."

"All right," said Senior Fernando. So, we offer this lord Guy the right price, perhaps gold then?"

"Oh no, no, no Monsieur. You do not understand he has access to all the gold in England...he won't bulge for that. What he requires, and we must offer him, is a Crown. That is what he wants more than anything. The power of the king, in fact, to be king."

"Okay...but, how can we sway him to think, that we could give him the throne of England?" asked Orin.

"My friend, persuade him that you are the rightful heir."

Then Orin interrupted and said. "...But I am England's rightful heir."

"Then it will be easier to convince him, now won't it Monsieur?"

"I guess you are right, but, how would I even get to see him, to convince him?"

"I know this man, the one he's paid for years to do all of his handiwork. Hawk, is his name. I will get word to him to meet with you, and open the way for you to be introduced to lord Guy."

"It sound good so far, but I don't want Orin caught in a snare. How will you accomplish this senior?" asked Fernando.

Before Jon Bolene could pull out an answer, Alberto spoke up.

"Seniors, we will make sure, that Senior Orin is not harmed. We do not fear this Hawk you speak of. We shall be as an eagle, hey men? They swallow the hawks. Hey?" And the men all laughed in agreement with Alberto.

"So then we are agreed. This will be our approach…and may God go with us!" said Bolene.

Then Raul remarked. "…And if He does not go with us, maybe He will send us help. You think, maybe?" All the men laughed and grabbed shoulders in complete accord.

"All right then," said Bolene. "We will leave in a week. Give me the money, and I will take care of all the supplies."

"I will bring what you need, just wait a moment," said Fernando. He left to gather the money needed for the trip. All seemed to be going well.

Jon Bolene sent a courier to deliver the message to Hawk. It should not be long until Orin is able to meet the man responsible for his trouble.

But perhaps there may yet, be another surprise awaiting him in England.

Lyonus, his father, the true king of England, is also waiting to vie for the throne.

In England, he too makes plans to repay their treachery.

CHAPTER SEVENTEEN
A Banquet in England

To celebrate the arrival of King Emanuel of Spain, king Luis and Queen Anne, prepared a great banquet. Every peasant in the land was invited, and given new clothes to prove to king Emanuel, that the country did not stand in ruin as he had heard.

King Luis was also happy, because this was his son, prince Edwards' seventh birthday.

Now Lyonus, and Jacob had made plans to deliver the wine to the castle. When they arrived at the door, they were ordered to hurry in.

"Thank goodness you've arrived, the king has been waiting for his guess to sample your almond wine!"

"Well," announced Jacob Corley. You would be late too, if you had someone who worked for you like this fellow. Took him two days just to pick enough almonds for the wine."

"All right then, just sit it down here, and take the rest of the wine to the cellar," said the cook, moving them out of his way.

Lyonus asked Jacob about the dark man that stood by the cellar door.

"Jacob, is that lord Guy standing there?"

"Yes, that's the black hearted crook."

"He seemed to stare directly at me when we walked in. So do you think he recognized me?"

"I think if he did, you and I would both be dead." Jacob replied, all the while hurrying to get out.

"Come Lyonus," he whispered Let's get out quickly. We don't want to have to talk to him now."

"Why don't you call me Jonathan, I think it will prove better, if anyone were to hear you."

"Right…you are right my boy," then he said in a loud voice, that lord Guy could hear.

"Hurry along there. I haven't got all day!" then lord Guy called out.

"Stop! You…stop there. I want to speak with you a moment."

Both Lyonus and Jacob took deep breaths and stood perfectly still. Then Lyonus said.

"What can I do for you my lord?"

"I was wondering…have we met before? You look so familiar."

Then just as quickly Jacob added. "Oh he couldn't my lord Guy, this boy came to me from my brothers farm. They just couldn't get him to do much work there, so I promised to help him out."

Then Lord Guy starred a moment more, and dismissed them.

"Well in that case, move out of my way. Go then and take care of your business."

"You see?" said Jacob. He is very suspicious."

"Well so am I," remarked Lyonus. Let's get the rest of the wine unloaded."

"Move quickly Jonathan" said Jacob. I just don't trust that man."

So they continue to unload the wagon, when they looked around, and there standing by the door was lord Guy. There he stood, waiting to once again interview Lyonus.

"Good evening again my lord," said Jacob. We seem to be running into each other tonight."

"Well I don't know about that. But I would like to ask your man here a question."

"You would like to ask a question my lord?"

"Yes, and…I'd like for him to answer," said Guy.

"But of course my lord." Jacob starred at Lyonus to watch his words.

"Yes your majesty," said Lyonus, pretending to be ignorant.

"Your majesty. Ha ha," laughed Guy. What is your name?"

"My name is Jonathan sir," he replied with his head lowered.

"Well Jonathan, you seem to have a face that is familiar to me. I know you can not be anyone I know, if you think me to be king." He and Jacob laughed together, and then Jacob added.

"I told you my lord, the boy is not too bright, but he can handle those heavy barrels. He is good for that," said Jacob.

"There are so many peasants here today, the king must be out of his mind, giving them clothes to impress king Emanuel. It's a ridiculous notion anyway."

"What notion is that my lord?" asked Jacob.

"He's tried to dress up a bunch of misfits to impress a king. That wouldn't matter a bit in the end."

"Well I see what you mean, my lord" said Jacob, with a frown. Well then, good evening my lord, we'd better get finished, the roads will be filled with peasants tonight."

"Then once again, I'll let you get back to it." Lord Guy seemingly satisfied that the face he thought he recognized was not the face he sought.

So Lyonus finished the last barrel, said.

"Jacob," said Lyonus. I would like to look around a bit while everyone is business at the banquet."

"I don't know if that would be such a good idea. You see how we kept running into lord Guy to night, maybe it's a sign not to go further."

"Or maybe it's a sign to dig deeper…I have to find out more."

"Then be very careful," warned Jacob.

"Look!" said Lyonus. There is my old apartment."

"How do you know from here, they all look the same to me?"

"Well, I do have my memory back, remember?"

"Oh yes. Well, I'll stand watch."

"No that's even more dangerous than getting caught. We'll both go in together. There is another way out of that room to the outside. I discovered it when I was a young lad."

So he opened the door. One could tell no one had occupied the room for a while. There were spiders and insects that roamed about with dust everywhere. Cobwebs covered the things in the room. Then Lyonus said.

"Do you see Jacob? It is just as I said, no one has been here."

"Yes, but what are we doing here?"

"Oh, looking for something, anything, that can help me."

"There is nothing here my lord, let's just go, this makes me a little nervous."

"I agree we should go."

When Lyonus opened the door, he heard voices in the corridor. He hastened to close the door.

"It seems you were right Jacob, we are in trouble. There is someone out there."

"What about the way out you spoke of?"

"All right let's try it. Stand back." whispered Lyonus, while he searched for the lever that opened the compartment.

"There." Lyonus huffed. He concentrated all his efforts on opening the fireplace wall. Help me Jacob, this wall is heavier than I remembered."

"Yes, I see what you mean. There now, we have it," said Jacob breathing as heavy as Lyonus. Now let's go from here."

"Just follow me, I recall this path leading to the outside garden wall."

It was most fortunate for them that the path led to the wall closet to their wagon. Once on the outside, they scurried to join themselves to the wagon.

"I told you Lyonus, we can't take those kinds of chances, it's just too risky."

"I'm sorry Jacob. I didn't mean to frighten you that way, I only wanted to find out something that could help me move closer to the throne. A document, or a letter…something I left behind that would be of some assistants."

"Listen to me Lyonus, The only thing that will help you do, is to find money and lots of it. Gold my boy."

"Then I need to go back in."

"What, go back in?" yelled Jacob. Whatever for. I just told you, there is no need to go creeping around the place…and you'll only get caught."

"Jacob, I know where the money chamber is."

"Now I think you have been sipping my almond wine."

"No. Think about it. Tonight is perfect."

"Did you say perfect?" questioned Jacob. Every guard is at his post, we will be sure to be seen."

"…Not if we are dressed like them."

"…And just where are we to get these uniforms."

"Well," said Lyonus, with a big grin on his face. Remember, I know where things are now. It will be easy to get there. We will go back in the way we came out. We will slip into the sewing room two doors over, where they put the uniforms that are in need of repair. Then we can take a couple…well…borrow them just for tonight, and then ease inside the money chamber. You and I can fill our bags, and leave once again the way we came in. Don't you see Jacob, easy?"

"Easy!" shouted Jacob.

"Jacob, quiet." cautioned Lyonus. Clam down. Listen, I will go in alone. No one will notice just one person. Anyway, if I'm caught it's only me. So you wait here with the wagon, if they question you or something, make up an excuse for not moving your wagon."

"I think I like that idea better Lyonus, I'm an old man, I can't take chances the way I used too. Please don't think ill of me."

"Of course not, you're the man that saved my life."

Then: Lyonus started for the garden wall, turned back and whispered to Jacob

"Keep a sharp lookout for me my friend, I'll return with the gold."

Lyonus took off through the path that led to his old room. Once inside, he searched the desk, and tables for any clues. He found some clothes in a chest that stood tall. Then he whispered to himself. "These look as if they might get me safely through the hallway." So he put on the garments, and fixed his hair, using water from a flowerpot to groom. Lyonus gradually pulled on the door, until he was sure no one was moving about. He headed straight for the sewing room. There, he found a uniform that had been freshly mended, and put it on. After he found a hat, he started down the corridor. Just then two guards were patrolling the hall. When they came near to Lyonus he pretended to talk with someone in the room, while he held the door slightly ajar.

"Ha, ha," he laughed, closing the door, and nodding his head at the guards as they passed by. What a close one," he whispered. Now where is that gold?" He tried to remember exactly what room it was in. "Ah ha," he sighed. Here it is." Lyonus watched the corridor and decided what to do about the guard at the door. He walked over to the guard, and then said.

"Evening."

"Hey there."

"With all the festivities around here, it took me all night to get a decent drink—with all the peasants about—I've had to watch everything."

"Hum." replied the guard. Then Lyonus, rubbing his head as if he had a great idea, said

"Listen, why don't you go and get something to drink, then come back and relieve me. Surely there are not likely to be any peasant up here."

"What…you mean leave my post?" scoffed the guard.

"Well," said Lyonus straightening his hat. You'll only be gone for a few minutes, and I'll be standing right here in your place. No one will be the wiser. Unless of course you want to stand here all night alone, while the peasants take all the wine. You know the banquet is just getting started. It will be a long thirsty night sir. But…I understand if you are afraid of being caught and all. Just forget it."

Lyonus started to walk away, then said. "I'm sorry, I should not have offered the drink. You just looked so thirsty. Well have a good night, I'll go and see if I can relieve someone else for a while."

"No wait!" called the guard. Are you sure you're authorized to relieve me?"

"Am I sure?" Lyonus replied taking off his hat in protest. Why, I would not have come otherwise. Don't bother, just forget it. Wait for someone else to come along, maybe in an hour or two!"

"No," said the guard. I think I should like to have that drink now, besides…there is no way to tell if or when another guard will come that I may be relieved."

Then Lyonus waved his arms toward the way the guard should go, and watched until he was out of sight. When he was sure not to be caught, he opened the door to the money room, and started to fill his bags with gold. Then he found rings and all kinds of jewelry he could put in his pockets, and he even placed some inside his hat.

After he had taken all he could carry, he crept back to the sewing room, picked up the clothes and returned to his old chambers.

Once inside he found a huge bag, and emptied all the gold inside. He decided to take a chance and go back again. And then Lyonus whispered.

"This may be my only chance, so I must do it all the way. So he went back to the money room, making sure no one saw him, and then loaded up again with all he could carry. Then he rushed back to the chamber and set it down. He decided if this was to be successful, he needed to go all the way. So he went back and stood at the door, to wait for the guard. Shortly after, the guard came staggering back, thanking Lyonus for his help.

"Oh you're still here. I was a little worried, but I feel great now."

"Well I'm glad," spouted Lyonus, "brave men like yourself need to have a drink now and then…you know to help relax you."

"I'm glad I listened."

"Anytime I can help, my friend," said Lyonus. I'd better go and see if I can help someone else"

"All right, good night."

"Yes, yes goodnight."

Then Lyonus made his way to his old chamber where he had hidden the gold. It was just in time too, for he could hear the sound of voices in the corridor. He opened the fireplace wall and hauled the heavy bags of gold and trinkets through the path. When he opened the door, Jacob was standing there waiting.

"Oh my boy, you made it!"

"Yes Jacob, it was rough going there for a minute."

"I was so worried, I almost came in. In fact I got down from the wagon, and decided I would come in. I was standing here getting up enough nerve."

"Not to worry, I think I have plenty. Hurry and help me get them aboard. We must hurry away. I think I heard voices in the hall when I was leaving."

"Right, right you are."

Then Jacob leaped upon the wagon, and took off like the wind. He was so happy to see Lyonus, and the gold.

"How much do you think we have here Lyonus?"

"I think quite enough to buy all the help we need, especially with the jewels."

"Then you can start putting things into action my lord."

"Let's just get this gold safely home, then we can talk about a plan."

"Right, my lord. Get you up there ladies," he called out to his pair horses drawing the wagon. "We need to get home fast."

He and Lyonus smiled at each other, feeling rather proud, for they had made a great accomplishment, one they never dreamed would be completed in one night.

CHAPTER EIGHTEEN
A Plan Set with Gold

Ivan, Jacob, and Lyonus, sat down together, to decide what should be done with the gold and jewels they were able to steal from the money chamber.

"My lord," said Ivan. Why did you ever think to try your hand at thievery?" Laughing a little, at Lyonus' expression of shame.

"I merely did what you said I should. Be strong, and do whatever it would take, if I wanted to succeed."

"Well my boy, you really surprised me."

Suddenly Ivan came in.

"You should have seen him going in and out of the castle. He tricked the guards into letting him replace them at the door, then went inside and took what he needed. It was something to see." Jacob and Lyonus laughed together. Then Lyonus said. "It is time to start playing the game, the way lord Guy does. He seems to have been successful at it for years."

Then Ivan said, with such a voice of distain. "There is one thing we most certainly know, Guy needs to be brought down. He needs to be shown how it feels, to be deceived and cheated. To have that sense of helplessness, and be unable to prevent the effect."

"Don't worry Ivan, I shall find for him a fitting end. Now, Ivan You and I shall go to the tavern in a few days, and wait there, until we can find enough men to accomplish our goal.

"Sounds good," said Ivan. We may have to visit them all…to find those still loyal to the king."

"What do you mean…to Luis?"
"No my lord, I mean you…the true king of England."

So after four days had passed, Ivan, and Lyonus, thought it was time to go. They made their way to the taverns, all over the highway, trying to solicit fighting men. It took several days to visit all the taverns.

By this time they had amassed a great number of men sympathetic to the cause. But still, there was one more left to visit. The last stop was called Flowers Row Tavern. Named for the road it occupied, located near the shore. Once there, Ivan and Lyonus went inside.

Ivan ordered ale for every man. Then Lyonus began to speak.

"Countrymen, I am a friend, one who desires England be returned to her first days of glory, and her since of fairness for the people. The way it is now, no one is happy, and some have been robbed of their lands." Then a man yelled out. "Yes and some…their lives!" Then another. "…And don't forget the outrageous taxes." Still another said. "That devil lord Guy stealing your soul, and the soul of your daughters."

"Lyonus waved his arms for them to all quiet down. "Now men, I'm glad you understand why I'm here."

"Well now…that my boy, you haven't made quite clear."

One man yelled out. "What are you going to do boy, help us drink our problems away?"

All the men in the tavern began to laugh, clapping their mugs together, while they stood to their feet.

"Wait, just wait, here him out!" Ivan shouted, motioning for the men to sit down.

"You need each other…now settle down, and listen, you will be surprised at what he will tell you." The men were calmed a bit more. I'm sorry my lord," said Ivan, turning to bow then winked at Lyonus. Please finish your proposal, I think these men are ready to listen now."

Lyonus smiled at Ivan and continued.

"Men, if you fight with me, I know we can be victorious in defeating lord Guy, and win back the crown." Then a man asked, "Win back the crown for who. Luis is king, who will get the crown then?" Then another said, "Maybe someone else who cares nothing for the people." Then yet another named asked, "What if we fail, then our burden will be twice as hard."

"My good fellows, there is a great risk here, I can't deny that. But keep in mine you won't be the only ones risking all. We have grouped together many men like you, soldiers that are still loyal to the crown. They too would fight to see it restored to the rightful heirs."

"Where is this heir you speak of? The children of Lyonus have long since been done away with. King Lyonus himself left for the hunt one day, and never returned. So whom are we fighting for?"

"Now that is a legitimate question....But what I am about to tell you, cannot leave this place. Agreed? Swear it, on the lives of your children!"

"We swear!" chanted the men, as they raised their hands in accord.

"What I say now, will change things? My life will be worth much, I am now willing to risk it, so you will trust me. But I am trusting you now, to keep loyalty with England."

Then Lyonus pulled back his coat. He wore the clothes he took from his old room in the castle. Then said boldly.

"I am Lyonus Warwick, II, The son of Lyonus Warwick I, King, High lord and Sovereign of all England!" Then Ivan shouted "God save the King!"

The men stood with their mouths open and eyes glowing. Then one said.

"If you are truly the king, why have you waited so many years to return?"

Then one soldier stepped forward and charged in. "Let me get a good look at him. I served in the kings army." Then he walked closer to Lyonus, and looked him over carefully. He looks all too much like the king, but...I can't be sure."

Lyonus knew him too. Then the man announced. "My name is..."

At the same moment Lyonus said along with him. "Miles."

Then Lyonus finished by adding. "You were one of my personal guards."

Miles said in great awe. "Oh men, he is good, he looks so much like the king, and it is the king!" He fell to his knees. A few of the others were not quit convinced.

"Ask me anything," said Lyonus. Anything at all."

Then a young man named Cole, asked, "What happened to your queen?" Then a man said, "No...it's no good. Everyone knows what happened to the queen and her children. Poor lady."

"Well, where are they now?" asked Cole.

Then Ivan chided in and said. "I can not reveal all these things now, but I can say, that both are here in England."

Then Lyonus looked at Ivan, and said. "Here! Both my children are here in England?"

A man spoke out and then said. "He still hasn't proved it to me."

"Then what can prove it?" Erik insisted. Just at that moment, Ivan spoke out and said.

"Your majesty, show them the ring, with the great seal of England."

"All right," he agreed, as he walked around the room to show the men his ring. They understood, that only the true king would hold such a thing.

"He is, he is the king." called out the men, and fell to their knees. Then Cole vowed. "Your majesty, I will give you my oath this day, if you will let me serve you, as your personal guard."

"Rise, please rise my good countrymen. I have spent many years without a memory of the past. I was badly injured on the hunting trip—in an attempt by my brother and others—to take my life, and my throne. But now, I am ready to take it back!" He raised his mug, as if for a toast. Will you fight with me men? I swear this day to pardon, and reinstate those of you charged falsely. Banished brought home, and your lands given back!"

Then one asked "What about pay?"

"Ha, ha." laughed Lyonus, and then turned over the bags of gold. What you see now, will be doubled…tripled, all you can carry—if you here today pledge your loyalty—and fight for me…your king!"

"We will, oh true king of England. My name is Bradmore, Sir Bradmore. I was banished because I would not stand with them against queen Miria, to have her murdered. I was striped of my lands and rank. I left with my life, but I never thought I would have the chance to fight for England again. My lord, you have my sword and my life, for the privilege to fight."

Then another said. "…And mine!" They continued, until all the men agreed.

"Wonderful men, and thank you!" They all took a drink to seal the oath.

Then Lyonus warned. "Now men, be cautioned. What has been revealed this night must be kept, till we are ready to strike? You will be informed soon, on what to do."

Then he called Cole over and said. "I will need someone I can trust to be my protector, when I am on the throne again. I shall remember your oath. "…But until then, be a friend, and a soldier and fight with the others. They will need your zeal."

"Yes my lord, I shall," said young Cole, now only about eighteen.

Lyonus began to wonder, and commented. "You know my son and daughter are just about your age." Then walked away from him. Ivan said to Cole. "Don't worry my boy, he will soon see your worth. He will not deny you his respect."

Cole looked at Ivan with a look of confusion. He was unsure of what Ivan meant, but he was happy to fight for the king.

Only a minute or so later, a fellow charged in the tavern. He yelled with excitement.
"A ship has arrived! The Tempest, has docked here from Spain."
"From Spain, you say?" asked the barkeep.
"Yes sir, there are a lot of men headed this way, armed men they say!"
The barkeep, called for the maid to make ready several rooms.
Then Lyonus whispered. "Remember men, we don't know what this means. Quiet."
Suddenly a man blurted out, as he fell in the door.
"There is an army of men coming. They look like fighting men. But it's hard to tell."
Everyone remained quiet, and waited for the men to arrive. It took a moment for the coach to reach the tavern. When the door opened, it was Orin, and Senior Fernando, with Miguel and their men.
"Good evening sir," said Senior Fernando. "My friends and I have come from Spain. I seek one of your very important ministers."
The barkeep replied. "Misters? There are no important folk around here, just a few peasants, and drunks. There are a lot of you here to see one man."
"Well, my friend, one should not presume to travel in these times without protection. Now, where do most of the important people drink around here?"
"You can try the Inn a couple miles or so down the road, but you won't have as much fun. Ha, ha." Then the whole tavern joined him in laughter.
Orin looked around the place, and being irritated with the barkeep threw a bag of gold on the bar, and then said. "Perhaps, you could tell me how to find a man named Hawk?" There came such a hush over the room, you could almost hear them breath. "What is it?" he asked. Did I say something wrong?"
The barkeep motioned for him to come closer, while he explained. "Listen sir, around here the name Hawk and death, are used in the same breath. If you sought that fellow, you must be just like him, or worst. Maybe you've even signed your own death warrant."
"I think I could take care of him," said Orin. Now…have you seen him?"
"He…usually comes around close to midnight, after he's done his murdering and thieving."
"Good then…give everyone a round of ale please. I would have a small pail brought to my table." He threw a smaller bag of gold to the barkeep, and

then asked. Has that covered the debt sir?"

"Indeed!" said the barkeep, with a big grin on his face. Maybe two rounds."

Lyonus and Ivan decided to stay, to watch the meeting with Hawk. Ivan seemed to watch Orin closely, then said.

"Lyonus, I'm not sure, but I think that he might be your son."

"Whom do you speak of…that brash young man? You think he is my son? I don't know about that Ivan, how can you tell?"

"It's just a feeling I have. He does seem to have some of your features, yours and Miria's."

"Well, what should I do if it is? He obviously wasn't looking for me."

"Does that matter? If he found you in the process of whatever he was doing here…then he would have found both a father, and inherited a kingdom."

"Let us wait and find out what he's doing here, before any rash decisions are drawn, Ivan."

"That sounds fair to me." Replied Ivan.

So, Orin, Senior Fernando remained inside the tavern. Miguel, and the men they brought with them from Spain, joined them. Once inside, they all sat and waited patiently for Hawk to show up. Orin rose up and started talking to the men individually. He tried to solicit their aid. But the men he approached refused even his gold.

They told Orin, that he was too late; they had already sworn an oath to the king. The help Ivan and Lyonus had solicited, were not aware of their zeal, for they told the very thing Lyonus had bade them not.

When Orin approached Cole however, he wanted to know, exactly who paid for his loyalty.

"Hey, you." Orin whispered, so that Erik would respond to him.

"Yes, what do you want?" he asked, as he squirmed in his chair, and watched Orin lean toward him. "I would like to give you a little gold, for the answer to one question."

"Oh, well that depends on the question, and who's doing the asking."

"The man that sat a few seats over there, told me, he made an oath to protect the king. Are you also under that oath, and where can I find this would be king?"

Then Cole stood up, and slammed his mug on the table, then said. "He should not have told you even that much." Then as he stepped from the table looked back and said. "Oh…and that was two questions, neither of which, I am at liberty to answer. Good night."

"Well," said Orin, with a very discerning look asked. Is there not a man among you who would fight for a good cause, if that cause is your country?"

The men looked around at each other, and one by one, left the tavern.

"Wait!" said Orin. You can make lots of gold…just listen!"

Orin tried to stop all the men, but they ignored him. This of course, made Lyonus fill wonderful. For the first time in years, he felt, there was a chance he could return to the throne.

Senior Fernando saw the frustration in Orin' eyes, then said.

"Orin, please be patient son. We have many men already, and there are more taverns to visit. We will find the right group."

"I know Senior, but it is not the men that bothered me, it is what they told me."

"…And what was that, my son?"

"They all…well, those that spoke to me, said they had already made an oath to the king."

"It is only natural for soldiers to give their word to protect the king. Why do you find this so strange?"

"Because Senior, they were not talking about my uncle, king Luis."

"Then who? Did they say name this king?"

"No, they only mentioned that he was the king. I wonder who this man is, and where he can be found. Or is he just another usurper, greedy for the crown?"

"I wonder as well, Orin. But perhaps now we will find out everything. Look." He pointed toward the door. "I believe that is the one you seek."

They both watched a man open the heavy doors that creaked. It was very close to midnight, and just as the barkeep had said, Hawk strolled inside. He was with a band of what appeared to be rabble.

Hawk's perspiration was so heavy, that it looked as if water had been poured over his head.

He came in yelling for ale.

"Ale…and I mean plenty!" When he shouted, he caused everyone in the tavern to take notice of him.

Orin and Senior Fernando made themselves known to him.

"Good evening Senior," said Fernando.

"Yes Good evening," said Orin.

Hawk merely looked up at the two of them, and nodded his head.

Then Orin spoke up. "Sir, my name is Orin. My friend and I have come a great distance to meet a certain nobleman named lord Fredrick Guy. I have with me, a letter of introduction from a friend of his in Spain."

Hawk pulled the letter from Orin's hand and proceeded to read it. He finally said.

"So, you want to meet lord Guy do you? Well I will have to contact him tomorrow, and get back to you. He is not so easily seen, as you might have expected. But I think it can be arranged."

"I have it on good authority, that he frequents the taverns in these parts." marked Senior Fernando.

"Now, I don't know what you've heard…but lord Guy is a very proper man, he would not like being called common." Then the rabble laughed.

"That's just fine, sir." Orin replied, and then asked. Where would be the best place to meet him?"

"I'm not so sure what he would say, but I would think the Cradle Inn, a ways down the road.

"Good then, it's settled. You check with your lord Guy, then get word to me at the Cradle Inn."

Hawk lifted his mug, and then said. "All right here's to first meeting." Then Hawk turned away at his table and left Orin and Fernando standing.

Now it took just a short time later for news to spread, of a rich young nobleman from Spain. He would come to England and bring with him a large number of men. Just what his purpose was, only few knew for sure.

Of course Senior Fernando, and Jon Bolene, had a great hand in its purpose.

CHAPTER NINETEEN
Lord Guy Seeks a Kingdom

Just after the plans for the banquet, lord Guy saw his chance to turn things once again in his favor. He resolved to rid himself of prince Edward once and for all. The prince was about seven now and able to travel without the queen. So Guy thought of a way to make him disappear from the kingdom. One evening when everyone had gone to dinner, he slipped into the nursery and shook some of Rosa' powder over the fruit, and in the goblets, that lie around the room. Then he went into the queen's room and shook powder into her goblets, and on the fruit. He wanted to make sure; both of them were finished. With them gone, it would be easy now to manage Luis.

Lord Guy finished his work, and went to his chambers; there he was meet with a courier from Hawk.

"Yes. What is it you have there?"

"My lord, Hawk ask that I deliver this letter as soon as possible. He wanted me to return with an answer by tomorrow."

"He does, does he? Then, tomorrow it shall be. I won't read it now. I will send for you when I am ready. Now go!"

"Yes my lord," said the courier, and moved quietly from his chambers.

Suddenly, out of the blue stood Lords' Biltfry and Westmoreland.

"My lord Guy, we need to talk."

"About what? You and I have no disagreements, my friend."

No!" said lord Biltfry. "But I should like to stop this plot before you get started."

"Plot!" answered Guy. "If I plot now, it is because I am tired of waiting, while we're overrun with peasants everyday—and the army—fat from laying around."

"But Fredrick." replied Biltfry. You can not remove the king from power, at your whim!"

"...And why not?" he insisted.

"Well, it's just not done, that's all...Lord Guy, listen, Luis still has the queen...and then there is the question of his son prince Edward," said Westmoreland.

"Yes. Interrupted Biltfry. "Not to mention the true heirs were never found."

"Oh, that's right." marked Westmoreland. That could cause a lot of trouble...if."

"Oh quiet the both of you. Now you listen Westmoreland," said Guy. I've held back long enough. I will not wait another seventeen years for another bastard son to take the throne. It is my turn."

"Yes your grace," said Biltfry and Westmoreland.

"Oh don't patronize me. I think now...there is even more to do."

"No Fredrick." lord Biltfry pleaded. "This would break Luis' heart, or worst."

"Yes, if he found out, it would utterly destroy him," Westmoreland added.

"Then we won't let him find out...now will we friends?"

"Careful my lord, he guards the queen too closely," remarked Biltfry.

"He barely lets her out of his sight," said Westmoreland

"...And we will just have to find a way to do it. That boy will never know what it means to be king. And neither will any other bastard son."

"All right, Fredrick, then what is your plan?"

"I think I will ask my lord Biltfry to leave now."

"What? I...why is it I must go?" said Biltfry.

"Because I think it better if you know as little as possible, on this one."

"Now wait a minute lord Guy," he squawked. "You're not implying that I am not loyal, after all we've been through!"

"I'm implying nothing!" he said forcefully, and walked up to lord Biltfry. "I said...you are not included. I have my reasons, and that is that!"

Lord Biltfry looked at both Westmoreland and Guy, straightened his coat, and slammed the door behind him.

"Biltfry!" called Westmoreland.

"No! Just let him go. He can do no further harm."

"Yes Fredrick, but I think he remembered my lord Du'Voe," said Westmoreland.

"Lord Du'Voe became a threat to me."

"I know, but Biltfry…? He is not a threat now."

"No matter…he would be in the way. I have my reasons for excluding him! Now, there are bigger things to worry about."

"For instance?" asked Westmoreland.

"For starters, I want that nuisance Biltfry done away with. Then I want the queen and the prince, gone."

"That leaves king Luis."

"Yes it does…as you have said before my lord Westmoreland…He will lose his mind, or at least the rest of it, if anything happened to his family. There you have it man, everyone out of the way."

"I see then my lord."

Just then a sound came from outside the door.

"Sh…" said lord Guy. Quiet! Did you hear that?"

"Yes, I think I heard something."

Guy hurried to the door to discover who it was. He did not see the face, but he was in time to see a part of the apron rounding the corner. He came back into the room, and pulled Duke Westmoreland away from the door.

"Who was it?" asked the duke.

"It was that meddling nurse Jeanine…I'm sure of it!"

"Now what? Surely she will warn the queen. What do you suppose she heard?"

"I don't know, but what ever it was, I'll assure you, she will be sorry she held her hear to my door."

"She most likely didn't hear anything, lord Guy."

"That doesn't matter, I told you I can't take the chance. Now we must move even quicker."

"Be careful my lord, things like this take great planning."

"You just remember to do your part, and let me take care of the rest."

"All right."

"Now, go quickly, before you are discovered. We will speak again soon."

The next day, as he had promised, lord Guy sent for a courier.

"Yes my lord."

"Take this message back to Hawk. Make sure he's the only one to see it."

"I will your grace."

Then the courier headed straight for the Cradle Inn. There he would fine Hawk waiting.

When he arrived, he gave the message to Hawk, and awaited a reply.
"Sit, and have a drink, I'll be right back "
Then Hawk proceeded to Orin's room. A knock at the door aroused Orin.
"Who is there?"
"It's Hawk."
"Just a moment," he said while he slowly pulled back the door. "What news do you have?"
"Lord Guy wants to know if you would meet with him here tomorrow, and he also wants to know how many properties you want. Here is the message."
"Well tell lord Guy, I would like a rather large Baronet, and a few other smaller properties, but tell him also I have changed our meeting place."
"All right...what should I tell him then?"
"You should say, meet at the Miles tavern, at nine o'clock tomorrow."
"Then I will send the courier with the reply tonight," said Hawk.
"Thank you very much indeed," said Orin, with a smirk on his face.
"My pleasure," Hawk replied, who looked as if he knew a great secret.
Then, Orin rushed to tell Senior Fernando the news.
"Sir. I have sent the message to lord Guy. He is willing to meet wherever we say. I think he will have just what we need, by tomorrow as well."
"Then everything is set in motion, just as we've planned."
"Yes." Orin answered a little melancholy. "But I'm having a little trouble waiting. I really miss Teresa."
"I know I've missed her too, my boy. I sent her a post yesterday, so she would not worry."
"I will be patient, I know it is the best for all concerned."
"Good my son. I will talk with you after dinner."
"All right."

After dinner, Orin, Miguel and Senior Fernando prepared to leave for miles tavern. They gathered Alberto, and Mateo to go with them. They were not seeking to cause a great stir.
When they arrived at the tavern, there was no lord Guy, or sign he had been there. They waited, until at last they thought it was best to leave.
Then entered lord Guy. He came late bringing a few soldiers with him. When he walked in, the rabble in the tavern, became agitated. They started grumbling and mumbling. Then he spoke.
"Relax, you pack of cures." He waved for his men to spread out around the room, and then said. I'm here on another matter. It has nothing to do with any of you. Go back to your drinking, and drink while you can."

Then Orin walked over to lord Guy's table.

"Good evening my lord, allow me to buy you some ale.

"I'll buy my own ale, if you don't mine.

"My name is Orin, I am the one Hawk told you about," he said.

"Quiet boy!" said lord Guy, in a hostile voice. I don't know anyone by that name!"

"What…what did you say?" Orin questioned. At this point, he was quite confused.

"…And do not speak his name in my presence again." lord Guy insisted.

"Well I'm sorry, my lord…I did not know."

"I knew it would be a mistake coming here."

Then just as Guy stood up to leave, Orin plopped both his hands on the table in front of him, as if forbidding him to move. Then he said.

"I am here to make you an offer."

"I'm aware of your desire to buy land, the money means very little to me," said Guy.

"How did you know that fact…if not by the afore named individual, you care not to have named?"

Then lord Guy whispered, "That is how I want to hear of him, in a nameless manner."

"I see," said Orin.

"Surely you can understand that…my position and all."

"Yes, of course…of course," said Orin, while he cleared his throat.

Lord Guy bade him continue.

"Are you aware, my real offer is about more than owning land?"

Then he attempted to flatter lord Guy to gain his attention.

"Since I have been here, your name is all I've heard. Lord Guy this, lord Guy that. I tell you, I did not know what to make of you at first. You are a favorite among the people."

"So far boy, you have not said anything of interest to me."

"I've heard you have great influence in the kingdom, and also much power. They even say in whispers…you should be…king."

Then lord Guys ears perked up. "You mean, they speak of me as being king?"

"My lord, after meeting you, I'm not at all surprised why they are of that opinion."

"Well state your business. Be quick about it, I've grown impatient."

"You have power, right?"

"Yes, and you've said all that before. You're wasting my time," said Guy.

"Alright, then let me get to the point of it. In order to be king, you need a plan, correct?"

"What are you talking about boy? Spit it out."

Lord Guy' men began to muffle their laughter. Lord Guy raised his hand to silence them.

"Listen boy!" he said standing to leave again, when Orin interrupted him.

"My name is Orin, Orin Warwick, the rightful heir to the throne of England."

Lord Guy, glared, then placed his hand on his sword. Orin continued to speak.

"…But I am not here for the throne."

"You do not want the throne?" He looked at his men, then back to Orin, and said. Before I have your head…and I will have it. Give me one good reason why I should not."

"Ha, ha," laughed Orin. My lord, I told you I am not interested in the throne, at least not for myself."

Then lord Guy became eager to hear more.

"I want to give you the throne instead."

"What?" said Guy, "You say you are the heir, and yet you want to give the crown to me?"

"Yes. My interest is toward the prince. I'm not in the least bit interested in the crown."

Well I find that very hard to believe." Then he motioned for the men to let down their weapons, and sheath their swords.

"It seems to me you are fighting a losing battle," Guy announced. You can no sooner get to the prince, than you could the king. He is very well guarded."

"That is why I need your help."

"…And you expect me to help you take the prince?"

"I do," said Orin.

"Your battle can not be won, so easily, I tell you."

"Well, I will find a way to do this with, or without your help!" exclaimed Orin.

Senior Fernando, mouthing for Orin to continue.

"You see, lord Guy, it is only important to me to get gold and land…not to mention the ladies. I'm too young to try to rule a big country like England. I don't want the responsibility you see. I leave that, up to men more powerful…greater men than I. Those of course, who might want to become king."

"...And you care nothing for the throne then, nothing at all. All that power?" said Guy.

"I'll leave that to mightier men, perhaps, like yourself sire."

Then lord Guy said, "Suppose, just for a second...I listened to your crazy scheme. What assurance do I have, that you will not change your mind, and come up against me?"

"The same assurances, you have given to me...my lord."

"I have not consented to this madness yet."

"Then consent, and let's get on with it."

"Very...well," said lord Guy, dragging out his words.

"I want to hear, what you so graciously offer me."

"You are the kings trusted minister. We know you can find a way to set me up with the land I need." Lord Guy interrupted. "Yes, yes...we know all that. But you sir, have not yet said how you will make me king." He starred hard at Orin, waiting for a reply.

"My lord that part is easy. We simply make sure the boy goes off to a tournament or something, and then we snatch him! We hide him away in one of my estates, until you are vested king."

"That doesn't say what should happen to the king."

"Do I really have to tell you everything my lord?" he said leaning in to whisper. Simply...kill him, and be done with it. You can easily find a way. You are within an arms reach everyday, and I hear...not without resources."

"You are aware you speak treason, are you not?"

"Treason? It is not treason to take back what is already mine. Besides, I spoke of power, and a kingdom! As a gift, that is for any man with enough stomach to go after it."

"If you double cross me...Orin," said Guy, standing again to his feet, gritting his teeth. "You will not easily find a hole to crawl in. My retribution will be relentless."

"Ha," laughed Orin. "I fear only your betrayal of me, after you are king."

"Then my young friend, what shall our bargain be?"

"You are a man of your word I suppose?"

"I shall become that man today," said Guy.

"All right, let us bargain. I want all the land I can get, in exchange for the throne. As simple as that." Lord Guy thought for a moment. He searched within himself, and then asked.

"By what means would you have me acquire this land, and when?"

"That is your part in the bargain my lord, you will have to figure that out."

"You have not said how soon you will need this land," asked Guy.

"I need it now…yesterday! The tournaments are close. I need to have a place for the prince ready when he's taken, and a place to live."

"That can be arranged easily enough," said Guy. "How do you plan to see that the prince is where he should be, and when?"

"That is also, where you come in, my lord."

"But why keep the boy alive?" said Guy, "I do not want him, complicating things."

"I'd like to think of him, as leverage."

"Leverage, against whom…Me?"

"You have your way, and I have mine, there can be no other." Orin paused for a moment, then asked, "Are we then in accord?"

"Yes, I agree to your terms. However, taking the boy from the queen, will be difficult."

"Then bring her along as well, it matters not to me," said Orin.

"Perhaps as camouflage…it could work."

"Great! I will start to make the arrangements," Orin announced.

"Do you have any men?" Lord Guy asked, as he watched the room.

"I have many men to support me." Then he called to the men.

"Men stand up, show our lord Guy your number."

When the men stood up, the tavern was filled. Lord Guy and his men shied away. There were nearly, four times as many of Orin's men, and more waiting.

"You have a large number of men. Where did you get them?"

"They are men whom you had banished, and some whose land you took away, left rather, shall we say…needy. They demanded gold, and I paid. So there you are, it is no big secret. Some will sell their own mothers, or kill them." Lord Guy starred Orin in the face, and then said. "I have just one more question."

"What is that, my lord?"

"Something you said a moment ago reminded me. How did you get this letter of introduction specifically addressed to me…and who would write such a letter?"

"Oh, but that's two questions, and I'm not obliged to answer either," said Orin, then smiled, and lifted up his cup of ale. We will have total control of England, and long live the king! How does that sound to your royal ears, your majesty?"

"It sounds more than perfect," said Guy. "Why, it's what I have worked a lifetime to achieve."

"Now we will see to it, that you hear it for the rest of your life. Drink up men!"

"I can not wait. I will send a reply by courier, as soon as I get it."

"I trust you will, my lord. Until then?"

"Yes, until then," said lord Guy, pouring down his drink, and tugging at his hat. "Let's go!" he shouted to his men, and they rode back to the castle.

Meanwhile, in the tavern sat, Ivan and Lyonus, who stood up in the number for Orin.

Ivan stood and went over to Orin. He and Senior Fernando were enjoying their victory.

"I hate to interrupt this happy occasion," said Ivan. But I would like to speak with your young friend here."

"With me?" said Orin.

"It'll only take a minute. Please…just a second."

Orin put down his drink. "It's okay, Fernando, I will return."

Once outside Lyonus joined them. Then Orin announced. "I remember seeing you, the both of you when I first came here. I don't like this, I'm going back inside."

"No, wait! This isn't what you might think," said Lyonus.

"You sir, have no idea, what I might think."

Just then Lyonus began to laugh. "I like him Ivan. Ha, ha, ha. He has great wit about him. He reminds me of Miria." Orin spoke out and said. "Who are you gentlemen? I don't think you're here to rob me…and you spoke of Miria, my mother."

"No, we are not here to rob you," said Ivan. We are here to enlighten you."

"To what…what did you say?"

"I said we are here to enlighten you," said Ivan.

"And how do you intend to do that, sirs?"

Then Ivan stepped closer and said. "By revealing to you, who you really, and your family."

"My family, what about them? Nothing!" he blurted. They are all dead, dead!"

"That is where you are wrong," said Ivan. Your father is still alive, and in England."

"My father was king, and was killed for it. He is dead!"

"Would you believe your eyes, if I showed you the great seal ring of England?"

"What? Only the king himself could wear such a ring, and that fop on the throne is my uncle, not my father."

"Then if you are willing to believe, look." Ivan pointed straightway at Lyonus, as he stretched out his hand to show the ring

"Where did you get that ring?" Orin shouted. That ring belonged to my father!"

"I know," said Lyonus. For I am he."

"This can not be. You, you are my father, the true king? No! It can not be?"

"But it is my son," said Lyonus. We had to wait for the right moment."

"The right moment! I'm eighteen years old. Did you not think there could have been a right moment in all those years? The right moment would have been before my mother suffered and died. And why come back now? Is it because now I am ready for the throne, you won't to take it?"

"Listen to me," said Lyonus, almost pleading. "I've spent many years in darkness, not knowing who or where I was. I roamed from one place to another, in search of my past and myself. Then Ivan here helped me, along with others, to regain my memory. And now, he has helped me to find you, my lost son and heir."

"...And mother, what of her? She suffered for many years too, and she never gave up."

"I know son, neither will we. That is why we must work together, to avenge the wrong to her, and the entire House of Warwick."

Suddenly the tavern door opened, there stood Miguel and Senior Fernando.

"Orin," called Fernando. You were out a little longer than I thought." Stammering at his words. I came to see if you were okay Orin. Are you okay?"

"I am fine sir," said Orin, in a daze. "However, I want you to meet someone."

"Oh?"

"Yes. Let me introduce to you Lyonus Warwick I, king of England...and my father." Then with tears falling continued.... And this is Senior Fernando and his son Miguel, in-laws, from Spain."

Then Fernando looked at Miguel, and Orin and said, "So this is the true king. And you believe it?"

"I wear the ring of my fathers...of England!"

"Could not any man where this ring? Maybe it was stolen."

"The courage of any one to where this ring would be amazing. Men have lost everything they held dear because of it. No, I'm sure. It has to be him. Only a true king could wear it."

"In that case sire, I pledge my loyalty to you now, as I have your son," said Fernando.

"It means so much to me that you have brought back my son."

"On the contrary my lord. It was he who brought me here."

"Either way, I thank God this day."

"Father!" cried Orin, and fell in his arms.

"My son," said Lyonus. I have waited so long."

Then Ivan spoke. "There is one more thing Orin."

"What is that sir?"

"You have a sister, Jessica."

"Jessica! Where is she? She was not with us in Spain."

"And that is precisely why she may still be alive." added Ivan.

"They did not know of her whereabouts?" said Lyonus. "It was that fact alone that has kept her alive, thou they have made a diligent search of it. They have murdered innocent people to fine her, to find you both. Not to mention, my dear friend…lord Thomas Graybourne, and the Jeffers. That is why, I was surprised when lord Guy allowed you to live Orin. He's a greedy, self-serving man, hungry for the throne. He will allow anything…in order to get it."

"I offered him a chance, and well…he took it."

"Offered him? Orin, what do you mean?" questioned Lyonus.

"Oh…ah…Senior Fernando and I had a plan to flush him out. I would buy a lot of land, and pretend to kidnap the prince, and…make him king."

"What!"

"I know it sounds impossible now, but it was a good plan."

"My son, you can not toy with a man like that, he will not be so generous, even at his word. For his words are like the adder, they are poisonous. One bite from him, and it's over. He would give his life to be king," said Lyonus.

"That may very well be the case…but…"

"Oh Orin," said Lyonus, in frustration.

"I am no fool father, I brought men with me for protection, and I have since rallied many more."

"You don't understand Orin, he will get back at you by using the law of England. It can not be challenged."

"Yes it can! He used the law to send away my mother for her to die on foreign soil. Then I will use it…to give him his reward."

"It will not work that way my son. He will rally everyone he knows to partition."

"Hum. Not if he is disposed of."

"You must hear me Orin."

"Then what do you suggest we do father?"

"I say…let's pool our resources, and give him what he deserves for a change."

"…And what is that, a quick and painless death…no doubt?"

"There are more ways to die, than you might think. Trust me."

"You said pool our resources, do you need money?"

"We could always use plenty of that. I also want to hear what made him so convinced."

"We are to kidnap the prince, and even the queen, if she won't stay away. Then we are to keep them in one of my properties…I'm going to buy." Orin explained.

"Is that your great plan? It this what you risk your life and ours to do?"

"Well, he bought into it."

"Orin, don't be fooled, the only thing he bought into, was that you'd kidnap the queen and prince, and then he would have you hunted down." explained Ivan.

"He was supposed to kill the king and take the throne," said Orin.

"Yes well…if it were that easy, he would have done it years ago," said Lyonus

"He is right Orin," admitted Fernando. I'm afraid I did not know this fellow very well. I've dealt with greedy men before, but this fellow is a new breed."

"New breed or not," said Orin. A rat is still a rat, and can die the same way…going after the cheese!"

"Here's what we can do. Let him follow through on the properties. We will divide our men to guard it. Then when…"

Lyonus went on to discuss the rest of their strategy.

In the meantime, lord Guy is back at the castle. It seems just in time for dinner.

CHAPTER TWENTY
A Master Plan

Now it was time the court made their way to the dining hall. When lord Guy dashed to the kings' chambers. He knew everyone would be occupied for hours at the feast. Once inside the room, he began to search for the titles to properties, some of which were taken for back taxes.

Lord Guy searched carefully through the kings' chests, and desk draws. He had hoped to find just the right thing.

Consequently, he was able to get his hands on several prime pieces of land, which could draw a ripe price. He quickly folded the papers, and planted them inside his pocket. He hurried to take them to his apartment to hide them. Lord Guy summand a courier.

"You called for me my lord?" answered the courier.

"I did," he replied while his eyes searched the corridor, and then said. I want you to take this to the Cradle Inn. Do you know where it is?" questioned Guy.

"Oh yes my lord, I know the place well," he answered.

"Good, then go...and take your fastest horse. When you have arrived, give this letter to a man named Orin. Got that? No one else!"

"Yes sir I understand."

"I shall want the reply as soon as possible."

"I understand my lord."

As soon as Guy hurried the courier off, he spied Kathryn coming through the hall.

"Good evening my lord," said Kathryn, as she walked toward his apartment.

"Ah, good evening my dear, this is such a pleasant surprise. Come in and sit for a moment."

"I can't stay of course…you understand the king would be expecting me. Speaking of the king, I saw you when you left his chambers."

"I see," said Guy, as he wondered what was on her mind, and then asked her.

"What is it my dear? You look a little pensive."

"Oh no my lord, I only wondered if you got hold of that little something for me?"

"What are you getting at my lady?"

"I'll come to the point then my lord. I'm aware you were in the queens' chambers last night. And today I saw you leave the kings chambers. I happened to know he was not there, and you had not been with him all day and…he has been looking for you."

"Oh," said Guy as he took a deep breath before he responded. Is that all, well I was merely putting away some papers I collected for the king, and I did not wish to wait until dinner was over. It was nothing for alarm my dear."

"And the queen, why did you creep into her chambers. Are you holding back on me?"

"I told you, it was nothing," he insisted.

"Come clean Fredrick did you or didn't you?" Lord Guy just stood with a look of innocence. "Fredrick, we had an agreement!"

"Oh, well I see then…"said Kathryn as she turned to leave the room. I see you still fail to trust me my lord."

"Trust, my dear?" said Guy. You my lady are about the only person in the whole of England that I feel I can trust. You and I are so much alike."

"Are we my lord?" she questioned, circling him like a vulture. Perhaps you tire of using me in these little games you play for the throne…remember queen Miria?"

"Now…that had nothing to do with me, it just happened to work out to my satisfaction, that's all."

"I find you are such a liar. It was later that I heard Miria was dead…well…there was nothing I could have done to prevent it, however what does concern me is the matter of Queen Anne, " said Kathryn.

"Please, lady Kathryn, feel free to share your concerns with me, surely I can find a way to clear your mind," said lord Guy, holding her hand.

"Oh, will you my lord?" she replied, as she recoiled her hand.

"Then what my dear, what is it?"

"I know you Fredrick, but I don't want anything to happen to Anne yet."

"Why, my lady you both shock and hurt me, to think I would do that. Why, I could no more harm Queen Anne, than I would…an innocent child."

"Well." sighed Kathryn; in relief "I just wanted to make sure my lord….And I…"

Lord Guy cut her off in mid sentence, when kissed her.

"As I have said Kathryn, I have no such plans. Besides, you think too much of me. The queen has guards to protect her," said Guy

"Then I have your word you will abide by my…?" Then his kiss silenced her again.

"All right yes my lady," he said, as he kissed her hand. You have my word. You know I have never been able to keep anything from you."

He put his arm around her tiny waist, drew her to him and said. "Meet me tomorrow at midnight in the moonlight Kathryn. The garden is beautiful then."

"Why do I feel something isn't right Fredrick? But I will meet you tomorrow, at midnight."

"Wonderful, don't disappoint me my love…I'll have a surprise."

"Yes well, I will try not to. I'd better go now, I'm sure the king wonders what is keeping me."

"No doubt he would have guessed you've taken an extra moment to prepare. I tell you what my dear…I will come to dine as well. Go on ahead, I'll just put away some things, and I'll be right behind you all right?"

"I'll see you then Fredrick." Kathryn turned to look back at lord Guy, not trusting he would follow her.

While everyone finished supper, Queen Anne stood up ready to leave, and announced.

"Luis my lord, I will leave now, I want to spend a moment with Edward before I retire."

King Luis enjoying the laughter and dance said. "I desire your company, and that of our guest, stay a while longer." The king pressed her hand hard against the table for her to sit down. "But sire, I beg to leave," she said, with such disappointment that covered her face. My lord, you have your guest still to keep you company. I am a little worried about Edward." Then the king said with a voice that commanded attention. "I desire that you stay." he again, placed his hand over hers. My dear, let the boy rest, he has had a difficult day, and he has eaten well." Then with laughter in his voice, he bade the dinner guest to laugh. While Anne began to seat herself, through the laughter, she looked toward Kathryn who came through the door, followed by lord Guy.

Since Queen Anne, through her chambermaids, caught wind of a plot between, Guy and the lady Kathryn, she has been very careful to keep close watch on the young prince.

Anne was very close in council with Kathryn, and was very hurt to find her coupled in some intrigue with lord Guy.

While the laughter roared the queen watched lord Guy and became afraid all the more, then said. "Luis, I employ you, allow me to leave now, I have grown weary." Then lady Kathryn replied. "Why your majesty, would you like for me to accompany you to your chambers?" The queen failed to answer her. Then the king sensing the queens' discomfort said. "All right then my lady, we shall go shortly." Then he turned to motion for lord Guy to move closer. "Here, sit here my lord, and tell me what news from Spain. Have you eaten enough?" Then motioning for a servant continued. Bring more food, and fresh wine for lord Guy."

"Yes sire," replied the servant, as he eyed all the food that remained on the table in front of him.

"Your majesty, I beg your pardon," said lord Guy, with such a frown....The hour has quickly come upon me, and I like the queen, have had my share of indulgence for the evening." The queen nodded her head in agreement, and then said. "Thank you my lord for understanding." The king took a deep breath, and then asked. "Well my lord, are you quite sure?"

"Really sire, I am very well contented, just a bit tired." Then the queen added.

"Please Luis, the hour is late."

"Of course, of course. Forgive me for getting caught up in the festivities. You, I'm sure have had a tiring trip home lord Guy. Perhaps we can discuss the details of your trip at breakfast." Luis turned to Anne and said. "My dear, lord Guy has brought me to face the light, all too quickly. Let us retire together, my queen." then he announced. Good-night all."

He took the hand of the queen, and slowly stood. Everyone rose from their seats, while the king and queen left the hall. As they left Anne turned and gave one last look. She was just in time to see lady Kathryn, mouthing something to lord Guy. The queen turned quickly as not to alert the king. While Ann was unsure of exactly what to make of their relationship, she was sure however, that she would do all in her power to protect the prince.

"Dear, I am going to the nursery, for a moment to look in on Edward."

"All right, I will wait for you in your chambers."

So Queen Anne walked to the nursery and entered. Shaken by Jeanine's presence, said, "Oh, Jeanine you startled me. What are you still doing here?"

"I'm sorry your majesty, I had to speak with you. I knew you would look in on the little prince."

"Well, what's wrong? Tell me Jeanine."

"My lady I fear the rumor about the prince may be true."

"What do you mean? I thought you said you did not know of any rumors."

"No my lady, I said I had not heard who was behind them."

"…And now you've heard," said the queen, while she continued to think about Kathryn. She tucked the covers on the bed of the prince, and watched him while he slept.

"Please my lady, you must hear me."

"I do hear you Jeanine, I'm just thinking of what to do."

"I overheard lord Guy, and another talking about a trip to the tournament, and it should happen on the road. The words then became a little blurred."

"Could they have been talking about something else? Maybe he spoke of a trip he would be taking for the king, and he wanted to take Edward."

Please your majesty," pleaded Jeanine, as she held the queens' hand. "Don't let them do this to the prince. Lord Guy has made up his mind to harm him. You have heard him, he means to go through with his plans."

"What can I do? Luis will not believe me, and my hands are tied."

"Your majesty…sh!" cautioned Jeanine, with her ear pressed to the door. "I thought I heard someone outside." Then Jeanine walked over the queen and said. "I simply felt I had to warn you my queen."

"…And I am grateful for your love for Edward and your loyalty to me. Take this token of my gratitude." Queen Anne removed the ruby bracelet Luis had given her for her birthday. She wore it faithfully and rarely took it off. She handed it to Jeanine to repay her loyalty.

"Why your majesty, I can not take this, it means to much to you."

"Please take it, the life of my son means a lot more than a trinket."

"Trinket your majesty?"

"Well, I feel it is the only thing I have to give that would truly show my appreciation for your help."

"Then I thank you from the bottom of my heart," said Jeanine.

"All right…but I must go now, the king will be waiting for me. He becomes impatient when I am away too long."

"Yes your majesty, but please be careful."

"Yes...and you too should watch your step. You are not strong enough to take on Fredrick."

"I do not fear him, only the fact I can not fight against him."

"It is all the same," said the queen. Stay clear of his chambers from now on he will suspect you, especially if I talk to the king."

"I will be careful, my lady."

"Then again I will say good-night."

"Goodnight your majesty."

Jeanine finished putting away things in the room of the prince, and made her way down the corridor. The queen had arrived at her chambers where king Luis awaited her, but something was wrong. King Luis sat a little slumped in the red oversized chair.

"Luis?" she called. What is the matter? Are you asleep sitting there?"

The king only made moaning sounds that alarmed the queen.

"Guard!" she shouted. Help me...it's the king! Something is wrong."

The guard charged into the room to help the queen.

"What is it your majesty?"

"I don't know...when I came into the room, he was sitting here like this, and would not say a word."

Just then she spotted the goblet on the floor that had fallen from his hand.

"What in the world is this?" she asked aloud, as she took a sniff from the cup. This wine has a strange aroma."

"You mean someone has placed this wine here to poison the king?" asked the guard.

"No! I'm not sure what to think. They must have know the king rarely comes to drink from my chambers, but knew that he would be waiting for me tonight."

"I will call for the Surgeon my lady," said the guard.

"Yes...and go quickly."

When the surgeon arrived, they were able to get Luis into bed. When he was examined he was found in a comma. The surgeon announced it to the entire court.

Queen Anne struggled in her heart over what should be done. She was left alone to fight against the essence of evil itself.

The guard that stood at the door of prince Edwards' room waited until the queen had gone and then hurriedly walked to lord Guys' apartment to tell what he had overheard.

"My lord Guy," he whispered, with his face nudged in a crevice of the door. "I have news to share my lord."

"Oh?" he said, then opened the door and pulled him inside. Tell me what news have you?" Lord Guy hoped the news would be of help to him.

"Sir…I overheard Jeanine tell the queen, that prince Edward was in danger.

Lord Guy interrupts and then said, "What is that to me?"

"Well…because she named you as the one who would do him harm. I heard her say you and one other had planned it."

"Good man, wait here a moment," said Fredrick, while he searched for his purse. He gave the guard a few pieces of gold and then said. For your silence…and make sure you tell no one of this."

"You have my word my lord."

"Now go, and don't worry about Jeanine, I will personally take care of her. Go back to your post and act as if nothing had happened."

"Yes my lord, good-night."

"Yes…yes good-night," he said, almost pushing him out the door.

Not long after Jeanine had gotten back to her room, a soft knock made her heart pause all the more.

"Who is it? Who's there?" she said, with her voice trembling as she clinched the ruby bracelet tightly.

Then a cold steel voice answered in reply.

"It is I Jeanine, Lord Guy."

Jeanine gasped for a breath and without pausing slowly laid her head against the door.

"The hour is late my lord. Can't this matter wait until the morning?"

"Well as a matter of fact it could wait, though I thought you might want to be the first to know."

"The first to know what?" asked Jeanine. She thought maybe it would have nothing to do with the information she gave to the queen.

"All right my dear, I just thought you would be interested in the welfare of the king."

Lord Guy peaked her interest and lessened her fear of him. She slowly pushed back the long heavy latch that secured her door then carefully cracked it open.

"Now what is so important, that it could not wait?"

"Don't leave me standing in the middle of the corridor, someone might get the wrong idea. Plus I don't want the guards to see me out here, they will really give me a roust."

Jeanine was reluctant, but her curiosity was peaked, so she let her guard down, just as the queen had cautioned against.

"Very well then…come in but for just a moment, then you must go." Jeanine's voice trembled, as she stepped back away from the door.

"I'm afraid my dear a moment is all I'll need. Now come and sit in this chair."

He tightened the grip he had on her wrist to guide her alone.

"Why should I sit here?"

"Why? Because you are going to write a little note to the queen for me."

Jeanine hopped up from her seat in protest.

"What are you talking about? You said you wanted to tell me something about the king."

Then lord Guy pushed her back down into the chair. He pulled from his cloak a large dagger and placed it at her throat then ordered.

"You will write what I say, and everything I say."

"Ha…!" gasped Jeanine as she squirmed to get free of him. My lord what…?"

"Just listen and write." Then he adjusted her chair so that she would face the desktop.

"Now write, my dear queen Anne, I'm sorry I just could not live with what I've done to you and the king, **and then sign it."**

"No! I won't write such a thing…the queen trust me!" Then said Jeanine in defiance. What are you attempting to do? I'll never do what you ask"

He grabbed a handful of her hair, which almost pulled her from the chair and then said.

"Never takes a long time…time I'm afraid I don't have." Then she tugged even more, and placed the dagger at her throat again and said. You will write exactly what I say, and anything I want you to do servant girl. Now do it before I cut out your tongue, and serve it to the pigs!"

"Oh…oh." Jeanine cried in a whimper. What kind of man are you? You are an animal!"

"Yes that's right, the big scary kind. You just keep writing." When lord Guy removed the dagger from her throat, she began to scream even louder. "You are <u>and</u> animal!" He slapped her with a heavy backhand and snatched her around to face the paper and quill.

"Now do not stop again until you have finished and signed it, or I will not bother about your signature, I will use your blood. Is that understood?"

Jeanine hurried to finish the letter. She let fall from her hand, the ruby bracelet.

Lord Guy instantly spotted it and asked.

"Well what have we here…pearls for swine? A present from the queen no doubt? I wonder what tidbit warranted this as a reward? It must have been a juicy piece of information to acquire this. No matter, so she knows, I will have both the letter and the bracelet. You will die, and I will have the throne. Now get up!" he said, as he jerked her up from the chair by the end of her hair. He took her closer to the window that would give her a last glimpse of the garden. She would fall where her body would not easily be discovered. Then he turned the dagger and placed it in her hand. Jeanine fought violently to free herself.

"A dagger some quiet night…will be your further reward if you say a word. Is that clear?

Jeanine quaked in her shoes as lord Guy managed to shove her to the floor. He folded the letter and pressed it into his pocket and left the room. Suddenly a creaking sound came from behind her. Jeanine looked up.

"It's you…what do you want?" said Jeanine, as she wiped her tears and straightened her clothes. How did you get in here?" Then there came a struggle. Her screams became muffled, and over the window seal her body fell. It landed in a soft bed of hedges that was in a double row underneath her window.

Now lord Guy paused and thought of the bracelet. He was determined to get it, but remembered he was set to meet lady Kathryn at midnight. There was no time to go to his chamber. So he went down the corridor, and around the twisted stairs till he was outside in the garden. He went to the fountain that stood only a few feet from the two rolls of thick green hedges, where Jeanine's body had fallen. He washed his hands then proceeded further into the garden. Suddenly he heard a crackling sound.

He turned, and there stood Kathryn.

"My dear Fredrick, a midnight washing?" she said.

"Be careful Kathryn, I would not want to have to wash twice…my dear."

"Oh my lord Guy, I was merely making a joke. Where is your since of humor tonight?"

"…I have some things on my mind tonight, I'm sorry."

"It's just unusual to see you spattering about at the fountain."

"Come Kathryn," he urged holding her about the waist. Look…I don't have much time tonight so listen. The plans are being set into place as we speak. All the pieces are coming together. Within a fortnight I shall have all my dreams come true, and you…well…you will be by my side."

"Fredrick does this have anything to do with what we talked about earlier?"

"Forget about that night," he cautioned in a stern voice. You are either with me or against me. Which is it Kathryn?"

"Frederick…?"

"Pity then…I had hoped…you and I could share the throne together."

"Wait Fredrick! I'm just a little. Is this where the treason comes in?"

"Well it's not like you haven't been in on it before."

"That was different, I owed that to Lyonus, but Anne, my reasoning is different."

"Look, I need you Kathryn."

While they talked, the castle guards' who patrolled the garden wall passed by. Lord Guy flashed his hand in hello. He proceeded to passionately kiss Kathryn. He wanted them to think he was having a romantic evening. The guards simply laughed and continued their patrol. Lord Guy wasted no time spouting his affections.

"My darling, it is for us that I must do all of this. We can live as king and queen for a change, instead of always having to vie for the crumbs. If you were my queen, I would flourish you with jewels and fresh scented flowers everyday. All that you desire would be at your command."

"Even you Fredrick?"

"Especially me." Then they kissed again.

"My lord, you know by now there is nothing I would not do for you."

"I know but listen, you must do exactly as I say." He began to whisper in her ear. Do you understand what is to be done?"

Then Frederick caught sight of a shining object in her hand.

"What is that my dear?" Frederick asked, moving his eyes behind her to see what she held within her hand.

"Why it's nothing. Just a trinket I acquired."

"Oh?"

"What about you Fredrick…have you acquired anything lately?"

"I'm sorry, I don't have it tonight. Pity thou…it seems such a treasure."

"My dear sweet Kathryn, I must go now, but I promise you will grow tired of me soon enough. Be patient a little longer."

"I will see you soon."

"Yes Fredrick."

Lord Guy hurried from the garden, while Kathryn slowly strolled under the moonlight admiring the jewels in her hand.

Now all of lord Guys' plans were set for the day of the tournament. And Orin now in possession of the land he desired. The only thing left to do was to wait.

But…thought lord Guy…I have forgotten about Hawks men, and the queens' trip to her dressmakers? I wonder if I can stop them in time? Oh well, with Jeanine silenced, there will be nothing to tie me to it so no need to worry. The throne is as good as mine. Next, I'll find something for that Biltfry. I've had enough of his meddling.

CHAPTER TWENTY-ONE
A Proven Friendship

The queen decided she would take a trip to her dressmaker in Carlyle village. It was a little town on the outskirts of the province. Because of her concerns for the prince, she made sure she rose early to take him with her. She wanted to avoid any one knowing he was gone.

In the town of Carlyle, the dressmaker named Madeline De' Gant awaited the queen's arrival. Anne needed to update her wardrobe. So Madeline was ready to get started.

"My dear Madeline, how have you been? It's good to see you again."

"Yes your majesty and it's about time too! Come in please…it has been a great while." Then with a grin she bends to look him in the eye, to welcome prince Edward.

"Are you the very brave little prince I've heard so much about?" she asked.

"Edward your manners dear. Say hello to Madam Madeline De' Gant."

"Hello…my lady," said the prince, as he grabbed hold to the queen's hand.

"Oh don't be shy, your highness," she said.

Then the prince spoke right up. "I'm not shy at all madam, I am a prince."

"…And a find one you are too," said Madeline, as she motioned for the queen to sit down.

"Thank you Madeline…but do you have a place where Edward might get a drink? The road was very dry for him I'm afraid," asked the queen.

"Of course...all right them," she replied, pointed to her back room. "Oh I have some nice fresh scones and cold milk in the kitchen. Would you like some?"

"That would be quite nice thank you," said the prince.

"That would be lovely Madeline thank you," said the queen.

Then, Madeline called for her assistant Amy to attend the prince.

"Yes what can I do for you?" replied Amy. Oh good day your majesty, and your highness.

"Good day my dear," answered the queen.

""Would you please...?" said Madeline as she pointed to the back room.

"Oh most certainly. Come little prince."

"Go with Amy to the kitchen my prince, she will see to it that you get your fill."

"Go on dear," prodded the queen. You will enjoy it."

"Yes mother," said the prince, a little reluctant at first, but he found himself enjoying the fresh pastries.

As soon as Edward left the room, Madeline started to measure the queen. "Oh dear," said the queen, It seems I've gotten a little bigger since last I was here."

"Well your majesty, you have had a child, and it is sometimes hard to keep your figure, but you have kept yourself well."

"Thank you. I should like to choose some fabric now."

"Oh yes my queen, I have a beautiful yellow Spanish silk, I just know you will adore."

""Wonderful! Let's take a look at it."

While Queen Anne searched for just the right fabric, across the way at the Double Headed Hound Tavern, Melinda and Jessica were busy eating their lunch.

Seated behind them were four men who discussed the queen and her visit to the dressmaker.

Secretly, they listened in on their conversation.

"Ralph, how long will it take for the queen to finish her fitting. I'm getting tired of waiting around?" said Harry.

Then Ralph replied. "It should only take about an hour or so, then we will take the prince."

"What about the queen. What is to happen to her?" asked another.

"Whatever you want to happen, Lord Guy doesn't want them to return alive."

Upon hearing their conversation, Melinda and Jessica decided they would follow the coach of the queen, and try to intervene.

They watched the men carefully to make sure when they would leave.

"Get ready Jess, it seems you will have a chance to grant another wish."

Then Jessica chuckled, and said. "Your wish is my command." And then rolled her eyes, and they both laughed together.

"Looks as though they are ready to leave," remarked Jessica.

"All right I'll pay the tab and be right out," said Melinda, as she wiped her mouth on her sleeve.

Once outside they spied the queen and the prince, as they boarded their coach. Something didn't feel quiet right to Melinda and Jessica. They waited until the coach pulled off, and the men began to follow. Then, that they proceeded to tag along in short distances. The two of them waited to see what the men would do. After the coach had traveled for about a mile, the men picked up speed and began to attack the queens' escort. The guards were overtaken, so Jessica and Melinda gave a hand.

Jessica came barreling along side the man called Ralph. She used the butt of her stave and knocked him off his horse. Then through the window of the coach, Jessica shouted

"Stay down, and inside your majesty! Sit down my prince." She continued to yell through the coach window. The queen in fear began to scream. "Guards do something, we're being attacked!" The guard in the front named Alec immediately turned his horse to fight. He was off his horse in a moment battling with one of them. Melinda looked in on the queen, while she was still screaming and then said.

"Your majesty please we are only trying to help." Melinda added. Then one of the men jumped on top of the coach. Melinda spotted him and reached in her boot. She drew out her dagger, and flung it threw the air. It landed to reach its mark, in his back. He fell headlong to the road. There were yet two others to fin off. The queens' guards were badly wounded. In an attempt to save the guard named Alec, Jessica road toward him side saddled. She used both her staves as though to make the letter x, and cut the throat of his attacker. Melinda stopped the carriage while the last man named Harry tried to ride away. Then Jessica gave chase as she steadily rode after him. Then Melinda called out.

"Leave one alive Jessica…We want to find out who sent these men."

"Oh no fair..." Jessica mumbled, while she pulled up beside him, knocking him from his horse.

"Well Harry," said Jessica, looking down from her horse. "It seems you have a guardian angel watching over you." She kicked him in the face and then said. Oh did I forget to tell you...it wasn't me? Now get up from there...and walk!"

Then Melinda said as if chastising Jessica.

"Jessica, Jessica...violence is a very bad thing...a very bad thing."

"I know..."she replied. But it feels so good...wouldn't you agree?" Then they both chuckled. Melinda brought him over to the queens' coach.

When the queen saw him, she was furious. She walked over to question him.

"Sir...why would you do this to me and my son? Have you no honor?"

Then he answered. "Ha...honor is for thieves and whores." Then the queen slapped him very hard, enough to turn his head. "You are a pig!" she shouted....And pigs are fit for one thing, and one thing only...to be butchered!"

"Your majesty how is the prince?" said Jessica.

In all the excitement, they did not realize that the prince had been hurt.

The queen picked up Edward and saw his wound and began to scream.

"Why...? Who would want to hurt an innocent child?" The queen's voice was filled with tears.

"Your majesty...let's ask our friend Harry, he looks as if he has lots of answers," said Melinda. Then Harry said.

"I won't spend time talking to a winch that's the likes of you."

Then Jessica backhanded him with the handle of her stave.

She kneeled down close to him, and dangled the blade over his manhood, then said with a soft voice.

"Now Harry...listen very carefully...I'm not as patient, nor am I as peaceable as my friend here. So we'll ask nicely one more time, and this time...you will answer to our satisfaction, or you and the end of my blade will have a little chat."

Harry's eyes grew wide. He began to tremble, as he watched the blade swing slowly back and forward.

Then Melinda said. "So how about it Harry...still think your time would be wasted if you talked to a winch like me? Think long and hard before your answer. Oh and by the way Harry, the last person who didn't answer her question...ended up dinner for the wolves.

"Oh so sad…but true," Jessica taunted.

"Tell me…have you ever seen a man eaten by wolves before, when he's not quite dead…hum Harry?" asked Melinda. "Just kind of hanging on to that last…breath. Then a snarl is heard, and the worst pain imaginable is felt when those canines tare into the human flesh." Then she smiled a horrible grin and then said. "Oh it was so sad…but true my friend."

So Harry, frightened at what they had described, told them what they wanted to know.

"All right…all right!" he shouted. I'll tell you. It was Hawk who ordered us to attack."

"Why would this Hawk be willing to attack the queens coach, they weren't carrying any gold?" said Melinda.

"He told us, that some noble was paying him to do the job. Now that's all I know." Harry continued to breath heavy, while he still shook from fright.

"Good man Harry…"said Jessica. Now…you see what happens when you answer when asked?" Harry shook his head vigorously. "No I don't! What do you mean to do with me?"

"Oh well…I guess she forgot to tell you, today is your lucky day," said Jessica.

"What are you talking about?" he asked.

"Why today Harry, you get to live!"

Then Jessica tied him to the back of the coach. She intended he should run along with the coach.

"Wait!" he squawked. I can't run tied up like this! I can't go back to the castle at all! Do you understand what I've said? If I show up there…I won't escape."

"Well I personally think dead is dead." Smirked Jessica.

"Left to Hawk, there are worst things than being dead lady," said Harry.

"Hum…"she moaned, as she gave his words great thought. Then Jessica said. Although I'm sure you're right—and you most definitely deserve whatever he would do to you—but today, we will test your theory."

"What are you blabbering about?" he said, making Jessica even more cross.

"Well, I'm saying you idiot…let's just see, if what I plan for you is less painful…than that of this Hawk fellow you so fear…shall we?"

Harry continued to yell for several miles. "Turn me loose! Are you trying to kill me? You know I won't make it! Please!"

Melinda talked with the queen and tried to calm her. Suddenly the prince started to show signs of life fading from him.

"Oh no! I'm afraid of what's happening to him," cried the queen.

"He does look pretty bad, madam," Melinda explained.

Naturally the queen was quite upset. "Is there anything else we can do Melinda?"

"I'm not sure…but wait a moment. Jessica!" she yelled. Can you tie off your horse and take the reigns, Alec may need help getting us to the castle a little faster."

"Sure thing," she said.

Harry screamed out shallow words, till finally Jessica said, as she raised her stave.

"Since you insist on not coming along quietly…why don't you just take a rest here?"

She did not waiver one moment, before cutting the rope that held him to the coach.

Immediately, the coach jerked forward as though a weight was removed.

"Jessica, what was that? Where is Harry?" said Melinda.

"Well…Harry said something about…being dead tired."

"Hum. Go and take the reigns Jess."

"Sure thing."

Jessica climbed onto the seat.

"Hey, hand over the reigns," she demanded.

"What," said Alec in confusion?

"You heard me. We want to get to the castle before midnight, the prince needs a surgeon."

"Well…it's only because of that fact, I'm moving over," he added in defiance.

A silence struck for a moment. He stared at her almost captivated.

Jessica noticed his arm was bleeding.

"Hey…you need to wrap that arm," she said with a sharp tone.

"Thanks. Thanks a lot. By the way, what's your name?"

"What," said Jessica.…You want to know my name?"

"Yes," said Alec. What do people call you?"

Then she said with a smirk, "My friends call me Jess, but you…you may call me Jessica."

"That's a beautiful name you have. My friends call me Alec."

"Is that right? So what do people that are not your friends call you?" said

Jessica with a glance from the corner of her eye.

He hesitated for a moment. "Those who are not my friends…call me Alec," he remarked, with a wide grin on his face.

Jessica signaled for the horses to go faster. "Get up there, let's go," she exclaimed.

However in the distance, you could hear the call of the wolves, and just as subtle…the faint yell of a man.

Finally they arrived at the castle. Then who, but lord Guy should race to meet the coach? He was determined no doubt, to finish the job he started. He brought a knife stuffed in his shirtsleeve. When he opened the door, he raised his arm to reveal a knife. But when he looked in, there sat Melinda, on the seat. He jumped for a second, giving himself time to put away the knife. He pretended to be startled.

"Your majesty. Are you all right? I did not know you were not alone. Tell me what happened?"

"Later my lord, it's the prince."

Then she ordered the guards to take him.

"Get Edward inside to the surgeon please! I don't know if he's going to make it."

"Come your majesty, let's get you looked after as well," said Guy, sly as a poison adder. The queen turned to thank the girls.

"I just can't thank you enough…for your rescue today. If not for you, we might all have very well been killed. Thank you."

She motioned for the servant standing by to come over.

"Please…make them comfortable and see to their need. I believe the young man is hurt as well."

"He will be fine my queen don't worry about us, go and tend the young prince," said Melinda in sympathy.

Jessica jumps down from the coach and asked Melinda. "Who was that fellow with her majesty?"

"Him? I don't know. I didn't catch his name," she muttered.

"His name is Frederick Guy," said Alec, abruptly.

Then Jessica said, dragging out her thoughts.

"You know Melinda…I just don't think I'm going to like him."

"I think…once again we agree Jessica."

Now once inside the castle they were both amazed. Jessica, the first to speak said.

"Whoa…! Is this what the inside of a castle looks like?"

Melinda whispered, "Yeah…and just think…it's really all yours." They both chuckled.

Jessica, thinking out loud sighed and said, "I could use a nice hot bath."

At that time two servants approached them.

"If you will, please follow me young miss's."

Nervous, Jessica nudged Melinda forward. The servants led them up the winding stairs to their bedchambers. Along the walls, they passed portraits of the kings of old, King Darius and Kings' Lyonus I, and II, hung side by side. Jessica paused, stunned staring at the paintings. *My father, and grandfather…*she thought not quite sure if she should believe it or not.

Melinda watched Jessica from the top of the stairs, and knew exactly what she was thinking, "Jessica…come…your bath is ready."

Jessica turned her head and continued up the stairs, still in awe.

Meanwhile, the queen checked in on the prince. The surgeon informed her that the prince was resting peacefully. Satisfied, the queen went to her husband's chamber. If he was finally coherent, she wished to inform him of all that had happened. But as it remained, he was still unconscious.

Queen Ann became very frustrated.

"Open your eyes!" she demanded. Wake up! Your son is deathly ill! Will you not rise from your slumber…to go to him?"

Still he lay silent.

Now Jessica was drying her body when there was a shriek. She immediately grabbed her staves, and tied the large towel around her. As she burst into the adjoining room—ready to remove all threat—she saw Melinda with a dress held up to her neck, with surprise written all over her face.

"What happened…where is he?" said Jessica, as she searched for the culprit.

Melinda recovering from shock said. "Calm down Jess. There is no one here!"

Confused, Jessica said. "Why would you scream, if nothing's the matter?"

"I was not screaming. I was just excited over these beautiful dresses."

"A dress? I came running in…half naked…because of a dress?"

"What Jess, disappointed you couldn't use your staves…eh?" Melinda taunted.

"Very funny Graybourne. Just what exactly do we need dresses for?" said Jessica, grabbing a beautiful gown from the bed.

"Jess…we, have been invited to have dinner with the Queen," said Melinda, as she spun around holding up a dress to her body. Then Jessica, who could only think of her stomach said,

"Great, I'm starved…let's get to the food. "

Melinda and Jessica arrived at the banquet, each dressed in the most magnificent gowns they could find.

Melinda wore a gold dress, trimmed with white lace. Her fire red hair was piled atop her head with ringlets that hung down.

Jessica wore a cobalt blue dress. She had sky blue ribbons braided throughout her hair. When they entered the room they could hear the whispers.

"Who are they?" one group said. "Beautiful!" gasped, the others.

Alec panned through the crowd. *Could this be her?* He asked himself as he beheld her face. "Surely she is the most beautiful woman in all England."

By this time Queen Anne was ready to introduce the girls at court, when lord Biltfry proved most anxious to be the first to speak.

"It's a pleasure to meet such ravishing ladies. Please…regal us with your heroics."

"Yes! Please do!" Kathryn insisted. Lord Guy has told us of your exploits today."

"Ha ha!" laughed another. "It should make for wonderful dinner entertainment."

"Really," said Jessica, with a great frown on her brow.

Then Melinda, with her eyes closed slightly responded. "We were happy to help the queen of course…we…" Melinda seemed quite nervous. Jessica clinched her arm for support then, continued for her.

"There was nothing to it," she voiced. A simple flick of the sword, and there you have it…works wonders."

"Oh indeed…" they all said, and then continued to laugh.

"Well…speaking of wonders," said Guy. You ladies look much improved from this afternoon's shambles. Ha…ha, ha." Everyone except the queen joined him in laughter.

Anne noted every word, and then said. "Raise your goblets for a toast," she said, and then stood. "I am so proud of these women for what they accomplished today. Without their bravery, my son and I would lay waste in the forest, dinner for the wolves. We would not be here tonight, to share supper with all of you."

Then she added sharply in a whisper to lord Guy. "Or was that your intentions all along?"

"Your majesty!" he said, protesting by turning away his face.

Everyone joined in deep silence wondering what prompted the queens' attitude.

"Continue with the music…despite the un-pleasantries today, I would rather think of happy things now."

The music and laughter continued as commanded when lord Guy moved toward Melinda.

"Tell me my dear, what are your names, and where do you come from. Then Jessica stepped in. "Well…none so fine as you have sir, and my lady," said Jessica, watching the lady Kathryn. She studied lord Guys eyes, and then said. What is it they say…? What is a name…but a way of making people smaller or larger than they are? Would you agree…my lady?"

"Ha…ha, ha!" laughed Kathryn. She is a jewel…really Fredrick, as witty as brave. She's pretty too I think."

"Yes…quite," he said, sluggish of speech.

"What's the matter dear?" asked Kathryn, with a look of arrogance across her face. Has my lord Guy met his equal, in these young ladies? Ha…ha, ha." Lord Guy touched by her words, replied with an ill-tempered expression.

"It would take more than wit to best me I fear. But…I tell you truly…there seems to be more to them than they would care to share. However, I assure you…it will not be for long." Then Fredrick stood and turned to the queen. "I beg our indulgence, your majesty, I must take my leave."

"Oh?" the queen said knowingly. Matters of State my lord?"

"I have pressing affairs yes…that do pertain to those matters your majesty."

"Hum. Luis always found time to eat, and certainly not run out on guest."

"Well, madam," he whispered. Since his majesty, is not truly with us…"

"Certainly through no fault of his own, I might add," said the queen.

"I must assume some of his responsibilities my queen. I'm afraid sometimes, that may mean skipping out on the entertainment."

"Oh Fredrick, bore me no longer, go if you must!" The queen simply fanned him away.

He found himself slowly backing out, with the queen's anger kindled against him.

However the merriment continued, Melinda and Jessica seemed to fit right in.

But standing in the distance, were two young soldiers. Alec and Erik.

"I want to meet that girl," said Erik.

"Whom do you mean?" said Alec. It was as though he expected him to say Jessica.

"The one with the red hair," he said. She is breathtaking."

"Oh…that one," said Alec. He was both relieved and surprised by his own assumption. "Oh I thought you…Well…her name is Melinda."

"I should like to take her for a walk in our garden," said Erik.

"By all means old friend, take a chance. I don't think she's as hard as the other one."

"Perhaps I shall judge for myself old friend," he insisted, while walking over to greet Melinda.

Melinda spied him as he walked toward her table.

"Your majesty, who is that young man walking toward us?"

"Hum…handsome isn't he? His name is Erik. He's one of the king's most trusted knights. Would you like to…?

"No! I don't know…"said Melinda.

"Oh hog wash!" said the queen. Here he is now."

"Good evening your majesty…my lady." Nodding his head though his eyes never left Melinda.

"Oh good evening Sir Erik. We were just speaking of you, weren't we dear?" remarked the queen.

"No…I mean…yes we were," said Melinda, stammering.

"Well…naturally I thought…as such an exquisite flower, you might accompany me…on a short walk through our gardens?"

"Well…I…yah…the queen and I have to discuss…" Melinda stalled to keep from answering.

"Oh nonsense my dear," insisted the queen. It's a beautiful night…one brimming with stars…and the moon is brilliant. Go…and drink your fill. I will still be here when you return."

Then Alec who was determined to see Jessica alone, walked over to her.

"I need to speak with you. It is a matter of life and death."

"What, "said Jessica. Wait, I'll get my…!" Before she could finish, he pulled her up by the wrist. She tried to pull away, but he clinched her tightly. Because his voice was low and very alluring, she no longer continued to struggle, once they were outside.

"Why did you tell me it was a matter of life or death?"

"I'm sorry…maybe I shouldn't have lied."

"Then, perhaps it should be a matter of life or death…yours." Then drew her breast dagger.

"No my lady, put that away. You have nothing to fear from me," said Alec, who used a truly apologetic smile, to curve her anger. I wanted to be alone with you under a blanket of stars." Jessica began to blush.

"I knew it would take more than just a hello…to get next to an especially lovely woman like you. The moonlight agrees with me."

"Oh my bratty brother," said Jessica.

"No listen," said Alec. I thought the glory of all the heavens, would be the only thing that could soften the hard shell you've placed around yourself. Just give it a chance. Give us a chance."

"What is your plan then, to try and break the shell you say I've place around me? I'm ready to go back inside," she exclaimed.

"Jessica wait! Don't get angry I…I just…"

Jessica walked away. She did not want to face Alec's true reflection of her. She left in quite a huff.

Erik however, was having quite the opposite affect on Melinda.

"Thank you for coming Melinda."

"Oh I think your sky is wonderful," she said, picking from the garden as they strolled.

"No not my sky…my lady…ours." Erik took the flowers from her hand. He truly wanted to kiss her, then said. If I could place you in the heavens, you could outshine any one of the stars."

A sudden pause took over.

"Lets look at the roses just there," said Melinda, assessing his glance. Oh…breathless," she sighed in the voice of a whisper.

"What did you say my lady?" he knowingly asked.

"Hum…um," clearing her throat. I said the roses are…ah…breathtaking."

Erik stepped closer to her with each breath he drew, said. "…And like you…you simply take away mine." Then he leaned in to kiss her.

He stepped back suddenly, not meaning to offend her.

"I apologize Melinda, perhaps I shouldn't have kissed you."

"Oh you talk too much," she said, reaching up to press her lips against his. Now what was that again…something about…taking you away."

"Indeed my lady…"

A starlight night did wonders for Melinda's sense of belonging.

At the end of the meal, when everyone was ready to retire, the guard made his nightly rounds. He managed to stumble upon the body, of the nurse Jeanine.

It was obvious; her body had lain there for at least two days.

The queen however, had already retired to her apartment, when the guard began to call out.

"Your majesty!"

"What on earth is it at this our?" she said. Can't you let one of the ministers handle it?"

"No your majesty, it's about the nurse of the prince…Jeanine!"

"What about her?" she said. The queen turned pale as a ghost, for the lack of air, when she realized she had not spoken with her all the day. The queen; could not help but to remember what Jeanine had warned her of. So she held her breath.

"Madame Jeanine was found outside in the garden, just below her window," said the guard.

"…Yes…" said the queen.

"Dead my lady…"

"No! Why that murdering…!" The queen was filled with indignation, and sent for Melinda and Jessica.

"Send those girls to me. The ones from today…hurry! The rest of you get out!"

"Yes your majesty."

The queen began to sob bitterly. There came a thump at the door. The queen searched for silence within her, to gain composure in order to answer.

"Yes…Melinda?"

"Yes madam, Jessica and I are here."

"Please come in. I've had some horrible news," said the queen.

"I'm sorry your majesty, we just heard. The entire court is buzzing."

Jeanine Numero, was a wonderful confidant. I had grown to trust her. She was great with Edward as well. Poor Luis…"

"How is that your majesty?"

"Oh you did not know. Jeanine was his nurse; she was—the only women, he could ever trust—he used to say. Oh I wish he were here now."

"What can we do for you your majesty?"

"I'm sorry I…I was lost in memories. I called you here to help me with a small problem."

"What is that your majesty?" said Jessica. My staves are yours."

Then Melinda said. "Jessica everything can't be handled with a blade."

"Oh I know Graybourne," said Jessica.…But it is worth the trying."

"Graybourne?" questioned the queen. "Thomas Graybourne, was your father?"

"Yes. And this is Jessica Warwick, princess, and daughter of Lyonus Warwick II.

"Ha…daughter of Lyonus?"

"Yes my queen," said Melinda. "I'm saddened, I have not had a chance to confide in you before now your majesty.

"Nor have I…in you Melinda," she said pacing.

"You have nothing to fear from me your majesty," said Jessica.

"Oh my dear, all I have feared for…is now all ready gone."

"I don't think we understand Madame…but we don't won't anyone to know about us for now."

"Don't worry…your secret is safe with me," said Queen Anne; Now, on to the matter at hand. I am in terrible danger. I now must flee for my own safety."

"Your majesty what are you talking about?" asked Jessica.

"I'm talking about, a little coo to usurp the throne is now in place, and I seem to be the only one standing in the way of it."

"What…? Well…what about the prince?"

The queen burst into tears, and dropped to the floor.

"Why your majesty. What else has happened?" asked Melinda.

Then the queen pointed to the nursery.

"Who the little prince?" Jessica questioned, with tears flowing. Is the prince also dead?"

"Yes…he died an hour ago. Now I mourn all I've loved…and it seems in one night, all I've known in one lifetime is destroyed. Poor Luis I fear he will never recover."

"It may just be better for him that he does not," replied Jessica.

The queen once again regained her composure, and then said.

"I need for the two of you to escort me out of the city."

"Your majesty, where will you go? Will you just leave the throne in the hands of that murderer?"

"I have no choice. I have not strength enough to fight him now."

"We will help do whatever we can, my lady."

"Good…now listen. In a fortnight, the tournament of champions will take place in Lantern Bury; about three days ride from here. I was scheduled to take the prince."

"But now your majesty," said Jessica. With the prince gone?"

"Only a few people have knowledge of the condition of the prince. I have paid for their silence."

"Why to Lantern Bury?" asked Melinda

"I want to take him from this place. If they think he is still alive, they will try to attack and we will force the hand of that mad man. Instead of a live prince to dangle over the throne, he shall receive a dead one…useless to his cause. And then I shall kill him myself."

"Oh…but first he will receive a taste of my stave," said Jessica.

"…But your majesty, then does it not serve his purpose to have the prince dead?" said Melinda.

"I only know this; with that mad man gone, the entire kingdom will be free, just as my little boy is now free." Then the queen began to sob softly.

"We shall remain here with you your majesty, until you are ready," said Jessica.

"We shall also be your body guards," replied Melinda.

Just then a soft thump was heard at the door.

"What was that?" questioned Jessica.

"No doubt…some of lord Guy's ears. But our business is concluded. Come let me show you something." The queen walked over to the fireplace wall. It opened to reveal a hidden passageway.

"Oh look!" said Jessica, eyes as a little child. This is great!"

"This is necessary," said the queen. When we are ready, we will leave through this passage. It leads to the gardens below, directly beside the gate. It is great for coming and going when you want to be unseen."

"Perhaps my queen, we should stay with you tonight?" said Melinda.

"I want to be alone with my son tonight my dear…but if you leave through the passageway they will think you are still here. I'm certain Guy has my room watched already. He knows you are here. He has many eyes and ears in this castle."

"No matter!" exclaimed Jessica. Soon those very eyes of his, will no longer see daylight. I will see to it!"

"For now go…I will see you in the morning ladies. And thank you for everything. Oh! I almost forgot. Take these…there is one for each of you."

"They are beautiful your majesty!" said Melinda.

"Diamonds!" Glared Jessica.

The queen presented each of them, with a solid gold chain necklace that had diamonds in each loop.

"We can not take from you such treasure my lady."

"Please…do me the honor of accepting these, as reward for your help and valiant efforts. I shall never forget what you have done for me, and my Edward."

"But your majesty we were not fighting for love of reward, but love of country," said Melinda.

"…Then it is all the same my dear. Accept them on behalf of prince Edward. He would have wanted you to have them."

"All right, thank you…"

"You had better go now."

"Yes. Good-night your majesty."

"Good-night ladies, and thank you."

So it appeared everyone had a plan that would a wait the right moment.

CHAPTER TWENTY-TWO
The Final Conflict

Now it would be two days before Teresa, the wife of Orin, would arrive in England. This was one time she would not obey her father. She was brought directly to Orin at the estate of Westbrook. He had already set it up with servants, who worked the land and took care of the home. Orin was making it ready for his wife, who has now added another surprise.

"Teresa, I am so glad you are here!" Orin proclaimed.

"I could not bear to stay away any longer my husband. Besides, to have the three men I love most in all the world away from me, was very frightening."

"It is okay, I was hoping to send for you in a few days any. But you said you came early because of?"

"My darling, I did not want to send you the news in a letter."

"Oh is it what I am thinking?"

Then she exhaled.

"Yes Orin, we are expecting!"

Knowing every beat of her heart, he asked, "Have you told Senior Fernando, or Miguel?"

"No! Not yet. I thought we could break the news together."

It's now two days before the Tournament of Champions held in Lantern Bury England.

Just outside Lantern Bury, there is was an estate with a tower. It would serve as a point in which Orin and his army would await a signal.

About noon, a rider would charge down the road to the estate, he would carry a red flag. His job would be to wave it back and forward as a signal that Lyonus' army was ready.

Back at the castle, the queen spent the night preparing prince Edwards body for transport.

Jessica and Melinda, were summand by the queen to get ready for the trip to Lantern Bury.

Melinda confided in Erik.

"Erik, I really feel I can trust you."

"Of course, more than you might think."

"Then I must share something with you, that no one else must know, at least not yet."

"Tell me what is it? There are none more trustworthy than I."

"All right. I am the daughter of Thomas Graybourne and Jacqueline is the daughter of Lyonus II."

He was so surprised by her statement that he could not speak for a moment

"You are the daughter of (Thomas of the Blade). Then no wonder you are so well versed. You come from a long line of skilled swordsmen and Jessica the daughter of the king?"

"Remember…no one is to know."

"I can hardly believe it myself," he said, not quite expecting to hear that news.

"So now what?" he asked, for lack of anything else to say.

"Well now queen Anne needs us."

"The queen? What could possibly be the matter…well, aside from finding out about poor Jeanine last night?"

"You surely know very little, about what goes on in your own castle," said Melinda.

"I make it my business to take care of my own…my lady."

"Well…today the queen is your business…our business. She has asked for our help to take the prince to the tournament." Melinda went on to explain the plan.

"I told her we would help, Jessica and I….But we need others we can trust."

"I serve the king my lady, what if he should awaken and need me?"

"Then I'm sure he would forgive you, for protecting his queen."

"I'll need Alec, and a few others?" he said.

"Only alert those whom you can trust…Erik," said Melinda.…For now, it's more than just the life of the queen…it's all of our lives as well."

He quickly moved his sympathies to the queen, and then gathered men loyal to her, to accompany them to Lantern Bury.

Each of them in the queens' party snuck through the hidden passage. They brought the body of the prince along with them. Once outside the gate, they took a different coach than that belonging to the queen. She had planned to surprise her assailants.

Everything was set. All was in order and ready to proceed. They set off for the tournament.

It was a very difficult journey. They stopped twice to change horses and for food.

"I must stop here," announced the queen, calling from the coach. I need food and drink."

"Yes your majesty," said Erik, who was made captain over the men.

"We will stop at the inn an take a breather."

Once they stopped at the Black Stallion Inn. Neither the queen nor the ladies; had enjoyed a hot bath or change of clothing. It was a real treat for Melinda and Jessica. They had become accustomed to days without a real bath.

The Stallion Inn; is where the army would discover prince Edward is already dead. They could not totally understand the queens' reasons for bringing his body, but they were sworn to protect her.

Subsequently Melinda and Erik became closer during their journey. They pledged their love one to another.

Jessica however, gained a greater sense of herself from Alec, and they became friends.

She still had not admitted, Alec truly discovered the shell that had encapsulated her. Perhaps one day, he would come to know why the shell remained.

Now after they had eaten and rested, they bought more horses for their needs. The troop had prepared to take to the road. They were very near to Lantern Bury.

It took two days to arrive at the Chantey Bridge, just on he outskirts of Lantern Bury.

Once there, a rider passed them barreling through, and across the bridge. He was waving a red flag. Somehow Erik knew it had begun.

Erik road back to the coach and announced.

"Ready yourselves men, that rider must be to the others, a signal!"

"Men?" said Jessica. I'm no man my friend. She continued glancing over at Alec.

"Believe me Jessica he knows," said Alec, and then who thought to himself. *She must be softening up.*

"We must expect something any moment," said Erik

"Most likely as soon as we come cross this bridge," said Melinda.

They moved cautiously across the bridge, and then drew their weapons waiting for the attack.

"Wait...hold yourselves steady. They must come to us."

"There. I see the tower from here," yelled the queen, for she could hardly be heard through the charge of the horses, and the sound of the coach.

"Yes your majesty. That is likely where they will take you," said Alec.

As they made there way closer, riders began forging from the tower.

"Here they come!" yelled Erik, and then he said to Melinda. Marry me when this is over?"

"You can bet your life on it," said Melinda.

Then the battle cry began. Orin's men met their opponents with swords in hand. The wagon containing the prince and the queen were overtaken.

The men belonging to lord Guy took the queen, and the body of the prince, to the tower as she had hoped.

Shortly after, Lyonus and his army emerged onto the field; each one taking many lives, that could not be easily be counted.

Lord Guy sent the lady Kathryn to the tower. He wanted her to watch the queen. They met in the hallway, and Hawk snatched the queen in the room. He called his men to take the body of the prince.

"Lay that rotting corpse on the bed," he ordered.

In walked lord Guy

"Well I see all are here. Your majesty," said Guy, bowing to the queen.

The queen spat in his face, as a way of retaliation.

Wiping his face he insisted, "Your poor attempt at a manful action will be of no avail," he muttered. Kathryn...keep an eye on our pair here, we don't want them to come up missing."

Kathryn turned her head in disgust. "Fredrick, the prince is dead," she said, as if saddened by the thought.

"What! No matter. She'll serve to better my purpose. Just watch her, and don't let her out of your sight!" He proceeded to slam the heavy wooden door.

"You!" said the queen, with indignation. You were a trusted friend."

"The prince your majesty?" she asked in sympathy. What happened?"

"No! Don't touch him!" shouted the queen, lain out across his body. He is all ready dead, there is nothing you can do to harm him now."

"I only meant…"

"I care not what you may or may not have meant, you are a traitor and traitors like pigs, are only good for one thing…to be butchered."

Then Kathryn pulled out a knife and walked toward Anne.

"What is his plan now, that you should be the one to take my life…coward?

"No your majesty, I thought maybe you would want to…well"

"What…to kill myself? That's for weaklings and cowards, and I'm neither weak nor a coward. Move away from me."

"I understand why you feel this way, but I had nothing to do with Fredrick's plans, at least not today."

"I don't believe you. You have been with him and his scheming, since poor Miria was exiled." A look of surprise covered Kathryn's face.

"It is true, I hated Lyonus' father the first king, but I never really suggested that they take things as far as they did. She was after all innocent."

"…And Edward…what was he in all this?"

"I've told you, he was a pawn in the game of power. He made the stakes a little more challenging."

"Why don't you just leave me, I'd rather be alone with my son."

"You know I can't do that."

"Look at them, they fight for England and he thinks that I am leverage?" said Anne, as they both stared out the tower window. "It's a battle not won with just manpower."

"Oh…Fredrick will win." Kathryn insisted.

"Yes he will win, but only a nice spot at the chopping block, as will you. That's what happens to those who commit treason."

"He will kill you your majesty."

"And he will kill you!" spouted the queen. Do you think, that as his power would grow, and you age, that he would keep you around? The young maidens will delight his eyes, and you my dear…will become disgusting to him. Kathryn, you will become devastated."

"No! Never…he loves me," she insisted.

"Love? He loves no one but himself, he never has. And now he's dragged you into his power hungry treachery."

"He would never leave me."

"I can't wait for that realization, I hope you remember the words I have spoken."

"Take the dagger your majesty. He will not kill you quickly. It will be slow and painful."

"I don't fear him or what he will do. He has all ready destroyed everything I have ever loved. So nothing else matters."

"Well I no longer want to continue with this little farce. If you must know, I'm the one who talked Biltfry into forging those papers about Miria. Worked like a dream."

"Ha," gasped the queen. And what about lord Du' Voe and my Edward?"

"A great piece of work I must say. Du' Voe was really in the way, and as for the little prince, poor thing, the way he squirmed just before his little feet stopped moving. He, like his mother, had little fight in him.

I knew with him dead, you would fall apart and Luis…well, he was never a threat. It wouldn't have taken much for him to crawl away into the shadows. Ha…ha…ha.

As for that loathsome nurse Jeanine, she was a pleasure. Imagine Anne, really…this bracelet on a servant? How preposterous." She slipped on the bracelet to admire it, and then said. I've always wanted it for my own, and what do you know…now it is."

The queen began to see red. The more Kathryn bragged about her exploits, the color deepened.

"You do understand behind every powerful man, stands an even more powerful woman," she said, as she toyed with Anne. Miria had power, and she could wield it…I must say though, I did think she would make a come back….But you, a weakling, I could hear you carrying on with those vagabonds…I don't have the strength to fight lord Guy," she said tauntingly. You were pitiful, whining and whimpering. Who were they to you, your champions…to come to the rescue? Don't make me laugh. You could never have defeated me, and Fredrick could never have gotten this far without me. Why if it weren't for my planning, he would have still been wet-nursing that idiot husband of yours. All he could think about was love. But you see power, like some men, can become twisted without the right woman to sort of…guide it along."

"Well…that's surely something you certainly would know nothing about!" the queen replied with a look of anger. Taunted enough, the queen saw her chance. It sounds as though the battle is coming in here," she said, as she moved closer to Kathryn.

Outside however, the battle raged on. Erik was wounded, and Jessica received a slash on her shoulder. Jessica found Melinda standing guard over Erik, while she made her way to the tower. Something made her look and turn back first, there was Hawk to consider. He crossed over the battlefield to get to Melinda, just as Jessica rushed to get to him.

"I've heard you are the brat of Graybourne's. I missed you the last time I was at the old estate. That mother of yours was sweet too," said Hawk, all the while trying to anger her and throw her off balance. I personally didn't get a taste, but my men talked about it for days."

"More is the pity then…for now, I am sure after today you will never touch another woman…unless of course, those in hell find your breath bearable." Hawk riled by Melinda's chatter said. "Then maybe we both can ask your mother when we get there?"

Now, Melinda tired of his bantering came in to him swinging her sword and said. "You should have finished me then, because now I will slice just enough of you and leave the rest as food for the wolves. Ready yourself you one-eyed piece of trash!"

They went around and round, showing their skill with the blade. But it was Jessica, that gave Hawk something to remember her by.

"Melinda I can't give you all the pleasure," said Jessica. Then she swiped him across his side. That was for the Jeffers you fop. Hey Melinda!" she called. That slice should give you a place to start." And with a grin of satisfaction on her face, she headed for the tower with a voice that stirred. "Don't forget Melinda, leave some for the wolves."

"Oh, that's exactly what I plan to do," said Melinda, as her voice echoed across the field. She then shouted with force, as she began to wield her sword.

Inside the tower Orin and lord Guy fought along its' spiral staircase.

"You!" said Guy, with a sense of irony. I knew there was something about all of this."

"You should have listened to your own mind," said Jessica.

"You brat, there won't be anything left of you when I'm finished."

Then Jessica stepped in. "…And finished is just what you are."

"Oh it's you…the winch in shambles who pretends to be a lady."

"No…I'm Jessica Warwick princess of England."

Fredrick's eyes closed for a moment, it could be seen that he was caught completely off guard.

"Well no matter, you will die and I will have your throne!" Then they continued the fight.

Meanwhile inside the room, Kathryn had taken things as far as she could.

"Well now it's time to end this House of Warwick for the last time. Finally I will have gotten rid of the last of you."

"Come then," said Queen Anne. You say I'm easy, then it should be no problem to kill a weakling."

"I don't want to hear anymore. Maybe I should just do it for him...I promise to be kind."

By the time Kathryn drew back, Anne was all ready upon her. She slapped her and made her drop the dagger. Anne picked up the dagger and plunged it into her stomach. Kathryn tried to speak, but she was only able to mumble. "How?"

Then the queen remarked. "Because you underestimated the power of self preservation."

Kathryn fell onto a table, stretched across it and then went sliding off onto the floor. Anne's retaliation for Edwards' death was still incomplete. There was one more that remained.

Frederick Guy out numbered in the corridor, turned over a lamp stand to block the path of Orin and Jessica who were right behind him.

He made a dash inside the room and bolted the door. When he looked around she saw that Kathryn was sprawled out on the floor. He immediately dropped his sword, and went to her. He placed her head in his arms and began to scream in such agony.

"Kathryn...no! You can not leave me!" He voice rang out with every bit of his being, the sound of devastation, he had prompted so many times, in others.

"No my love!" he cried. The crown is nothing without you!"

"Now you know how it feels to lose someone you love, for no good reason," said queen. Then in search for retribution said. I am satisfied. Now I pity you."

Fredrick reached for his sword intending to kill her, but Orin and Jessica erupted through the door.

Orin jumped in to try and save her, but Fredrick cut him across the arm.

Then Jessica moved in and was pushed behind a table. Fredrick grabbed the queen.

"Stand back both of you...or I'll slit her throat! I mean it get back!"

"No!" shouted the queen. Kill him, don't let him live!"

"Stay back, I will leave...and take her with me. Don't try to follow me," said lord Guy, as he took queen Ann out the door and down the stairs.

"Don't let him." Screamed the queen as the sound of her voice muffled.

"Let him go Jessica," said Orin. He won't get very far with the queen. There is a surprise awaiting him."

"Are you okay Orin?" asked Jessica.

"Yes, I'm fine, just a little scratch."

"You?"

"Never better, just a little bump," she answered, rubbing the side of her head.

Jessica went over to see if Kathryn was okay.

"Looks like she didn't make it, she's dead."

"How about we go and catch a rat?" said Orin.

"I'm right behind you." Then Jessica and Orin rejoined the battle outside where Lyonus was waiting. As soon as lord Guy made it to the queens' old coach, he thought surely he had succeeded. When he opened the door to put in the queen. Lyonus was seated, waiting.

"Going somewhere? The battle is out there my friend…not in here."

"Oh…! Now who are you?" he asked in exasperation.

"Why I'm the king…your king to be exact."

"What?"

"Lyonus Warwick I, of the House of Warwick," he answered. And you my friend, are about to feel the foundation come down around you."

Then in an attempt to get away, he slit the throat of the queen, and started for a horse that was near by. Lyonus ran after him and they began their volley with the sword, until Lyonus tripped backward over a stump and Fredrick thrust his blade into to him.

When Jessica and Orin arrived, each one began taking a turn with lord Guy.

Jessica spotted Lyonus and went to him.

"Oh no!" she said saddened. You are my father?" she said, with eyes full of tears.

"Yes, and you are my beautiful daughter, whom I never knew."

Lyonus failing said. "Don't kill him, lord Guy…let him live, death alone is not good enough."

"When Orin, finally took the sword of lord Guy, he ordered his soldiers to hold him.

"No! Finish it," he yelled. Let's finish it you upstart! Do you lack the courage to kill me now?" he asked, knowing it was better for him to be killed in battle, than face his punishment for treason.

"No lord Guy," said Orin. I think the king has special plans for you. Take him away." Fredrick went away screaming for death.

Erik commanded his army, to gather up the remainder of lord Guys' men.

"Alec, please make sure Guy doesn't get away," said Jessica, and then she called for Orin. Orin rushed over to Lyonus.

"Father!" said Orin. I'm sorry for everything."

"It isn't your fault. It is I, who am sorry...for Miria, and...you both growing up without me."

Lyonus coughing, nearing his last breath said to Orin. "Here, take it. This is something you might need as king."

Lyonus pulled off his ring, with the royal seal of England.

"No father!" cried Jessica. Not yet! We have so much to learn together."

"Maybe we will pass each other in the night when you reach that city of death. Look in my shirt," said Lyonus. The papers you have, are my last act as king. They will reward those who have helped you today. There were many lives mingled together to win back the kingdom. Son remember there are some things worst than death."

"It's our kingdom father."

"Yours and Jessica's, rule it well great king." Then he rose just a little and pointed saying. "Look...Miria!" his eyes were fastened toward the sunset. Can't you see her? She is just as I remembered...I will be with you soon," he whispered, just as he took his last breath.

"What is he saying Orin?"

"He's speaking of mother I'm afraid," said Orin....But now he's gone to join her."

"No! No!" Jessica cried, as she pounded her fists on the ground. Please don't go!"

Everyone standing around paused.

King Lyonus II is dead...Long live the king!" said young Cole.

Then several of the men raised Orin in the air, as the men all encircled him. They made a victory round with him, while the men cheered and shouted.

They took the bodies of Lyonus, Queen Anne, and prince Edward to the castle.

Orin stopped by his estate and picked up his wife Teresa.

The entire court and countrymen gathered at the castle to hear Orin, and to honor Lyonus II.

Orin was saddened by the death of his father, but he knew that justice was incomplete.

"My father left instructions, on what I should do with his enemies. Alec you know what to do with him?" Nodding his head at lord Guy.

"Yes your majesty, I will take care of it."

"Fredrick Guy will be striped of all titles and lands. He will spend out the rest of his days thinking about his crimes with no mercy.

Jacob Corley, you will be given the estate of Duke Westmoreland, with all rights and titles. And as much gold as you can carry in your wagon:

Skunk, you shall have the Biltfry title and estate, and as much gold as can be carried: Samuel Devereux, you will be appointed the kings surgeon, and a substantial reward along with your servants.

The Graybourne estate will be given back to his heir, Melinda and restored back to its' charm. She has asked permission to marry here in the court…granted. Melinda and Erik, also with as much gold as can be carried.

Not to leave out Richard Graybourne, to be knighted with all rights and titles, and given the post as trainer for the king's army, and…"

Then everyone joined in unison with voices that filled the great hall.

With as much gold as can be carried.

"Quiet friends…please. My father had something special for you Ivan. Ivan Fellows, you will be appointed special reagent and advisor to me, along with all titles and rights, and as much gold as you would ever have need of, and many thanks to you from Jessica and I.

I'd like to present to my special friends in the army of England a well deserved reward, please bow," he commanded. By the power invested in me by my state as England's king. I hereby dub you knights of the realm. Rise sir knights of England!"

"Yeah!" shouted the men.

"And unto my sister Jessica Warwick, Princess of England…I bestow all rights and titles, and to help over see the land.

To my wife and queen Teresa, I bestow all my love as I introduce you to your new queen. We are expecting an heir."

The room rang with shouting and applause.

Then in faintness, there could be heard, a slight sound of a voice pleading. It was Fredrick Guy locked in the lowest dungeon, in the dark and, alone.

"Come back boy!" You know me; you know I can get you gold, silver jewels whatever you want…Let me out!"

"The only thing I want sir…is for you to stay locked up, where you are, for the rest of your life. Here is where I'm sure you can do harm to no one but yourself." Then he closed the door to the cell.

Frederick Guy's screams could still be heard....But with each step, they became softer and more faint.

Alec rejoined everyone in the great hall

"Is it done Sir Knight?" asked Orin.

"Yes sire, as was your will," he replied, with a huge grin on his lips.

The House of Warwick would still stand and was made as strong as ever by the efforts and blood of many.

"Long Live Orin!"

"Long Live the King...!"

King Lyonus Queen Anne and prince Edward were given royal burials.

Hanging in a small room of the castle, lord Biltfry was found by a guard. He had been there for several days.

Lord Westmoreland, and other Ministers along with the King's surgeon, were banished for England, never to return.

The soldiers, who had followed Fredrick Guy, were also banished.

Senior Fernando, Miguel and Jon Bolene, went back to Spain, taking with them a shipload of cargo. It was mostly for the men of Spain who fought.

Margarete, Consuella, Jacqueline and Ricardo were also sent gifts from Orin.

Margarete was offered a way back to England; she refused and elected to stay in Spain.

...And as for Luis...well...he was found in his secret shrine built for his mother Rosa. He was in a corner clutching her journal drooling and babbling, his mind gone.